Bits of String

V. good

ALSO BY AMANDA MACANDREW

Passing Places
Party Pieces

BITS OF STRING

A Novel set in England and
Scotland 1953–1988

Amanda MacAndrew

Century · London

Published by Century Books in 1997

1 3 5 7 9 10 8 6 4 2

Copyright © Amanda MacAndrew 1997

Amanda MacAndrew has asserted her right under the
Copyright, Designs and Patents Act, 1988 to be identified as
the author of this work.

First published in 1997 in the United Kingdom by
Century Books
Random House UK Limited
20 Vauxhall Bridge Road, London, SW1V 2SA

Random House Australia (Pty) Limited
20 Alfred Street, Milsons Point, Sydney,
New South Wales 2061, Australia

Random House New Zealand Limited
18 Poland Road, Glenfield
Auckland 10, New Zealand

Random House South Africa (Pty) Limited
Endulini, 5A Jubilee Road, Parktown 2193, South Africa

Random House UK Limited Reg. No. 954009

A CIP catalogue record for this book
is available from the British Library

Papers used by Random House UK Limited are natural, recyclable
products made from wood grown in sustainable forests. The
manufacturing processes conform to the environmental
regulations of the country of origin.

ISBN 071 2676759

Typeset by Palimpsest Book Production Limited,
Polmont, Stirlingshire
Printed and bound in Great Britain by
Mackays of Chatham Plc, Chatham, Kent

For Sally and Ferret
with all my love

Many thanks to all those who have helped and encouraged me

Thirty-one people died in the King's Cross fire of November 1987. One man's body was never claimed, never identified. White, uncircumcised, of middle years with a scarred skull and artificial teeth, he had been a smoker and that is all that was known of his life. He was not tall, was probably slim with fine features possessing, as the forensic team discerned, 'a good strong English face'. Forty missing persons were reported after the fire but none of these people fitted the description of the man whose reconstructed face gazed hauntingly from hoardings and newspapers in early spring 1988.

He remained unknown.

Part One

I

Kilbole June 1953

FELICITY CAMPBELTOWN WAS eight and knew that things were wrong when adults spoke in French. The French themselves would have been equally mystified by her parents' conversation on the afternoon of Coronation Day.

'Pas devant les enfants. Si vous understandez moi. Le mari de votre cousine est up to ses tricks habituelles,' Sheila Campbeltown had whispered loudly to Magnus her husband as she washed up the bowl which had contained offputting red, white and blue jelly.

Something had gone on between Uncle Lionel and Wolfgang Duncan's German nanny in MacBrayne's potting shed. It had happened just as the new Queen was going home in her crown and doing an awful lot of waving. Auntie Fay had been dozing at the time. The sitting room of the Shieling was fuggy. Not only had hours of television watching been quite exhausting what with all those rays beaming out of the screen and wrecking the eyes and brains of viewers, but Magnus had generously opened two bottles of champagne to cheer the day along. He wished now that he had been less lavish and kept them for Sheila's next birthday as he had originally planned.

'Cousin "L" est un vieux goat, et pas de mistake,' said Sheila. 'Pauvre Hanne. Je ne think pas qu' elle est to blame.'

Hanne had lingered in the garden after helping Felix Blackburn retrieve his cricket ball from next door and taken refuge from a shower in the lean-to, which was where Lionel had found her brooding over some discouraged geraniums. Hanne was pensive and withdrawn, she had enjoyed the gala atmosphere of royal pomp but mass celebrations brought back memories of a time

3

when she would wag a flag and be showered with sweets as she stood in her dirndl and cheered to order. Her childhood heroes had transpired to be monsters.

Preparations for this day had been frantic: souvenirs proliferated amongst exploding bunting and everything but everything came in red, white and blue bearing the Queen's head, except, as Hanne had pointed out, the paper for the lavatory. Secretly Felicity had found the whole affair a bit of a disappointment. Apart from the music which had thrilled her and the sight of all those jingling horses the rest of the ceremony had been far too drawn out. Besides, her father had become cross and she always hated that.

Magnus resented the invasion of his house by spongers. Had the Blackburns, the Braids or Clarice Duncan invested in television sets of their own they wouldn't have been cluttering his territory giving gratuitous advice.

'Will you leave off fiddling this instant, Magnus,' said Fay. 'Just because you are a doctor you don't know everything. Besides, if you wreck that device the wee Queen will never get crowned.'

'Do try not to be silly, Fay,' said Miss Clarice Duncan.

The grown-ups had become much nicer to each other once the corks were pulled. Felicity Campbeltown, Felix Blackburn and his adopted cousin Wolfgang Duncan had settled down to watch while Felicity's little sister Ailsa had tossed her imaginary mane and neighed as she cantered off to play at horses in the Shieling garden with Penny Blackburn.

One robed peer looked very like the next and Felicity found the idea of anointing with oil utterly horrible; furthermore, the Queen's golden robe looked just like Auntie Fay's nasty mustard mackintosh that felt slippery and smelled of the dentist's tooth mug.

Miss Duncan's housemaid Isa had told Felicity that all that fancy carry-on was just a load of popish rubbish and not at all the sort of thing to happen on the stone of Scone. Felicity wasn't up in either popery or grudges about the stone beneath the throne but agreed with her anyway and was rewarded with a slab of tablet made with evaporated milk.

'If three of my relations were dead my father could be a marquess and I could be his page,' said Felix Blackburn.

'Don't brag, darling one,' scolded his mother, Joan, who had cultivated her voice to sound like an *ingénue*. She referred to herself as 'little me', so silly, so very much in need of a clever man to put all these horrid things right. Her prettiness was made of bubbles. Joan ate men, who were often quite prepared to be eaten. She was a snob and did not care for women much. If crossed she got a headache without delay. The Campbeltown television encased in oaken cabinet was an object of mirth between her and the other senior officers' wives but it didn't stop her, or her sister Clarice, spending Coronation Day transfixed by such a marvel. Major Blackburn, splendid in his uniform, had called in on his way to the Barracks and Magnus had demonstrated another of his exciting acquisitions, a camera with a timer that allowed the photographer to get into the picture too.

'But it is true, isn't it, Aunt Clarice about me being a lord one day?' Felix continued, making sure everyone had heard.

'Yes, Felix dear, you are fortunate enough to have been born into a most distinguished family, on both sides. After all, your mother and I are Duncans who once were on the throne of Scotland.'

'I wish we had a most stinkish family,' said Ailsa.

'Never fret, sweetheart,' her father replied. 'There has been a Campbeltown on the foot of Kintyre for hundreds of years.'

It had been while Felicity and Wolf were playing Chopsticks on the play-room piano that it had happened. No one said what had gone on in the potting shed but it must have been bad. Bad enough to make Miss Duncan send Hanne home to Glamis Towers before tea. Bad enough for Sheila to make Felix Duncan promise never, ever, ever to say anything about what he had seen going on upon the fruit nets to anyone. Felix promised with his fingers crossed and told his little sister Penny who told Ailsa Campbeltown who, wide-eyed and breathless with incredulity, told Felicity.

'German ladies aren't only hairy under their arms, you know. They have hairy bottoms too!'

All children seemed to love Hanne. She was plump and blonde and fun. She could sing songs about *Kinderlein* and sleepy sheep, bake gingerbread men, draw hearts and proper stars, cut out cardboard snowflakes and make Christmas really beautiful with candles and wonderful wreaths of delicious-smelling greenery. She also took children swimming in the sea. She never sat on the sands huddled up in woollies exhorting the young to enjoy themselves in the bitterly cold water that was said to have got heated in the Gulf Stream which washed the coastline near westerly Kilbole. Hanne would strip to her substantial bathing dress and pounce upon the waves, singing, 'Oh Vot a Beautiful Mornink,' even when most of Scotland was storm battered. Her armpits were intriguing.

Felicity had heard her mother talking to Joan Blackburn about them. 'Could not your sister buy Hanne some Veet, or maybe a razor?'

'Oh I couldn't. Clarice is so stern, not like me. She never did think that sort of thing mattered even when we were little. She likes foreigners and their horrid habits. Look how she found that unpleasant little boy in the first place.'

Joan Duncan had married Digby Blackburn during the war and given birth to Felix in 1945. Six months later her sister Clarice, who was being mighty yet merciful on behalf of the Red Cross in defeated Germany, had come across a little orphaned boy, whom she adopted as her own. So the story went, though Clarice herself never denied that she worked for the Secret Service, in fact she positively encouraged such speculation. No one ever dared suggest that little Wolfgang was her own by-blow. Clarice seduced, Clarice aroused or Clarice submitting to indignity were all most unlikely. She upheld the community and kept most of Kilbole's institutions on course, having a highly developed sense of duty and quite an inflated idea of her own importance.

Wolf adored Hanne. She was the nearest thing he had to a mother. Some people even wondered whether Clarice had been like Pharaoh's daughter and hired the foundling's own mother as nursemaid. Wolf called Miss Duncan 'Mutti' and kissed her whiskered cheek each night after she had read him a Bible story and bade him sleep tight beneath the gaze of a soppy Gentle Jesus being kind to some waifs with rabbits. Beyond that Wolf was not prepared to go. Hanne was the one he loved.

Felix hated his adopted cousin; he resented him as an impostor and loathed the way the younger boy seemed brighter and more clever at school. Felix was still too young to realise that he, with his blond hair and his mother's fair complexion, was conventionally the better looking of the pair, though he did know he was stronger and far more nobly born.

Each child had been given a Coronation crown and a Coronation mug to mark the day. In addition, Clarice Duncan gave Wolf a gold half-hunter watch that had belonged to her father.

'Mutti has given me this to mark this suspicious day,' said Wolf to Felicity. 'Look, she has had my name put on the back. I am not allowed to keep it though, it has got to live in the safe.' Wolf longed for a proper watch that he could consult ostentatiously by shooting his wrist out beyond his blazer cuff like the other boys at school. He was quite used to being considered somewhat odd though he did yearn to be, just a little bit, less different. Joan found her sister's gift to her ward utterly inappropriate. 'That was Daddy's watch Clarice, it should have gone to Felix, who is real family.'

'The watch was bequeathed to me, Joan, to bestow as I choose.'

The fireworks were meant to be an added delight for big children only. Penny Blackburn and Ailsa Campbeltown were far too small to stay up till it was late enough to be dark.

'Me and Ailsa don't want to go anyway. So!' said Penny boldly to her mother.

'Don't talk like that, Penny, you sound like a nasty tripper's child,' Joan replied while inspecting her teeth for lipstick marks in her regimental powder compact 'And stop giggling behind your hand, sweetie. Only common little girls do that.' How Joan longed for a new posting, somewhere other than in her native Kilbole where it was so hard to meet new and interesting people who didn't say pardon with an accent.

Her elder sister Clarice had inherited Glamis Towers when their mother died and lived there in draughty, battlemented and highly uncomfortable splendour with little Wolfgang looked after by Hanne and Isa, the long-suffering Duncan house-maid.

Once Digby's post-war tour of duty in Singapore had ended

7

the Blackburn family had been issued with purpose-built 'married quarters' which were cramped and unimaginative, but better for Joan than sharing Glamis Towers with her sister Clarice once more, as they had been forced to do in wartime, when matters had been made worse by the largest rooms being requisitioned for the Kilbole and District Food Office.

Felix Blackburn had cornflower eyes and was his mother's blue-eyed boy. Wolfgang Duncan's eyes were also deep blue but no one, except possibly Hanne, appeared to have noticed them. Plump little Penny had amber eyes.

'I wish I didn't have to go to the fireworks,' Felicity confided in Ailsa.

'Don't go then.'

'I've got to. It is a treat.'

Felix sidled up to his mother as they stood waiting for the set piece to explode into E II R beneath a fiery portrait of the Queen, who appeared to be weeping sparks.

'Is Aunt Clarice going to send Hanne away, Mum?'

'Maybe, darling. Now be quiet . . . Oh look at that pretty golden rain! isn't it lovely?'

Felix wasn't listening, he was whispering to Wolf. 'Your nanny won't be there when you go home.'

Major Blackburn saw that Wolf was crying and put a kind hand on his shoulder. 'Cheer up old boy. Don't you like the bangs? You'll have to get used to that sort of thing, you know, if you are going to be a soldier. Lots of banging in the army. Come on, buck up! This is meant to be fun. You are lucky. Most of the grown-ups here have heard bangs go off in anger.'

Wolf did not want to be a soldier, he wanted to be a musician, and most of all he wanted Hanne.

Felix was right. Hanne was gone when Wolf got home. Her room was empty except for the lingering scent of honey and fir cones. Even her Polyfotos of Wolf as a toddler had disappeared.

One quiet moment, the following day, when they were alone in the subterranean kitchen, Isa gave Wolf the present Hanne had left for him. It was her father's violin, her only keepsake of the only other male she had ever loved.

'Here, Master Wolf' – Clarice insisted on formality with staff – 'Hanne asked me to gie you this. There's a wee note wi'it, only I canna read it, it is written in foreign and in yon green ink.'

'*Auf wiedersehen, mein kleiner Liebling . . . Hanne. x.*'

Wolf was too old to have a nanny. Hanne would have had to go at some time and Clarice Duncan had leapt at the chance of sacking her. Clarice was also jealous. She wanted and also felt she deserved to be loved by her ward. It was Wolf's duty to love her. She had invested in him and so far the return was paltry. Without Hanne there would be nothing to stop Wolf doting on her as a son should dote upon his mother. Clarice was not in touch with much of normal family life. She had already found out that expensive presents did little to encourage devotion. The final barb tore at her heart when she saw how much Wolf missed Hanne and how his only comfort was gained from trying to play her violin. In the end Clarice relented: Wolf could have music lessons, she would arrange for Sheila Campbeltown to give him tuition after school. Then, just for a moment, Clarice felt loved. Wolf flung his arms around her neck and gave her an unbidden kiss. 'Thank you, Mutti. Thank you. I will be a great musician, the very very best. Better than Mozart, better even than Yehudi Menuhin. Mrs Campbeltown says I have got lots of talent.'

'Now then, young man, pride comes before a fall, never forget that.'

The spell had snapped. Wolf was once more subdued.

'Yes Mutti.'

'I don't believe that Hanne could have tried to seduce Lionel, do you, Magnus?'

Sheila and her husband were sitting in the Shieling garden enjoying the last pink rays as the sun set behind the hill separating Kilbole from the coast.

'Lionel is an awful bantam cock, Sheila.'

'Oh I know that, Magnus.'

'You do?'

'Oh yes. A woman would need three heads and to stink of skunk to stop Lionel making a pass. He is a shocking flirt.'

'I don't expect Fay gives him much exercise,' said Magnus. 'I would imagine it was old man John's fortune, all those nuts and bolts, that attracted young Lionel rather than Miss John's winsome ways.'

'Fay keeps both her legs bolted together in the same stocking,' said Sheila. 'But that's no excuse for jumping on poor wee Hanne.'

'Hanne was a fine big lass,' said Magnus. 'And my cousin's husband fancies himself the Lothario.'

'Your cousin's husband is no better than a lounge lizard, Magnus. No woman would be that driven to want to entice such an oily kind of fellow.'

'Don't be so sure, Sheila. After all, look at Joan.'

'The war has much to answer for, Magnus.'

'That episode, to my certain knowledge, happened in peace-time.'

'Ah yes, but rationing was an awful burden. Look what girls would do for nylons.'

'Sexual urges can be mighty compelling too.'

'Involving Lionel, my love? A woman would need to be desperate.'

'You are right, my darling, as usual.'

Felicity had heard this conversation from the open playroom window. Her only ambition then was to be as happy as her parents were that summer. That was what she wanted. It wasn't so much to ask.

Wolf and Felix both started at Gantry Close in the autumn of 1953. On clear winter days the cranes of Ardrossan could be seen from the top of the school's tower which was encircled by a stone inscription in medieval script: EXCEPT THE LORD BUILD THE HOUSE THEIR LABOUR IS BUT LOST THAT BUILD IT which came in handy for sermons and other harangues. Gantry Close was a traditional establishment believing in team games, cold baths and beating backsliding small boys with slippers.

Hanne had sent Wolf an advent calendar via Isa. Taking it to school had been a mistake. Each morning he had opened the little doors surreptitiously and hidden the calendar, painted all over with ruddy-cheeked and chirpy shoemakers, chimney sweeps, flaxen-plaited *Mädchens* and other un-manly ephemera, under his mattress safe from the scorn of fellow boarders. He hadn't counted on mattress-turning Sunday, when his secret was laid bare.

'You are a weed, Duncan One,' said Felix, who was now known as Blackburn One. Matron was really nice about it, but Wolf felt humiliated. Had he been beaten like Forbes Two who had a copy of *Men Only* beneath his mattress, things would have been fine. Sentimental Germanic folksy kids were despicable. Wolf put the calendar in the furnace despite having most of the doors left to open and despite missing Hanne more and more as Christmas approached without her *Kristkindchen*, *Engeleins*, decorated fir cones, spice cakes and beeswax candles sent from Ulm. Miss Duncan gave him games suitable for his age like L'attaque, Contraband and Tell Me; she was advised from department store catalogues as to what he should want.

Father Christmas had never called at Glamis Towers on account of St Nicholas doing so early in December and leaving goodies in Wolf's shoes. Hanne used to tell him that wicked children found sticks in theirs. The year that Hanne left neither St Nicholas nor Father Christmas showed up.

Sheila Campbeltown taught music part-time at Gantry Close. Wolf and her daughter Felicity were her greatest hopes. To have two such promising pupils in her charge at the same time was something for which she had not dared hope, and for one of them to be her own flesh was sheer bliss.

The next year Wolf received a letter from Hanne, which Isa smuggled to him as all mention of Hanne was expressly forbidden at Glamis Towers. Sheila offered to help him decipher the difficult boxy green script after his violin lesson. Hanne, according to the letter, was now Frau Doktor Claus Schmidt. Dr Schmidt, in her words, was having a wife who was dead already and one son who is much reminding her of Wolf who is also having the same age as you. She was happy, she said, but was much fearing that her English was becoming an atrocity. She was sending many kisses and a picture of her so charming husband and stepson. Wolf scowled at the picture of the Schmidts squinting into the sunshine, the tall doctor with his lanky son in lederhosen and Hanne with a big belly between them. He tore up the photograph and hid the bits in his fiddle case. The advent calendar that had accompanied the letter he gave to Sheila for her daughters, who fought each other to open the double doors of Christmas Eve. Wolf was staying at the Shieling for this battle because Clarice had been called away to London and would only get back on Christmas Day itself. She was going to fly into Prestwick, a frightfully dashing thing to do in 1954.

'Why have we got to have Wolf and his Mutti for Christmas here?' asked Ailsa. 'They aren't even family like Aunt Fay and Uncle Lionel.' Family was something you put up with like verrucas.

'I like having Wolf here,' said Felicity. 'We can play carols together and give you all a concert.'

Showing off would be fun; having to endure Clarice Duncan would be grim. Her idea of a good time was asking general knowledge questions and organising a spelling bee. The last time she had been to Sunday lunch she had insisted on giving the children a quiz.

'Now Ailsa. Horse is to stable as sty is to . . . ?'

'Eye,' said Ailsa.

'No, Ailsa that is silly. The answer is pig, isn't it?'

'No. Horses live in stables and sties live in eyes.'

'Dear me, I know one little lady who is so sharp she might cut herself. Now who can tell the first letter of Knee?'

Wolf was silent, he refused to perform.

In desperation Felicity gave the correct answer.

'Very well then,' said Clarice, glaring at Wolf. 'How does pneumonia start?'

'With damp feet,' said Magnus who hated pedantry and said he only enjoyed games that involved violence, cheating and big prizes.

'Pneumonia starts with a pee,' said Ailsa, 'like everything we ever do. Mum always says we are not going anywhere till everyone has spent a penny. Don't you, Mum?'

At this point Sheila packed everyone off into the garden where instead of looking for interesting plants as instructed by Clarice, the children lobbed slack handfuls of gravel over the wall to spatter passers-by.

Actually, the reason why Clarice and Wolf were spending

Christmas at the Shieling was because the Blackburns and their quarters were full to bursting with Digby's cousins. 'Aha, that explains it,' said Magnus, laying down his copy of the *Radio Times*. 'Maybe these relatives are the ones that have to be eliminated before Dingo gets his title. I suspected Joan was laying in rat poison when I met her in McCreath's last week.' He started reciting in a singsong voice.

'Joan is having a Borgia orgy.
Isn't it sickening, she's run out of strychnine,
So she'll thicken the gravy with ground glass instead.'

'Magnus . . . Really. Not in front of the children please,' said Sheila giggling.

'There are only three cousins left now before Felix's daddy turns into a tent,' said Ailsa.

'A marquess you twit, not a marquee,' said Felicity. 'You end it like hiss, unless you are French in which case you get your head chopped off.'

'That's enough Flicky. Wolf and Miss Duncan are going to be here for Christmas and that is that. After all, Auntie Fay and Uncle Lionel are going away this year.'

'Are they really going all the way to Strathpeffer to stop Uncle Lionel doing his trick with the balloon, the bucket of water and the feather duster?'

'Whoever gave you that idea?'

'Dad told me. Is it true?'

Magnus was a large, rubicund, balding man, the antithesis of urbane Digby Blackburn whose dark, curly-haired and navy-eyed good looks were only marred by his lack of height. (Joan Blackburn would have preferred her Dingo to have been more of an operetta ambassador in stature but comforted herself by thinking of other military shorties, Napoleon, Nelson and Monty, even wheeling in Alexander the Great, about whom she knew nothing.)

In a parody of self-importance, Magnus smiled at his daughter and flung out his substantial chest. 'One is a martyr to truth, Flicky.'

Felicity giggled. 'Oh Dad, you sound just like Major Blackburn.'

No one questioned Clarice Duncan's business in pre-Christmas London. 'Please don't ask me, I am not able to tell you,' she had said with a smug look of one privy to momentous information, but nobody cared.

Clarice had been lucky to secure a seat on the northbound plane, a Stratocruiser. The name alone sounded dashing and exotic, something not to be sneezed at by Dan Dare, Pilot of the Future.

Felicity and Ailsa had stockings to hang up.

'I don't believe in Father Christmas,' said Wolf.

'Nor do we,' said Ailsa. 'I don't believe in anything, not even Hell. I don't believe in fairies or Old Nick or Noah's Ark, but I still have a stocking. We all do, even the grown-ups. Let's help you fill one for your Mutti.' Together they found a variety of adult treasures that might permit Clarice to experience a smidgen of joy, things like soap, lavender bags and bookmarks. Up until then Wolf had only ever given Clarice a hankie and a hand-painted card for birthdays and Christmas.

An airport, even one as little used as Prestwick, was a temple of thrills with passengers newly arrived from the States in sharp bright clothes knowing first hand about hot-dogs and popcorn and going to drive-in movies in their Cadillacs. However, everyone was too busy to take the children to greet Clarice and anyway she was not the sort to relish a noisy reception.

MacBrayne would collect and transport her to the Shieling.

Wolf didn't mind whether Mutti arrived or not. He was having a wonderful time with the Campbeltowns and told Sheila he wished she had chosen him to be her ward instead.

Felicity could never trust Christmas to be heavenly again after the hell of that year. The bells didn't ding-dong merrily, they tolled a grim tocsin because the Stratocruiser crashed on landing.

Twenty-eight passengers died, including Clarice, which left Wolfgang Duncan quite alone, unclaimed, without known moorings.

When Sheila and Magnus broke the news to Wolf, he did not cry, he had just stood still and looked out of the window towards the wintry coastline in the direction of the airport almost as if expecting to see the column of smoke rising to heaven.

'I had better give Mutti's stocking to Isa,' he said in a matter-of-fact way. 'She doesn't have anyone either.'

Sheila had cooked the festive lunch and served it in a silent dining room, no one pulled a cracker and the pudding wasn't brought to the table in flames. Only Wolf appeared to act normally. He was a quiet child, not used to funny hats.

Later, when Felicity found him, he was playing 'Für Elise' on the playroom piano. She picked up her fiddle and tried to accompany him but it wasn't that sort of piece. She could think of nothing to say.

Eventually Wolf stopped playing and went to open his violin case. He took out the fragments of the photograph Hanne had sent him of herself and her new family. 'I'm going to live with Hanne now,' he said. 'I know she doesn't love that other boy as much as she loves me.'

Wolf didn't go to Germany: he moved in with the Blackburns, on account of Miss Duncan having been Joan's elder sister. This was horrible for everyone. Only Dingo Blackburn with his first-hand knowledge of shooting wars as well as domestic conflicts seemed able to rise above the turmoil and make the best of things. Even the new and bigger quarters that went with his greater rank and larger family didn't console Joan, who had no room for cuckoos however vast her nest.

Glamis Towers was put on the market. Once it was safely sold it became of enormous sentimental value to Joan who simply couldn't bring herself to pass her childhood home now she had been forced to part with it. She disapproved of all aspects of the new ownership. 'What would Mother have said? I can't bear it. All Mummie's sweet Dorothy Perkinses, all put on the beastly bonfire. Poor little flowers, poor little me, I'm the only real Duncan left,' she wailed dabbing her eyes. She hissed with disgust, on hearing rumours of Glamis Towers being fitted with pastel sanitary ware, carpeted bathrooms and a specially created television lounge. 'Lounge!' she shrieked, raising her azure-lidded eyes to heaven. 'If Clarice was alive she would die!'

Apart from a tea-set and a hundred pounds to Isa, most of Clarice Duncan's fortune was left in trust for Wolf. It wasn't much. There was no evidence whatsoever that she had ever been employed by anyone as a spy. Clarice had probably just been a plain and bossy spinster with a bent to be dutiful and a meagre supply of human warmth.

The sale of Glamis Towers was essential if Wolf was to be educated privately according to her wishes. This became another convenient thorn in Joan's already well punctured flesh. 'I hope you appreciate, Wolf, that we have all had to make lots and lots of horrible great sacrifices for you,' said Joan. She was checking through his school trunk and had been most put out to find he had outgrown his rugger boots and that his corduroy shorts would expand no further in any direction.

'Yes, Aunt Joan.'

'You are a very lucky boy. You might have had to go to the Quarriers Homes like Isa. How would you have liked that?'

'I want to go and live with Hanne, Aunt Joan.'

'With Hanne? That German whore? Don't be silly and ungrateful.'

'What is a whore, Aunt Joan?'

'Wolf! You naughty boy. You must never use that word again ever. Do you understand?'

'Yes, Aunt Joan,' said Wolf, still quite at sea.

Rugger boots and shorts were essentials, music lessons were not. Dingo did try to persuade his wife that a few guineas per term was not outrageous expenditure on a child with such great natural musical aptitude. After all, he pointed out, when all was said and done and all things considered, it wasn't as if Wolf wanted a pony.

'Now you are just being mischievous, Dingo. Wolf riding . . . what a silly joke! The next thing will be that you expect him to come skiing with us.'

'Well yes. I mean, we can't leave him behind, Joan.'

'Oh Dingo! Don't be so cruel. Can't I have a little time with my own darlings alone? Please, Dingo, ask the Campbeltowns to have him.' Joan put on the pouting face she used for wheedling, then brightened as a thought struck her. 'We can't take Wolf to Switzerland, he hasn't got a passport.'

When he was not at school, Wolf spent a lot of time at the Shieling. He was happy there amongst the messy domesticity of a family home with cats and Scottie dogs called Haig and Johnnie Walker, whereas he felt out of place with the Blackburns, even disliking Bomber, their irascible labrador through whose veins coursed the blood of Sandringham.

Almost all of Kilbole had passed through the care of Dr Magnus Campbeltown either as baby, child, adult or corpse. All secrets told in the surgery or from the sickbed were safe; most were forgotten. Magnus had been able to deduce several secrets concerning the Blackburns, one of which he felt should be made known to Wolf. Wolf wasn't told, however. He was too young, said Joan. He wouldn't understand.

Magnus did not agree. He told Digby and Joan that, in his opinion, a child of ten understands, knows and feels far more than may be apparent and that it would be a comfort to him to know who he was and where he came from.

'Rubbish,' said Joan. 'Consider poor darling Clarice's reputation.'

Clarice dead was much mourned and had, by dying, become the closest and most missed of sisters, whereas in life she and Joan had been no more than stiffly civil to each other for years.

Wolf replaced Clarice as pariah in Joan's private chamber of horrors and the only person she could find to sympathise with her was her own little boy. Felix loved to hear how his mother hated Wolf and got great joy from agreeing with her wholeheartedly.

W OLF GOT USED to sudden brisk cheer and bright comments on the weather whenever he appeared. He did not seem disturbed by Clarice's death, which got him a reputation for being either a brave young chap or a heartless little lad, depending on who was talking about him at the time. Wolf knew what had happened and never asked why. His life was like that. He got told he was lucky. Holidays with the Blackburns were awful.

Joan Blackburn did deserve a little sympathy. She possessed just enough maternal feelings to nurture her own brood with none left over. She was not a simple ewe to be gulled into mothering alien lambs.

Ailsa had an aptitude for fractions and called Wolf's new home the Half, on account of the pebbledashed box being twice the size of the Blackburns' previous quarters. He missed Glamis Towers for its nooks and corners, senseless turrets and battlements created many centuries too late for sieges. He had loved the mystery of the dark musty cupboards and revelled in a Gothic background for his invented adventures.

At Glamis Towers he had never been discouraged from reading and had spent hours quietly absorbed amongst the fusty books of Grandfather Duncan's library, which had now been sold to a dealer who dignified new houses with yards of venerable books or else removed the literary meat of them to create novelty boxes and cupboard doors.

The Blackburns didn't own many books: army life was too peripatetic for shelf filling, and reading was not something a healthy person did in daylight anyway. Those fit enough to be up and doing got on with life and didn't vegetate with a book. Military biographies, sporting memoirs lay about in their virgin bliss from Christmas to Christmas; the likes of Agatha Christie were provided for the convalescent sick and wounded.

Felix Blackburn felt ousted by Wolf. If he couldn't get himself noticed by being a joy he was bloody well going to make himself important as a pain. He made it his aim to be a phenomenal irritation and prominent thorn, especially in Wolf's well-bruised flesh. Even his younger sister Penny, whom he had always affected to despise, followed Wolf about adoringly and no longer seemed to be in awe of her own brother.

Long after the grass had begun to sprout on the victims' graves the wreckage of the Stratocruiser remained a macabre reminder of Christmas turned nightmare. There had been diamonds on board and experts were sent to sift the cinders; quite a few of the everlasting stones were recovered. The Nazi Diamond Rumour kept Kilbole humming throughout all early spring and had originated when someone mentioned that several stones had been found lying apart from the rest like Christ's grave clothes. Instantly it was accepted that these gems were a gift from Wolf's fugitive father and had been hidden in Clarice's sturdy crêpe stocking tops. It made a good story for an unusually dull time in the dreariest part of the year. Tales grew more and more lurid about Clarice until all Kilbole was satisfied that not only was Wolf her child but that his father, the provider of the diamonds, had been the highest of Nazi monsters, there being no accounting whatsoever for German taste or capability. Had the liaison occurred in France, Clarice Duncan would have had her head shaved for sleeping with the enemy.

There were very few musical boys amongst the Gantry Close pupils so the orchestra had to be plumped up with outsiders. Felicity, as the music teacher's daughter, sat next to Wolf and led the first violins, the boilerman who played in the Kilbole Skifflers strummed a battered bass and Matron upon the viola made hopeless eyes at the nervy Bursar on the cello who had never got over the war.

Felicity and Wolf were the stars. Felix was pretty bad at the violin but sometimes, especially when it mattered, he made it his business to be excruciating. Felix aped Godolfin Horne and held the human race in scorn, which showed in the slight sneer that grew upon his handsome face. Wolf was all amiability, a dunce at games and a great clown. Felix excelled at sports provided he was on the winning side and in the best position.

'Our family have always been Etonians,' Joan informed Gantry Close's headmaster who was sceptical about the divine right of Blackburns to rule the world regardless of intellectual ability. Her eyelids fluttered while she let a sweet smile sit trembling on her glossy lips. 'It is a tradition, you know,' she explained helpfully. 'Of course, dear Felix will get in. Eton wouldn't dare fail a Blackburn.' She quoted the slight marquess as a further example of family loftiness.

The Campbeltowns had no such pretensions. Ailsa was bright and might perhaps be able to follow her father and grandfather into medicine via the Academy and Glasgow University. Felicity was aiming to get a place at Fairweathers, an English co-educational boarding school for the musically gifted. A scholarship would be useful but not essential: the Campbeltowns were prepared to sacrifice much and to work hard for their daughters' futures.

Sheila suggested to Joan Blackburn that Fairweathers might accept Wolf too. Actually she knew the school would be eager to have him: his talent was extraordinary, of the kind that might even get him attention as a prodigy.

Digby was appalled at the idea of Wolf making a career in music. 'No child of mine goes to stage school,' he told Joan firmly.

'It isn't a stage school, it is a public school for gifted musicians. Wolf wouldn't be a tap-dancing tot in the Gaiety pantomime,' Joan replied. 'And anyway, Dingo sweetie, Wolf is not your child.'

'He is my responsibility,' Digby replied dutifully.

'The child is an impostor.' Joan spoke like this only after a couple of gins. 'And anyway he might get a bursary or something. Think of the economy, Dingo.'

'This family does not rely on handouts, nor does it countenance its young being turned into performing monkeys.' Later, when sober, Digby relented. Wolf could try for Fairweathers and if he got a scholarship, well and good. If not, he was off to Seaforth Crag as planned.

★　　★　　★

In 1957 Joan Blackburn's world shuddered. The crack of doom wouldn't cause her greater anguish than Felix failing to pass into Eton. Nothing that Khrushchev, Grivas or Nasser perpetrated could be quite as calamitous as this monstrous act of inhumanity by the Common Entrance Board. Something must be done. The Governors, the Head Man, the MP, the Queen – somebody must be able to pull a string and put things in their proper places. Would a legacy, an offer to rebuild some crumbling fabric, a reminder of the Duncan royal descent and the Blackburn proximity to the nobility bring the powers to their senses? No, nothing could be done: Felix had failed very badly and no votive offerings could change Eton's mind.

'It is wrong to laugh,' said Sheila to Magnus within Felicity's earshot. 'But do you not think Joan is going a wee bit over the top? It is not as if anyone's dead.'

Magnus had read a small bit of psychology and had acquired much patience from listening to the little troubles that become so great to others. 'I dare say Felix is as good as dead in her eyes. There is much of the Roman mother in Joan.'

'What do you mean?'

'Well she is the sort of woman whose first question would be whether her menfolk had sustained their fatal wounds gallantly in their fronts or shamefully in their retreating backsides. Social acclaim matters more to her than achievement. She'd be quick to the hemlock in the event of family disgrace.'

'Oh Magnus . . . you don't think . . . she wouldn't, surely?'

'No, Sheila. Digby will bring her to her senses. Also, he has asked me to refer her to a man of the mind. A really expensive one, away down in Harley Street: a sort of psychiatric equivalent to Fortnum and Mason, purveyor of sanity to the nobility and the crowned heads of Europe. That should fix her.'

The man of the mind was worth every guinea. Joan was a martyr to nerves and stricken with repressed grief for her deceased mother. To endure the violent trauma of her beloved sister being killed in an air crash on top of all this was intolerable. Subconsciously she blamed her sister's ward for the accident. She felt herself and her family to be threatened by a murderer. Her dreams, her childhood and Digby's ready cheques were all very enlightening. It was clear that all threats to her tranquillity and recovery must be distanced until such time as she could sublimate her fears and cope with her neuroses.

The further Wolf was sent away the greater would be poor Joan's equanimity.

As for Felix and his education, there was nothing that all psychiatry could do to make him an Etonian, but in view of the lad's delicate lungs and weak chest would it not be preferable to send him to school in Switzerland instead?

Indeed it would. This seemed like a perfect solution.

In January 1958 Digby was to be posted to Germany. Joan would go with him and Felix would start at a villainously expensive establishment on the shores of Lac Lucerne. Penny would board at the preparatory department of the school to which both her mother and her late aunt had gone on the south coast, and Wolf would either start at Fairweathers or, if he failed the scholarship, get sent north to tough it out at Seaforth Crag.

'I didn't know that wee Felix had a problem chest,' Sheila Campbeltown said to her husband on hearing of the poor delicate boy's new school.

'Neither did I,' Magnus replied. 'Which isn't surprising. I am only his doctor, after all.'

Felicity was too anxious about her own entrance to Fairweathers to dread the changes planned but Ailsa was miserable. Penny was her best friend. Nothing, she said, would ever be nice again.

Lesser parents than Magnus and Sheila might have been rather smug. Their children had the knack of pleasing without being unbearably pleased with themselves. Felicity's musical talents came from her mother; Ailsa's cleverness came from her father. Neither questioned nor resented the way their lives were shaping.

Magnus, who found Penny Blackburn spoilt and bossy and not a little stupid, couldn't believe that it was just her departure which was distressing his little Ailsa. 'We can't all be nightingales, my wee lamb.'

'I don't want to be a nightingale, Dad. I don't want Penny to go away.'

'Is that all? And here's me thinking you were bothered about not being a musician like Felicity.' He kissed the top of her head. 'Everything changes all the time, that is what makes life exciting. I'll not be able to look down on your nice straight parting much longer with you growing up so willowy. You will find lots of new friends quick as winking, see if you don't. I'm no nightingale either but we wise old ravens know a thing or two even though we just croak.'

Magnus let her listen to his heart with his stethoscope and she cheered up. For now, at least, he still had the power to be a comfort. Ailsa was practical, she liked to know what things were for and why. Between them, she and her father had their doubts about the usefulness of music and nothing delighted her more than to have Magnus explain the purpose of all his instruments and to let her shine lights down his ears and take a look at the site of his absent tonsils.

'I expect you will get to see Penny lots of times when she has settled in her new home and she can come and stay here too. Won't that be grand?' Magnus added, fishing his trump card out of its case to Ailsa's horrified delight: his very largest syringe for jabbing Kilbole's hugest haunches.

Compared to Ailsa Campbeltown, Penny Blackburn was a lump. However, Joan hoped the puppy fat would dissolve just as soon as her ugly duckling met all those thoroughly sweet girls at her new school in Sussex, girls who spoke nicely, who rode their own ponies and had mothers who opened fêtes. Only the thought of these mothers visiting their Etonian sons on auspicious dates like the Fourth of June stabbed Joan in her disappointed heart. Still, with poor Felix and his chest, what else could be done but to send him to the clean Swiss air? Heaven knows what microbes might have leapt out of Datchet Mead or Queen's Eyot to do her golden boy dirt.

Jock Otway liked to be known as the Captain. His wife was Little Eva and together they kept themselves in spirits by running a sort of outward-bound holiday home for schoolchildren whose parents, for one reason or another, couldn't have them at home during the holidays. Only the children with parents stationed in the furthest postings stayed for all the time: even they generally had a friend or relative of sorts prepared to cope with them for a week or so. Though the Blackburns had yet to move to Germany, Wolf spent most of his last summer holidays from Gantry Close near Whiting Bay skirmishing about the coastline with his new friends throwing sheep droppings and putrefying sea urchins at intruders, while Digby introduced Felix to the superior joys of fishing and throwing lead at furry and feathered game.

Penny Blackburn broke her arm at Pony Club camp. Some of the autographs on her plaster were quite rude, as were the things relayed to her by the other campers before her accident. Of horse management she learnt nothing but of sex and boys and glories to come she learnt lots and lots. She was utterly fascinated by it all and resolved to get hold of a boyfriend the minute her flat front erupted.

Joan was becoming increasingly distant towards the Campbel-towns the more her Dingo got promoted. Sheila put this testy behaviour down to nerves. Magnus said Joan's nerves couldn't stand being blamed for much more, it wasn't fair: too much to expect of them altogether, poor little things.

Felix spent his last term at Gantry Close being a thorough nuisance. Idle and superior, handsome and supercilious, he exuded a magnetism that was not at all what was wanted. His newly established infirmity gave him a mysterious air of the exotic, like limping Lord Byron. Weaker and younger boys flocked in his wake. He had reached an age of bothersome late childhood and early puberty. Girls and sex troubled not only him but all the top form of Gantry Close: carnal disturbance was not dispelled by cold showers or muddy exercise.

Felicity was bewildered by her feelings and her changing body. Sheila's attempts to tell her the facts of life had been crude and embarrassing for both of them. Ailsa had gone straight to her father and demanded to know the lot in every scientific detail no matter how absurd and unlikely the information seemed. No stork or gooseberry bush was to be tolerated. Facts were what Ailsa wanted, and Magnus had obliged her. Felicity had been much more reticent and reluctant, unable to imagine how Ailsa's pragmatic biology could be involved with emotions. She marvelled at how all the songs on the wireless were about love, love and marriage, everlasting love and secret love, except on

Saturday mornings when Uncle Mac had nothing to do with love and concentrated on Laughing Policemen, Tubby the Tuba, Four Legged Friends and someone called Eddie whose trumpet was golden. She and Ailsa used to sing rounds of 'Frère Jacques' at full pitch to drown out creepy Sparky and his pesky Magic Piano.

Felicity Campbeltown was the most prized female to go near Gantry Close. A great giggling and shoving took place every time she came to play in the orchestra whose repertoire sounded ever more discordant as the Founder's Day concert approached. Parents and friends withstood the grinding rendering of 'St Anthony Chorale' and the plodding tootles of 'Trumpet Tune and Air' and were all busy planning their escape when the evening was saved by an astounding performance of an adaptation of the Largo from Bach's Double Violin Concerto in D Minor. Wolf and Felicity played with such feeling and musicianship that the audience was transfixed, suddenly afflicted by watery eyes and lumpy throats. Two twelve-year-old children absorbed and delighted by their skill had nothing whatsoever to do with infant prodigies or freakish precocity. Their ability was God given and miraculous. Such a long silence at the end made Wolf anxious. He looked at Sheila enquiringly: had he done wrong? Sheila was crying quite openly and Felicity, who had seen and understood, took Wolf's hand in hers. 'Come along, we ought to bow or something.' The applause was deafening and delightful. Wolf raised his eyes and saw the rows of friendly faces. He had never felt such warmth before and grinned back disarmingly.

'Go on, give her a kiss!' yelled Magnus from his seat at the back. Even he had been galvanised by the performance and he felt inclined to burst with pride not only for his daughter but also for his wife, who had been such an outstanding teacher.

'Kiss her. Kiss her!' the audience repeated.

'Shall I really?' Wolf asked the hall.

'Get on with it!' someone's father yelled back. 'Or I'll come and do it for you!'

With the joy of friendly laughter echoing round, Wolf kissed Felicity and then she kissed him back.

He felt a surge ignite him. His face glowed red as he realised how perfect it is to be loved. Since Clarice had died, hardly any-one had touched him; kisses were things that had only happened when he was little enough to have a nanny. Hanne's kisses were all in the past: a kiss from Felicity promised a wondrous future.

'Lucky sod!' said Forbes Two with envious admiration.

'I wish I was Felicity,' said Penny to Ailsa who was rather bored.

Only Felix felt a knife slide into his guts.

As autumn turned from gold to glum grey Felicity had a date to dread. Felix had asked her to come to the school party on November the 5th.

She refused. 'No thank you, Felix. I can't, I have to practise,' she replied rather priggishly.

She always tried to get out of Bonfire Night at Gantry Close. Year after year she had employed various ruses, every one of which had failed. This year with the Fairweathers entrance test only a fortnight away, she must succeed in avoiding the horrible event.

'Nonsense,' said Magnus. 'You deserve a bit of fun, Flicky.'

'I don't want to go, Dad.'

'Rubbish. You work too hard altogether. I won't have you missing a good time. What else did we fight the war for than to have our children grow up being able to enjoy themselves?'

Felicity knew she was defeated, and joined the others out of duty.

Despite the unusually mild night she wore earmuffs. They were made of fake leopardskin, bought from the penny surprise bucket at the Kirk Jumble and smelled quite nasty, having once belonged to Dafty Cora. Felicity tried not to think about that as she plugged her ears further with pill-bottle cotton wool, hoping that this added protection would make her deaf to all explosions. She could shut her eyes and pretend Guy was not being burnt. She hated that most. She wanted to rescue him and save him from the gloating frenzied mockery of children dancing around the grizzly execution. Christ upon the cross without a city wall never moved her as much as treacherous Guy on his sinner's pyre.

Ailsa came to the party too and so did Penny Blackburn.

'This is the last time I shall ever enjoy Bonfire Night in my whole life,' said Ailsa. 'I shall go into a recline.'

Penny was looking forward to moving south. 'I've got a boyfriend, Ailsa. Do you want to know who he is?'

Penny put her mouth to Ailsa's ear.

'Stop that at once, Penny!' said Joan, then added to her husband, 'What did I tell you, Dingo?'

'What did you tell me? You say so much, my dear that a poor straightforward soldier like me gets quite overwhelmed.'

'I told you that those doctor's children, the Campbeltown girls, are a really bad influence on Penny. Look at her giggling like an assistant in Woolworth's.'

Sheila wanted to check over both violins before the journey south to Fairweathers. Neither Felicity nor Wolf had ever been to England before.

Felix was in charge of creating the guy. It was a harmless occupation and kept him and his toadies quite well entertained. The effigy was dressed in incongruous castoffs including a cardigan that had once belonged to Clarice Duncan. 'Look, Duncan One. We are going to burn your Mutti in her stinking woolly. Don't you mind?'

Wolf shrugged. He had long since learnt to ignore Felix and his jibes. He had his own friends now and a life of his own in which the Blackburns were increasingly peripheral.

'Your Mutti loved Nazis, didn't she? That is why she bought you. All Germans are musical. That is why they had an orchestra at Auschwitz. You are a Nazi, Duncan One.'

'And you, Felix, are utterly pathetic,' said Wolf walking away.

'Wait, you scum! How dare you call me by my first name. Where are you going?'

'To see Felicity.'

'Felicity isn't coming, so hard cheese to you.'

'Yes she is. She brought me some crisps and I've got to take my fiddle along to her mother's car.'

Some other top form boys heard this and smirked. 'Woe Bet Blackburn. Woe Bet!'

'No one calls me pathetic and lives,' said Felix. His gang agreed that Duncan One should be wiped out.

*　　*　　*

The Coronation fireworks in Duncan Park had been but a fizzle compared to the annual blast at Gantry Close. The more bangers the better. Tame golden rain and pretty popping flashes were despicably girlish, something even a girl would hate to be called.

Felicity's ear-blocking devices were useless. The sausages were burnt on the outside and coldly raw within, a nursery for tapeworms which fascinated Ailsa and made Felicity cringe. Parents stood about pretending to enjoy the fun while longing for home and gin. Joan Blackburn was wearing a new coat made from an inside-out sheep which curled at the edges and was much too hot but greatly admired.

Penny and Ailsa had been given sparklers and ran about writing their names in the night air.

'What are you writing, Ailsa?'

'P-E-N-N-Y.'

'Why?'

'Because you are my best friend. You write my name now.'

'Why should I?'

'Because I'm your best friend.'

'No you aren't. I love my boyfriend much more than you. I'm going to marry him. He is going to put his thing inside me and we are going to make babies!'

Penny wrote W-O-L-F, shouting out the letters as the sparkler traced the name of her beloved. Joan clasped Ailsa by the forearm, her grasping scarlet nails quite painful through the duffel-coat sleeve. 'You silly, dirty little girl. How dare you fill Penny's head with nonsense? Thank goodness you won't see her again after this Christmas.'

Releasing Ailsa's arm, Joan addressed her husband. 'Dingo, listen. Do not expect me ever to have that horrible boy under my roof again. Wolf is evil, do you hear? I'm telling you he is the devil. Horrible little Kraut bastard.'

'Surely not, Joan sweetheart. He is just a young lad yet.'

'He is perverted, he is corrupting my children. You must get rid of him.'

'I'm doing my best, Joan. We can't shut him out of our lives completely.'

'Yes we can, Dingo. We must.'

28

Ailsa refused to tell her mother why she was crying. There was no point.

The fire was lit. Felicity was pleased that at least the fireworks were over apart from the odd squib inserted amongst the heap of scrap timber and stench-producing tyres. Sheila had told her children that the smoke had stupefied Joan of Arc long before the flames had begun to roast her. This comforted Felicity somewhat, though Ailsa said it was rubbish.

The guy's mask leered indifferently as the flames licked his clothing and Clarice Duncan's cardigan shrivelled and smouldered before catching alight.

Wolf stood alone, hands in his duffel-coat pocket amongst his Beechnut gum, conkers, caps and jacks. He was far away, imagining himself on stage at the Usher Hall and didn't notice Felix come up behind him accompanied by a party of his followers.

'Vell, Vell, Vell. Vot have ve got here?'

'Get lost, Felix.'

'Who is this vot is telling me to get lost? I think he should be taught a lesson. Come vith me, mein baby Führer.'

Felix, confident with the backing of his posse, pinched one of Wolf's prominent ears and twisted it till the younger boy squealed with real pain. Then he kicked his backside and forced him towards the fire. 'Hold him for me, Forbes Three. I want him to see what I'm going to do.'

Forbes Two's younger and less enterprising brother held Wolf from behind by pinioning his arms. There were at least three other boys. There was no question of escape.

'Look what I've got! Your precious violin, your silly fiddle that your nanny gave you, only it didn't belong to her father. Oh no, it belonged to your mother who used to play it while everyone else was being gassed. Didn't she? Answer me – didn't she?' Felix was shouting, his face inches from Wolf's nose. Behind him the flames of the bonfire shone like a halo round the black silhouette of his head: his features were obscured except for the reflected flashes off his tooth-straightening plate. 'Didn't she, Duncan One?' he repeated bringing his knee up to Wolf's groin.

'If you say so, Felix.'

'There, he's said it! Did you hear, everyone? His mother was the Witch of Auschwitz!'

'Felix. Stop being such a prize idiot.'

'Idiot? I'm an idiot, am I? We'll see about that! First we must burn what is left of the witch!' Felix waved the fiddle above his head. 'Will you throw this on the fire or shall I do it for you?'

'Stop it! Don't, Felix. Stop!'

No matter how loud his screams nothing could be heard above the crackle of flames and the other children's shrieks.

'Ha ha. Now I've got you!' Felix skipped towards the fire, singing.

> 'Rickety Tickety Tin.
> She danced around the funeral pyre,
> Playing the violin.'

Felix was now quite beyond reason, bewitched by his own strength and delirious with power.

> 'All they ever found were bones
> And occasional pieces of skin.'

He looked at Wolf, then returned to where he was held and peered into his face. 'He's crying!' he announced in triumph. 'Herr Hitler's little baby boy is blubbing! Let's make him really cry, shall we? Come on everyone. Let's burn his precious fiddle now. Let's give it to good old Guy.'

'Guy, Guy, Guy . . . Stick him in the eye. Put him on the bonfire to die die die!'

'Go on, Blackburn,' urged Forbes Three. 'I can't hold him much longer.'

'Here goes! Bye bye!'

Felix flung the violin far into the middle of the fire. It landed on the remains of the guy and burnt like tinder. The strings snapped apart and it was all over in a moment.

'Burn, burn, burn!' chanted the boys and then realising what had happened their vigour deserted them, bravado died and they became quiet and sidled off to be absorbed in the silenced crowd, leaving Felix to be faced by a tormented Wolf alone.

'That violin wasn't mine. You have burnt the wrong one, Felix.'

Only the crackle of the dwindling blaze could be heard as Felix was ordered home in disgrace, never to be seen at Gantry Close again. Being expelled upon the spot meant that at least he departed in style. Digby rang to apologise to Magnus and Sheila on his son's behalf. He had no idea why Felix had decided to burn Felicity's instrument, but there it was. Boys will be boys, youth must have his fling, nothing like a dose of high spirits, didn't they agree? No they didn't but accepted the offer of compensation with good grace: the violin, unlike Wolf's, was nothing special, there were plenty of others that could be got in time. Digby explained that Felix was highly strung like his mother.

'Infectious devils nerves, you know.'

'Oh I do,' Magnus replied.

The porch of the Shieling had been lightened by the insertion of knobbly glass panels in the outer door. Jelly danced upon by kittens was how Felicity had described it once, before Felix had told her that she was wet and probably thought she had fairies at the bottom of her garden with elves at home in toadstools.

Wolf was quite short for his age and she had known that it must be a child by the height of the distorted shape behind the obscured panes. As usual the Scotties had set up a snarling chorus of barks and howls when the bell was rung. It was a day or so after the bonfire party and Felicity was alone in the house. Her father was in his surgery, Ailsa was with Penny and Sheila had gone to Glasgow chasing an instrument for Felicity to play for her audition. Felicity was stage struck and liked the word 'audition'. It thrilled her like the exotic life led by the Fossil children in Noel Streatfield's *Ballet Shoes*. There were days when she only answered to the name of Pauline and made Ailsa crumple her toes walking on her points in gym shoes blocked with wodges of Bronco.

Wolf was holding his violin case. 'Here Flicky, this is for you.'

He presented it to her as if it were a coffin for a very small dead baby. 'Take it. I don't want it.'

'But Wolf. What about you? What about Fairweathers?'

'I'm not going to Fairweathers. I'm going to Seaforth Crag.'

'Why?'

'Because I want to.'

He turned and started to walk away, shuffling through the heaps of fallen leaves upon the gravel.

'Wolf, I can't have this. It is yours.'

'No, it is yours now. I don't need it any more,' he said. 'I want you to have it.'

Wolf had been looking at his scuffed shoes while he spoke to Felicity; only as he ended did he look at her with clear big eyes and a slight smile that showed his somewhat crooked teeth. 'I'm fine,' he said. 'I must go or I will miss the bus back to school. Goodbye.'

Felicity knew she should have followed him, made him stay at least until one of her parents came home but instead she let him go, watching him walk away in his outgrown school uniform with saggy grey socks crumpled round his thin ankles. He turned once more at the gate and waved, then broke into a run and scampering down the road skittered a stick along the neighbours' palings.

As she had stood on that porch step holding Wolf's precious violin she supposed that life from then onwards would be different. The Laughing Policeman was no longer funny, maybe he never had been. She had felt like crying because suddenly she knew that, now she was growing up, there were other things too that she would never find funny ever again. She didn't understand what there would be to take their place.

Part Two

I

London, April 1966

'I WANT TO dye!'
  'Madam?'

'Shoes, satin, plum. I wish to dye my daughter's satin shoes a pretty plum.'

That voice, with its coy sweet lisp, was unmistakable. Joan Blackburn sounded the same as she had nine years ago. Only her looks had sagged a bit despite her yet blonder hair being backcombed ever upward and lacquered to withstand any hurricanes happening about Belgravia. Joan's repeated request for shoe dye was peevish, uttered between stiffened lips that shone glossy peach as her duck-egg eyelids narrowed with intolerance. Bernice, the haberdashery assistant, was a bit stolid but selling 'notions' was a most pedestrian job. If it hadn't been for Felicity Campbeltown working three days a week Bernice might have jacked the whole thing in, given up her dream of becoming a buyer on lampshades and gone to work in a Wimpy Bar. Felicity lightened the load and gave Bernice an ear into which she could confide her troublesome romances.

'I can't bear it!' Joan wailed. 'I will go mad if I have another disappointment. It is too bad!'

Felicity heard this exchange from behind the display of zips where she was trying to get the lingerie repair kits into some semblance of order. Poor Bernice sweated when flustered. Peering over the carousel of embroiderers' requisites, Felicity saw that Joan was typical of most Sloane Square customers, complete with gilt trimmed shoes to match her patent bag, a harness-printed scarf knotted on its handle.

'Plum, madam? What variety of plum, may I ask? Victoria

35

or maybe a pleasant prune?' said Bernice, horribly aware that sweat stank.

'Can I help you, Mrs Blackburn?'

'Please do,' said Joan, turning on her spiky heel and smiling ingratiatingly. 'This young lady seems *distrait*. I am sorry, do I know you?'

'It is Felicity, Mrs Blackburn. Felicity Campbeltown from Kilbole.'

'My dear! Such a surprise.' Joan looked Felicity over in an instant. 'You've grown,' she stated as if her observation were wholly novel. 'How clever of you to recognise me.'

'You haven't changed,' Felicity lied, ignoring Joan's flabby throat and heavier figure.

'You are the image of your sweet mother, Felicity. How fortunate you took after her and not, well, not after anyone else,' said Joan with a girlish giggle. 'Penny doesn't look anything like me.'

'Major Blackburn is awfully handsome, though,' said Felicity. 'Maybe Penny looks like him.'

'Oh gracious no! Colonel Blackburn has a moustache. Perhaps you didn't know he has been promoted. He has such an important job now, in Whitehall at the War Office, or rather the Ministry of Defence, the same thing only less cross sounding, don't you think?'

It certainly was lucky that Felicity hadn't inherited her father's dumpy chubbiness and crinkled hair. At twenty, she was lovely. Tall, almost too slender with dark, near black, long hair, a clear complexion and large well-fringed brown eyes. She was nearly a beauty, only her over-big mouth and long nose prevented her from being fashion-plate material. Of her good looks she seemed charmingly unaware and unconcerned. She could neither afford, nor did she much wish, to look like a swinging Londoner. She had shortened her own hems and wore old shrunken jumpers instead of splashing out on miniskirts and skinny sweaters.

'Is this what you are looking for?' Felicity showed Joan a tin of wine-coloured dye.

'Yes, exactly, you clever girl. Tell me, what you are doing here anyway? I thought you were going to be a great musician, not peddling spare suspenders.'

'I'm waiting to go to the Royal Academy of Music. This is just a temporary job. I earn my money where and how I can.'

'What else can you do?'

'I can type. I learnt that while I did music in Glasgow. Dad made me learn, he wanted me to have something to fall back on.'

'How wise. I keep on telling Penny she should do a secretarial course. After all, even she might want to get a job one day. One never knows. Tell me, do you do shoe trees?'

'Plastic or wooden?'

'Plastic will do, and have you got those frames for putting under headscarves?'

'You mean one of these?' Felicity showed Joan a nifty device in canvas. 'You'll need some spray starch.'

'You are good at your job. What else can you do?'

'Apart from the violin and piano?'

'Yes, of course, I mean useful things, like flower arranging.'

'I can cook a bit. I've been going to Westminster Tech part time – the Bride's Course.'

'A bride! How time flies. Who are you marrying – some gorgeous Scotsman from dear old Kilbole?'

'No, no. That was just the name of the course. It cost less than a tenner and I learnt to souse herrings and make a cake look like a chicken.'

'How charming.'

'It was repulsive.'

'Where are you living?'

'With my godmother near Battersea Park.'

'South of the river?'

'Just.'

'Oh dear. Well, never mind. We live in Thurloe Place,' said Joan triumphantly. 'Awfully near Harrods, actually. You might like to come and see Penny some time, for coffee perhaps. Give me your telephone number.'

Preparations were already under way for the Chelsea Flower Show as Felicity walked home past the Royal Hospital. It was raining but she had spent the bus fare on sausage rolls. Aunt Myra Pennyfeather was kindness itself but Felicity was a carnivore and the never-ending nuts and pulses that were served up in the second-floor flat in Prince of Wales Mansions made her even envy the dogs their Pal, if not their boiled lights. Myra tolerated bloodiness in nature and her three rescued dogs were old, beyond being taught new dietary tricks.

White smoke rose into the glowering skies above the power station. Only a garish display of well drilled tulips erupting regularly amongst the wallflower carpet at the park entrance cheered the dank scene. London was brighter than Kilbole but hardly vibrant and throbbing for Felicity.

It had been her choice to come south. She had needed to get away before she took root in Scotland. There was no future for her there. She had also wanted to lose Rob. She liked him; once she'd thought she loved him, but there was no magic to be had in the back of his Land Rover and only tedium to anticipate at his side. Rob was kind and steady and loved her. He was also rich and competent, an ideal husband for anyone and Felicity was considered quite mad by all Kilbole to ignore such a brilliant opportunity to get settled. Only her parents understood why she had turned him down in favour of a most uncertain musical career and the gamble of finding herself a better man.

Felicity was still going to be a star. She was good; extremely good in fact. With a place at the Royal Academy, now only the occasional doubt about whether she was top flight troubled her. Myra Pennyfeather bothered her too, for she represented exactly what Felicity wanted to avoid: a good, competent musician but without luck or flair who eked a living by teaching and being second fiddle in a last-gasp ladies' string orchestra playing teatime medleys while other ladies shovelled up fancy pastries with dainty forks.

She trudged up the stone flights to Myra's flat. The first-floor baby was bellowing in competition with the baying dogs. It was Felicity's job to put all three mongrels on leads and take them to pee in the park. As this mixed bag squabbled and got muddled she felt like a battered maypole danced round by delinquents. Meanwhile Myra would prepare some vegetable wholesomeness which they would eat listening to the news before settling down to an evening of practice.

'It is very good of you to play for me,' said Felicity, who often wished Myra had more meetings of the Battersea Labour Party or CND to attend.

'I do it as a penance,' said Myra, who amongst other things had taken up Catholicism since her student days with Felicity's Presbyterian mother.

'I'm as bad as that?'

'No, my dear, you are good. I offer up my jealousy as an act of contrition.'

Some nights they went to concerts, often standing throughout the performance while Felicity dreamt of the day when she would be taking bow after bow and Myra tried to forget the time when she too had hopes.

It was a life, but not all that high.

'It's for you,' said Myra handing the phone to Felicity.

'Is it Rob?' Felicity mouthed back. She was fed up with his pestering pleas to her to return north.

'No. It is a lady. A very hoity-toity one too,' said Myra, forgetting to block the receiver.

'Hello.'

'Felicity?'

'Yes. Who is it?'

'Mrs Blackburn. Incidentally, who answered this first?'

'My landlady.'

'Is she mad?'

'Yes,' Felicity replied and then waited. 'What can I do for you, Mrs Blackburn?'

'You can cook, sweetie, can't you?'

'Well yes, a little bit.'

'You went on a course, didn't you? Something like Winkfield or the Cordon Bleu?'

'No, not exactly. I only learnt about herrings and covering yellow cakes with desiccated coconut, Mrs Blackburn.'

'Marvellous! I knew you would say yes.'

'What to?'

'Doing me a debs' mums' lunch.'

'What?'

'Not to worry. Colonel Blackburn says I can borrow Corporal Bolsover.'

'Oh good,' said Felicity.

'Come and see me tomorrow about eleven o'clock. Are you free then?'

'Yes,' Felicity replied weakly. 'I only work part-time.'

'Excellent. Here's the address. Top floor, mind the lift gates and don't be late, I must be off at noon for my feet – or is it my face? – no it's feet, I remember because I'm lunching at Lady Ravelston's.'

'Keep it simple, make it pink, pretty and possible for a fork. Corporal Bolsover has a brother in gulls' eggs.' Those were Joan's instructions to bemused Felicity, who was given no time to question or protest before a fiver and two pound notes were thrust into her hand and Joan left for the chiropodist saying, 'That should cover it, we will only be about twenty-five. I will expect you early next Tuesday.'

As the day of the lunch approached Felicity felt the kind of panic rising inside her that she always experienced before giving a performance. At least with cooking it is impossible to go blank and forget every note and how to play it, she thought – though she could still be incompetent. She had a recurring nightmare in which she was unable to open the piano lid or found the violin case empty as a packed concert hall awaited her recital.

'Coronation chicken and a nice trifle. You can do wonders with a swiss roll and custard powder,' said Sheila Campbeltown on the telephone when Felicity rang home almost in tears.

'Aunt Myra only allows dog food into her kitchen.'

'Dog food? You're never eating dog food! Are you?'

'No Mum, the dogs eat dog food. Aunt Myra says people should know better than to eat dead animals. She found me with a ham sandwich last week and went on for half an hour about how I had deprived this dear pig of the joys of life.'

'You must get married, Flicky.'

'What? Mother please, I want help with cooking this beastly lunch, not a husband.'

'People who don't marry take up weird ideas. Myra was never cranky at college. It is being a spinster that has turned her head. I understand she's a papist too.'

'And a Fabian and a pacifist. She goes on marches.'

'Flicky, come home. Come back here. Your father and I miss you terribly and poor wee Rob looks quite mortified.'

'Rob is never wee, or poor . . . he is a big blustery farmer.'

'He misses you.'

'Tell him to go and shoot something. That will cheer him up.'

'It's the wrong time of year.'

'It is?'

'Yes, Flicky. Even I know that! You will never make a farmer's wife.'

'I have no intention of being a farmer's wife, Mother, so stop match-making.'

'Please come home, darling. You can go on studying in Glasgow.'

'No, Mother. I like it here.'

'Oh well, please yourself. Your father sends his love and suggests tinned salmon and baked beans – wait a second Flicky, he is shouting something at me from the surgery . . . Right you are, Magnus, I'll tell her . . . Darling, he says there is nothing wrong with beetroot sandwiches.'

'Mother! They look like swabs. I must go now, Aunt Myra needs the phone.'

'I'll pray for you, darling.'

'Thanks, Mum. I wish you would cook for me instead.'

Laden with two cooked chickens from the Rotis-O-Mat, sliced ham, sausages, a pot full of pre-mashed potatoes, a giant jelly still in its basin, and a great many tomatoes, cream and shop-bought mayonnaise, Felicity spent most of her remaining earnings on a taxi from Battersea to Knightsbridge. Here it took her three jerky lift journeys to get all her kit into the Blackburns' flat. Corporal Bolsover was already there arranging flowers in fine tidy pyramids and folding napkins into water-lilies. He was about to embark on rose-shaped butter pats when Joan Blackburn returned from some beautifying appointment and announced that no less than thirty women were expected and had Felicity remembered about Mrs Goldmark?

'I am doing coronation chicken as well as ham cornets.'

41

'Oh dear. Not that ghastly dish again! What will people think?'

'It's pink, Mrs Blackburn, like you said, and fork-upable.'

'Yes dear, but also impossibly common.'

'Steady, Mrs Colonel,' said Corporal Bolsover. 'Why don't you go and lie down while I bring you a nice cup of tea.'

'Oh Corporal, you are a treasure!'

When Felicity went to boil them, most of the gulls' eggs, buoyed up by noxious gases, floated bobbing in the saucepan like dangerous Hallowe'en apples.

'Did your brother say when these were laid?' Felicity asked dubiously.

'Search me,' replied the corporal. 'It's hard to tell with a gull, not being your battery bird, you understand.'

Felicity boiled the eggs for fifteen minutes. She dismembered the chickens and coated the stringy flesh with pink sauce, then piped potato into the ham cornets. There was a lot of potato over so she put a frill of it round the chicken and the two dishes of sausages. Having washed the piping bag she refilled it with whipped cream and covered the giant jelly with ridged streams and blobs till everything looked as if it were trimmed with white fur and about to perform a pretty turn in *Holiday On Ice*.

One look at Joan's pained face told Felicity that this was not what Mrs Digby Blackburn had in mind when she had invited the cream of the Season's débutantes' mothers to her socially advancing luncheon. It was too late. The lift gates could be heard cranking shut and a vigorous humming of Waygood Otis tackle announced the imminent arrival of the first guests.

They fell upon each other with such enthusiasm that Felicity thought this must be a reunion of long-lost best friends until she saw that the kissing women never sullied their lips with fleshy contact and used the brief moment of embrace to scan the room over each other's shoulders for guests more fascinating, or gazed at their own immaculate reflections in one of the gilded mirrors that so cleverly added a spacious dimension to the cramped flat.

Dressed in a white stockman's coat (a present from Rob) Felicity did not present the right front-of-house image and was sent back to the kitchen while Corporal Bolsover dealt with coats and drinks. The ham cornets were uncurling in a sneering way, matching the lips of those who saw that the buffet was not from the same social echelon as the champagne which was being constantly poured into their glasses. 'The trick' – Corporal Bolsover told Felicity – 'is to keep them all topped up. That way they drink less but think they have drunk more and become far easier to handle, if you know what I mean.'

Corporal Bolsover was quite in charge and capable of handling twice the number. Felicity felt defeated. She could catch snatches of conversation through the hatch between kitchen and dining room. Most of the women had met each other before but were still prowling about in search of fresh addresses to add to their books and, most importantly, news of suitable young men to dance with their daughters once the cocktail season ended. Partners were vital for the forthcoming balls.

The gulls' eggs that weren't full of well-boiled baby birds were solid rubber, the gobbets of potato shot from the ham cornets like cannonballs and the coronation sauce had developed an odd wrinkly film. At least the sausages were inoffensive.

Felicity was summoned to mop a tomato-spattered pussycat bow belonging to a woman who, though well drenched with Jolie Madame, did not much resemble her scent, having the face and the stance of a doughty mule.

Felicity was invisible as she dabbed. The mule's conversation continued unabated throughout. 'I understand that Joan has got some sort of a nephew as well as a son,' she confided in a shout to a cerise greyhound.

'Really?' said the greyhound, metaphorically pricking up her ears and brightening like a mariner sighting land, before scrabbling in her bag for notebook and gold pencil. 'What is he called and how can one find him? Is he about?'

'My dear, he has the most dreadful German name, his father was evidently something quite awful but the poor child can't help that, and one cannot afford to be too picky or else our girls will end up dancing with each other as one understands they do in dance halls. Thank you, that is fine now,' said the mule, dismissing Felicity, who retreated to scrape off rejected food and wash up heaps of plates. The telephone rang and she shook her arms free of suds to pick up the receiver in the hall.

'Hi. Corporal Bolsover?' said a female voice.

'I'll get him. Hold on.'

'Who is that?'

'I'm the cook, madam,' Felicity answered.

'Flicky! It's me, Penny. How are you? I was just ringing to find whether it was safe to come home yet.'

'It depends what you mean by safe.'

'Is the flat still full of vultures?'

'Fit to burst, I'd say.'

'Damn. I'm fed up with traipsing round the Natural History Museum. Bloody sponges!'

'Who?'

'Sponges in glass cases, they're frightfully boring and I've done the dinosaurs to death.'

'Why can't you come home, Penny?'

'Because I'm meant to be getting groomed, and I hate all those screeching mummies. I hate watching them be thankful that I'm not their daughter.'

'I've seen your photograph, Penny, you look lovely.'

'It's a fake.'

'Come and hide in the kitchen with me.'

'Can I? Will you smuggle me in?'

'Of course. Ring twice and then I'll know who it is.'

'No need, I've got a key. Just make sure Bolly stops anyone spotting me.'

Even without the ghoulish make-up Felicity would never have known Penny Blackburn, who had swollen from cumbersome little girl to hefty young woman. She was right: the misty studio portrait of dewy delicacy *was* a fake. Penny's rosy cheeks were plastered with pancake to cover the lumps of massed spots. Her eyes were encircled and extended with spikes of eyeliner and her lips were thickly matt coated in palest marshmallow pink. Her miniskirt concealed none of her far from mini thighs, and her hair had been geometrically cut, presumably by a sadistic drunk.

'Don't tell me! I know! I'm a wreck. This is all such hell.'

'But Penny, it's heaven to see you again. Ailsa will be so excited when I tell her.'

'Where is Ailsa?'

'She is just about to do her highers. She's going to come and stay once this last term ends. She is very clever. She wants to become a mathematician. She even knows about computers.'

'Good for her! I only understand my times tables if I start at one two is two and work up. Ailsa won't want anything to do with me.'

'Of course she would love to see you,' said Felicity uncertainly. Ailsa and Penny now lived on different planets.

Things were sour. Joan's luncheon had not ignited and her own address book still remained top heavy with heavy top-drawer girls and light on suitable men. Her popularity depended on the production of her scrumptious son but plummeted when those who asked Felix to their parties were obliged to invite his clod-hopping sister too. There was to be no having of one without the other. By mentioning the possibility of another male, Wolfgang Duncan, whom she described as having belonged to her late widowed sister, she had regained some ground but regretted the introduction the moment his name tumbled off her tongue. The champagne was to blame: it always made her over-chatty and prey to hung-over regrets and headaches.

Joan's dislike and resentment of Wolf had, if anything, increased over the years, though Digby Blackburn had respected the psychiatrist's opinion and seen to it that Wolf spent the minimum of time with his adopted family. Once he had left school he had become virtually independent. He had got a place at London University and lived in digs off Warren Street. By playing the piano in clubs and pubs Wolf managed to finance his second greatest passion – rock climbing. The rest of the time he waited tables or took temporary shop jobs down the Charing Cross Road.

Joan hadn't seen him since Christmas when she always felt compelled to be kind, if only to bring up the subject of how she missed her dear, dear sister Clarice, the saint who had plucked Wolf from the horrors of defeated Germany and who had been so tragically killed on another Christmas Day in 1954. Everybody cringed as year after year Joan succeeded in ruining all vestiges of jolly good will by becoming tearful even before the drink made her maudlin.

Still, desperate situations demand desperate measures and, short of hiring a gigolo, there was no option for Joan but to wheel in Wolf as Penny's partner for Queen Charlotte's Ball. Penny had said she would die rather than be escorted by her brother. Felix was not available anyway as he had already been asked to partner at least three other girls.

Once the last guest and Corporal Bolsover had left, Joan lay down in her darkened room with weary cucumber slices on her tired red eyes. As Felicity put the place to rights, Penny ate her way through most of the leftovers and declared herself delighted with the jelly.

Officially at four, Penny was due to leave for a tea party where she would make nice friends. Unofficially, she was going to lie low in the V & A.

'It is big, I'll say that for it.'

'What is?' Felicity asked.

'The Bed of Ware. Big, but not really what you'd call great. It palls after a while like standing round at bleeding cocktail parties trying to look cool talking to yourself, puffing on your thousandth cigarette, praying for a man to fancy you while pretending that you don't want anyone to ask you out to dinner and that you are proud of having more fat and more spots than anyone else in the whole of the western hemisphere.'

'Is it really that grim? I've never been to a cocktail party,' said Felicity.

'Lucky you. Actually you would be fine, no juicy spots, no spare tyres, and you've got loads of long hair. You would be snapped up and taken off to a bistro to eat *coq au vin* by the light of a candle in a bottle before anybody even got round to asking whether you were going to have a dance or if your father owned a grouse moor.'

'My father owns a hen run. What is the point of all this if you hate it so much?'

'Fun, Flicky dear. Fun and making sure that virginities get lost in nice places. Only some of us can't lose them anywhere, not even nasty places.'

'Do you get to meet the Queen?'

'No, not any more, not like Mummy. We have to curtsy to a cake.'

'I don't believe you.'

'It's true. I've been to special cake curtsying lessons with a woman who farted.'

Crabby but rested, Joan reappeared in a scarlet dressing gown. She was quite shattered and asked Felicity to make her some China tea.

'Then go home, Felicity dear. I am sure you have busy things to do.'

Felicity hadn't been paid.

'Shall I send you a bill, Mrs Blackburn?'

'What for? I've already paid you. I gave you seven pounds last week, don't you remember?'

The vase on the hall table was the antithesis of a useful pot. Naked putti clasping garlands encircled its slender neck above roundels depicting frolicsome half-dressed, half-baked Arcadians loafing about to no good purpose. The artefact was a hideous liability and a hazard to display, fragile as it was precious, and worth heaps.

Felicity packed her stuff and prepared to leave. She had no money at all: it would take at least an hour to lug all her kit back to Battersea. Her sleeve caught on the table corner as she tried to lift her box of empty dishes. Yanking it free, her arm flailed and tipped the vase. She watched it slowly topple: her arms were full and she could do nothing to stop it tumbling. Over the edge it rolled and dropped. The thick Turkish rug would have limited the damage; all might have been saved. The vase landed upon the uncarpeted boards, scattering its cherubim and embellishments all about like rubble.

'What is going on? What has happened?' Joan's voice shrieked from her sitting room. Felicity looked in horror at the wreckage, dumbstruck and tearful. There was nothing at all she could do.

'Whoops! That was silly of me, Mother!'

A fair young man, not tall but lean and handsome, had caught

47

hold of Felicity, and prevented her from speaking by putting his hand over her mouth. 'I've broken that bloody pot, Mother, dreadfully sorry and all that.'

He winked at Felicity and she recognised him. It was Felix.

2

FELIX DROVE A low, open car, all wood and leather inside with a British racing green exterior. As he ran Felicity home to Battersea they passed Bernice at the bus stop. Waving to her from the two-seater was a rare treat and delightfully sinful, the sort of behaviour that would have sent Godmother Myra hot-footing to confession, but didn't rattle Felicity. Not to have been seen would have been a catastrophe, like playing to an empty house.

Joan had lamented the value of the shattered vase. 'It cost your Cousin Cedric thousands,' she wailed.

'Oh balls to that, don't bang on! It was one of his rejects. I would have inherited it anyway one day, so it was mine to smash. Can I have a fiver please, Mother? Actually, make it a tenner.'

'Darling, you are so extravagant,' said Joan, wagging a sunset-tipped finger in mock admonition and delving into her purse where Felicity caught a glimpse of many more banknotes, none of which were coming to her.

Felix braked outside Myra Pennyfeather's mansion block.

'Thank you, that was wonderful.'

'What was wonderful, Flicky?'

'The lift home, the car, everything.'

'Me?'

Much to her dismay Felicity felt herself going red. She always said she never blushed. She was wrong; she did.

'You've gone scarlet!'

'Sorry.' Felicity felt her cheeks were on the boil.

'It is lovely, just like the rest of you.'

'Stop it, Felix.'

'You sound like a shop girl!'

'I am a shop girl.'

'No you aren't. Tonight you are going to be my girl. Have

49

you got something a bit less grotty to wear? I want to show you off.'

The stench of sauerkraut and curried eggs wafted from Myra's kitchenette and the disgruntled dogs scratched themselves irritably, peeved to have been kept waiting for their evening airing. Felicity was late.

'I've cooked us something really special tonight,' said Myra. 'We can eat it before the film show – the Clapham Internationalists have obtained a copy of *The East is Red* and the Battersea Socialists have been invited to see it with wine and cheese.'

Felicity explained that she had been asked out. For a moment Myra allowed herself to show her disapproval and disappointment before mustering her Christianity and saying she quite understood, that she herself had once been young and that it would be her pleasure to lend Felicity her best *petit point* evening bag that had been much admired in its day.

Felicity's one dress had been christened 'The Grave Error'. It had come from Wallis in Glasgow and was utterly plain, terrifically short, making her the image of Jean Shrimpton at the Melbourne races. Aunt Fay Braid had been outraged at its brevity and quite mortified by the delight it provided the Kilbole Institute when Felicity had lifted her fiddle to her chin and given the audience an eyeful of her lovely legs. 'Lionel, I forbid you to look!' Fay had hissed at her salivating husband. 'This is a charity concert, not a night-club.'

The dress was purple and did well against Felicity's dark hair. As usual her legs were bare: tights cost too much and stocking tops would have shown beneath the hemline like a Ronald Searle St Trinianite.

She wore very little make-up and her concert shoes, which were flat and safe. A doleful locket containing the hair of a long-dead, long-forgotten Campbeltown was her only bit of jewellery. 'This is the best I can do, Felix.'

'Christ!'

'Sorry? Is anything wrong?'

'No, nothing, absolutely nothing whatsoever.' He kissed her on the cheek. Felix smelled expensive.

'We will start at the Cavalry Club and work downwards to the

Lords via the Zoo, which should be fun. Later on we might take in the Goldmarks' do at the River Room. Thursdays are always such a rush.'

'What do you do, Felix?'

'I'm at the Royal College.'

'I'm going to the Royal Academy.'

'Mum is frog-marching Penny there next month, in a hat.'

'Really? She never said, I didn't know Penny was musical.'

'Penny is tone deaf.'

'What are you reading at the Royal College?'

'Timeform mostly.'

Felicity laughed, not sure why. She was baffled by this new world filled with frivolous and prosperous improbabilities. 'I can't go to these parties, Felix, I haven't been invited.'

'Don't worry, it's easy. Just answer to the name of Penelope for the first one; after that it will be a piece of cake.'

'What if Penny is there?'

'She won't be, I've given her enough money for another ticket to *Dr Zhivago*. Hardly anyone knows Penny and absolutely no one will miss her. She hates these things anyway and always goes home by herself. She can't talk and looks like a tip. If it wasn't for our joint party in Scotland later this summer Penny wouldn't have got an invitation to anything. Don't fret, Flicky, it will be plain sailing once you're through the first door.'

They were early for the Cavalry Club party where Lady Adelaide Trencher-Turpin and her puzzled husband, Colonel Hartley Trencher-Turpin were At Home for their horsy daughter Griselda. All three Trencher-Turpins were lined up at the door and what must have been a retired drill sergeant was announcing the guests.

'Damn,' said Felix. 'This requires tactics. Wait here.'

Felicity studied a print of pig-sticking, which looked like no fun for anyone. Felix returned with a thickset redheaded youth. 'Rescued by your fellow countryman, Flicky! This good man will fix it for us, won't you, Mungo? I'll sign you in for a whole week of lectures. This is Mungo McInlay, we are old muckers.'

Mungo sidled up to the announcer. 'I say,' he said, 'I wonder whether you would be so good as to direct me to the In and Out.'

'Certainly sir, just continue up Piccadilly in an easterly direction.'

'Sorry, where is the east? I've no bump of locality.'

'Towards Piccadilly Circus, sir.'

'Which way is that? I'm from Scotland, you understand.'

'Very well sir, I'll show you.'

Felix pushed Felicity through the door towards the hosts. 'Quick, Flicky. Now's our chance.'

Down the reception line they travelled, handed from one Trencher-Turpin to the next as in a dance. It was easy if taken at speed. Horsy Griselda took after her mother, the mule, whose pussycat bow Felicity had mopped only six hours since. As a servant Felicity had been invisible; as a guest she was the centre of attraction. Even Colonel Hartley Trencher-Turpin cheered up: maybe all this ado was not such a waste of precious funds.

A tray of drinks was offered and they helped themselves to champagne.

'Hold on to your glass, Flicky, we'll take it with us.'

'Why?'

'You'll see.'

Groups of girls dressed as abbreviated Regency dolls stood about smoking and eyeing the sparse amount of men who were knocking back the drink as if the world was ending shortly. Felix steered Felicity towards a fellow with the half-closed eyes of a languid reptile. 'Chat to Flicky, Malcolm. But hands off, she's my bird.'

'Hello Felix,' said a girl with extra hair. 'Why didn't you ring?'

'I lost your number,' he replied pushing past her to another dolly with artificial flower earrings. 'Hello, you're new. I'm Felix. Are you having a dance?' he asked bluntly. When the girl replied in the negative he moved on to a side table and filled his gold case with the cigarettes on offer.

'Are you at college with Felix?' Felicity asked Malcolm.

'Christ, no. Do I look like a mud student?'

'What is a mud student?'

'Felix is at Cirencester, the agricultural college.'

'He is never a farmer!'

'He is certainly never there. I don't think he would much like to be called a farmer; more of a landowner-in-waiting. I'm in Lloyd's myself.'

'Which branch?'

Malcolm looked at Felicity with disbelief and then burst into laughter. 'Are you wearing a bra?'

Felix returned. 'Watch out, Flicky, I think we're rumbled. One of those harpies was at school with Penny. Have you got your glass?'

'Yes.'

'Put it in your bag.'

'It won't fit,' said Felicity indicating Myra's *petit point* reticule.

Once in the descending lift Felix put both glasses in his pocket and they set off in Mungo's tracks to the Naval and Military Club where a desperate mother had invited everybody she had ever heard of. Only nonentities had turned up, none of whom were known to either her or her daughter.

Felicity longed to have a look round but nobody seemed in the least bit interested in the architecture or the history of the place and all the talk was of where next they could go. The Trencher-Turpins' party was obviously a flop, and this unknown hostess was serving shoddy champagne. Anybody with their wits about them was off to the Zoo.

Driving through Regent's Park Felix put his hand on Felicity's knee. 'God, Malcolm was right – you are naked underneath.'

'No, I'm not,' Felicity replied, recalling her none too perfect washed-out knickers, and how ashamed her mother would be of her should she be in an accident wearing them.

'Do be careful, Felix.' They missed a pedestrian on a crossing by inches.

'Stop fussing, woman.'

The trick worked again. By entering a room holding a used glass everyone assumed that the gatecrasher had been admitted earlier and was now just returning from a visit to the loo. The party was in the boardroom of the Zoological Society and some socially acceptable beasts had been brought along to meet their human equivalents. The brute race won the prize for amiability and good manners. Felicity was asked to stand beside a gregarious macaw while an elegantly coiffed man took a photograph.

Felix grabbed her and pulled her away. 'Take care, you tit.

You may be the prettiest girl here but no gatecrasher gets her face in the glossies and lives. Avoid that woman with the yellow hair and velvet bow too: she's licensed to kill.'

Somehow Felix couldn't remember where he had parked the car and Felicity thought it wiser to pretend ignorance also. Six revellers in each of three taxis then swooped down upon the House of Lords where an avuncular but firm constable said that Lord and Lady Ravelston's party was over. Only those in evening dress could hope to get into the Goldmark do: the Savoy staff were famous for vigilance.

Five stragglers, including Felix and Felicity, sheltered from the drizzle beneath the hotel awning as they determined what to do next. It was too late for the cinema and much too early for bed. Besides, they were still hungry despite eating mountains of canapés which had emptied whole rivers of salmon and most lumpfish of their roe. (Only the Goldmarks would have real caviar but even that would be spread as thin as one rabbit's droppings on a golf course.)

'We could go to the Saddle Room.'

'Great! Is anyone a member?'

No one was.

'How about the Marquee?'

'Christ no.'

'I'm starving. Let's go to the Unity.'

'And pay? You must be barking.'

'Felix, I think I had better get home now,' said Felicity. 'Aunt Myra will worry.'

'Let her. I know what – we'll go up to Little Venice. I happen to know those awful Von Hoffers are having yet another thrash tonight.'

'How come? They had one last week for Angelica.'

'Scraping the barrel. If you had a daughter like Angelica you would give a party every night. I keep my ear to the ground, I do,' said Felix.

Money was getting short so they took the Bakerloo line. Felicity studied the advertisements for Speedwriting and the Ring Road To Bravingtons, trying to disassociate herself from Felix and his friends, who seemed to enjoy irritating their fellow passengers by talking in blasé voices, giving the plebs a treat.

Nevertheless, for all the party's bravado, only Felix and Felicity were left to get off the tube at Warwick Avenue. Felix seemed determined to get to the Von Hoffer party: it was as if he had something to prove. Felicity had drunk more in one night than in her entire previous life and felt fit enough to vanquish all obstacles until she saw the scale and grandeur of the Von Hoffer establishment. Then even she, soaked in champagne, became apprehensive.

The Von Hoffers were rich, generous and considered a bit vulgar: ripe victims for poorer, meaner and older established predators and sponges. Angelica von Hoffer was a quiet serious girl, whom nobody much liked; she was short-sighted with eyes that appeared vast behind her thick glasses. She had no frivolous conversation and Felix insisted that crashing her party would be doing her a kindness. She only seemed stupid because she was so clever. Angelica wanted to study physics, her mother wanted her to retrieve a title to compensate for the one the Von Hoffers had forfeited by fleeing Hungary and her father was discovering, rather too late, that hurling money at problems merely caused them to multiply. This latest Von Hoffer bespoke extravaganza had already been running its dismal course for a couple of hours by the time Felix and Felicity got to Clifton Villas. Flowers, food, wine, glasses, staff – maybe even some of the guests – were hired for the night. Tomorrow they would be gone and Mr von Hoffer would be left with the bill, his wife seething with disappointed frustration and his daughter happily back in her room plotting polar curves.

'Not the front door, you ninny. We can get in through the kitchen,' said Felix taking Felicity's hand and pushing her through a side entrance.

'Don't, Felix, we can't. I mean it isn't right. I thought you said you knew these people.'

'I do. But we need to be a bit subtle. Trust me.'

A girl dressed as a waitress was leaning against the dustbins having a smoke.

'God, but you are gorgeous,' said Felix.

'Who are you?' she replied, not visibly flattered.

'Go and find your bartender for me, there's a good girl. Tell him some friends want to see him, friends from Scotland.

55

Whatever is a girl with your glorious legs doing in a pisspot job like this?'

'Earning my keep.'

'There are easier ways.'

'Like gatecrashing?'

'Run along my dear, I'm getting bored.'

She stubbed her cigarette out and ground it with her heel before disappearing into the busy kitchen. 'You'd better come in and wait inside,' she said. 'It's about to rain again.'

A brown-haired young man in an ill-fitting white coat came through the kitchen swathed in steam generated by epic washing up.

'Oh it's you, Felix. Sorry I can't help. Please go.'

'Wait little cousin, I've brought someone to see you. You remember Flicky, don't you?'

Wolfgang was not much taller than Felix, and apart from being darker, could have been his brother except that where Felix had thick lips and a loose mouth Wolf had an altogether less louche and self-assured demeanour. He smiled enchantingly, showing his uncorrected crooked teeth.

Something about him made Felicity feel horribly ashamed. She felt in the wrong: she had been stupid, blinded by Felix and his sophisticated veneer.

'You'll get us into this bash, won't you, Wolf?'

'No, Felix, I'm sorry I simply can't. You wouldn't enjoy it anyway.'

'Of course we would. Besides, we are hungry.'

'There is tons of stuff left over, I'm sure we can fix you up something in here. Perhaps you could lend a hand? They haven't hired nearly enough staff to cope.'

'Don't make me laugh, Wolf. Me, wash up? You must be mad.'

'Let's go, Felix, please,' said Felicity grasping his sleeve.

Felix shook her hand free. 'Go and find Angelica. She will be so pleased to see me, I mean, us. I want to do the poor girl a favour. She will have us in there like a flash.'

'You don't understand, Felix, it isn't that kind of party.'

'Do what you are told, Wolf!'

A stout woman expensively dressed in slippery magenta had

come into the kitchen. Like Joan, her hair was styled in a stiff dome with ends curling outwards. 'What is the trouble?'

'Nothing, Mrs von Hoffer,' said Wolf.

'Who are these people?'

'I am a friend of Angelica's, Mrs von Hoffer.'

Felicity hadn't heard what had been said as Felix signalled her to follow him and Mrs von Hoffer upstairs. While Wolf was sent to find Angelica she lost her nerve completely and blurted out, 'It was very kind of you to ask me, but I think I ought to go.'

'Wait there. Did I ask you, my dear? Are you sure?'

Numb with fear, Felicity couldn't bear to look at Mrs von Hoffer. Through the door she could see a baby grand.

'Oh what a lovely piano,' she exclaimed.

Wolf returned with a wan girl wearing glasses. She had been to the same photographer as Penny: her portrait, which stood on the Bechstein's lid, was virtually unrecognisable.

'Angelica, darling!' Felix swooped on the poor girl and planted kisses on her pallid studious cheeks, unsettling her spectacles.

'Did you invite this young man, Angie dear?' her mother asked.

'No,' Angelica replied bluntly.

'Well, in that case I must ask you to leave. Show him out,' she commanded Wolf. As Felix was hustled away Felicity found her arm firmly held in Mrs von Hoffer's diamond-encrusted grip.

'Not you. You stay. I presume you are the person sent to play the piano.'

'Not entirely,' Felicity answered.

'The agency must have found us a pianist after all. Splendid, we are all agog.'

Felicity realised that Mrs von Hoffer was trying to exact revenge, to get her own back by humiliating her in public.

The thrilling dread of pre-performance apprehension churned her innards. The champagne anaesthetised the agonising panic that otherwise she would have felt had she offered to play without either music or rehearsal before a houseful of strangers. She seemed removed and remote from the event as she took her seat on the stool and shook her hair back before attacking the keyboard. Inside her head Aunt Fay's voice nagged, calling her a show-off. Damn Aunt Fay, she thought, I like showing off.

The notes jostled and tumbled over each other as if hurrying to shelter. The initial clumsiness of Felicity's performance dented her carefree exuberance: she must grip herself, purge her befuddled mind and stop her fingers stumbling. The music she played was from her familiar examination repertoire: Chopin's waltz in A flat major, Liszt and Debussy *études*, a flourish of Rachmaninov – pieces she could have done upside down or blindfolded, all played with over-confident careless enthusiasm.

She stopped and looked up to desultory applause. Most of the guests who had gathered to listen looked ancient, nowhere near Felix's age group. Wolf had been right. This wasn't an affair that should have been gatecrashed – it was grandmother Von Hoffer's eightieth birthday party.

'You play quite prettily for one so young,' the old woman conceded. 'Given time and much more practice you might, just might, make a competent second-class accompanist.'

'You have probably heard of my mother-in-law, the most celebrated soloist of her day in Budapest,' said Mrs von Hoffer, then mentioned a name that was etched in Felicity's mind. Someone for whom no one would dare play when sober, let alone half drunk.

'Oh my God!'

'Yes. Well, there you are. You had better go now. Goodnight to you.'

It was no longer raining but the spring night was chilly, as Felicity headed for home. With luck she might pick up a 137 bus if she got to its route in time; if not she would have to walk. From Warwick Avenue to Battersea must be about the same distance as Kilbole to the nearest beach, a long pleasant walk on a summery day but arduous by night. Fear of being attacked didn't worry Felicity, not now that all her emotions were smothered by overwhelming embarrassment.

'Stop, Flicky. Wait a second.'

Wolf in his bartender's coat caught up with her as she reached Blomfield Road. 'Wait in the kitchen, I'll take you home on my bike once I've cleared up.'

'I can't go back in there. I'd rather be murdered.'

'You played brilliantly, you know, if that is what worries you.'

'I played like a cow. I've been a prize idiot. God, I'd have died rather than do that in front of her, of all people.'

'She was jealous.'

'Her – jealous of *me*? Never. She was quite right. I had no business playing like that. I had no business being there either.'

'Listen, Flicky. I tell you she was jealous. She is an old woman and, what's worse, she can no longer play herself. Did you see her hands? She is crippled with arthritis, nothing works for her any more. Being horrible to you was her best birthday treat.'

Wolf was being kind and Felicity knew it. 'At least I didn't disgrace myself on the fiddle.'

'My fiddle, the one I gave you?'

'Yes. That's the most important thing in my life. If I got so I could no longer be a violinist I would want to be put down.'

'Well now you know how that poor old woman felt about seeing a beautiful young girl achieving something she would never be able to do again herself.'

'Thank you, Wolf.'

He took her hand and gave it a reassuring squeeze. She felt his warmth flood through her and she looked up to see him smile. 'None of this matters, Flicky, does it?'

'No, but I should never have gone gatecrashing.'

'That wasn't your fault.'

Felix must have remembered his earlier parking place in spite of not yet being sober. His brakes squealed as he stopped where Felicity and Wolf were standing.

'Flicky is with me, Wolf, not you.'

'Then I suggest you look after her.'

'Run along little cousin, get back to your work or you will get the jolly old sack.'

'Thanks to you, Felix, I expect I already have. Goodnight.'

They drove home without speaking as Felix shot down Park Lane and round Hyde Park Corner and Belgrave Square at close on seventy miles an hour. Only a few stragglers outside the Royal Court saw him hurtle through Sloane Square before taking the turn towards the river.

It was pure luck that got him safely to Prince of Wales Drive.

'You'll kill yourself, Felix, driving like that.'

'Good. I intend to die young. Didn't you enjoy that, Flicky?'

'No. You did that on purpose.'

'I always drive like that.'

'I meant you knew perfectly well where Wolf was working. You set out to humiliate him and to make fun of us both. Good-night, Felix.'

'That isn't true. I never meant to make trouble. I thought it would be fun.'

'Is it fun tormenting people? Was it fun to make me miserable, to lose Wolf his job?'

'Flicky, please, I meant well. It is just that no one understands me.'

'I understand you, Felix.'

'No you don't. You are being most unkind. I have an awful life.'

'What on earth do you mean? You have got everything you want dished out to you on a plate.'

'That's the point – I need some excitement, something more. Hey, wait! You can't leave me like this.'

She tried to worm out of the car, but it was so low that its door only jammed on the pavement. Felix put his hand gently round her shoulders and said quietly, 'You must at least let me kiss you.'

'Goodnight, Felix.' She gave his cheek a quick peck and felt tomorrow's stubble grate on her lips. He leant across her and, pulling the passenger door shut, placed his mouth gently over hers. He tasted rich, of wine and tobacco. She couldn't struggle, and she didn't want to escape from such surprisingly wonderful pleasure entwined in that cramped car which smelled of leather and horse. Like eating fudge and listening to Haydn's *Andante Cantabile* it made her tingle and her whole body responded with shivery thrills.

'There now. That wasn't all bad was it, my angel?'

Felix had childishly blue eyes hooded by adult lids and a skilful mouth that could be cruel or could pout with an injured innocence. His hair was thick and fair, and he was a miraculous kisser, which made it worse because she knew she shouldn't even like him. At least she could have been fond of good Rob though his kisses had been forgettable, the sort during which she could plan what to do the following morning. Felix was a rather pathetic, spoilt, stupid, conceited young man, but oh God, being held by him was bliss. He whispered silly things about how lovely she was.

She broke loose, scrambled out of the car and ran up the steps to where Myra was waiting for her in a mothy kimono, her long hair plaited for the night.

'You forgot to take your key. I wasn't spying.'

'Thank you, Myra. I am so sorry. I have made a complete ass of myself.'

'No Felicity, not completely. You have many years left for doing that.'

3

WAVING AT BYSTANDERS from smart cars is for royalty only. Five minutes at the shop the next morning and Felicity knew that for certain.

'I hate those open cars,' said Bernice. 'I said to my Brian that I wouldn't ride in his MG not after what it done to my hairpiece. Mind you, Alan has got an E-Type and I don't care for that neither but then I don't like Alan no more and I said to my friend Corinne – you know, the one with the Vidal Sassoon haircut done at Derry and Toms? – I said she could have Alan any time and see if I cared. Flash cars don't mean nothing, Felicity, nothing at all. What you wants is love.'

'How is Brian, by the way, Bernice? I haven't heard much about him for a while.'

'I'm through with him. If he can't be bothered to ring me, I can't be bothered to go out with him. It's Kevin for me, he looks like that Peter Noone.'

'Well I hope for his sake he doesn't drive a sports car,' said Felicity.

Things were quiet in Notions between the early panic shoppers in dire need and the leisurely browsers with time they couldn't fill and purses they couldn't empty. Felicity wished Bernice would shut up. Her world of pop stars and chat-up lines sprang entirely from the copies of *True Romances* she devoured nightly on the bus to Turnham Green. By noon Felicity's thirst was cruel. Half an hour till her lunch break and her mouth felt like a desert while her head ached and throbbed. She had never had a hangover before nor had she ever experienced such remorse and embarrassment: the memory of the previous night kept returning to prod her damaged self-respect.

'Well hello.'

'Felix, please go away.'

'Why? I've come to shop.'

'You have come to be a nuisance. Go away.'

Felix stood, arms folded, head on one side and stared at Felicity, blocking her path between the shelves of haberdashery. He was in the uniform of the off-duty young upper-class male, the tweed jacket, cravat and cord trousers which, combined with his floppy blond hair, heavy lids and large thick-lipped mouth, completed the image of aristocratic cad he had been at such pains to contrive.

'Please let me pass, Felix. I have work to do.'

'You look so severe with your hair up, Flicky. Like a schoolmistress. Do you beat naughty boys, by any chance?'

'Felix I will get you thrown out of the shop if you don't behave.'

'They wouldn't dare. My mother has an account, I'm here on business. I want to buy some of these.' He picked up two packets of dress protectors. 'Tell me, Miss Campbeltown, are these satisfactory? Do they protect all dresses from all attacks on all sides? Aha! A travelling coat hanger – Have hanger will travel! What have we here? . . . a boudoir cap! Well, I won't be wanting that, my boudoir has already got a cap. Talking of which, do you do Dutch caps? Those rubber gloves are so provocative. Tidgey weenie clothes pegs, just the job for fairies . . . Flicky you work in an Aladdin's cave!'

'That will be three and fourpence,' said Felicity, putting the dress protectors in a paper bag.

'Wait, I haven't finished. Who is this? Where have you been hiding all my life, you living doll? You will do me nicely, my dear. Make my day!'

Bernice giggled and her striped grey shirt was instantly in need of protection.

Knicker elastic, bra straps, nappy pins, kirby grips . . . Felix made Bernice scuttle about and find the lot, which he built into a heap on the counter. 'Shall I have this in pink or blue?' he asked, latching on to a cache of nasty nylon bags euphemistically called Sanitary Pochettes. 'You must give me your number, my dear, I am sure my photographer friend would kill to use you. Has anyone ever told you what a rare beauty you are?' Bernice, already shimmering with greasy sweat, blushed a deep red in patches.

'Stop being so cruel, Felix,' said Felicity in a whisper.

'Me cruel? You are just envious. Isn't she Miss er . . . ?'

'Bernice,' said Bernice, having spotted the floor supervisor approaching. 'Will that be all, sir?'

'Apart from you, Bernice? Yes I think so. No, silly me, I almost forgot — I want black suspenders and some good stout corset laces and of course these.' He picked up a pair of foam rubber breast supports. 'Now I wonder if these are the right size? Let's see, I think I am looking for something between your gorgeous squashy buns and Felicity's pimples. Perhaps you would try them for me.'

'Is anything wrong, Miss Pry?' the supervisor enquired.

'No, Mrs Prentice,' said Felicity in an attempt to help. 'Nothing is wrong here. We are just fine.'

'This gentleman is Miss Pry's customer, is he not?'

Felicity nodded.

'Then let Miss Pry deal with him. There is a customer over there looking for lingerie guards. Go and help her at once.'

Even if Felicity wore glasses (the ones Felix had asked Bernice to remove so he could see whether her eye colour was right for the movies) Mrs von Hoffer would be bound to recognise her, despite the tied-back hair. As Felicity sidled away feigning a suddenly catastrophic stomach, she heard Felix instructing Bernice to charge his accumulated loot to his mother's account. 'Get it sent,' he drawled. 'To the Honourable Mrs Digby Blackburn of Thurloe Place.'

When both Felix and Mrs von Hoffer had gone Felicity went to rescue Bernice.

'I'll help you put this junk back, Bernice. He is a silly boy, just out to make trouble.'

'But he's going to help me get started in modelling.'

'No, Bernice. He won't. Felix isn't like that. He was making fun of you.'

'And you're just jealous,' Bernice snapped.

*   *   *

64

Felix was waiting at the staff entrance. 'Let me buy you lunch,' he said.

'No.'

'Supper, then?'

'No Felix, nothing. I don't ever want to see you again.'

'Flicky, please.'

'No, you are a self-centred, arrogant, spoilt bastard.'

'I am not a bastard. Anyway, all women love me.'

'No they don't.'

'Remember last night, in the car, outside your flat? You loved me then.'

'That wasn't love.'

'Oh wasn't it?'

'All women do not find you irresistible. Look at that poor Von Hoffer girl, she wanted nothing to do with you, she got you thrown out. Remember that? Or were you too drunk?'

'Now you are being silly, Flicky. I can make Angelica grovel at my feet begging for it.'

'I doubt it. Now please go away. You are nothing but a boring nuisance, and a very stupid one at that.'

Felicity returned to Myra's flat after work, exhausted. Her feet were sticky and she imagined that her ankles were ballooning like those of Mrs Prentice whose purple mottled legs were ill-concealed by support stockings. At least her headache had dissolved by the time she crossed the river, which somewhere to the east became the sea, unlike at home. In Kilbole last year, she and Rob had walked on the hills to watch the sun setting behind the westerly islands.

There was a man with Myra. Felicity hoped it wasn't Felix and that Myra wasn't offering herself for his mockery by plying him with either her politics or her herbal cigarettes.

'We have been having such an interesting conversation about student unrest.'

Wolf was well into a heap of wholemeal scones and a tumbler of the house liquor, Myra's potent and numbing beanpod cordial.

'How did you know where I lived?' Felicity asked.

'I didn't. I was just returning this bag that I found under

the Von Hoffer piano. It had Miss Pennyfeather's name and address in it.'

'Oh I see. That was silly of me.' More pride, more stupidity. There was no reason whatsoever for Wolf to have sought her out, none at all.

'It was excessively kind of him to return it, don't you think?' Myra asked without a trace of reproach in her voice.

'Of course, of course, I am so sorry. I have been behaving like a cretin. Thank you both very much. I am grateful, really I am.'

'You'll get over it, Felicity. One always does,' said Myra. 'Felicity is anguished,' she explained to Wolf.

'Discovering that you lived here too was a bonus,' said Wolf. 'I was telling Miss Pennyfeather how well you played last night.'

'Didn't you say rather what a fool I made of myself?'

'I too have played in front of that old witch,' said Myra. 'It was years ago and she was still at the height of her career. She was scathing then when she could afford to be generous, so we must forgive her rudeness now she is decrepit.'

'Why are you both being so nice to me?' Felicity asked.

'Because we don't want you to be hurt, isn't that right . . . er . . . Ludwig?'

'My name is Wolfgang or Wolf, Miss Pennyfeather.'

'You may call me Myra, provided you associate me with Hess not Hindley. You will stay to supper? Sauerkraut reheats like a dream, and with a name like yours I expect you to appreciate it. Now off you both go and take the dogs for a widdle.'

The sauerkraut wasn't bad, better even than the boiled beef and carrots Wolf normally ate on Friday nights when he played a pub piano for tourists.

'I've got a most unconvincing cockney accent but I'm better at it than Dick van Dyke even though I have to dress like him. Everybody expects Swinging London to be full of chirpy chaps with their thumbs stuck in their weskit arm'oles, wearin' titfer tats on the back of their loaves of bread, gassing abaht apples and pears to bobbies on bicycles two by two.'

'What do you play?'

'The usual stuff: "Daisy Daisy", "Any Old Iron", "The

Lambeth Walk". I do requests too. Last week I was asked to sing "Milord" which was pretty daft, a sham Scots cockney barrow boy singing about being a tart in French. Still, it makes them happy and I get paid.'

'What will you do when you graduate?'

'Look for something sensible in banking or insurance I suppose.'

'What would you like to be?'

'An explorer, a mountaineer, a musician, a writer and to live for ever.'

'Now that is what I call a really worthwhile young man,' said Myra after Wolf had left on his bike for Russell Square where he was due to pound a specially honky-tonked piano in a recently brassed up and mahoganised cocktail lounge.

Felix was not used to unpopularity. No female had ever refused an invitation from him. Normally they clamoured for his attentions and squabbled over him. To have been rejected by two women, one hideous and the other a social inferior, within the space of a few days was an enormous and sobering blow to his self-confidence. He could not understand it. Something was wrong with Angelica, anyone could see that. She was quiet, studious and profoundly hideous, a lesbian maybe, but Felicity was a stunner exuding sex appeal by the ton. Yet she refused him. He rang nightly to ask her out and nightly she gave the most pathetic excuses: she must practise, she had promised to help Myra defrost the fridge, one of the dogs was sickly, she was expecting a telephone call. He sent flowers and she gave them to the woman downstairs whose teething baby was causing despair.

Though Felicity was determined to resist him, the temptation to experience something more exciting than Myra's company was wearing her down. They had seen *The East is Red* after all: there had been a second showing by popular request. As Felicity watched the massed dancers pressing ever forward brandishing red flags and declaring themselves for Mao she felt no joy of universal endeavour, no enthusiasm for world brotherhood. Rather than toiling for fulfilment she fancied a lot of champagne and a chance to wear her new dress from

Bazaar. All over London people of her age were having the time of their lives while she was sitting on a stacking chair watching quaking, gibbering capitalists being vanquished by swarms of single-minded workers gleefully keen on selfless struggle.

Neither the weather nor Felicity's social life improved. Sheila Campbeltown was quite hurt by her daughter's brusqueness when she phoned for a dose of her London news. Magnus guessed his daughter's trouble wrongly and comforted his wife by saying it was love, adding, as if referring to an outbreak of head lice, that there was a lot of it about and quoted his leghorn cockerel forever crowing and climbing aboard the compliant hens whose necks and backs were becoming bald from frequent rutting. When Magnus observed to his cousin that springtime was so invigorating with the sap spurting upwards and all, Fay Braid had replied that there were times when nature was utterly revolting.

Ailsa never rang for just a chat. She was as straightforward and pragmatic now she was almost grown up as she had been as a child. Her call came during off-peak rates after six.

'Don't worry, Flicky, I won't be long. I just want to ask if I can come and stay with you for a week after Highers. I want to lose my virginity.'

'It isn't like going for a haircut.'

'That too. I'll get both done at the same time.'

'Why?'

'It is in the way.'

'I didn't mean your hair.'

'Neither did I.'

Felicity didn't have time to wish her little sister luck before Ailsa hung up. Luck had no place in the life of an aspiring scientist. Ailsa would pass her Highers provided she worked hard and remembered the relevant facts. Horseshoes, mascots and black cats formed no part of the equation. Likewise her curiosity was a burden: she needed to know what sex was about then she could look at the problem with informed detachment.

By the next week Felix seemed less ardent. Felicity tried to convince herself that she was relieved but she had got used to being pursued and now found his cooling a bit hurtful and began to understand how he must have felt now the boot was changing feet. She went with Myra to a concert on Monday and to *The Silence* at the Academy cinema on Tuesday. Wednesday was Fabian night, when Myra sipped cocoa in Clerkenwell with two ancient sisters who had once cycled with the Webbs. Having longed to be without Myra, Felicity now found solitude irksome as she played sad ballads and looked out across the park where the new leaves obscured all sight of the river and the Chelsea bank.

'Ye Banks and Braes' was interrupted by the doorbell. Even an Avon lady or an Adventist would have relieved her boredom. Felix would have been better company than the radio. If the caller was him she would relent, but it wasn't, it was his sister Penny in an exploding frock of flower-besprinkled tana lawn.

'I'm at the Hyde Park Hotel, since you ask.'

'Come in, Penny. Won't you be missed?'

'Who by? I made myself recite the whole of "The Lady of Shalott" three times through before I ran away.'

'How did you get on, curtsying to the cake?'

'It was a bloody disaster. Fabulous! Some idiot released a whole lot of white mice. I felt sorry for the mice. I didn't get to tow in the cake, which Mum took as a personal snub, and got all nettled with the ball chairman who told her that as an officer's wife she should learn to take these slights manfully. Mrs Goldmark told Mum that she thought her son was charming and Mum purred with pride till she found that Mrs G meant Wolf, at which point Mum said in a really loud voice that Wolf was just something her late sister had got lumbered with and she shuddered to think of his origins. Everybody heard – they were meant to, so was Wolf but he said he couldn't give a damn and Dad said that was the spirit and Mum said there was nothing worse than a hunter who ran with the fox. Wolf was the very best thing there, he danced with me all the time and took me to Covent Garden for a big greasy breakfast amongst all the fruit and veg.'

Penny looked better, more confident and less defensive. The rotten shape and complexion seemed less overwhelming now she appeared to be happier. Perhaps the rising sap was working its spell on her.

'Go on. What else happened?' Felicity asked. There may have been less than three years between them but Felicity felt decades older than Penny, who seemed less perceptive than even Bernice for all her exposure to a more advantageous life.

'Nothing, sadly.'

'Oh.'

'Well nothing between me and Wolf, if that is what you mean.' Penny looked wistful. 'You don't know how much I adore him.'

'Oh Penny, do you?'

'You aren't carrying a candle for him too, are you, Flicky? If you are I might as well throw myself off a friendly bridge and be done with it. I wouldn't stand a chance against you. You are gorgeous.'

'No, Penny I am not in love with Wolf.'

'Who, then?'

'No one. You haven't told me how the rest of the evening went.'

'Well, Dad got really bored until Felix made him cross.'

'Why was he cross?'

'Oh, you know, the usual thing. Felix put ice cubes down Sexy Lexy's cleavage and refused to dance with anyone on our table.'

'Even Sexy Lexy?'

'Especially her.'

'Why is that?'

'It is his way. The moment anyone falls for him he ditches them.'

'Where is he now?' Felicity felt she had to ask.

'He is meant to be at Cirencester.'

'Ah yes, of course, the Royal College.'

'Only he isn't,' said Penny. 'He is wrapped round Angelica von Hoffer at Boulestin's.'

'Really?'

'Yes, why?'

'Nothing. I just thought . . . oh well, never mind.'

'He has to get all his women lying down with their legs in the air.'

'What?'

'Figure of speech. Like a fawning dog, showing all its private parts, adoring and submissive.'

70

'I see,' Felicity replied.

'Then he dumps them.'

Felicity thought of poor, good Tess of the D'Urbervilles and all the ranks of misused women who had let themselves become playthings of heartless squires who chucked them beneath their winsome chins and then into the gutter once the simpletons had been seduced. Felix was just another dastard, calling all women angels and kissing them magically so that the memory caused turmoil in their poor misguided hearts. A confusion from which Felicity herself was not immune. She couldn't quite banish the image of Leporello reading out the list of Don Giovanni's conquests: princesses, baronesses, citizenesses and peasants. She had led the orchestra at Fairweathers and enjoyed the Don's philandering route to perdition but despised all the silly baggages who let themselves get embroiled with such a brute.

'Will you do me a favour, Flicky?'

'Sorry Penny. What did you say?' Felicity had never been to Boulestin's but imagined a sort of *fin-de-siècle* mirrored salon filled with young blades and smooth bounders drinking champagne out of actresses' slippers amongst much gilt and plush.

'Flicky, please can you have Wolf to supper.'

'Me, here? Why?'

'I'll pay, really I will.'

'Is Wolf hungry?'

'No, I don't think so.'

'Well then why are you offering to pay me to cook him supper?'

'I want you to have a supper party and invite Wolf, and me as well. You will have to have several others to make it look authentic.'

'You want me to be a match-maker?'

'In a way, yes.'

'Who else shall I invite? I don't know anyone.'

'Neither do I, only other wallflowers. And Felix, of course, but he doesn't count.'

'No?'

'No. Emphatically not Felix. He hates Wolf.'

'Why? Surely Felix has no cause to loathe anyone.'

'Oh but he has.'

71

'Why? When he has got everything.'

'Felix needs to be admired. Wolf is not jealous of Felix, in fact he is indifferent to him, that's why. Nothing Felix thinks important means anything to Wolf. You know the sort of stuff like having titled relatives, shelves crowded with stiff invitations, cool wheels and lots of notches on his gun.'

Before they could decide how and when this dinner party was going to happen Wolf appeared in person, letting himself into Myra's flat with a key she had lent him.

He had rung earlier but Myra had quite forgotten to warn Felicity about his proposed visit. Myra could be a schemer but it wasn't part of her cunning to forget the message. After all, Wolf wasn't coming to see Felicity: that was well established. Myra had invited him to use her piano whenever he liked, which was why she had given him a key. Wolf was, as she had said rather too many times, an extremely worthwhile young man.

'Wolf! This is a surprise!' said Felicity.

'Sorry. Were you not expecting me?'

'No, Myra never said.'

'Am I disturbing you? Were you not going out tonight?'

'Me, Wolf? No, not me,' Felicity answered. 'Come in. Penny and I were just talking about you.'

'No we weren't,' said Penny giggling foolishly.

'Penny! How are you? Have you got over it yet?'

'Over what?'

'The ball and all that.'

'Oh yes, all that has been well got over. Well got over indeed. Very well. Oh dear I must go to the loo. Excuse me. Oh gosh!'

'What is up with her?'

'The usual,' Felicity replied, meaning love.

'Oh,' said Wolf, assuming the usual to be gynaecological. He opened the piano lid. 'I want to try something out. Do you mind?'

He played with untrained vigour, having had no lessons since the age of twelve. He had taught himself to vamp at Seaforth Crag and had only been given tuition on the bagpipes.

'That is lovely,' said Penny. She had returned newly repainted, her mouth once more a pasty gash, her eyes outlined in navy pencil.

'It is Handel,' said Felicity. 'Silent Worship.'

'You know it?' Wolf asked.

'Of course, but not played like that.'

'Is it sacrilege?'

'No, it is wonderful. Can I see if I can improvise on the fiddle? On your fiddle, Wolf, I should say.'

Felicity was classically taught, her playing obeyed the rules of score and scale, but she found that by playing beside Wolf she could also make a wonderful sound without the bars and staves of others to restrict her.

Penny watched and listened, eaten with envy and hatred of her own lack of artistic ability, yet hopelessly transfixed with admiration. Wolf and Felicity looked beautiful as they played with unique harmony. She knew something, even if they didn't, and it hurt her badly. It was bloody sickening, like being fat, like being stupid and lazy and stuck with spots, addicted to chocolate and cousin Wolf.

They left together at nearly midnight, Wolf to bus home to Warren Street and Penny in a taxi to Thurloe Place. Myra was late home: the Fabians could get heated on occasions and talk long into the night especially when they replaced the cocoa with harsh Bulgarian wine.

Felicity gazed out of the big front window and listened to the traffic. She loved being in a city where people lived and worked, racketing about throughout all days and nights. She could never settle back in Kilbole where the only sound at night was a demented bird singing in the day-like beams of a street lamp. She loved knowing that, even as an anonymous ant, she was at least part of the capital anthill.

4

'I AM MUCH liking your Beatles. Please will you sell me that hat with the hair, it will be an amusing present for my son.'

Frau Hanne Schmidt and her daughter Lotte were visiting London before travelling north to look at Edinburgh and Loch Lomond about which Lotte could sing a song. It was thirteen years since Hanne had been dismissed by Clarice Duncan and she was now forty, stout and strong, the happy mother of Lotte and little Hans. Her stepson Dieter was in his early twenties and set to be a student till middle age. Dieter studied Youth Culture very seriously and was preparing a paper on 'The Role of Liverpool in Post Colonial Music' for some unspecified date in the distant future. Dieter was also well up in high fidelity and the latest ways of tape recording and disc cutting. Hanne bought the Beatle wig for Dieter knowing he wouldn't wear it to be silly but might do so in order to note his findings and express the entertainment factor of absurd hair in the form of a graph. She almost bought an 'I'm backing Britain' T-shirt for little Hans, then decided a Union Jack mug might be better received in Ulm.

Amongst the trivia and souvenirs on the Carnaby Street stall Hanne found something that had not been about in 1953.

'Now even your lavatory paper is patriotic,' she remarked in astonishment to the lean jacketed youth in charge. 'In Germany I am thinking such a thing would not be possible.'

'Yer, well that's yer British sense of 'umour for you.'

'This I remember. Thank you. Come, Lotte we must go to the Tower.'

Lotte could sing 'London's Burning' and 'Oranges and Lemons'. Hanne was determined to expose her daughter to the maximum of interest in the minimum of days. Lotte was exhausted but her mother was indefatigable. London wasn't like it was in *Mary Poppins* and her mother's stories of life as nanny to little Wolf quickly palled. Little Wolf who was so good, so obedient and so very clever would have been better off, in Lotte's opinion, beneath a big red bus.

Hanne had lost touch with all Kilbole apart from Isa, who was a rotten correspondent and generally sent no more news than the basic in her annual Christmas card. Last year she had said she was well and in outside catering, which puzzled Hanne considerably till stepson Dieter explained that Isa must have become a manufacturer of picnics. Hanne remembered several windswept excursions to eat fruitcake and jam sandwiches huddled behind rocks and ruins, and concluded that there might be a market for Isa's services amongst the stoic Scots. She could still taste the metallic tang of pre-milked tea poured into plastic beakers from a thermos flask.

She had received no news of Wolf since he had been sent away to boarding-school when the Blackburns had been posted abroad. It was as if he had disappeared just as mysteriously as he had arrived.

Hanne had written to Isa again in March to tell her of her proposed visit to Scotland but she had, as yet, received no reply. Nevertheless the Schmidts, mother and daughter, had every intention of visiting Kilbole. Much time had passed since the awful episode with Lionel Braid; much had changed. Hanne was a woman of status now, greatly respected as Frau Doktor Claus Schmidt, wife of one of Ulm's foremost citizens and herself a pivot of local affairs. She was admired, not feared like the late Miss Clarice Duncan, though she could be of colossal embarrassment to her daughter.

'Go and request a tune. One of the typical folk songs that I have been teaching you, *Liebling*.'

'Nein, Mutti.'

'Lotte?' Hanne could be withering if crossed. Lotte with-out her little brother as ally knew when she was defeated. Things would be worse if she persisted in defiance and got sent up to bed in the stuffy hotel room that looked out upon the inner well, echoed with kitchen clangs and reeked of fishy cabbage. It was already well past her usual bedtime and probably worth the compliance if it meant another glass of Coke.

'Why do you not suggest he play "My Old Man Says Follow the Van". I am thinking that is most suitable.'

Wolf took a mouthful of his beer after playing the final chords of 'Maybe It's Because I'm a Londoner'. Penny Blackburn had appointed herself his personal waitress for the evening and sat nearby, adoring him as he played, which was incredibly irritating.

'*Bitte*, please.'

'Hello,' said Wolf to the girl with her hair scraped back in tidy plaits. The child looked about twelve, rather too old to be dressed like a modern Gretel. She smiled back at him but couldn't remember her words.

'What is your name?'

'Lotte.'

'Where are you from, Lotte?'

'Bitte?'

'Deutsch?' Wolf asked.

'Ja.'

'Well, Lotte from Germany I will play you a German song. Would you like that?'

She smiled at him again and Penny became all bouncy and motherly. Wolf's natural charm with children was enchanting; maybe he would find her irresistible if she too behaved in the same way. Maybe.

'Come and sit on my knee while Uncle Wolf plays for you.'

Lotte backed away as Wolf struck up 'The Happy Wanderer'.

'Mein Vater war ein Wandersmann, und mir liegt's auch im blut!'

Hanne's face glowed with delight. 'How kind of the young man to play one of our own songs! Do you know what he is called, Lotte?'

'Wolf, Mutti. The lady said his name was Wolf.'

Of course Wolf recognised her, but as he did, he lost sight of the Hanne of his childish heart. The real Hanne had worn and swollen, bloused out and got herself some frizzy lemon hair; the woman he had kept alive in his imagination had been an unwrinkled girl without flaws in her complexion or bags beneath her unspectacled eyes with wavy untidy hair the colour of sand. He understood how orphans, when recalling dead mothers, remembered them as icons of loving serenity, awesomely beautiful and bathed in sweet scent when the reality was probably more crude, bad tempered and flustered. Hanne still smelt of fir cones and beeswax candles, honey and cinnamon, but her fingers were thick and the flesh bulged either side of her wedding ring.

Hanne would never have recognised Wolf. He was twice the size and weight of the little boy she had been forced to leave. Wolf had grown into a fine man too dark to be Wagnerian but far more attractive than most of the fair short-shorn youths who were her stepson's friends. She had often longed to see Wolf again, and had nursed hopes that one day he and Dieter would meet. She said that she would never have succeeded as stepmother or parent without having practised on poor little Wolf, who was denied nothing except mother love.

Hanne made their meeting easy, with spontaneous exuberance and a great deal more ecstasy than she would have permitted herself had she been prepared. Wolf bore the kissing and hugging with fortitude despite his natural disappointment in finding his angel to be a little shoddy and entirely human. Hanne had been the nearest thing to a mother to him, but he had grown up and survived well since the times when she would let him sit on her knee as she told him happy stories of Max und Moritz falling into the sausage machine and chubby Augustus who died after five soupless days.

They parted late that night after all the excitement of the reunion. Lotte fell asleep leaning against Penny, who refused to leave because she hoped vainly that Wolf would kiss her goodnight upon the lips and not peck at her fat cheek like a dutiful brother. Tomorrow night, after Hanne had carted Lotte round Hampton Court and all sights west of Hammersmith, they would meet again and go to supper with Felicity. Hanne could hear her fiddle played and catch up on news of Kilbole. Penny took it for granted that she was included in this invitation but Wolf forgot to kiss her goodnight at all, not even on the air behind her ear.

*   *   *

77

Two years ago, on his eighteenth birthday, Wolf had been invited to visit the offices of the Blackburn family lawyer in Gray's Inn. The appointment had been for midday with Mr Bastion. Wolf had taken the tube to Holborn and arrived slightly late: he was living in a schoolfriend's basement at the time, working as a washer-up and film extra while waiting to go to LSE. He also played piano for a skiffle group of medical students called the Contractions.

Mr Bastion, an elderly junior partner of Fry, Pride and Harping, had been looking out upon the wintry lawns and was clearly not in the business of being kept waiting: time was money and his paymasters were not generous. However, Mr Bastion had managed a smile and a hearty handshake before inviting Wolf to take a seat in the leather upholstered chair opposite his leather-topped desk. Life forms throve in his water carafe.

'I have been asked to see you today by our client Colonel Blackburn on a matter of some delicacy concerning your birth,' said Mr Bastion. 'You may smoke if you wish.'

Mr Bastion sat with his back to the window. Wolf offered him a Cadet which was refused with ill-concealed disdain, then sat back in his seat looking out upon the plane trees that may once have shaded Dr Johnson, William Blake and Handel. Coram's Fields were nearby. Wolf had decided long ago that even if he did tire of London, which was highly unlikely, he could never tire of life.

Mr Bastion spoke carefully, shuffling with agitated anxiety as if searching for an elusive truth amongst his heaps of paper. He began with the known facts.

'Throughout your brief life you have been reared and nurtured by Colonel and Mrs Blackburn following the most unfortunate death of Miss Duncan, Mrs Blackburn's eldest sister.'

Thus far Wolf could find nothing controversial in Mr Bastion's information. He nodded in order to show interest. Outside, a nesting bird flew by with straw in its beak; there were still a surprising amount of working stables in central London in the early sixties.

'It is my duty today, Mr Duncan, to inform you as to the identity of your mother. Mr Duncan?'

'Yes, sorry Mr Bastion, I was just watching those ducks. Do you suppose they come from Regent's Park or Buckingham Palace?'

Mr Bastion was not a man to be gripped by ducks. He rose and drew down the blind. 'Mr Duncan, I require your total attention,' he said.

'Sorry,' said Wolf, stubbing out his cigarette and leaning forward attentively, fixing the lawyer with a rapt stare. Mr Bastion sat up and took off his glasses to add moment to his words, then was struck by a fit of spluttering coughs. 'I do apologise, Mr Duncan, please excuse me.'

Still erupting, Mr Bastion embarked upon his revelation.

'The fact is that you may have been misled into thinking that you were adopted as the ward of the late Miss Duncan when you were in fact her –' Mr Bastion's face was turning purple with the exertion of subduing his choking long enough to make his announcement – 'When you were her . . . er . . . natural son. Do you understand?'

'Yes. Can I pour you a glass of water?'

'No! . . . Thank you. Do you understand? . . . Mr Duncan?'

Eventually Mr Bastion stopped coughing with one final giant sneeze that doused the whole district. Wolf wondered if it would be rude to mop himself of Mr Bastion's million microbes or whether such a soaking should be ignored like spit sprayed in conversation or broken wind.

'I have here your birth certificate which I will now hand you.'

Mr Bastion was holding a single sheet of paper, a shortened version of the normal birth certificate, a cheaper document for a bastard. 'If there is anything you feel I should explain to you, please do not hesitate to ask,' said Mr Bastion, applying a large ill-laundered handkerchief to his nose. It bore a school name tape: BASTION C.H.E. 948 MARYATS. Mr Bastion needed lunch and, more than that, he needed the sherry that always preceded it.

Wolf took the certificate and read it for himself.

Mother – Clarice Dorothea Duncan. Father – Unknown.

The male child registered as Wolfgang Duncan had been born in Plymouth on the 16th of February 1946. No Germany,

79

no foundling, just a bastard: a mistake, an embarrassment and encumbrance.

It was a harsh truth to know that he had not been chosen by but inflicted upon Clarice Duncan. She had carried him in secret and given birth to him in obscurity. He had grown in the belly of a woman he only remembered for rigid order and absence of love and laughter, whose womb must have been as secure and comforting as a locked filing cabinet. Worse still, no one, least of all his mother, had wanted him. He had been a horrible accident, a vile catastrophe. Miss Duncan, the most upright of women, had fallen. Her reputation mattered more than her child. She had turned disaster into triumph by having the world believe she had adopted Wolf as a supreme act of charity. That really hurt.

Father unknown. Clarice must have known his father unless (and this was the most terrible possibility) he had been the result of rape. Wolfgang Duncan, criminally created, conceived in hatred and shamefully born.

Money had been sent from the Blackburns, then stationed in Cyprus. A covering letter hinted at further funds should Wolf keep the dark secret of his birth quiet, but meanwhile this birthday present should go to buy a decent suit and tie so that he could lunch with Digby Blackburn at his club on his next London visit.

Wolf used the money to have a party, after which his first hangover somewhat obliterated the memory of his first woman.

He wrote to his aunt and uncle from Arran where he had spent most of his school holidays and where he loved to climb: 'Please do not worry, I see no reason whatsoever to boast about my birth.'

A year passed before he lunched with Digby, by which time tons of dirty dishes and a stint in the crowd of *Tom Jones* had bought him a fearsome trendy suit from Lord John and he was well into the first year of his degree.

To mark the occasion, Digby gave Wolf a gold watch chain for the half-hunter Clarice had given her son on Coronation Day 1953. TO W.D. FROM C.D.D. had been engraved on the back beneath the initials of Clarice's father who had been, of course, Joan's father too and grandfather to Felix and Penny Blackburn and also grandfather to Wolf. However, Joan Blackburn persisted in pretending that Wolf was a foundling, selflessly rescued by her late and sainted sister.

From his earliest years he had known that he must make his own way and his own life; that he, having been disowned by his parents, had no need to live up to some tediously virtuous or noble ancestry. Being independent and free of family obligations could be quite a relief, not a handicap. The good fairies had given him enough of their best gifts – brains, courage, skill and looks – to compensate for the bad.

'What was my mother doing on VE Day, Uncle Digby?' Wolf asked at the end of their rather stilted lunch in St James's Square.

'Why do you ask?' said Digby, quickly adding, 'How the hell should I know?'

'I thought you might be able to tell me where she was. I must have been conceived then.'

Digby had drunk quite a lot of port. 'Make no mistake, Wolf, I am very proud of you.'

'I can't imagine why,' Wolf replied.

In Myra Pennyfeather's flat, the night following their meeting the initial sparkle of surprise between Wolf and Hanne was a little less intense.

'Who is your Mutti?' Lotte asked with childish directness. Wolf's German was as rudimentary as Lotte's English. Both knew songs in each other's language but were short of small talk.

'Mutti ist tod,' Wolf replied.

'Vati?'

Wolf shrugged.

'Why are you called Wolfgang?'

Wolf shrugged again. 'Why are you called Lotte?'

'My Mutti's name is Hannelore Lotte. Is your Vati a Wolfgang?'

'Maybe.'

It had been quite a burden, that name. Wolf Gang: it jarred, and implied a nasty faction amongst Boy Scouts gone bad. At school Wolf had changed his first name to Wilf but now Wolf had become a great name, better far than Ringo, more exotic than all those boring Daves and Micks and Pauls that made brief marks on the sixties scene. Wolf liked his name, it was the best thing his mother had given him and added to his happiness. He was also falling in love, or rather he was carrying forward a love whose seeds had been planted before he knew or understood any such thing.

Hanne had been disappointed to find that Wolf had given her father's violin to Felicity. It had been none of her business, Wolf was free to do as he liked with his own property, but she did feel she had retained some thread of ownership, that somehow the instrument's future was still in her gift. Wolf told her that Felicity had needed the violin more than him. He did not say that, even at the age of twelve, he had wanted to offer his most precious possession in an act of adoration.

Once she had heard them play together Hanne knew that Wolf had been right.

'I am content,' she said, examining the cherished fiddle after their performance of 'Silent Worship'. 'My father would be most pleased. One day I am thinking that this will be again living in the household of Wolf.'

Only Penny heard and bothered to understand what Hanne was evidently trying to say. 'Bloody hell,' she muttered. 'Trust a German to state the obvious.'

The tape recorder was temperamental and the day was scorching hot. It had been Hanne's idea to get Wolf's Handel interpretations taped. She was sure she had seen the future and it was bright with success. Dieter would fix it. She had been quite bewitched by the songs and especially taken with 'Silent Worship': the combination of piano, fiddle and Wolf's strong yet tentative voice made her nerve ends fizz.

Downstairs the baby still had agonising gums, its teeth continued unsprouted and its furious bellows resounded about the stone stairwell of the common parts. Myra's dogs were fractious too and snapped at each other for want of better entertainment. Having tried to get a decent recording at least a dozen times it was tempting to jack in the project and take off for the park to enjoy the first really hot summer sun.

'"Rivalling the glittering sunshine with a glory of golden hair!"'

82

Wolf sang the verse once more. It sounded fine; the baby was lulled and the dogs munched quietly on biscuits thoughtfully supplied by Penny who was in charge of recording and keeping the sound at a level neither too soft nor so loud as to make the indicator take a fit and set its needle vibrating with stressed rage. Just as Wolf reached the final bars a great jet flew over Battersea bound for Heathrow.

'I can't bear it! I give up.'

'No Wolf. You can't. Come on, one more time please,' Penny pleaded.

'What is the point?' said Felicity. She didn't feel twice as fair as anything, let alone a rose or lily. Her chin and shoulder were red where the violin had rubbed the sweaty bare flesh.

'Let's call it a day. It's hopeless.'

'It is not hopeless. This time it will work, I know it will. Just wait till I get this lot set at nought.'

'Isn't that a hymn?'

'Probably,' Penny answered. 'A prayer might be handier. Come on – ready, steady, go!' Felicity knew the recording was working and she could feel Wolf's eyes looking at her, into her, as she played. She smiled and kept his eyes held in hers. She was right, so was Penny, it was very good. Wolf sang without once shifting his gaze. The performance was faultless, the world for once, was hushed. Blackbird and thrush were silent.

'"Oh saw you not my lady? . . . Though I could never woo her, I'll love her till I die . . . Rivalling the glorious sunshine . . ."'

He had got it wrong.

Wolf had forgotten the words after so many, many repetitions. Glittering sunshine, it should be glittering sunshine that was rivalled by his lady's golden hair. For a moment Felicity hesitated and raised her eyebrows in a stab of exasperation before seeing Wolf smiling back at her as he completed the line with words of his own.

'. . . with the loveliness of her hair.'

The final cadenza and it was done. Near perfection: anything better would have been divine, the music of angels only for the blessed dead. Silence. Wolf and Felicity were still staring at each other when a loud sob broke the spell.

'Oh Penny. Don't cry.'

'I'm going to die. Now.'

The door opened and Myra, who had been listening at the keyhole, entered. She too had been moved; her envy was difficult to suppress. She was dressed in a droopy long dress, more green now than in its youth when it had been her best concert black. The long kid gloves looked quaint in the afternoon, she was wearing them to keep them in shape while they dried. 'A friend of yours has just arrived. Come in, my dear.'

A young man pushed past her without a word of thanks. 'Well, well, well. What is all this about then?'

'Felix! What are you doing here?'

'What are you doing here, Wolf, is more to the point?'

'We were making a recording, Felix,' said Penny. 'It is utterly and completely fabulous. You should hear it. Sit down, let me play it back to you.'

'No! Penny, don't,' Wolf commanded. 'Here, please give me the tape.'

'Wolf?'

'Please, Penny. Thank you. You have been marvellous. Flicky and I are really grateful but I don't want anyone else listening to it yet.'

'Oh go on. Let's hear it. Be quick though, I've come to collect Penny. Father is berserk.'

'Why?'

'They are carting you off to Glyndebourne, you twerp. Have you forgotten?'

'No, I haven't, but there is still plenty of time.'

'Glyndebourne, how extraordinary,' said Myra. 'Isn't life full of coincidence? I myself am going this evening. Dear, kind friends are taking me, hence this finery,' she said indicating her lifeless draperies and threadbare satin buttoned shoes with her damply gloved hands. The evening bag she had lent to Felicity dangled from her wrist bulging with her most treasured relic, a pair of enamelled opera glasses.

Felix didn't seem awestruck by this.

'Penny hurry, for God's sake. It will take hours to get your horrible body disguised.'

'That isn't kind, Felix,' said Wolf, putting his arm round Penny who did look worse than ever. Streams of mascara had flowed over her puffy cheeks either side of her shimmering nose and her lank hair had been made greasier by the stuffy heat.

Felix looked beyond his sister at Felicity. The contrast was cruel.

'Flicky!'

'Felix.'

'You will play that tape to me, won't you?'

Felicity looked at Wolf. She was holding the reel. 'Shall I, Wolf?'

'No!'

'Please, Flicky,' said Felix. 'I will be as good as gold, I promise. After all, if you are going to make millions out of music you are going to have to be heard. Come on. You need an agent. I have masses of contacts. Really, honestly I would like to help, please.'

'Please, Wolf,' said Felicity. 'Felix is quite right.'

'No!'

Felix turned to Penny. 'All right, be like that. Come on, Miss Monster let's get you home.'

Felicity wished she didn't find Felix quite so physically attractive. 'Are you going to the opera too?' she asked him to change the subject.

'Christ, yes. Worse luck.'

Wolf had never been to any opera but knew most scores intimately. Despising himself for his curiosity he asked which one was on that night.

'Some rubbish about a caterwauling madwoman.'

'Lucky you,' Wolf muttered.

'You think so? I'd almost pay not to go.'

'*Lucia di Lammermoor* is magnificent. You will enjoy it. It is about Scotland.'

'God, the White Heather Club sung in kraut or frog, what hell.'

'Italian, actually.'

'Bloody Eyetie, that's worse. No battles, just a load of yellow gigolos eating spag bog.'

'Wolf is quite right, Felix,' said Felicity. 'It is wonderful.'

'Well then, Cinderfella, you shall go to the ball! You can go in my place and change at the flat. Penny will fix you up with my DJ and all that crap. Father will be delighted to take you instead of me.'

'What about your mother?'

'She will do what I say.'

Wolf's grin was enough to convince anyone of his genuine delight at the prospect.

'There is one condition, though,' said Felix like a tormentor allowing his victim a vision of release before resuming the torture.

'Not the tape, Felix,' said Wolf. 'I won't let you hear the tape, not even if you offer me a whole season of operas.'

'No, Wolf, not that. Flicky, you must come out with me tonight.'

'No, Felix.'

'Very well then, sorry Wolf. No outing for you after all. Shame. Still, never mind. I'm told the waiting list isn't more than ten years and the tickets only cost a fortune.'

Wolf shrugged and lit a cigarette, betraying no vestige of his thumping disappointment. Felicity couldn't bear it. 'All right, Felix. I will go out with you provided there is no gatecrashing.'

'I promise. On my honour,' Felix replied giving a mocking Boy Scout salute. 'Come along both of you. I'll be back for you later, Flicky, I promise.' He took her hand and brought it up to his lips. 'Pretty hands, no claws,' he said kissing her musician's stumpy fingertips.

5

T HERE HAD BEEN quite a clear-out of superfluous Blackburn
kinsmen lately and the current marquess seemed so disin-
clined to breed that Digby, and after him Felix, looked certain
to get the title. Joan let this be known. To have written
Felix's expectations in neon would have been more discreet
than Joan being subtle. Apart from clambering ever closer to
the aristocracy the Digby Blackburns had done really well from
recent wills. Their family was shrinking, members of the older
generation were dying without issue and the clan was dwindling
to a point with Digby's brood firmly poised upon it.

'Such a shame that Felix is missing all this,' said Joan. 'He is
too sweet, far too kind, so thoughtful. I only hope that Wolf
appreciates the sacrifice.'

'Felix said he would rather be boiled in oil than hear a
Scotswoman screeching in Italian,' said Penny. 'He would have
bribed Wolf to take his place if necessary.'

'What nonsense. Felix was being a dear. Is there a Scotswoman in this opera? I had rather thought that Queen sang
her song in German. Never mind. After all, Glyndebourne isn't
about singing it is about everything that is best in being British.
Do you not agree?' Joan beamed at the Von Hoffer party with
which she and Digby, Penny and Wolf were joining forces
for a picnic supper. This chumminess had been engineered at
Angelica von Hoffer's request. The Blackburns had contributed
no more than two bottles of regimental champagne to the party,
but Mrs von Hoffer had stripped Fortnum's and Harrods of deli-
cacies and provided everything else including silver candelabra
and icy damask cloths starched to rigidity.

'Whatever next?' Joan trilled. 'How spoiling!'

Earlier in the evening, Myra Pennyfeather had clasped Wolf's arm, which was rather too short for his borrowed dinner jacket.

'What a relief to find a real friend amongst all this!' she said, indicating the gardens teeming with elegance, as if pointing out a scrapyard. A fan and her reticule dangled from her gloved wrists; the best concert black had travelled badly. Myra was the guest of a grateful pupil's parents who admired her long-term dogged persistence in attempting to ignite musicianship in their bored child.

Wolf introduced Myra to the Blackburns. Digby was civil and jocular as he had learnt to be over years of inspecting Other Ranks. Joan was somewhat put out. There was no need to air inferior acquaintances in front of the Von Hoffers.

'It is an honour to meet you again, Madame,' said Myra to Grandmother von Hoffer, who nodded graciously but did not extend her arthritic, lace-covered hand, agreeing entirely about the honour being Myra's.

Later, when Mrs von Hoffer asked who the strange woman so droopingly festooned had been, her mother-in-law dismissed Myra as 'One of one's public.'

'Your son is a credit to you,' said Myra to Digby within Joan's hearing but not loud enough to be heard by Wolf. 'I do admire the way in which you have brought him up, so unspoilt, so industrious. A diamond amongst rhinestones.'

'I'm glad you appreciate him,' Joan interrupted. 'We all miss him most awfully tonight.'

Myra looked perplexed. 'But surely Wolfgang is your son? He bears such a striking resemblance to you both.'

'Oh no, not him. Wolf look like my darling Dingo? What nonsense! Wolf is just a most obscure cousin, if that. Our son is Felix.'

'Dear me, how unfortunate.'

Digby beamed, not having absorbed a word but set upon a course to charm. 'I do hope you enjoy the performance.'

'I shall, I shall. One only longs for all this to be available to all. For the people to get their just share. The masses should have access to culture.'

'Quite,' Digby replied.

Joan took his arm and steered him towards Wolf who had

been instructed to open the first bottle of champagne. 'Don't be silly, Dingo. The working classes don't need these things, they want holiday camps and bus trips. They simply wouldn't understand about dressing properly and being civilised.'

'Quite,' Digby repeated, 'but all the same, Joanie, you can't expect people to enjoy good music if they never get to hear it or see it done well.'

'Don't say you are a pinko, Dingo! Everyone gets more than enough music. If the masses need more the government should dish out record tokens with the dole. Anyway you are talking nonsense, I am sure that some of those people in the orchestra are from very humble stock. Wolf, do you think you could persuade your friend not to pester us any more? Ah, I see she has gone to join her party. Who is she anyway?'

'Myra Pennyfeather, Aunt Joan, she lets me play her piano. She is Felicity Campbeltown's godmother, Felicity is her lodger.'

'Ah yes, that girl said her landlady was mad. I remember now.'

'We meet again,' said Mrs von Hoffer, inclining her head kindly towards Wolf. 'I am so glad you have found other employment. I told the agency that I felt I had been too harsh on you after that misunderstanding at Mother-in-law's party.'

'Think nothing of it, Mrs von Hoffer. May I offer you a glass of champagne?' Wolf replied.

'Really it is too bad of you,' said Mrs von Hoffer to Joan. 'I certainly didn't expect you to go to the trouble of hiring staff though it will be nice to have our picnic spot guarded during the performance. Incidentally, where is Felix? He has been so kind to Angelica.'

Angelica looked different. She was fresher all over, no longer exuding the weary damp pallor of one who spends hours in close study like a rabbinical scholar. Even her glasses were gone and her eyelids coloured blue to match her eyes, the whites of which were as pink as her rouged cheeks due to the unfamiliar contact lenses.

'What has happened to Felix?' she asked Penny.

'Oh he said he didn't want to come.'

'But he promised.'

'He asked Wolf to take his place.'

'But he is a waiter!'

'He is my cousin,' said Penny.

Angelica's eyes began to water in earnest. First one and then the other lens got dislodged. 'Oh my God! I've dropped one.'

'Is this it?' said Wolf. 'I saw it fall. Look, why don't you put them back in the case then you will be able to enjoy yourself without worrying. Your glasses suit you.'

Angelica looked at Wolf with gratitude despite knowing he lied. 'Are you really Felix's cousin?' she asked.

'Sort of,' said Wolf.

From the first note to the final victory chorus Wolf was transfixed. He knew *The Magic Flute* even better than *Lucia di Lammermoor* but its familiar tunes were an additional delight. The performance was magnificent, his eyes and ears were drowning in pleasure while his heart and mind were steeped in love. Only the woman beside him might have marred this heaven. Penny grabbed his hand and held on to it but she could have sat on Wolf's knee quite naked and still he wouldn't have noticed. Digby saw and got worried. Apart from Grandmother von Hoffer, no one did justice to the supper set out beside the water, a Watteau *fête-champêtre*, with midges. Joan and Mrs von Hoffer were dieting, Mr von Hoffer's ulcer was troublesome, Wolf was transported, Penny was infatuated and poor Angelica felt sick. Digby, for all his switched-on *bonhomie*, was profoundly disturbed. Hand-holding was only a symptom of a hatching disaster. Copious smoking calmed the nerves and deflected biting insects.

'Wolf, would you mind driving us back to London after the performance?' Besides feeling weary himself, Digby thought that by making Wolf drive all furtive backseat groping with Penny could be avoided.

'I'd love to, Uncle Digby, but I can't drive.'

'Can't drive! Why not?'

'I've never learnt, there has been no need.'

'Everyone must drive.'

'Driving lessons are expensive,' said Mr von Hoffer who had been listening and kept accurate accounts.

'Damn it, Wolf. I will pay for you to learn if that is the problem.'

'I am not asking for money, Uncle Digby.'

'I know, Wolf.'

'Is that young man related to the one who has been squiring Angelica?' asked Grandmother von Hoffer. 'The one with a title to inherit?'

'Yes, Mother. Hush now.'

'Don't hush me, you are only my daughter-in-law. Has this one also got expectations?'

'No, Mother.'

'What a pity. Why not?'

'I am a bastard, Madame,' Wolf·explained helpfully.

'All my best lovers were bastards,' she replied.

Felicity was glad of the opportunity to wear her new dress. If she was firm she would keep both Felix and herself in order. The rules must be laid down. No gatecrashing and no groping.

'Flicky, you are a prude. I promise no gatecrashing. The groping will be up to you. I will give you a good time, entirely at my own expense,' said Felix. He was wearing a silk jersey polo neck that would have offended Joan's ideas of good taste but suited him beautifully. Felix always glanced at his reflection as he passed plate-glass windows and was invariably delighted, with justification, by what he saw. 'Tonight we are hitting the heights.'

'Boulestin's?'

'God no! Whatever gave you that idea? I wouldn't be seen dead in that pretentious hole.'

'You took Angelica von Hoffer there.'

'Flicky, you have been spying! I think you are jealous, how marvellous! Didn't I tell you I could get that woman to dote on me. All it took was one evening out; the rest was simple, a pushover.'

'You are callous, Felix.'

'Of course, but only with people like Angelica and only if I am coerced.'

'What do you mean?'

'You challenged me, you doubted my ability. Of course I had to prove you wrong. Anyway I succeeded, if that is what you wanted, and now Angelica is on the pile of dead leaves.'

'Poor girl.'

'We are not going to talk about Angelica Boring von Huffer Puffer tonight, not now I've booked us a table at Hurley.'

'But that is in the country.'

'Yes, we could stay the night if you like.'

'No!'

'All right, I was only trying to be funny. I will get you home all safe and sound like Cinderella. Why does your flat smell like festering pumpkins?'

Felicity wasn't sure how pumpkins did smell even in best condition but she understood what Felix meant: Myra's flat had quite a bit of the compost heap to it.

Felix had enough magnetism to keep Felicity happy for an evening. He was being sweetly considerate but she had a feeling his charm was a mere film of oil.

'Before we go are you going to let me hear that tape?'

'No, Felix, I'm sorry. I promised Wolf I wouldn't play it to anyone.'

'Fine. I understand. Oh Flicky you do look lovely tonight. Is that a new dress?'

'No, not exactly.' The orange dress wasn't new as such but it had hung about in the curtained corner that served as a wardrobe in Felicity's bedroom for three weeks, an unsullied virgin, waiting to be worn. It had cost far too much.

'Don't you think you should cut off the price tag, then? Or do you like everyone to see how expensive you can look in cheap tat?'

Before dinner they had a drink by the river in Henley. 'What are those tents for?' asked Felicity.

'The Regatta, of course.'

'What is that?'

'Ascot with boats going backwards instead of horses going forwards and fat old men in pink socks. Lots of champers and tarts in hats, you know the sort of thing.'

'No, I don't,' said Felicity throwing crisps for a swan who owed its bulk to extracting snacks from picnics. 'This is near where Mr Toad lived.'

'Mr Toad? Who on earth is he? You do know some funny people, Flicky.'

'I meant Mr Toad of *The Wind in the Willows*. He had a gentleman's riverside residence.'

They hired a boat and Felix rowed upriver towards Shiplake. He was most solicitous in warning her to be careful not to squash her fingers between the boat and dock. 'You mustn't hurt your precious hands, not now you are going to be a famous musician.'

The lawns of mansions rolled down to the river's edge fitted out with gaudy beds of lobelia, alyssum, tagetes and scarlet salvia created by tidy gardeners with faultless precision shouting the conspicuous and self-conscious prosperity of riverbank dwellers. No Mole, no Ratty or Badger messed about amongst this contrived prettiness. It was too late to row downstream to Temple Island; besides, the Glyndebourne midges had cousins in the Thames Valley who were quite immune to cigarettes.

'Felix, can I ask you something?'

'Of course.'

'Why are you so awful? So ghastly when really, deep down, I am sure you are not nearly so dreadful?'

'Meaning me?'

'Yes. Why do you set out to be such a boor?'

'A bore?'

'Well yes, but I actually meant a boor spelt with a double "o".'

'Your accent shows.'

'So?'

'Oh nothing. I'm not boring, am I?'

'No, not always.' Felicity smiled.

'When, though? Why? I want to know. No one has ever said that to me before.'

'Perhaps you are the one who is bored, Felix.'

'The only thing that is boring round my life is not being able to please you. If you could stop being so bloody superior and aloof I would be really happy and really good.' Felix looked at her with a kicked puppy expression that had hitherto pulverised all women.

'Poor Felix,' said Felicity. 'You are so young.'

'Oh yes? How come you are so old when we are the same age? Flicky, you have no sense of humour.'

'Great! Well now that we have established ourselves perhaps we can be friends.'

'Of course, Flicky but you can't stop me wanting more.'

'Well you can't have it, Felix.'

'Are you sure?'

'Yes, quite. I'm hungry.'

Shadows were growing when Felix drove Felicity up the hill out of Henley through the beech woods towards dinner. She was happy; only a faint nagging warned her that she was being softened for capitulation and fattened for slaughter.

True to his word, Felix drove her home to Battersea without once being brash, loud, bullying or ostentatious. It had been like dining with a different man from the uncouth lout she had seen earlier in the day. As they crossed Chelsea Bridge Felix asked once again to hear the tape of 'Silent Worship'.

'No, Felix, I am really sorry. I must keep my promise.'

'Very well. I am going to drive the wrong way round the roundabout.'

'No! Felix don't! Stop it!'

'Here goes!'

Heaven alone knows why there was no traffic coming from Nine Elms or Queenstown Road just then.

Felicity screamed and hid her face in her hands.

'The tape! I want to hear the tape. It is for your own good,' Felix shouted through clenched teeth.

'No!'

'Very well. Here we go again!'

This time he managed to avoid a Mini and a Triumph Herald. The 137 bus was collecting passengers at the stop.

Felicity was just capable of hoping she hadn't wet herself in terror.

'Flicky, shall we dice with death again? Look, the traffic is picking up nicely. This should be fun! Or what? It is your choice entirely. The tape or the roundabout, which is it to be?'

'Oh damn you, Felix. I'll play you the tape,' said Felicity shaking with petrified sobs.

'Good girl. Come on then, we have wasted enough time.'

'Do you always get your own way, Felix?'

'Always.'

94

'Christ I hate you!'
'No you don't.'

All the way home from Glyndebourne Digby twitched. Joan twittered on and on about the inconsequential trivia of her existence while Wolf dreamt sweet dreams of love and sour ones about his forthcoming finals. Penny swore silently at her father for placing the bottle basket and picnic rug between her and Wolf.

Bowling down the Mall within minutes of their journey's end, Digby, ever vigilant, turned to see what was heaving on the back seat. Before he could realise that Wolf was merely fidgeting as he slept Joan had seized the steering wheel in panic on seeing their Bentley headed plumb centre for a jaywalking tourist scuttling across the road from St James's Park. The car skidded on state horse droppings, bounced off a crowd barrier and cannoned into a stand left up since the Trooping of the Colour.

The Bentley looked as if its feelings had been hurt and was only slightly dented, though the impact had bust the radiator which steamed in hissing disapproval above the shrieks coming from Joan, whose arm was almost certain to be broken. Digby was silent, knocked out against his genuine walnut dashboard. No harm whatsoever had come to the passengers in the back.

Myra was spending the night with her friends. Felicity knew Felix was aware of that, so there was no point whatsoever in pretending they must be quiet. Apart from the dogs, who were overdue for a lamp-post visit, the flat was theirs. The dogs must wait, they could empty their bladders when Felix left. She had no wish for him to stay any longer than necessary. It was also useless to pretend the tape was lost as it was still sitting in full view on top of the piano beside the recorder.

'Let's be having it, Flicky.'

'OK, hold on, Felix while I get all this machinery sorted. Listen! Isn't that the phone? I had better answer it. Make yourself some coffee.'

Felicity's heart gave a jolt when she heard Wolf's voice. How could he have known that she was about to betray his trust? He sounded quite agitated.

'Is Felix there, Flicky?'

'Yes. How did you know?'

'I guessed. Please, Flicky, I need to talk to him. It's urgent.'

'I'll get him. He is just making coffee. Hold on.'

Felix wasn't making anything; he was bending over the tape recorder studying the mechanism. Nothing had been played.

'Wolf wants to talk to you, Felix.'

'God, that jerk is a creep. What does he want?'

'I haven't a clue, he sounds rather worried.'

A couple of minutes later Felix returned from the hallway where the phone lived on its 'Chippy' telephone seat.

'I've got to go, Flicky. There has been an accident and the parents are in the casualty department of St George's. The Bentley has been pranged. Mum has done something to her arm, Dad has had a knock on the head and, according to Wolf, has gone off his rocker.'

'Shall I come with you?'

'Christ no, it sounds as if my little sister and the blessed Wolf are behaving as if they have just won the Duke of Edinburgh's sodding gold award.'

'Are you sure there's nothing I can do? Please tell them I will do everything possible to help, anything at all – shopping, driving, typing, I could even do very plain cooking at a pinch.'

'I'll tell them. Now I had better fly before anyone does anything stupid like using my inheritance to endow a bed.'

As she lay soaking in a brimming bath which had squandered much of the geyser's gas in heating the water Felicity felt satisfied and grateful to whatever it was had saved her from playing the tape to Felix. She wished his parents no ill but their accident couldn't have come at a better moment.

After a wonderful night's sleep, she just had time for a sneak listen to her performance before going to work. Aunt Fay would have disapproved of such vanity. She took her toast into the sitting room and switched on the tape recorder . . . The tape was not there.

6

'PLEASE COVER FOR me, Bernice. Say I've gone to the dentist suddenly, in agony. Say my grandmother has died, anything at all. It is urgent, really it is.'

'What is urgent, Miss Campbeltown?'

Felicity turned round to find herself facing Mrs Prentice, wobbling on plastic patent court shoes and quivering with agonised indignation.

'I'm sorry. I must have some time off now, please. It is a matter of –'

'Life and death? I doubt it, Miss Campbeltown. However, I am prepared to believe you. You may go.'

'Thank you, thank you very much.'

'You may go, Miss Campbeltown, but you may not come back. Your cards and wages owing should be ready for your collection at close of business today. Recent reports and observations of your performance have been most unsatisfactory. Goodbye Miss Campbeltown.'

Oh but Bernice did look smug.

At Thurloe Place Penny answered the door. She was up and doing, brisk to a fault. Last night's crises had been her road to Damascus. 'Oh Flicky, I'm so happy!'

'Penny, I must see Felix.'

'Don't you want to know what has happened?'

'Yes of course, I mean no. Later please, Penny. I must find Felix. He has got the tape.'

'Felix isn't here.'

'Oh God. Where is he?'

A voice, somewhat weak and quavery, but authoritarian for all that, came from a bedroom. 'Who is it, Penny?'

'Felicity Campbeltown, Mum.'

'Oh good, that is one problem out of the way.'

'Problem?' Felicity was puzzled.

'Yes Flicky. Mum is really pleased about your offer to help. You see she has sustained a fracture to her right ulna and won't be able to drive or write or do anything for weeks, she may even have to have it plated,' Penny announced joyfully.

'How awful.'

'No, not really, it is quite a common procedure and entails removing a small amount of bone from the pelvis. Recovery, apart from some inevitable scarring, is nearly always a hundred per cent. It has all been absolutely fascinating, you have no idea how exciting a casualty department can be. I was gripped. I am called, I am going to be a nurse!'

'Oh good. Penny, that is marvellous. Now please help me. I must find Felix.'

'Penny darling,' Joan called. 'Is that Campbeltown girl going to do the job or not?'

'You are, aren't you, Flicky?'

Felicity wrinkled her brow and looked more confused than ever.

'Yes Mum. She says she would love to work for you,' Penny shouted back.

'Penny, I never said that.'

'Oh yes you did. Now come in and help me give Mum a blanket bath.'

'No Penny. Not that. I type, drive, maybe boil eggs, but emphatically no baths or bedpans, ever. Do you understand? Now please, I must find Felix.'

It was impossible really to tell whether his bed had been slept in or not. The daily lady was ill, his room was in chaos. Felicity found heaps of tapes and records, both singles and LPs, some with centres, some without and none of the tapes with legible labels. A stud box, crammed it seemed with cufflinks, watch chains and other precious junk, stood open on his dressing table beside a pair of ancient ivory brushes. Torn cigarette packets jostled for space alongside silver cases and a bowl full of loose change and defunct betting slips. It was hopeless. Felix had last been seen at St George's, where

Digby had recovered consciousness and was being kept in for observation.

It seemed quicker to run to Hyde Park Corner than to wait for a bus. Digby was in a private room at the end of a male surgical ward. Felicity tried to keep her mind off blood and knives and throbbing entrails as she passed bed after bed of prone men with Nil By Mouth notices above them. Unlike Penny, Felicity loathed illness and hospitals; malfunctions and deformities made her feel sick, she actually disliked the afflicted. It was hard to guess she was a doctor's daughter.

'His son is with him now,' said Sister in a starched pimple of a cap and important navy blue uniform.

'Thank God for that,' said Felicity. 'Can I see him?'

'Are you another daughter?'

'Yes,' said Felicity. She was another daughter, of another father.

'Don't worry Miss Blackburn, the Colonel will be fine. Just a nasty knock on the head.'

Sister showed Felicity where to go, just as a bleeper called her to the phone. A trolleyload of patient needed to be shoved off to theatre. It didn't bear thinking about.

Digby was lying half propped up in bed wearing white like an aged Nativity play angel. The room overlooked the gunners' memorial where a bronze corpse lay beneath a bronze cape and bronze tin hat. Standing with his back to Digby, gazing at the treetops of Buckingham Palace was Wolf.

'Oh, I'm sorry. I was told Felix was here. I was looking for him.'

'Don't worry, Felicity,' said Digby. 'Young Wolf and I have finished our business. What can we do for you? Felix hasn't been here since last night. Can I give him a message?'

Wolf turned towards Felicity and smiled. His eyes were sad and tired but he used them when he smiled. Because it was hot the window was open at the top.

'Don't worry, Flicky. It doesn't matter.'

He could barely hear her reply above the continuous roar of circulating traffic.

'You know? About the tape, I mean.'

'I guessed.'

'I am sorry, really sorry.'

Just then Sister opened the door. 'Well, Colonel, I congratulate you on your united and loyal family. If only more of our patients had such dutiful children. Here is your other son, come to take you home.

Felix looked dishevelled and weary, either hungover or exhausted, maybe both.

'Well look at all the little vultures gathering. You two had better be off before Sister Death finds you out. Incidentally, I expect you were looking for this.'

He held the tape out and pulled it back beyond Felicity's reach. 'Now then, say please nicely.'

'Please, Felix. Please can I have the tape.'

'Did you give it to him, Flicky?' Wolf asked.

'No, he took it.'

'Right then I will take it back,' said Wolf coming towards Felix with his fists clenched.

'Now now, little Wolfgang, no need for that,' said Felix throwing the reel at Wolf like a discus. 'Have it back with my love and a kiss. It is crap. Utter crap.'

Wolf reached to catch the tape but missed. It skimmed through the open window soaring before it fell back against a pediment to drop from ledge to ledge till it bounced out into the traffic and was squashed beneath a bus, as dead as the bronze soldier on the plinth beyond.

'Boys, boys, please. What is all this about?' said Digby. 'I've had more than enough. That will do!'

'Sorry,' said Wolf. 'It is nothing to worry about.'

'Too right,' said Felix.

For a while they walked in silence. The day was going to be hot but as yet no one basked upon the park grass. Ice-cream vans were drawn up like tanks before a battle. A string of riders, slumped inexpertly upon resigned hirelings, thumped their heels against their horses' sides until these mounts, who knew what happened when and where, broke into a bumpy, hobbledehoy trot and later on, at the correct spot, lumbered briefly at the canter. The riders shrieked with delight or fear at such intrepidness, hair bounced, jackets flapped but their hats stayed on, anchored by elastic beneath the chin. Only the Household Cavalry with shimmering jingling harness, horses and riders groomed and polished to a sheen, gave credence to the tradition of elegant riding in Rotten Row.

Still they walked, over the grass towards the Serpentine. Lilac and philadelphus scented the morning. Beyond the trees London was working; the sound of traffic had become a muttering groan. All but the highest storeys of the overlooking buildings were concealed by leaves. At the centre Wolf stopped and took Felicity's hand. Famous men, for whom there were memorials, stood sentinel round the park's perimeter and had no business with common man and woman: Shackleton, Prince Albert, Wellington and David who slew his tens of thousands. The god Achilles attacked the new Hilton. Peter Pan to the west and Tyburn to the east provided reminders of human innocence and guilt, childhood and morbidity, fanciful and actual macabre brutality.

'I love you, Flicky.'

'Oh Wolf.'

The coffee was tepid by the time it reached their outside table; the buns belonged to yesterday.

'I am going away, Flicky. I have got to get through these last exams and then I am going climbing in Skye.'

'Alone?'

'No. Not alone. With friends, it has been arranged for ages. After that I promised to lead a climb up Goat Fell. I will be back in time to hear my results. Will you wait?'

'Of course, we have got time. Lots of it.'

'Yes, I can hear it now. Your parents, everyone, will take you aside and tell you that you are too young.'

'You are young too, Wolf.'

'Yes but I'm different. I don't have a family to make me see sense.'

'The Blackburns?'

'No. To the Blackburns I am a nuisance or an embarrassment. Felix hates me, as you know.'

'Penny loves you.'

'But not as a brother. That is the trouble. I don't love her in any way, except to pity her and that is no love at all, of any kind.'

'What are you going to do, Wolf?'

'I don't know. I expect I will have to re-sit my exams or, if I am really lucky, try for a doctorate.'

'Here, in London?'

'If I can, if that is permitted.'

'What is there to stop you?'

'I have been asked to go away, to leave, quit England altogether. I don't need to be bribed. Presents given without conditions are the only ones worth accepting. I can manage without being corrupted, though I would like to travel and I have been promised enough money to live abroad.'

'Why, Wolf?'

'I haven't got a fitting face.'

'Will you go, Wolf? I've never been abroad. In Kilbole we used to look on England as a foreign country.'

'Are you saying you would come with me?'

'I thought you were asking me.'

'If I was, would you come?'

'Yes,' Felicity answered.

'But I wouldn't let you, Flicky. You must go to the Royal Academy even if I have to deliver you there each day.'

'Will you stay, then? What about the world?'

'The world can wait. We will see it together. We can make our own ways together, if . . .'

'If what, Wolf?'

'If that is what happens, I suppose.'

'Of course it will happen,' said Felicity.

'I am poor, really poor. More so if I stay here, as my rent will not be paid after this summer whether I graduate or not.'

'Don't worry, Wolf,' said Felicity. 'There are ways round that.'

'Waiting tables, tending bars, thumping joannas?' he suggested.

'Selling socks, typing, cleaning, scrubbing corpses even,' she replied. 'Oh I hope it doesn't come to that. No, even that I'm sure I could do if I had to.'

'So you don't mind being on the breadline? It won't be for

ever. I will make money, I will make my own success but I will not be a remittance man, living in exile on handouts. I will keep quiet and out of the way but I won't be discreet for money. I will wave two fingers at the bribe and spit at the incentive to disappear.'

'Who has asked you to go? Your uncle?'

'He is not my uncle, Flicky.'

'Adopted uncle, then.'

'Can you keep a secret?'

'Wolf, there is something I must tell you. I nearly broke my promise to you last night. If you hadn't rung up when you did I would have played that tape to Felix. I was frightened.'

'That no longer matters. Not at all. If Felix wants to behave like an idiot with a death wish for God's sake let him do it on his own. Just remember, Flicky, whatever people say about me, I love you, only you, for always. I always have.'

'Oh Wolf, how wonderful.' Felicity thought for a bit. She had not expected this and yet, now that it had happened, it was as if it had been booked from years ago. Suddenly practical, she said, 'Shall we make a new tape? I am sure we can do it again.'

'Wait till I get back, we could have another go when Hanne's stepson comes to London. Anyway I've got to get my head down and do these finals. I'm bound to fail, I know.'

'But you are clever, Wolf.'

'Idle Flicky, I haven't done enough work recently. I feel stupid and distracted. Your little sister has the right idea.'

'Ailsa? Oh yes she knows exactly what to do. She works and plays with equal dedication. Did I tell you she is coming down to stay when her last term ends?'

'Yes, to have her hair cut and lose her virginity.'

Felicity threw crumbs of stale bun to the cocky sparrows jostling amongst the table legs. Wolf put his hand over hers. 'Flicky. I meant it.'

'I know.'

'I'm going now, Flicky. Wish me luck.'

'Goodbye, Wolf. Good luck.'

She watched him walk away. His hair was too long now to see whether the sun still shone through his protruding ears as it had when he was little. Then suddenly she discovered what she had been looking for. She found what had been hiding and knew what she had always known. She loved him. He ought to be told.

'Wolf!' She ran to the edge of the pavement and called after him. He turned.

'I love you!' she shouted over the belching rattle of a diesel taxi.

'Good!' He waved and blew her a kiss before breaking into a run, crossing the road and vanishing. Felicity sat in the café till the tables began to fill for lunch then she walked back down Exhibition Road towards Thurloe Place.

Being Joan's right-hand woman was quite a good job, especially as Digby was most meticulous about wages. It didn't worry Felicity when she overheard him telling his wife that by paying her staff she could keep a proper distance and feel free to give them the sack, without embarrassment.

Penny was delighted with her new role as nurse. She also enjoyed making invalid meals, even though eggy dishes and milk puddings were not really the stuff to nourish mere broken arms and mild concussion.

There was to be a ball. Felix would come of age and Penny would come out with maximum *éclat* in August to coincide with the grouse-shooting season. The dance was to be held at the home of the current marquess, a bachelor of middle years, from whom Digby would inherit, barring accidents. Cousin Cedric lived in Dumfriesshire and doted on dachshunds, porcelain and the cultivation of rare orchids. The threat of the accidents the Blackburns dreaded befalling Cousin Cedric dwindled with each year as no sign of the mating urge appeared to bother the immaculate proprietor of Tulliebrae.

Felicity's job was to make lists, write invitations and carry out orders regarding the procurement of caterers, florists, tent erectors, bands and car-park attendants. It was all enormous fun, especially as it involved watching other people spending their money on wonderfully silly things.

Aunt Fay Braid would have been quite appalled at such profligate squandering. For all her inherited wealth she had never let her fortune from John's Bolts and Rivets be wasted by herself or Lionel with either generosity or ostentation.

Myra Pennyfeather was also disapproving. 'You are a lackey of capitalism. You have no business being involved with such ephemera. That Felix is a liability, an over-privileged parasite who throws things. Buns or bullets, it is all the same to that sort. Don't go, Felicity, I'm warning you, you will regret it.'

She had accompanied Felicity playing 'Elisir d'Amour' and the sentimentality had agitated her. Felicity's playing had been sublime.

'It is harmless, Myra and apart from that, it provides employment.'

'Who says?'

'My father. He told me that if it were not for idiots like the Blackburns the labour exchange would be swamped with out-of-work oyster openers and gossip columnists.'

'What does Wolfgang have to say about it?'

'He has gone away. He left after the last of his finals.'

'For ever?'

'No, not for ever.'

'Cherish him, Felicity. He is the only man who will ever be worthy of you.'

'Aunt Myra, what are you saying?'

'The truth. Now let's have a go at the Debussy, despite your lack of flaxen hair.'

Felicity was helping Penny pack for the weekend. She had been invited to a most sumptuous ball in the Dukeries. 'It is all so hellish. A wallflower is still a wallflower, whether the party is in village hall or palace.'

'Oh Penny, come on. I expect you will have the time of your life.'

'Not according to my stars in the *Evening Standard* I won't.'

'Buy the *News* then. One of them is bound to say what you want to hear.'

'Flicky, have you ever had your fortune told?'

'Only by Isa in the tea-leaves. She was hot stuff on parcels at Christmas but a bit shaky on dark strangers. Why?'

'Nothing. I just wondered. If you had been to a clairvoyant, a proper one I mean, would you believe what they said?'

Felicity thought for a moment as she threaded a needle to stitch back a dangling button. 'It depends, I suppose, on what I was told. I would hate to hear that I would never find happiness or that I was not going to make it as a musician and I was going to be squashed by a bus at an early age. I do tend to believe everything I hear so I think I would be better off steering clear of crystal balls just in case. Have you had your cards read, Penny?'

'No. Not my cards.'

'What then? Go on, tell me.'

'My palm. That old woman near Godfrey Street.'

'I've heard of her, she is meant to be good. Tell me, what did she see? I bet she said you'd make a wonderful nurse.'

'I can't remember anything about that. She was awful, Flicky. She had this really crumby furniture and ducks flying up the wall, honestly I couldn't believe it. How could a woman with a crinoline lady over her telephone know what was going to happen to me?'

'You tell me. This yellow dress is really pretty.'

'Not on me it isn't. Felix says it makes me look like an alcoholic baby chick.'

'That is just Felix being silly. Treat him with disdain like tatty horoscopes.'

'I can't get what she said out of my head, bloody old hag. She even had antimacassars.'

'The woman must have been a rogue and a charlatan.'

'Don't mock me, Flicky, please. It was horrible.'

'I'm sorry, Penny. Tell me what she said.'

'Loads of old codswallop all about strife and having to settle for second best, needing to be cunning, hoeing my own row and that motherhood would be hard won. It isn't fair.'

'Oh Penny, try not to brood on it. You must have caught her on an off day and consulted her at the wrong time of the month. Maybe you didn't cross her palm with enough silver.'

'Silver be damned, it cost me a fiver.'

'Well then, that only proves that money isn't everything. Come on, tell me your star sign and I'll read you what Celeste is saying about you this month.'

'I've looked already, it is all jolly discouraging.' Penny held up a tent of ribbon lace more suited to a well pregnant bride. 'What do you think of this?'

'Isn't it a bit too like a doily? How about that puce dress?' said Felicity. She took the hanger out of the wardrobe and laid the ball gown on Penny's bed, overturning the pillow.

'That is mine!' said Penny snatching a photograph of Wolf, which must have been taken before he had started to shave. 'That is a secret. Tell Mum about it and you're dead.'

'I won't breathe a word, Penny. I promise.'

Felicity only had memory to conjure up her love. The more she thought of Wolf the more she knew that she was one of the very few who are lucky enough to become victim of the real thing. She was felled by thumping, overwhelming, swamping, lasting love.

A week or so later Joan's plastered arm stopped hurting but Digby fretted despite his mended head.

Felicity was typing the list of potential guests when Penny came to see her in considerable agitation.

'Flicky, have you ever seen Granny's emeralds?'

'I've never even seen your granny, Penny,' Felicity replied. She had typed 'incitation' instead of 'invitation' and was scratching at the error with a dirty disc of rock-like rubber. 'Why does your mother want to have this stuff engraved? Surely there must be a cheaper way of printing.'

'There is, but it is social death not to have bumpy invites. People rub their thumbs over the writing even before they read what it says,' Penny replied informatively. 'Granny is dead, it is only her emeralds that are still about somewhere.'

'What do they look like, apart from being green?'

'Thoroughly unpleasant. I'm supposed to inherit them.'

'You could always sell them, couldn't you? If you really don't like them, that is. What are they, necklace or brooch?'

'Neither. There is a socking great ring, a green glacier mint set about with diamonds and a bracelet to match, like a strap. I hate them but I won't be able to sell them if they are lost.'

'Oh, I see. Are they lost?'

'Well, no one can find them. Mum wore them to Glynde-bourne and kept flashing them about in front of the Von

Hoffers. Even the blind would have known about them, they rattled horribly, it was quite embarrassing in the quiet bits of the opera.'

'Which hand did she wear them on?'

'The right, the broken one.'

'Perhaps someone removed them at the hospital. Have you asked?'

'No, Wolf took them off, I remember. Just after the accident, before the ambulance came. He said it would be better to remove them before Mum's arm got too swollen.'

'Maybe he put them in his pocket and forgot about them. What was he wearing?'

'Felix's dinner jacket. Anyway he didn't do that, he put them in Mum's bag and gave the bag to me. After that I went to the hospital with my parents, he stayed with the car then followed us. He arrived at casualty just as Dad was being admitted and Mum had been X-rayed.'

'Is that when he rang for Felix?'

'Yes.'

'Then what happened?'

'He brought me and Mum home in a taxi. We got out. I was helping Mum but Wolf hadn't enough money to pay the cab so I handed him Mum's bag and told him to take the fare out of that, which he did and then gave it back to me, I'm sure about that. We then came up here. He changed out of Felix's kit and left.'

'How did he get home without money?' Felicity asked.

'I don't know, Flicky. Walked I suppose. Anyway the point is the bloody emeralds are missing.'

'Where do they usually live?'

'In the safe.'

'Well then maybe they have been put back there.'

'No, they aren't there. Dad has had a look. Anyway, no one else can work the combination except Felix and he hasn't been here at all since he brought Dad home from hospital.'

'I had noticed. Where is he?'

'He's got exams, or that's what he says. I think he is running away from Angelica but that is neither here nor there. The point is that Wolf is suspected of nicking those jewels.'

'Penny, he wouldn't do that. Surely you know that. Are your

parents going to get the police? I am sure there must be some other explanation.'

'We will never know.'

'Why?'

'Because the police are not going to be told. There is to be no investigation ,nothing. Wolf isn't even going to be asked. I have had a long lecture from Dad about it. He says that he wants nothing done at all. He just wants it to fester like a bloody time bomb. Where is Wolf?'

'On the Isle of Skye, climbing up the Cuillins. You don't think he did it, do you, Penny?'

'I don't know, Flicky. Anyway, why didn't Wolf tell me where he was going?'

There wasn't really an answer to that. 'Look Penny, Wolf will come back, you can ask him then, about everything.'

'I'm not allowed to mention it to anyone, ever.'

'You have told me. Why?'

Penny looked confused. 'Because I wanted you to know.'

'Have you told Felix? Penny, does Felix know?'

'Well, I might have mentioned it to him when he rang up. Just sort of in passing while he was asking whether Angelica was still chasing.'

Felicity put the cover over the Imperial and got up. 'I'm going to take myself off for a sandwich in the park now. I will be back in time to drive your mother to Harley Street.'

'Can I come with you, Flicky?'

'No, Penny, I need to be alone.'

'Flicky, please, you must tell me. Is Wolf in love with you?'

'There is nothing that I must tell you Penny.'

Felicity hated driving in London. 'You must assert yourself,' said Ailsa when she rang to say her exams were going quite well.

'Thank you Ailsa. You can't even drive.'

'I know how it should be done, though. I can't play the piano, but I can spot your mistakes.'

Manoeuvring Joan's Rover was a stately business, rather like driving a drawing room. Felicity felt a bit more secure behind the high solid instrument panel than she did in her mother's Austin 1100, but being assertive required nerve, especially at Hyde Park Corner and even more so with Joan giving commands from behind. Penny sat in the back with her mother and Felicity wondered whether a peaked cap and a cockade might give her greater confidence and gravitas in negotiating Park Lane amongst the other chauffeurs.

At Harley Street she pulled up and got out to help Penny with her invalid. She left both Joan and Penny on the steps of a pink brick edifice embellished with superfluous stone frills and a front door gleaming with brass plates. It would appear that at least two dozen doctors had consulting rooms in there, a bill for every ill.

'Come back for us in half an hour, Felicity,' said Joan imperiously.

Fully expecting to have been addressed by her surname, Felicity suppressed the urge to touch her forelock. She used the half-hour to go to Warren Street, to see where Wolf called home. She missed him and was riddled with rage about what was being insinuated. She managed to find a parking place on the corner of Fitzroy Street. There were two pubs in Warren Street and she knew his digs were next to one of them. She decided to ring the bell of the house nearest Evans's Dairy with its blue tiled shop front.

A woman whose bosom had dropped to below waist level opened the door. She wore fluffy slippers, a flowered overall on top of a flowery dress, and appeared to be feeling the heat, at least she smelled that way, rather like Bernice but without the camouflaging cocktail of all the free squirts available in Perfumery.

'Excuse me. Does Wolfgang Duncan live here?'

'You're the second one this afternoon. What's he done?'

'Nothing. I'm a friend. He does live here?' Felicity persisted.

'Not for much longer he doesn't. Anyway, he's not here.'

'I know. Could you just direct me to his room? I want to leave him something for when he gets back.'

'His other visitor left something there too. What's up?'

'Nothing,' Felicity repeated. 'I expect he has lots of friends.'

'Enough. Come with me, I'll show you. He is a good lad. I'll miss him.'

It took a while for Mrs Crease to climb the stairs to the top floor where Wolf lived in an airy bedsitter that ran from front to back of the house. 'Have you got a fag?' she asked, gasping as she unlocked the door.

'No, sorry. I don't smoke.'

The ceiling appeared lower because of the size of the room, which seemed vast because the only furniture in it was a bed, an armchair, a chest of drawers, a table and a couple of chairs, one of which was used as a stand for a gramophone. An ancient radiogram stood in the corner. A curtain concealed some coat hooks and shelves. The back of the room, from the window of which the newly opened Post Office Tower could be seen looming, had been crudely converted into a sort of kitchen with a Baby Belling, a sink and a fridge.

'He's got every luxury,' said Mrs Crease. 'And a view of the back of St Luke's Hospital. It's for the clergy,' she added as if sick clerics were an asset.

Felicity had never seen so many records. A lot of them were old 78s stacked beside heaps of books and sheet music. The walls were covered in posters for concerts and pictures of mountains. Above his bed, with its black-painted iron frame, he had stuck some photographs. She felt like crying when she saw the middle one, the one with pride of place. It was familiar to her too, having been taken by her father on Coronation Day. Everybody was there. Digby, quite splendid in uniform, Felix scowling at Penny who was smiling up at Hanne holding Wolf's hand beside Joan, a plumper version of her sister, Clarice Duncan, standing at the rear between leering Uncle Lionel and Aunt Fay with lips pursed in acid smirk. Felicity and her mother, who looked so young and pretty, were sitting on the floor at the front. Magnus Campbeltown had only just managed to run round and get himself included in the shot and had attempted unsuccessfully to look nonchalant as he put his arm round little Ailsa who was gazing, unblinking, at the camera.

Felicity saw that Wolf had drawn a circle round her own face.

There were papers all over the table which doubled as a desk, so she stuck her note on the cracked mirror beside the sink with stamp paper.

Dearest, darling Wolf, Welcome home. Ring me immediately.
Very important. All my love Flicky. x

'You will see he gets my message, won't you, Mrs Crease?' she said as she left.

'Are you sure you haven't got some ciggies?'

'I'll go and buy you some if you promise to make sure Wolf sees my note.'

'Bless you dear. Of course I will.'

Miss Evans in the shop was most helpful about which brand to buy. 'You're the second person in this afternoon buying cigarettes for Mrs Crease.'

Apart from Miss Evans's Morris Minor most other cars in Warren Street were for sale, it being a market overt.

'Fancy a change of motor, dear?' asked a sharp young man in creaseless Terylene and drip-dry shirt. He was working for one of the dealers who had strangely apt names – Wheeler, Ringer, Graff and Bluston.

'This isn't mine,' said Felicity. 'Sorry.'

'Pity, I could do you a lovely TR4, just the thing for a glamour girl like you. Young fellow brought it in this afternoon, it's perfect. One careful owner.'

7

I N KILBOLE DIGBY had been the Major. Now that his dark hair was grizzled he was the Colonel and shortly, if plans worked well, he would get promoted yet further. Felicity found this neat, erect and correct example of military dexterity far more approachable than his fluttery wife and half as intimidating. His hair and forehead were corrugated and concerned. He laughed to put people at ease and not to mock. He knew he had gone wrong more than once in his own life and certainly couldn't understand his children. He worried for them and their happiness while retaining his soldier's sense of duty and was well acquainted with how misfortunes should be breasted. Above all he wanted a home life free of unnecessary strife. He had seen enough of that in the course of his career.

'Can I talk to you, Colonel, please? In private.'

Digby was at home for the morning while his wife and daughter had gone out to squabble over shoes for Goodwood. Joan insisted on pumps from Rayne and Penny wanted short white boots that made her look like an inflated mortuary attendant.

'Come in, Felicity. What can I do for you?'

Digby looked at Felicity with wistful admiration. That was what he wanted for a daughter-in-law. She was just the ticket, he thought. Gentle, capable, funny and lovely. Come to think of it, he wouldn't have hung about himself, given the chance. That was a wicked thought which had to be smothered double quick. 'Is something wrong, Felicity, are my wife's plans being tiresome?'

'Oh no they are just fine, Colonel. It is about the missing emeralds.'

'But only Penny and her mother should know of them,' he

exclaimed, thumping his fist into the palm of his other hand, gritting his tombstone teeth.

'Penny told me, Colonel,' said Felicity.

'Oh damn! I swore her to secrecy. Blast this modern education system, nobody respects the importance of discretion any more. It's not surprising this country is crawling with traitors.'

'The thing is, Colonel, I do not think it is fair for you to let Wolf be thought a thief. After all, I could have stolen the stuff and no one has suspected me. Why not?'

'Because I know you didn't take them, Felicity.'

'And I know that Wolf didn't either.'

Digby looked at Felicity steadily. She had the prettiest eyes he had ever seen, clear and honest, unpainted and heartbreaking. 'Did Penny believe the story, Felicity?'

'Then it is just a story?'

'Yes yes, of course it is,' said Digby impatiently.

'Why though? Why did you want Penny to think Wolf is a criminal?'

'It is a private affair. A family matter, Felicity. No one else is meant to know.'

'I do, and I think she might have told Felix. That makes two of us.'

Felicity remembered a sermon at school about secrecy. If one person told another that was two ones, which looked like eleven, then one hundred and eleven told, and so on.

'Bloody hell!' said Digby. 'I am sorry, Felicity, please excuse me. This is not what I planned.'

'What did you plan, Colonel?'

'I just wanted to discredit Wolf in young Penny's eyes. She seemed to have a crush on him.'

'She has,' Felicity answered. 'But that is no reason to brand an innocent man a villain. Or is it a snob thing? Is Wolf not good enough for Penny?'

'No Felicity, I don't think that,' said Digby sadly. 'Her mother might, but I don't. I think Wolf is a splendid fellow, but you see they are cousins.'

'That isn't against the law. There is nothing wrong with that.'

'I know.'

'Well, Colonel Blackburn, I think you should know that Penny is not and never will be loved by Wolf. He told me that himself and I believe him. He is honest, I know.'

'Yes Felicity and so are you. Thank you.'

Digby rubbed his hand over his orderly waves and stroked his neat moustache. 'One day, Felicity I will tell you why. One day you might understand. Meanwhile I would like to apologise to you.'

'What are you going to tell Penny and Felix? Is your wife going to find the emeralds mysteriously back in her jewel box?'

'I'm afraid not,' said Digby. 'They have gone for good. I don't quite know how to figure this all out. Are you going to spill the beans? If you do there will be a right old shindig.'

Felicity looked at the leader of men and saw a well-intentioned, muddle-headed inadequate man of middle years. She felt saddened and could afford to be compassionate. She wasn't accustomed to this much potential power and had no urge to wield it. There was no point. Let the Blackburns sort out their own cesspit.

Wolf was innocent and all hers. At least she hoped he was still all hers. If only he would write or ring. She had received no word of him for over three weeks.

When Ailsa came to stay the Blackburns had already decamped to Sussex for Glorious Goodwood so Felicity never did discover whether the chasm between the two girls had become too wide for their old friendship to bridge. Ailsa and Penny were at the opposite end of all manner of scales, social, academic and physical.

Ailsa's friend Senga had taken mumps. That didn't stop Ailsa from coming to London on her own, nor did it deter her from going to Senga's cousin's party. Ailsa, at seventeen, saw no point in being shy. Unseen blooming got you nowhere.

'What does B.A.B. mean?'

'Bring A Bottle,' said Felicity. 'I've got Bulls Blood or Blue Nun. I won them on a raffle. Which do you want?'

'Both, please. I have got to bring a partner. Who have you got for me?'

'I haven't.'

'You must know someone who would do.'

'What for?'

'A partner, of course.'

Felicity didn't like to bring up the subject of her little sister's virginity. Maybe she had forgotten. She had not.

'I won't get my hair cut till afterwards. That will make it more of an event, a rite of passage like *Coming of Age in Samoa*. You must find me a man. Who have you got on that paper? Surely there is someone suitable amongst that lot.' Ailsa was looking over Felicity's shoulder at a much scribbled over list of invitees to the Blackburn ball.

'I'm not sure that half these men even exist – they certainly haven't replied to the invitation and Mrs B. is going batty as all the girls have accepted. Sorry Ailsa, you will just have to go on your own. None of these would be any good at a bottle party in Shepherd's Bush.'

'Senga's cousin has got a tent and a live band.'

'That doesn't sound much like a bottle party to me, unless the tent belongs to the Scouts and the band is made up of friends.'

'Could be. Anyway, I need a man. Now! What about Wolf?'

'No! Certainly no. Anyway he is still away.'

'Are you sweet on him, Flicky?'

'Ailsa I'm shocked. I didn't expect you to think like that.'

'I don't. You do,' Ailsa replied.

Felicity brooding about Wolf got Ailsa no nearer to finding a partner. 'Concentrate, Flicky,' she implored. 'Approach my problem methodically, there must be an answer.'

'Short of hiring a man by the hour or one of Myra's old socialists I can't think of any spare men.'

'You are hopeless, Flicky. What with me coming so well prepared, it is a great disappointment.'

'What do you mean, Ailsa? Are you really determined to go through with it? Why not wait?'

'I've brought precautions. Four in all.'

'Four French letters?' Felicity asked.

'Four packets.'

'That should do for one night.'

'Stop being silly, Flicky.' Ailsa wasn't smiling. 'I bought them at the chemist's. The assistant was most helpful.'

'Not in Kilbole surely?'

'Of course not,' Ailsa replied. 'I'm not stupid.'

Indeed she wasn't, she had got Grade A in all her Highers.

There had been no word from Wolf yet about his results, nothing at all. It was all most worrying. There was nothing Felicity could do but wait for him to contact her. She had written to him once more at Warren Street but received no reply.

The telephone rang and Felicity's guts somersaulted. They did that every time.

'Please can I speak with Miss Felicity Camp Bell Town. My name is Dieter Schmidt, my *Stiefmutter* has instructed me to call.'

'Dieter, you are an answer to prayer.'

'Please?'

'Come here at once. Have you got the address? Good. We shall be waiting for you.'

Felicity hung up the receiver and turned to Ailsa. 'There we are, my little sister, the Lord hath provided. A man comes for you within the hour. Are you sure you want to go through with this? We could all play Scrabble. There is no need to go the whole hog.'

'How else will I find out whether I like it?'

'What will you do if you don't?'

'I haven't, thought. Maybe I might prefer roller skating or keeping bees. But I need to know first.'

Dieter, when he appeared, brought flowers: six sad roses in a paper poke. Stiff and proper, he was thin, immensely tall and blond, a humourless white tulip in steel-rimmed glasses. At least he and Ailsa shared a taste in spectacles.

The following morning Ailsa was ecstatic. They had danced till their feet gave out, she had never had such fun.

'I am glad you are getting on so well,' said Felicity lamely. 'I take it the hive and roller skates can be shelved.'

'Maybe. I haven't found out yet,' Ailsa replied. 'But I am still going to have my hair cut. It will be more practical for travelling. Dieter has asked me to go back to Germany with him to stay with his family. Don't look so shocked,

Flicky. Mum and Dad have known his stepmother since long ago.'

'Yes, Mum said Hanne had called in with Lotte.'

'Well there you are. It is all fixed.'

Felicity gave her sister a kiss.

'What's that for?' Ailsa asked.

'For being so uncomplicated,' Felicity replied.

Short hair suited Ailsa. Dieter said so too as the three of them ate Myra's leftover chickpea risotto after seeing *The Knack* at the Essoldo the following evening.

'Dieter says you have got some music to play to him,' said Ailsa, offering her plateful to an already windy dog.

Having explained about the wrecked tape, Felicity offered to pick out the melody of 'Silent Worship' on the piano.

'That will not be necessary. I think I am already knowing this aria from Ptolemy. The group last night was playing many parodies of older works, maybe they are also including this air or one similar.'

'The group was called the Bloody Brothers, or something like that,' said Ailsa. 'They were all friends at some college, actually they were really good.'

'Musically they were inept,' said Dieter. 'But they are having a strong beat and are making a pleasant sound which is good for dancing.'

Two days later Felicity met the downstairs tenant as she dragged her baby's pushchair up the stone flight. How she would manage when her lump turned into a second baby was not to be imagined.

'Are you Felicity Campbeltown by any chance?'

'Yes,' Felicity answered. She longed for the time when such an answer would trigger a request for an autograph. One day maybe.

'Oh good. I've got some mail for you. The postman keeps putting it through my door.'

Without an apology the woman gave Felicity no less than seven postcards, all from Wolf. One had been posted over four weeks ago. He had put no address on any of them so at least he had not been waiting for a reply. He was well, the climbing was fun, was hard, was thrilling, the weather was good then bad then finally improving and all the time on every message he missed Felicity and loved her more and more. A grim photograph did nothing to make Whiting Bay look inviting but his second-last postcard came from there where he was staying with old friends who were in need of his help. The most recent card was of the Esplanade at Ardrossan but had been posted on Arran. In block capitals he announced that he had just passed his driving test. He went on to say that he couldn't return to London till his friends, the Otways, were better. Squashed at the bottom, under the photographer's name, he had written 'Great News! I got a First!'

Goodwood over, the Blackburns moved up to Scotland to stay with Cousin Cedric and transform his harmonious aesthetic existence into a frenzy of preparations for the great ball. It was extremely good of the marquess to tolerate such an intrusion but Joan felt no qualms. Cedric Tullie was a childless bachelor, the least he could do was to let his heir have a taste of his inheritance. 'Let the dog see the rabbit!' said Digby by way of most inadequate palliative, though who was the rabbit and who the dog was not explained. Corporal Bolsover had left the army and had gone with his wife to work for Lord Tullie entirely on Digby's recommendation. That favour was surely worth several weeks of shattered peace and all manner of loud celebrations.

Felicity was expected to travel north too. Joan's arm was mending well, there was no need for it to be plated, but she had grown to rely entirely on Felicity's secretarial and organisational skills as well as her infinite capacity to withstand being bullied.

It was time anyway that Felicity went home: she missed her parents and was homesick. She couldn't imagine what it must be like to have no one to miss and just a bedsit to call home.

'You look thin, my wee girl,' said Magnus. 'Are you pining?'

'No, Dad, don't worry about me. Are you going to prescribe a tonic? Halibut liver oil or Radio Malt?'

Sheila Campbeltown had gone grey early, which is often the way with near-black hair. She was still very pretty; only her eyes occasionally betrayed her anxiety. She missed her daughters more than she could say but at the same time she was ambitious and knew that neither would come to much if they stayed at home. To see Felicity a star of the concert platform was her greatest hope, it had sustained her throughout her own mediocre career. Felicity promised she would return to Kilbole for a longer visit once the ball was done with.

'You are practising aren't you, darling?'

'Yes, Mother, I promise. Every day.'

Tulliebrae had escaped the wilder fantasies of the prospering Victorian merchants who had established themselves amongst the wooded hills of Dumfriesshire. It stood plain in peach-coloured sandstone upon the rising ground above the river whose brown peaty waters glided and scuttled between mossy rocks. Oak and beech trees were interspersed with tall Scots pines and Douglas firs with giant cones that bounced when they dropped on the damp ochre earth. The walled kitchen garden was upon the flat spit in the river bend and had been let go to a gentle ruination. The paths had all but disappeared beneath creeping weeds and unfettered, erstwhile cordoned fruit trees spread enthusiastically over the mellow walls till pears and peaches, plums and nectarines mingled their branches and delighted the birds who gorged at will without being trapped by shielding nets.

Falkirk, the head gardener had been at Tulliebrae since birth and had lived his life in the same cottage, having seen as many change of monarch as change of marquess. In 1966 he was too old to care about the dishevelled vegetable garden but, like his master, he was devoted to the cultivation of orchids. Together they would potter and gloat over their cosseted treasures that throve in perfect conditions. The glass houses at Tulliebrae were renowned. They were heated by sonorous cast-iron pipes from a greedy furnace and watered with rainwater collected in cisterns; the tiled floors were never muddy and no staging harboured mite or bug.

Up at the house itself Lord Cedric Blackburn, Marquess of Tullie, kept his immaculate Sèvres, each piece perfect and carefully protected behind glass, well away from the tails and paws of the eight prize dachshunds which, apart from Falkirk, appeared to be the only living creature to benefit from Cedric's conversation.

Poor Cedric: he winced at the mention of tents, of bars and caterers, of night-clubs in his cellars and floodlit trees. He fretted at the thought of fireworks frightening his dogs and the thumping band shaking his fine china. His only comfort was that Bolsover and his staunch wife were both capable and trustworthy and would still be with him after all this loud vulgarity was over and things could subside again into harmonious serenity and deaf Nanny Fount could return to the kitchen to cook his favourite shepherd's pies and rice puddings once more.

'Excuse me, sir, would you mind very much if I played the piano.'

Felicity was alone in the house with Cedric. Bolsover had taken a party to Dumfries in search of paper sunflowers and Digby was trying to introduce Felix to the joy of golf.

'Go ahead, feel free,' Cedric replied in a resigned voice. 'I am going down to see my orchids, come along you lot.' Eight shiny sausages trotted after their master, tails erect like a team of irritated scorpions.

Felicity had been playing for about half an hour when she sensed that she was not alone. The piano was kept tuned but the keys were stiff with lack of use. She indulged in a luxurious melancholy, thinking not about the music but about Wolf and was near to tears when she looked up to see Cedric watching her from the doorway.

'I'm sorry, I didn't realise you were there,' she said as she began to shut the lid.

'Please go on. I haven't heard that piano played properly since Mother died. You have given me a great treat.'

'Thank you. I've finished now. I have to go and do some phoning for Mrs Blackburn.'

'No more panic about smoked salmon, I trust.'

'No, that is resolved. This is about Pipe Major Duchal who is to stand at the head of the front steps as the guests arrive.'

'One shudders,' said Cedric clutching his pink bald pate in mock exasperation.

Felicity laughed and he smiled back. Cedric must have been a bonny baby but it was less appealing for a man to look as if he flourished thanks to Cow and Gate.

'Do you play the piano, sir?'

'No, alas, I do not. Please call me Cedric or I will have to call you Miss Campbeltown.'

'Mrs Blackburn would prefer that, I think.'

'Very well Miss Campbeltown, we must not torment Auntie Joan's nerves. Do you play other instruments?'

'I have my violin with me but I won't play it now. The dogs, you know, they hate fiddle music.'

'Some time when Bolsover takes them for a walk, will you play for me then?'

'Yes, if you really want me to. It can sound acid on its own – without accompaniment I mean.'

'Do you like performing?'

'Yes, if I know what I am doing.'

'Is that your ambition?'

'I start at the Royal Academy next term. I want to be a soloist if possible.'

'What is there to stop you?'

'Lack of talent in an overcrowded profession mostly.'

'And lack of money?'

'Well it would be nice not to have to work, I suppose, provided I used the time to practise. Yes, I suppose money might help. It generally does. Now, if you will excuse me I must away and sort the Pipe Major before the others get home, sorry, I mean back.'

'Don't apologise. One day Tulliebrae will be their home, Miss Campbeltown.'

Felicity took out her fiddle, having made quite sure that she was alone and the dogs all gone out and about to do whatever it is that thrills animals ten inches tall with stomachs skimming the ground.

Felicity was already wrapping the violin in its silk handkerchief before putting away when Cedric appeared, having been listening out of sight.

'Can I see that violin, please.'

Felicity gave it to him carefully.

'You deserve a better instrument than this.'

'I never want to play any other. That violin means the world to me.'

'But it is scratched.'

'Music is never perfect.'

Cedric thought for a while and said, as he handed the violin back, 'I agree that nothing is perfect but some things get very, very close. Come with me and I will show you.'

The Sèvres was splendid. Cedric told her so. Felicity felt awkward and insufficiently ecstatic as plate after vase after urn was shown to her and her admiration invited. She remembered the time that Felix had taken the blame for the vase she had knocked over in the Thurloe Place flat and felt exonerated. With this lot to inherit, Felix would have pots in plenty.

'My mother has a monkey band. I used to love it, I still do. She would let me dust it and rearrange it when I was little, if I was good.'

A look of revulsion passed over Cedric's cherubic face. 'I hate that sort of thing. You see, I detest any kind of imperfection. Freaks and deformity, clowns and midgets, animals dressed as people and vice versa are all abominations to me.'

Cedric insisted on taking Felicity to meet his orchids. He talked of them as if they were his children, or at the very least, living, breathing creatures with a duty to perform for their master. Discreet yellow and small rust-speckled specimens received the same devotion as huge white and pink butterflies and mauve, deep purple flowers which were so contrived and exotic as to look too theatrical to be natural. Felicity preferred flowers that were less precious. There was none of the cabbage rose's generous exuberance amongst these stiff plants: they were beautiful, like models advertising ball gowns costing ransoms, and just as unreal. One orchid in particular thrilled Cedric as it had only just chosen to bloom again after several years of sulky torpor. It was a greenish bilious yellow with a white tongue spattered with what seemed like a rash of diseased sores.

'Which is your favourite?' Cedric asked Felicity.

She thought for a while, knowing she should pick something subtle before indicating a plant with large white flowers blooming upon a long slim stem. 'It looks like *Les Sylphides*,' she said.

'You like the ballet?'

'I've never been. I have just seen pictures and I know the music.'

'I will take you, next time I am in London. Would you like that?'

At last it seemed that the guest list was taking shape and the lack of men was becoming less obvious. Wolf had not been invited. Felicity had seen his name on the original list but then it had been scratched out. It was easier in a way if he did not come. There was less to long for, less to dread and she could concentrate on her job and watch a world she didn't wish to join, at play.

Every substantial house within the neighbourhood and well beyond had their spare bedrooms filled with guests for the dance. Twenty gallant hostesses had volunteered to give dinner parties for those not dining at Tulliebrae, where every room was taken and all beds occupied.

The dancing was scheduled to start at ten though no one would risk arriving till at least half an hour later which would mean that for the first hour or so the band would play to an empty marquee. At one, the group would take over while the dance band and the elderly guests had a supper break. Reels would alternate with flat dances in the first part of the evening to please the natives, as Joan called her fellow Scots. Felix had been born at 3 a.m., which was when the fireworks were to be let off. (One of Felicity's most ticklish jobs had been to circulate everyone within earshot of Tulliebrae and warn them that their repose would be wrecked by happy explosions.) Breakfast would then be served and the nightclub's jukebox would stomp on till dawn or till there were no more survivors.

As the night of the dance approached crises succeeded problems in a relentless string, causing Joan to do much lying down with aspirins. The steps from the upstairs drawing room to the marquee were too long for the awning, moles had dug up great barrows all over the rose garden paths, the chief florist sprained her ankle, the car-park field flooded, no one could agree a table plan and Nanny Fount insisted on being in charge of the cloakroom despite being stone deaf and liable to drop asleep (or

124

dead) at any time. Pipe Major Duchal had not been sighted sober for a month.

The only thing on which the Bolsovers and Nanny Fount could agree was the total incompetence and undoubted dishonesty of the temporary staff and caterers who were all murderous lunatics and likely to poison everything they didn't break or steal.

Felicity walked about with a clipboard and wrote down all complaints, grievances and suggestions. When her sheet of paper was full up she threw it away. This was not the first of such parties these experts had attended; everything was bound to come right in the end. If it didn't, the whole affair would be over and gone in a flash, consigned to the memory, a page of photographs and a mention in the social columns.

The police were alerted and the AA put up signs. Arrangements were made for all outside staff including security men to be fed and watered by Mrs Bolsover in the stables, which didn't please her much but made a change from her usual work of chopping firewood, butchering, gutting and plucking, all of which jobs turned her husband's stomach. Bolsover thought little of the flower arrangements and said so but kept himself happy making a mountain range of butter curls.

Penny had lost enough weight to look quite elegant in electric blue satin though the dress from Belleville et Cie would have suited a woman twice her age. A hairdresser was coming to set her hair in coils and add some more that had been shorn from European nuns before they took their vows and not, Joan had been assured, from the heads of impoverished oriental prostitutes. Joan would wear emerald green. No mention was made of the stones that would have been the natural accessories to this formidable creation. Had they been available, she would have had to wear them on her left arm; her right one, still in plaster, was to be supported on the night with a matching emerald satin sling.

Meanwhile Cedric spent a lot of time with Felicity. She felt sorry for him: his house was being overturned and quite obviously he didn't care at all for its eventual inheritor. Felix was behaving abominably. He dashed about in his new car making ruts in the gravel and scaring the under-gardener, who was a bit simple, by practising handbrake turns in the avenue when the poor lad was meant to be tidying the verges. He sometimes came to meals, and sometimes he stayed out all night at parties he had told no one about. The only bit of the dance he had organised was the hiring of the pop group which he planned as a surprise. Cedric was nearly ill with worry about this: he had read much of uncouth doings amongst pop groups and wished he had never consented to this awful party without first stipulating that his valuables be removed or boarded up.

Nanny Fount started the rumour. She told Mrs Bolsover who told Bolsover who relayed it to Penny in deepest secrecy which meant that, very soon, everybody except Felicity and Cedric was well aware of what was hatching. Nanny Fount knew all about Cedric. She had raised him from the cradle and was an expert on all his moods and whims. The rumour reached Joan, who shrieked with horror at the thought of all her son's expectations being snatched from him by a scheming harpy. 'Do something Dingo!' she pleaded.

'There there, Joanie. You are worrying about nothing,' Digby replied.

Digby had much more to worry him than his old cousin's unlikely infatuation. Mr von Hoffer had rung from the Central Hotel in Glasgow on a matter of the gravest importance.

8

Felicity was neither guest nor servant. Her position as Joan's right hand was hard to define though she spent most of her time being ordered about like poor Cinders with Penny and Joan cast as the ugly sisters and Bolsover as Buttons. Joan, however, wasn't ugly, she saw to that, whereas nothing – no lotions, clothes, pills or hairstyles – did anything much for Penny. Gratification and self-confidence would make her bloom; neither would happen without the other, and Penny lacked both. Mother and daughter shared a need to chase men. All men were targets for their frantic flirting and most men fled.

'Of course you must be at the party,' said Cedric to Felicity after he had scanned the list of guests and seen that her name was not included. 'I insist.'

'Do you?' said Felicity and they both laughed. It was a private joke they shared about Joan, who was getting more insistent with every minute. 'I insist,' she had remarked at breakfast, 'that it is a cloudless night. I insist the moon shines through the cedars. I insist no one gets drunk and has a car crash.'

'I insist on no stiletto heels,' said Cedric.

'Oh do stop being so tiresome, Cedric,' she had replied.

Cedric had helped Felicity with the placement at dinner, making sure that he at least was near the few old friends he had been permitted to invite personally.

'I don't mind her being at the party, Dingo, provided she is useful and not obtrusive,' said Joan after her husband had raised the subject of Felicity's role. 'She mustn't wear anything loud and I insist that she remains at my beck and call.'

Penny was torn between excitement and dread. Also, as regards Felicity, between colossal jealousy and a longing for friendship. She envied Felicity her looks, her talent, her confidence and her total indifference to her own impact on her surroundings. Felicity skimmed over the waters of her life while Penny floundered in her own troublesome sea. Both girls longed for Wolf but neither mentioned him nor had heard from him since coming north.

Penny enjoyed the gossip about her fat ageing cousin and young and beautiful Felicity and got great pleasure from strumming upon her mother's already taut nerves. Cedric might be old but not beyond everything, especially with an electrifying young girl with many breeding years to go and hoards of eager lovers prepared to lend a sperm.

Cedric and Felicity were in utter ignorance of the whispers.

'Mum wants to know what you are going to wear to the party,' said Penny, knowing full well that Felicity hadn't got a long dress.

'I've got a sort of shroud for choral singing, or I suppose I could wear one of those,' said Felicity pointing at the distant washing green where Nanny Fount's flannelette and Mrs Bolsover's pink brushed nylon nightdresses billowed in the breeze.

Sheila Campbeltown came to her daughter's rescue with a black velvet sheath she had used to bewitch Magnus in 1939 and which, because of its colour, had escaped being made into children's clothes or lampshades. 'In fact, my darling, I doubt if you would exist at all if I hadn't worn it to the Graduation Ball.' Magnus claimed that black velvet was Sheila's secret weapon. 'I was lured,' he said. 'Lured and ensnared, it wasn't fair.'

'What nonsense, Magnus. You seduced me away from Hector with sweet talk and silver buckles on your patent pumps.'

Isa was one of the caterer's team and agreed to bring the black velvet dress to Tulliebrae from Kilbole on the morning of the dance. Bolsover reassured Felicity that there was nothing he couldn't do with a kettle and a stiff brush to revive velvet that had lain dormant for a couple of decades.

The day of the dance started grey and a bit blustery. The marquee sides flapped noisily making the breeze sound like a junior gale. The stripy lining was going to be hung later and a final team of florists was due to encircle the tent poles with swags of greenery and dangle flower baskets from the ceiling just as soon as the trouble with the lighting was cured. There was trouble with the gas blower and the loudspeakers too, as well as trouble with the coconut matting and the dance floor which Bolsover insisted was on a slope. Digby had shut himself in the morning room to think. He needed a confidant, someone like Horatio or Jeeves to attend upon him and listen to his woes then encourage and commend him in a sturdy laddish way, a Colonel Pickering or a dear Dr Watson. Someone to give advice and keep him straight. Tactical warfare was a dream compared to this latest quandary, which he felt incapable of handling alone. Sometimes even the Padre comes in handy but not in this case: the Tullie minister was not sympathetic with the flesh, consigning philanderers to torment perpetual in nethermost Hell, lesser agonies being reserved for mass murderers and other irritants.

Digby paced about the Turkish rugs and brooded. Anger and fury were fruitless; besides, he wasn't sure where he stood, his own past was not open for probing. He must talk to Felix and get him to face his responsibilities. His eldest child was coming of age with a thud.

Felicity, when asked, told Digby that Felix still had not returned. He had last been seen scorching down the drive in a tremendous hurry bound for who knew where with two bottles of whisky and a gun.

'Where is my wife, Felicity?'

'She is lying down with one of her heads.'

'Which one?'

'The thumping one, not the hot sick one or the clammy shaking one, so Penny says she should be just fine after a couple of hours and a couple of pink pills. Is there anything else I can do for you, Colonel B?'

'No, Felicity, thank you.' He watched her walk away, calm and capable with quite the most delightful bottom he had seen for years. If only it had been her, she would have added grace and charm to his stumbling family.

Digby was in such despair that he almost wished there was

truth in the rumour about Felicity and Cedric. Ridiculous as it seemed, stranger alliances had happened. But the thought of Felicity inflicting herself with such an unattractive physical prospect in the cause of material gain seemed impossible. She had greater integrity than that and no one could possibly imagine anyone taking up with Cedric for any other purpose than to become nobly rich.

Felicity met Bolsover in the kitchen corridor. He was holding a box marked MONTAGU BURTON THE TAILOR OF TASTE. 'I've got your frock,' he said.

'Oh great, where is Isa?'

'I'm here, hen.'

'Oh Isa, what a mountain of potatoes,' said Felicity giving her a hug even though hugging Isa was like embracing a roll of chicken wire.

'I've peeled mair tatties than any other body in Scotland, I reckon.'

'You look very well on it, Isa.'

'Aye, well, I've had nae chance to look well not on it. Your folks send their love by the way and your uncle has taken impetigo. Your aunt blames the lassie who delivers the butcher meat.'

'Isa, really?'

Bolsover returned and interrupted them before Felicity had time to find out more delightful misfortunes. 'A Mr and Mrs von Hoffer and their daughter have arrived.'

'Whatever for, Bolsover? Fun?'

'Blood, more likely, Miss by the look of them. They are seated in the hall.'

'Have you told the Colonel?'

'Yes, Miss. He climbed out of the morning-room window.'

Half an hour later they were still there, in a row upon a wooden banquette like the god-fearing attending church whilst others revel. Behind them hung a painting of an earlier clutch of Tullies ascending to Heaven.

'Can I help you?' Felicity asked in her best shop assistant voice.

'We wish to see Colonel Blackburn.'

'I believe he has had to slip out. Mrs Blackburn is ill and

Felix isn't here at all. I could find Lord Tullie for you if you like.'

'We will wait,' said Mrs von Hoffer.

'I could make you some coffee.'

At the mention of coffee, Angelica leapt to her feet clutching her mouth and started running towards the front door. Felicity went after her and managed to steer her into the downstairs cloakroom, which was stacked high with hired gilt chairs and boxes of table linen amongst a century's worth of sporting tackle and hunting trophies. She looked on in horror as Angelica heaved and projected her breakfast down the stately lavatory. 'Wait there!' she commanded, throwing the poor girl a monogrammed towel.

Penny was reading something slim called *Romance on the Ward Round* while waiting for her nails to dry: she had painted them to glitter like tarnished Christmas baubles. Another half-hour and she would apply ice to her mother's head. Apart from that she was bored. 'Penny, come quick. Angelica von Hoffer is being sick everywhere.'

Penny could cope: the more mess the better, it seemed.

Leaning against the lower branch of a cedar Felicity breathed the fresh damp air and watched as the morning grew warmer and plans took shape. Lights had been placed to illuminate the upper branches of the glorious trees and the sad garden boy had swept away the mole hills from the grassy paths that defined the overblown rose garden. She sniffed the smell of recent mowings. In the tent someone was testing the sound system. 'Mary had a little lamb, one, two, three.' Real sheep bleated on the hill above Tulliebrae, pigeons murmured from the woods.

'Beautiful, isn't it?'

Felicity started and turned to see that Cedric had come to stand behind her. Eight dachshunds followed, bobbing up the path and panting. His footsteps had been silenced by the mossy grass.

'I would find it more beautiful without all this,' Felicity replied indicating the mass of canvas, guy-ropes and cables.

'It can be arranged.'

A couple of men were constructing a frame for the firework display. 'Where are you going to put the dogs tonight?'

'Falkirk will keep them in the garden cottage.'

'I hate fireworks too,' said Felicity. 'I wish I could hide with them.'

'You can go down to the orchid house if you like, I'll give you my spare key. You will be quite safe down there. The path is lit but the rest is out of bounds and well away from the bangs.'

'Thank you. I know it's stupid but I am terrified of them.'

'Don't worry. Your secret is quite safe.' He patted her hand with his podgy pink paw; the crest upon his signet ring was quite worn down. Felicity thought how immensely old he must be.

'Cousin Cedric!' Penny called as she led the Von Hoffers from the house. 'Cousin Cedric, Mr and Mrs von Hoffer would love to see your orchids.'

Cedric jumped as if shocked and snatched his hand away. Felicity looked up and smiled.

'There you are, Mrs von Hoffer,' Penny hissed behind her hand. 'What did I tell you?'

'Don't be ridiculous. He is old enough to be her father.'

'But not too old to be a father,' Penny replied.

Felicity wrote out the absolutely final dinner table plan only to have to do two even more final ones before anyone was satisfied. She also had to move into the Bolsovers' cottage to leave her room vacant for Angelica. As a result of some very intense negotiations Mr and Mrs von Hoffer also got themselves an invitation to the party but they had to make do with a room over the public bar in the Salutation Arms. Digby had been found hiding in the kitchen garden and had spent a miserable afternoon being harangued.

Felix returned at six. Only Felicity was still downstairs, writing out place names in her best italic script.

'Hello,' he said. 'How is my favourite girl I've never rogered.'

'Get lost, Felix,' said Felicity. 'Where have you been? There is mayhem here, the Von Hoffers have turned up.'

'What – all of them?'

'All except the grandmother.'

'Bloody hell! Why?'

'I don't know except Angelica isn't well, she was horribly sick this morning.' Felicity shuddered.

'Bloody hell! Oh Christ!'

Felix was awfully young to have got his face so outworn, but for a man, bags beneath eyes, a moody mouth and wrinkled brow serve well.

'There, that's done,' Felicity said. 'I'm off to change, I'll put these cards round later.'

'Where am I sitting?' Felix asked.

'Between Angelica –'

'Oh Christ!'

'. . . and the County Surveyor.'

'The County Surveyor?'

'Yes, apparently the County Surveyor is an old friend of Lord Tullie. He is sitting the other side, by special request.'

'The Countess of Ayr, you tit. Now you will have to do the whole plan all over again.'

While Felicity was zipping Penny up, Joan appeared demanding help with her sling. 'Felicity dear, I've seen your sweet mother's dress and I don't think you should wear it. It is far too old for you my dear and as you aren't having dinner with us I feel you would be better off wearing a nice jumper and skirt, especially now you have had to move out to the Bolsovers' cottage. That way you won't get yourself confused with the guests. We are awfully grateful to you but I am sure you understand.'

Felicity understood perfectly and longed to have someone to comfort her. The knowledge that spite was caused by jealousy was no compensation for a treat denied, an evening ruined.

She left Penny's room and went to find Isa. At the bottom of the stairs she met Cedric. 'Where is Bolsover? I can't get this tie to work and Nanny is being obstinate,' he said.

'Shall I do it? I used to have to tie all the boys' bow-ties at school when we gave concerts.'

'You are an angel.' Cedric raised his chins for Felicity to get at his throat. 'Shouldn't you have got your glad rags on by now?'

'I'm to stay like this, sir.'

'Why, for heaven's sake? And stop calling me sir, I am Cedric and you are Felicity. To hell with Joan.'

'Mrs Blackburn doesn't want me to get muddled with the guests.'

'Well I do. It is my house and you shall be my guest. Go and get changed this instant.'

'What about Mrs B? She will explode.'

'I can fix her. I know a thing or two that will make her putty in my hands. Of course you must go to the ball.' Cedric had grown rather too fat for his tails and his waistcoat no longer covered his trouser waistband. He looked more Humpty Dumpty than Fairy Godmother.

Felicity had just ten minutes to change in the cottage's damp-ceilinged bedroom. At least I'm clean, she thought as she brushed her dark hair and inspected her short nails for grey tips. The dress fitted superbly. Bolsover had done a great job with the kettle and Mrs Bolsover had put a good strong stitch through the small gash in the cross-cut fish-tail which was its only departure from being totally plain. She put on the gold chain without the mourning locket, then twisted her hair into a knot and pinned it up securing the chignon with a comb which belonged to Myra, who would undoubtedly disapprove thoroughly of these capital-ist frolics.

Most of the dinner guests had assembled when Felicity entered the drawing room. She accepted a glass of champagne and went over to where Penny was standing. 'You look lovely,' she said. Penny's hair and that of the Sister of Mercy had been contorted into a confection of medusa ringlets with the mechanics cleverly concealed behind several white carnations.

'Why have you changed, Flicky? I thought Mummy told you to stay as you were.'

'Lord Tullie insisted. I'm sorry.'

'No you aren't,' Penny replied.

Felicity could feel eyes all round her; she could hear the rustle of mass whispering. Everybody was looking at her and she loved it. She knew that she was beautiful that night and looked forward to years of adulation when she would be famous as well as beautiful.

Cedric walked towards her. 'You will have to come and sit next to me at dinner.'

'But what about the Countess of Ayr?'

'Sick, I'm afraid and frail, too ill to come. She is well over eighty and mad as a snake.'

'Oh dear. I'm sorry.'

'I'm not,' said Cedric.

9

CEDRIC HAD A word with Joan. A most effective word, it seemed, as from then onwards his cousin's wife took to smiling upon Felicity with a fearful benevolence and even complimented her on her dress. It could not have been just champagne that caused this turnaround or that Felicity had suggested Robert Green as a last-minute replacement for a precious male casualty.

Felicity heard Joan telling a twittering woman wearing dripping bead embroidery that Rob was surprisingly nice, just the right type to get asked to dances, his mother having been a schoolfriend of her dear late sister, Clarice. He was good-looking, well mannered and mature though how he was a friend of Felicity Campbeltown was quite beyond her. 'Life is full of surprises!' she remarked, inclining her face towards Digby and looking through her mascara at the photographer. Two glasses of champagne and plenty more to come plus loads of men of all ages all being most attentive served to make her utterly sweet. It was her duty as hostess to sparkle and be kind, even to Felicity, for the time being.

Cedric burbled on about table leaves, ancestors, his own coming of age and times when his father had given balls for the tenants. Felicity wasn't listening but nodded and murmured encouragingly, feigning avid interest. What hell it must be for the Queen, she thought as she stopped herself from grinning on realising that Cedric had switched from pheasant shooting to air crashes. He had known Clarice Duncan and remembered her death at Prestwick vividly. He also remembered how his cousin Digby had been expected to marry her, rather than her frivolous little sister.

'I was about ten when that air crash happened. I've never liked

Christmas much since,' said Felicity. 'Miss Duncan's ward was staying with us. It was horrible.'

'What became of the child? Didn't he have a rather odd name?'

'Yes, Wolfgang. He grew up.'

'Why isn't he here then?' Cedric asked. 'Or is he too uncouth?'

Felicity smiled and felt herself filled with butterflies. 'No, Wolf is couth.'

'Is he a friend of yours?'

Felicity said he was and the butterflies became a bag full of flapping birds.

Through the forest of candelabras she could see Penny at the far end of the table seated between a loud landowner in a mothy kilt and Rob Green. Happiness had done for her appearance what hundreds of pounds had failed to achieve. Penny laughed and was enchanted by Rob, who was telling her all about his new silos.

Felicity wondered how she had ever fancied herself sufficiently in love with Rob to contemplate marrying him. Last year she had been an ignoramus, muffled by a need for security, stability and adequate prosperity, none of which mattered to her any more. Without Wolf nothing counted.

Felix began to creep his hand up her leg gathering the velvet as he went. He was already very drunk.

'Stop that, Felix.'

'It's my birthday. I must be allowed a birthday grope.'

'Shouldn't you be groping Angelica?'

Once more Angelica was trying to get through the evening in contact lenses. Her eyes were red rimmed anyway, regardless of her tearfulness.

'They are trying to make me marry her,' Felix announced in a voice loud enough for Angelica to hear even though he had his back to her.

'Oh Felix, no. You can't.'

'Why not? Will you run away with me instead, Flicky?'

'No, of course not.'

'I didn't think you would, not now that you have caught a better fish.'

'What do you mean?'

'You know. Don't be coy.'

Felicity could see Angelica dabbing at her eyes trying to stop her mascara dribbling down her artificially pinkened cheeks. 'Felix you can't get married if you hate each other.'

'If I don't marry her, the baby gets thrown away.'

'I see. Poor girl.'

'Poor girl be damned. She asked for it. You don't imagine I enjoyed it, do you? You are to blame, Flicky.'

'Me?'

'Yes, you. It was you who doubted I could make it with Angelica. Well, she was a gift, a pathetically easy lay and the most boring virgin screw I've ever had.'

'This is obscene.'

'Obscene but profitable. I am being well bribed. She is an only child.'

'That makes it worse. You can't do it.'

'I have little choice, it seems. Anyway I have expensive habits and you are about to snatch my inheritance.'

'What are you on about now, Felix? Are you quite mad?'

'Probably. So I'm mad. I'm still right though, aren't I?' He pinched her bared knee with his hand till she winced with pain.

'Stop it, Felix! I don't know what you are talking about.'

'I'm right, aren't I?'

If he pinched any more she would be forced to cry out.

'Yes yes, you are right. Now leave me alone.'

Felix turned towards Angelica and smiled. 'There now, my sweet. From the horse's mouth as it were. You can marry me but you will never inherit any of this, you will just be plain Mrs Felix Blackburn, the silly tart whose parents had to pay for her to get married and write out socking great cheques to stop their grandchild, their only grandchild mark you, being a bastard.'

'I don't want you to marry me, Felix. I don't even like you any more.'

'Nonsense, of course you do. Everyone loves me. It is my birthday all the time.'

'I don't want to kill the baby.'

'Don't, then. Give it away. Have it adopted. I'm sure lots of people would like a nice white brat for Easter. A little fluffy chick popping out of its little egg to play with the bunnies. Do-gooders will all be dying to take away your baby and give it a home. You will never see it again, nor me. In fact I doubt if you will ever be bothered by any man ever again. You've had your treat. You'll have more fun in a nunnery from now onwards.'

Cedric's convoluted catalogue of antecedents and youthful memories shunted on. The candlelight twinkled through the glasses of claret, its bloody red matching the roses in the crystal bowl at the table centre.

Isa, now dressed as a waitress, was offering the hollandaise sauce. 'Excuse me,' she hissed into Felicity's ear. 'Excuse me, but Wolf is here.'

Felicity felt the blush surging up her face. 'But he isn't asked!'

'I invited him,' said Felix. 'It is my party, I wanted him to come. I have got something to show him. Where is he?'

'In the kitchen, Felix,' Isa replied.

'Good. Feed him, will you. Do I know you?'

'Ay, you do. I worked for your Aunt Clarice in Kilbole.'

'Oh really? I can't remember.' Isa left and Felix muttered, 'Wretched woman, why can't she call me sir? Anyone would think she was a friend.'

From then onwards there was nothing Felicity could force between her jaws. She smiled desperately to stop herself from screaming at the dinner guests to hurry while they, impervious to her agitation, spun out the pleasantries and loitered agonisingly through the succession of courses.

'You've eaten nothing,' said Cedric. 'You will never have the strength for our dance if you don't take nourishment.'

Felicity smiled.

Cedric had drunk quite a lot and was becoming bold. 'You must be in love,' he said.

Felicity said nothing and pushed a meringue about her plate. Cedric touched her cheek with the back of his hand. 'You are very sweet.' The whole table saw.

Felix's left hand was back again climbing up her leg; his face was turned to Angelica, whom he was addressing through a cloud of smoke. A hovering waiter kept changing the ashtray till Felix told him to stop being such a nuisance. 'You see, Angelica the big difference between you and Felicity is that you aren't sexy. Men don't want you, you have to beg them for it. Sad, isn't it?

Look here, I've nearly got my hand inside Flicky, I can't help it. It won't matter whether she has Cousin Cedric's child or not as there will be a queue of men frantic to give her babies. I only performed with you for a bet. I felt sorry for you, I did you a favour and don't you forget it. Bingo! Wow! Look what just sitting next to Flicky does to me. Ow! Christ, woman! You bitch, Flicky!'

Felicity had taken hold of Felix's little finger and bent it back till he let go: it gave a most satisfying crack.

Dinner over, the ladies retired to powder noses and to gossip; the men were told to be quick about their port. Felicity rushed to the kitchens where she found Wolf with Isa demolishing leftover salmon mousse.

'Watch yourself with yon pink gunge on that good frock.'

'It doesn't matter, Isa,' said Felicity. 'Oh Wolf, this is heaven. God, am I pleased to see you!'

'So it would seem,' said Isa.

Wolf could say nothing while he was devouring Felicity with kisses. She laughed as her hair fell down below her shoulderblades.

'Och, folks is awful unrestrained these days,' said Isa retrieving the dropped comb. 'But I always said you two belonged together.'

'Oh Isa, what nonsense, you didn't.'

'Maybe I didn't, maybe I did, but you'll do right enough.'

'Help! I must shove my hair up again or questions will be asked.'

'I'll help you,' said Wolf.

'Darling Wolf, you are everything wonderful except Mr Teazy Weazy. I'll just nip upstairs and look in a mirror. How did you get here?'

'In my car!'

'Wolf you've never bought a car!'

'Yes, remember you said the only thing you liked about Felix was his car? Well I found it in Warren Street and bought it. Are you pleased?'

'You bought Felix's car to please me?'

'I'd get you Felix's head if you asked.'

'Don't tempt me! A car – it must have cost a packet. Specially

140

something low and green and leathery. Where did the money come from?'

'A windfall. A prize for my results.'

'Oh yes of course. Very, very, very well done! That was marvellous. Who gave you the prize?'

'Mr Bastion, the Blackburns' solicitor passed it on from my father.'

'Your father, Wolf? I didn't think you had one.'

'Och away,' said Isa who had been listening throughout. 'Everybody has a faither. Even I had one though naebody kens who he was except he marched awa' to war and got himsel wiped oot. Anyway all Kilbole kens fine that wee Wolf's daddy was the German gentleman who gave puir Miss Duncan those diamonds. Am I not correct?'

Wolf looked amazed. 'No, Isa you aren't. What a shame. It makes a much better story.'

'Who is your father, then?'

'I can't tell anyone that.'

'Och well, that proves it. It is yon Bormann fella that keeps getting himself found in they jungle parts. Did I no always say that?'

'I must go, Wolf, I'll be back down once I've got straight. I wish we had known you were coming. I could have got you organised into dinner.' Felicity didn't want to discuss where Wolf would sleep.

'I only got back to London yesterday. I found your note on the mirror and rang Myra at once. She seemed to think you had betrayed your country and sold your soul to the devil.'

'I don't imagine old Sid and Bea Webb spent much time at deb dances, do you? I can't see the comrades approving of these high jinks.'

'She said she had a feeling that you needed rescuing.'

'Dear Myra. Mum said she was a stunner when she was young.'

'Oh dear. Does that mean you will be all mouldy greenery-yallery with witchy wild hair when you are older? What a lot I will have to put up with.'

'You won't, Wolf. I promise. Tell me, when did Felix send you the invitation?'

141

'It was there in my room, waiting for me. He had delivered it by hand, according to Ma Crease. He said he wanted me to come, he wanted to put things right. It sounds as if he got an attack of conscience.'

'That I doubt, but we shall see,' said Felicity. 'I'll be back in a second. Go through and see the others. I have got to go and stand behind your Aunt Joan in the receiving line in case she needs anything.'

'Like sal volatile?'

'Yes. If the Von Hoffers get their way she may need more than smelling salts. I'll tell you about that later.'

She sped off down the corridor and collided with Penny, who was a bit flushed but thoroughly enjoying not being a wallflower for once.

'Oh Flicky. Thank you so much for asking Rob. He is wonderful, he has promised to dance all the reels with me, and guess what: I haven't thought about Wolf once this evening. Well, not until now. Am I very fickle?'

'Yes Penny, but very wise. Rob is a real dear.'

'And Wolf is not?'

'I did not mean that, Penny. Anyway Wolf has come. Felix asked him.'

'Oh my God! How wonderful! You know what this means?'

'That you will have to dance with two men at once?'

'No, it means he is innocent. He can't have taken those emeralds. He wouldn't have dared turn up if he had.'

'Of course he isn't a thief,' said Felicity.

'You know that now,' Penny replied.

'I never doubted his innocence for a second, Penny.'

'God, you are a smug bitch, Felicity. I'll laugh when one day things stop going your way. Quick, you had better hurry, Mum needs you.'

Felicity was going to enjoy putting faces to people she had only known, up to now, as entries on a list.

Penny clasped Wolf and he kissed her dutifully, careful not to dislodge any bits of her hair. 'This is wonderful!' she gushed. 'I am so thrilled you came. Come on, we must go through to the library, the rest of the guests are arriving and I've got to shake them all by the hand. How many people do you think will kiss me tonight? You were the twenty-second and we haven't even started the dancing yet.'

Digby was talking to Wolf as they inspected the case containing the cream of Cedric's collection. They had their backs to the room; their reflected images were deadly earnest, not party-going faces. Digby appeared more distressed than pleased to see his nephew. He glowered like Napoleon when glorious things turned shifty. 'I'm sorry, Wolf, I really did not want you here tonight. It isn't personal . . . well, I suppose it is in a way, it is just that I don't want things to get sort of out of hand with Penny. It wouldn't do if anything happened, if anyone got hurt, you do understand?'

'Perfectly,' said Wolf. 'But you have nothing to fret about. Look behind you.'

Penny's rosy face beamed delightedly as she scampered off to dance Hamilton House clasping Rob's hand in hers. She waved at Wolf. 'You will dance with me later, won't you, Wolf?'

'I doubt if I will stand a chance. Too much competition!'

'You must take me to the night-club, there's a fabulous jukebox there.'

'Not likely, Penny. I don't want to get stabbed in the back in the dark by one of your jealous admirers.'

Digby touched Wolf's forearm confidentially. 'Do you think you could manage only to love Penny as a brother?' he said.

'I would never love her other than as a sister.'

'Well that is probably all right then,' said Digby, permitting himself to look slightly less harrowed. 'In that case, Wolf, I think I may have done you a great wrong, although for the right reasons. I hope you will forgive me.'

There was a moment's silence as they both continued looking at the faultless display of porcelain. Neither of them was sure how to end this stilted interview till a man's voice broke in from behind Wolf. 'Are you a connoisseur or a burglar?'

The two men turned to see who had spoken. 'Cedric, may I introduce Wolfgang Duncan. Wolf, this is my cousin Lord Tullie.'

'My goodness!' said Cedric on seeing Wolf's face. 'So you are Wolf. Wonderful Miss Campbeltown tells me you are couth, which is such a relief amongst this mêlée – and what an amazing likeness!'

Digby winced and clenched his eyes.

'Dear me,' said Cedric. 'I appear to have made a gaffe.' Then swiftly he changed the subject to general civilities. 'Well well, this is nice. Do you know these parts at all?'

'I was reared in Kilbole and later spent my school holidays at Whiting Bay. I've been there this summer.'

'Were you sent to the Otways' place?'

'Yes, I was.'

'Well I'll be damned! Old man Otway and I were in the same outfit during the war.'

'He is dead, sir. He died a month ago. I've been helping Little Eva, his widow.'

'The gallant Captain dead? Dear me, what of? Drink? Oh look here comes the light of my life.' Felicity saw the three men and came towards them hoping that she would be able to rescue Wolf. The drink had given Cedric courage, but unlike Captain Otway, he had not drunk enough for it to do him dirt. 'Come here my dear, I want to dance before it gets too wild.'

Digby and Wolf watched them leave the room, Felicity so young and graceful, slender and tall as a reed beside Cedric who was becoming more like a sweaty tomato as the night progressed.

'It mightn't be a bad thing, I suppose,' said Digby. 'It is not unknown and it could clean up this family to have a shot of fresh blood. Not that one imagines she would put up with him fathering her babies.'

'Sorry, I don't know what you are talking about.'

'You will, Wolf. The whole place is hotching with it. That and Felix's little trouble. Poor Joan, it isn't fair, her world is falling apart. You must excuse me, Wolf.'

At Seaforth Crag the pupils had been taught to dance reels. Leaping and jigging to music kept them warm and was said to come in handy for frightening the enemy whenever Scots set out to subdue pagans and get the Empire into shape. The school was a male preserve so the least enormous boys had to dance as women, which required adjustment when they grew up. However, Wolf felt equal to the challenge especially as most of the visiting English were making havoc with the ordered ranks of Scots. Angelica was sitting alone on a windowseat looking out on to the garden over which the harvest moon had risen, a dimpled orange, bright and huge.

'Would you like to dance, Angelica? I am sure I can remember enough to get us through without disgrace.'

She had taken out her lenses, the tears were too much for them. Putting on her glasses she smiled wanly at Wolf and said she would rather not dance.

He sat down beside her. 'Aren't you enjoying yourself?' he asked rather pointlessly as her misery was obvious. 'What is the trouble?'

'You haven't heard?'

'No, I've only just arrived. What is it?'

'I'm pregnant and my parents are making me marry Felix. It is his baby, you see.'

'And what about Felix? What does he say about this?'

'He will do it if he is paid enough.'

'And you? Do you love him, Angelica?'

'I hate him. Now I hate him but once I thought I loved him. If I don't marry him they will make me have an abortion or take the baby from me. I couldn't bear that. Felix hates me too, except for my money. He needs lots.'

'But Felix is the richest man I know,' said Wolf. 'Anyway, isn't he going to inherit all this one day?'

'Not if Lord Tullie marries and has children he won't.'

Wolf thought back to the pink perspiring rotund person who had called Felicity the light of his life. 'Surely no one would marry him,' he said. 'He is far too old, and anyway, he doesn't look the kind to be keen on that sort of thing, much too set in his comfortable and precious ways.'

'He is getting married to Felicity Campbeltown.'

'What? That is ridiculous! Of course he isn't. She would never, ever do such a thing.'

'Oh but she is, Wolf,' said Angelica. 'She told Felix at supper, she was sitting on Lord Tullie's right between him and Felix. I was next to Felix and heard every word. I promise you it is true. Now I have told my parents and they are going berserk because they don't want me to marry Felix if he isn't certain to be a lord, and I want my baby.'

She started to cry again. Wolf was no longer listening. He passed her his handkerchief to mop her eyes and got up to leave. 'I don't believe this. It is a joke. I can't. It isn't possible.'

'Everyone is talking about them, Wolf. Penny is full of it and the old woman in charge of the coats upstairs has been telling everyone that this party is only a rehearsal for their wedding.'

Felicity was escorting Pipe Major Duchal to the kitchens in search of black coffee. She had removed him from his post at the front door on discovering him sitting in a tub which once had held a now demolished ornamental orange tree.

'Oh Wolf, please give me a hand with the Pipe Major. He and I have got different ideas about the way to the kitchen. Take his other arm, will you, he won't let go of his bagpipes.'

'Flicky, I have just been talking to Angelica. Is it true?'

'About the wedding? Yes I'm afraid it is.'

'It can't be. It just isn't possible. Tell me I am having a nightmare. You can't go along with that, it is outrageous, ridiculous, absurd. I refuse to believe you.'

'It is true, Wolf, ask Penny. Ask anyone – it is bound to be common knowledge by now. It won't mean anything, of course. It won't last longer than necessary.'

'But why? Tell me that, why? Why when everything was so perfect?'

'Necessity, convenience, ambition, the usual reasons. Anyway I don't remember much being perfect, what are you talking about?'

'Oh don't you? Well neither do I. Goodbye.'

'Wolf come back. I need you, Wolf please, don't go. Let me explain, you don't understand. I must talk to you, please. Come with me down to the orchid house during the fireworks and I will tell you everything.'

Wolf turned and saw her struggling to keep the drunk man upright. He came back and helped to heave the protesting Pipe Major on to a nearby chair. 'All right, maybe I will come to hear what you have to say. Will you be alone?'

'Of course. Please, Wolf will you dance with me?'

'No. I am going to look for Penny and have a duty dance with her, like a brother.'

The pop group's roadies were setting up their equipment and

the excitement was rising. Someone had spotted the Transit van and word had flashed around that the latest pop sensation, the Muddy Buddies, were going to perform. Their first disc had just got into the hit parade and was rising daily, jostling the Kinks and even nudging the Beatles. The performance started. The young clustered round the stage to hear these new heroes play. Four boys with the usual shaggy fringes had got themselves up in dungarees, collarless shirts and wellington boots. The yokel look was their gimmick. They had all met at agricultural college, hence the name. Now, if things continued well, they would escape the tedium of returning to farm their family lands. A precarious life pursuing stardom defeated the allure of dull husbandry.

A scuffle had happened earlier when some fans had tried to crash the party and had to be forcibly ejected by the police. All that added greatly to the charisma and star quality of the Muddy Buddies. Malcolm, their self-appointed manager, was delighted with the way things were going: hysterical teenage girls and a spot of unruliness make brilliant publicity.

'Where is Wolf?' Felix asked.

'I wish I knew,' Felicity answered. 'What are you doing with my violin?'

'Do what you are told and nothing will happen to it. Come with me.' He grasped her wrist and led her up to the stage where the closing notes of yet another reinterpretation of 'True Love Ways' was being played, none too tunefully by the Muddy Buddies, who concentrated on sex rather than musical appeal.

At the signal from Felix they struck up the first bars of their newest song. The audience cheered as a thumping rhythm pounded behind the unskilled playing of the posturing boys, plucking and strumming their guitars, crudely aping masturbation.

'"Did you not hear my Lady go down the garden singing? . . ."'

Felicity gasped. 'Felix, they have stolen Wolf's song. That's "Silent Worship". They must stop.'

'The song belongs to Handel, and anyway you let me take the tape, remember?'

'You stole it.'

'Nonsense. This will make Wolf famous. You too, if you behave.'

The song trundled on. It was not the 'Silent Worship' of either Handel or Wolf. It was a tawdry parody, a braying cacophony.

'"Surely you see my lady out in the garden there,
Rivalling the glorious sunshine with the loveliness of
   her hair."'

'They have even stolen Wolf's words. They have wrecked it.' Felicity grabbed Felix by the sleeve and he immediately put his arm round her waist and held her while he spoke into her ear.

'Listen, Flicky. If you want to do Wolf a good turn and get him some royalties you must do what I say. You do want to help him, don't you? Of course you do.'

Before she knew what was happening she was on the stage and Malcolm was addressing the audience. Flash bulbs went off and a strong light beamed down on her so she couldn't see beyond the platform's edge.

'May I present to you . . . the Lady. The inspiration behind the hit. Beautiful Felicity who is soon to be a real live Lady.'

The Muddy Buddies started to play again and this time Felicity was forced to stand beside them. She realised that somewhere in her mind she and Wolf were playing too.

'Play the fiddle, Flicky. Go on. Do it for Wolf.'

She lifted up the violin and started to play, though any note that was hers was quickly drowned by the ambient caterwauling. She played for Wolf, that was all, not for herself; she played as never before and as she never would again.

Once more the song ended. The applause was deafening. Felix was beside her with a glass of champagne. Her hair had fallen loose and shone beneath the lights. 'Here, Flicky: raise your glass. Propose a toast to the people who will make you famous.'

She shielded her eyes and saw Wolf standing alone in the middle of the dance floor. She raised the glass to him and said, 'To you, Wolf for your wonderful song.'

He watched her as she drained the glass before he answered.

'It is not my song. Nothing is mine.'

10

THE PALM HOUSE attached to the western end of Tulliebrae had been used by previous generations for wooing on wet days. Nanny Fount, in view of her great age, was just permitted to keep her busy lizzies and African violets in there along with Cedric's lesser orchids and large leafy plants, but he drew the line at her fuzzy-leafed geraniums smelling of tomcats which she placed instead about the back yard like queues of schoolchildren in red blazers.

This conservatory was an ideal vantage point for watching the fireworks, as only numb drunks and the sturdiest Scots could tolerate standing about outside on an August night, however mild for Dumfriesshire.

Wolf waited beside the spike-tipped tentacles of a monstrous succulent. Withy baskets crammed with tangled roots hung from the wrought-iron filigree ribs of the domed glass roof. There were few, if any, flowers but Wolf asked a woman who was enthusing over yuccas and she reassured him that the dangling plants were orchids. The conservatory filled but still Felicity did not come. With all these people it was going to be no place for a private conversation. Wolf seethed, unable to believe what he had heard and miserable about the rape of 'Silent Worship'. 'Though I can never woo her, I will love her till I die.' Nothing made sense. Felicity must explain, she must put it right. They must get away, leave this place: go off and be done with it all, except each other.

Felicity left her violin with the sober-looking youth in charge of the sound system and slipped out of the marquee through the back, to escape the clamour and get some air while the Muddy Buddies concluded their act of murdering music with a 'yeah, yeah, yeah'.

'Remember Cleopatra? She dissolved her pearls in wine.' Felix had found Felicity leaning on the lichened balustrade. He held her arms pinioned.

'The film? I haven't seen it. I must go Felix, let me go,' she said trying to shake off his grasp.

'Why don't you like me, Flicky? Look what I have done to please you.'

'Please me? That pantomime appalled me. You set me up.'

'All publicity is good publicity.'

'I don't want that kind of publicity. What did that Malcolm mean anyway? Or is he out of his mind on drink and purple hearts or whatever junk you all take?'

'You are a fine one to talk, Flicky.'

'I have never taken drugs, Felix, and never will.'

'Oh no? How very interesting. I should be careful if I were you. Now, are you going to let me have my birthday present?'

'I've got nothing for you. Sorry.'

'Well then I will have to take it from you.'

'Let me go! Do you want to make a scene here in front of everyone? Look, there are Mr and Mrs von Hoffer.'

Felix looked round and loosened his hold.

'My esteemed future parents-in-law. The least we can do is give them a demonstration, don't you think? Oh look, your lover is there too.'

'Where is Wolf? I can't see him.'

'Wolf? I never mentioned Wolf, my beautiful gold-digging tart.'

'As usual you are talking rubbish, Felix.'

'No matter. Nothing will matter, you will find, in the end. It will all be a great big Catherine wheel.'

Malcolm came up to them. 'Listen, Felix. The boys are looking for something a bit more stimulating than cat's piss. Have you got anything on you?'

'Sorry. They will have to wait. Blame the lady.'

'I don't know what either of you are saying. You are both as drunk as each other,' said Felicity, walking away.

'But gorgeous and kind. We only meant to be kind. I only

wanted my little bastard cousin to get some credit for this bumper chart-busting hit.'

'I don't believe you. You wanted to gloat, you wanted to defeat him. I tell you, Felix – Wolf is worth more than you, more than all the people here.'

'Silly Felicity. You have so much to learn. Run along and enjoy yourself while it lasts. Everything will be over soon. Enjoy the trip.'

The rockets whooshed up and burst into falling stars. The golden rain glittered and spent itself upon the grass as the jumping jacks leapt and cracked in fizzy fits. The spectators ooohed and aaahed as hundreds of pounds burnt themselves down to sticks and empty tubes. Wolf watched alone, listening and hearing things he wished he need not learn.

'Fancy Cedric falling for that old trick. I would have thought he had more sense,' said the woman who was up in plants.

'She is very pretty,' her partner replied.

'Honestly Roddy, you men are all alike. You never spot the serpent.'

'Finding the slow-worm might be her problem when it comes to fun in the sack, I would have thought.'

'That won't worry her.'

'Why not? She is very young to be disappointed.'

'Roddy, you are impossible. There will be droves of game-keepers aching to make daisy chains with Lady Tullie. She is just looking for a meal ticket.'

'Give us a light, Harry please,' said a young man to a friend. 'Caroline and I are down to our last ciggy.'

'It'll have to be a Dutch fuck,' Harry answered, handing over his cigarette.

'That's what Felix got when he had his end away with Angelfish-eyes.'

'He must have been mad. What a rotten prospect.'

'Still, plenty of bread about.'

'Not much once that gorgeous bird gets her claws into his expectations.'

'Christ, she can get her claws into mine any day.'

'She might, if you asked nicely.'

'Now now, Jamie, you are with me,' said Caroline.

'Well I'm warning you, if you have an off day you'll know where to find me, treating Milady to corn on the cob.'

'She used to go out with that man over there. His name is Rob.'

'Rob on the job? I bet he's got some tales to tell.'

Wolf could bear it no longer and went over to where Rob was standing with Penny. She had enjoyed every minute of the party, her face shone with healthy happiness and confidence. She held Rob's hand and linked arms with Wolf. 'My two most favourite men! Have you met each other?'

Rob shook Wolf's hand with reliable enthusiasm.

'You two have got Felicity Campbeltown in common,' said Penny.

'Dear me,' said Rob. 'Welcome to the club of has-beens.'

'Nonsense,' said Penny. 'God never slams the door without locking the window.'

Rob squeezed her comfortable middle and said that he thought the champagne might have got her a wee bit muddled there.

Wolf did not agree. Penny was speaking the truth: his hopes were shutting down fast.

Felicity took the path through the shrubbery down to the orchid house. She could hear the thrumming pop music from the night-club and the distant twittering of excited voices waiting to watch the hateful fireworks. Her fear amounted to a phobia which had got worse, instead of better, as she had grown up. She must get away in time. She ran regardless of roots that could trip her. She would explain everything to Wolf and he would understand; they would laugh together and he would hide her from all horrors.

She felt she was flying, a black bird swooping between the trees. The river swished as it trundled beside the garden wall, lights danced in the black silk water sprinkled with pearls. She could swim, she could be a mermaid on a rock and comb her hair and wave to sailors, only there were no sailors passing down the Lesser Waters of Tullie.

The first rocket went up and Felicity rushed to the orchid

house. Miraculously the door immediately yielded to the key and she was safe.

She couldn't find the switches but she could see quite well by the outside lights. Her eyes quickly adjusted to the dark and only the occasional trace of false stars exploding above made her heart pound and her hands grow clammy. Dimly, distantly she heard the thrilled cries of delight, the hisses and bangs, the rushing wind of skyward rockets.

Wolf had come. He had crept up quietly and was just about to open the door. She couldn't say anything, she wanted to greet him in silence while all the rest of creation filled the world with raucous noise.

The door didn't open. Wolf did not come in.

Falkirk, unable to sleep for the uproar, was patrolling his territory. He rebuked himself for leaving the orchids unprotected, locked the door and pocketed the key.

He will not come. The orchid with the fetid tongue licked Felicity's ear and whispered between her fallen hair. *He will not come.*

The little russet-speckled flowers giggled with their silly yellow sisters; white worms waved at her from the masses of writhing brown roots overflowing their cramped pots beneath the clumps of leaves, bundles of swords and daggers. Felicity stumbled and grasping a fleshy spear fell on the tiles; the plant pot tumbled too. A slobbering mouth met hers, she staggered to her feet and saw a chorus line of fairies waft towards heaven, turn and slide down a greasy string to Hell.

One for the pot. You are for the pot. You cannot get away. Nevermore, like the raven, black lady, black box, shut the box.' The flowers were singing right into the middle of her head.

She lurched towards the door and tried to shake it open. She thought she saw a face as big as a balloon staring at her, a dead face huge and smooth and quite transparent. Behind her the flowers had all conspired to laugh. 'You cannot escape.' The laughter threatened louder, her ears were full of waterfalls.

There was only one way out with the door locked and the balloon face standing sentry. She picked up a pot and flung it forward. The window smashed, she climbed on to the staging, which buckled and splintered till she fell down in a heap amongst the heating pipes, her torn dress soaked and dripping with algae.

The orchids screamed, dozens of them, hundreds all at once against Felicity. She grabbed at the shattered frame and with a monumental effort managed to haul herself up once more and out through the broken window into the cordite night. She stood upon the outer ledge and looked down. There was just a void, a chasm, a crater matt black, reflecting nothing, bottomless and ready to swallow her for ever. The plants behind were mustering to surge through the smashed glass and grab her. She must choose. Just before she was going to jump she turned on the ledge, lost her footing, stretched out her left hand and grabbed the jagged glass that was still lodged in the base of an upper frame. For a moment she hung by her torn hand, feeling nothing. Her grip slipped, her fingers surrendered and she dropped into the empty cold frame one foot below where her feet had danced on empty air. Her head cracked on the open latch.

Dawn was approaching. The party ended as the eastern sky became pale. A shaky chilled tiredness struck guests no longer warm with elation. Their ears still heard music and their feet tingled, too achingly tired to dance another step. Wrapped-up wrecks huddled in cars and prayed their drivers would hurry them home dodging the ditches and the keen police. The Blackburns and the Von Hoffers had assembled in the drawing room.

Digby suggested waiting till later to resolve their problems. Mr von Hoffer was delighted to agree but his wife was not. She had wanted the engagement to be announced during the evening but was prepared to settle for a notice in *The Times* to coincide with that of the ball.

Bolsover, sensing drama, had brought a fresh pot of coffee and put the last of the logs upon the fading fire to cheer the weary pallor of cold morning.

Joan and Penny, friends for once, were still ecstatic about the brilliant evening. Felix was virtually insensible and Angelica felt and looked like death though she was sure she sensed a vigorous kicking going on inside her slightly swelling belly.

Despite everything, Penny was utterly exhausted and fell instantly deep asleep upon the sofa.

It was both too late and too early but the men ignored the coffee and helped themselves to whisky. Felix no longer seemed to count as a man: he was slumped half comatose beside his gently snoring sister, the most dissolute and unappetising of fiancés, a silly child crippled by greed.

Joan looked at her son and was overwhelmed by the need to protect him. He was not to blame for anything, not her little boy.

'Well then, what is to be done?' said Mr von Hoffer. His only daughter's condition had distressed him beyond measure; castration of her seducer would have been his preferred option. But his wife had managed to persuade him that Angelica had been a compliant partner in the act. Furthermore she alone, ever the pragmatic matriarch, had been capable of perceiving any advantages springing from the catastrophe.

'Your son must marry Angelica,' said Mrs von Hoffer. 'There is no other course. Our grandchild is to be born in wedlock, come what may.'

'Quite,' said Digby. 'But there is no need to be hasty. Things might change.'

'Like what?'

'Well, things. Accidents, mistakes, those sort of things. Are you absolutely sure there is a baby? After all, there are lots of nasty viruses about.'

'Viruses don't make mice grow breasts or whatever it is they do when one pays for a pregnancy test, and accidents will not happen to Angelica. There are to be no hot baths or pints of gin or pushings down stairs. Angelica is carrying your son's child and she gives birth to a bastard over my dead body.' There was a lot of the warrior queen in Mrs von Hoffer despite her pouter pigeon appearance.

Bolsover coughed before entering. 'Excuse me, Colonel, I have just had this handed to me by the young gentlemen dismantling the stage.'

'Is that Miss Campbeltown's violin?'

'I fear so, sir.'

Wolf was standing behind Bolsover. He had come to say

goodbye. He asked to see the fiddle, the neck of which had snapped so that the halves were only attached to each other by the strings.

'It can be mended,' he said.

'What are you doing here, Wolf?' asked Joan. 'Haven't you got a bed to go to?' She looked him over with undisguised disgust, despising him from his hired suit to his gaping-soled shoes that he had attempted to mend with ineffective glue, her eyes focusing resentfully on her father's old half-hunter attached to what she knew was one of Digby's watch chains.

'No, Aunt Joan. I will sleep in the car.'

'Very well, off you go.'

'Wait a second,' said Digby. 'Have you got any more space in your cottage, Bolsover?'

'Well sir, Miss Campbeltown was meant to be sleeping there but according to my wife her room is empty.'

'Where is the girl?' Joan asked. 'She is never about when she is wanted.'

'Do you want her, Joan?' Digby asked.

'No I don't,' Joan replied.

'Well then.'

'She could have said goodnight.'

'That is another thing,' said Mrs von Hoffer. 'I have heard most disturbing rumours tonight. Where is Lord Tullie?'

'His Lordship has gone to bed, madam,' said Bolsover.

Felix sat up. 'Jolly good. I bet the old boy is having the night of his life. Look up, isn't that chandelier shaking? In out, in out, bang bang bang . . . better than the boat race and grouse shooting all at once, all to be had in a hot wet tight little hole locked in one's own big bed. Good luck to you, Uncle Cedric. Puff puff, heave, spurt . . . Yes yes yes!'

'Felix! What are you saying?'

'The truth, Mother. Little Flicky the sex machine will be a marchioness and you will just be the Colonel's lady. But don't worry, you will be sisters under the skin, which should be lovely for you.'

Wolf was still there waiting for Digby to let him go. He was holding the broken fiddle and felt final despair threatening. He looked at poor Angelica and smiled sympathetically, their misery knitting them in grief.

Angelica stood up from where she had been sitting huddled beside the fire hugging her unborn baby. 'I won't marry Felix. I can't,' she said.

'You will, you can, you must, for the sake of the child,' her mother replied.

'Felix isn't the father,' said Angelica. 'He is.'

She pointed at Wolf.

A gasp of horror came from Mrs von Hoffer. 'What nonsense. He can't be!'

'He is,' said Angelica. 'He is and he will marry me.'

Wolf was quite dumbfounded. He had never laid a finger on Angelica, never for one moment felt anything but pity for her.

'I told you it wasn't mine,' said Felix. 'Accidents happen on dark nights. You should get better glasses, Angelica, then you will be able to tell bastards apart.'

'I forbid you to marry him,' said Mrs von Hoffer. 'The baby will be disposed of. It isn't too late.'

'No!' Angelica screamed. 'No, no, you cannot make me have my baby murdered.'

'Don't be so hysterical. It is the only way.'

Mr von Hoffer intervened. 'Your mother is right: the only alternative is for you to go right away and for the baby to be adopted.'

'No! I want my baby. I won't give it away. I want it. It is mine. Isn't it, Wolf? You understand, don't you?'

'Yes, Angelica, I think I do.'

'You'll marry me then? Please.'

Mrs von Hoffer' voice was mounting to a scream. 'No! No daughter of mine marries a bastard.'

'You have a choice, Mother: a bastard son-in-law or a bastard grandchild. Say you will marry me, Wolf. You must. Please, otherwise you will be a murderer too. I will kill myself if I can't keep my own baby.'

Wolf thought he had never seen such an ugly, pathetic sight as Angelica, yet her professed longing to save her baby moved him. After all, he hadn't been scraped out and thrown in a bin, though now and again, especially now, he felt things might have been better if he had ended up in an incinerator.

'You will never have Felicity now. Never, you know that,' said Angelica. 'Please help me.'

'Yes, Angelica, I will.'

'Say you promise. Say it in front of all these people.'

He thought of Felicity, of how she had deserted and deceived him, of how she had sold herself to a higher bidder and of how little his love must have meant to her. He couldn't help loving her still but it was pointless, stupid romantic slush in a world where bank accounts in the black were all that counted. He might be miserable but at least it might make Angelica happy. His own happiness no longer seemed to be in the contest.

'Yes Angelica, I promise. I will marry you.'

'God, Wolf, you are slimy,' said Felix. 'A thieving, money-grubbing chancer. I hope it chokes you and I hope you both will be ever so bloody unhappy.'

Falkirk didn't care for dachshunds. He felt a dog should be large and useful, herding stock, hunting or fetching dead birds, not just being there and needing to be fed. Germans had used the breed to cull badgers but Falkirk liked badgers and knew no good whatsoever of Germans. At six o'clock he rose as usual despite his near sleepless night and let the dogs out to make puddles all over his best cut grass. They yapped more than usual and jostled and jumped about in a maddening way.

'Whisht whisht! Damn your nasty German tongues,' he said but they would not be silenced. Eventually he went to where they had gathered beside the cold frame he had emptied for overwintering semi-tender plants. They jumped and agitated while trying to hoist their torpedo bodies over the wooden edge like beached seals. 'What is up with ye?' Falkirk looked up and saw, with horror, the devastated orchid house. 'God Almighty, the place has been attacked!'

His eyes were drawn to the frame where the bolder clamouring dogs were clustered around a giant bloodied raven, soaked in dew.

They all came quickly and helped to lift Felicity out of the frame. She was unconscious, stunned but breathing. An ambulance was called and soon the bell was heard ringing through the morning, speeding down the woody lanes.

After Felicity had been stretchered away, Bolsover's wife remained behind picking through the wreckage, searching for something.

'What are you doing, woman?' asked Falkirk.

Mrs Bolsover straightened herself.

'Bloody dogs,' she said.

It was ages before Felicity was discharged from hospital. Shock, concussion and the effects of drug poisoning had combined to make her case more complex than that of accidental amputation. She had not been told about the fingers till she was considered strong enough to bear the loss.

Sheila understood. It was her loss too: her own ambitions now wrecked vicariously, another generation thwarted, all her hopes and sacrifices wasted, slashed, broken and chewed to pulp. With two and a half fingers missing Felicity would never fulfil her early promise. She wouldn't play the violin again.

The Blackburns agreed that it was sad but Felix pointed out that Paul McCartney fingered his guitar with his right hand and there was nothing amiss with his career.

'Look at Russ Conway,' said Joan. 'He manages really well and makes such a cheerful noise.'

Cedric Tullie sent a spare orchid with arduous instructions on how to keep it happy. Generously he waived all question of suing for the damage done to his glasshouse. That was the last Felicity was ever to hear or ever expected to hear from him.

All through her illness, when she was at her most sick and delirious, Felicity had asked for Wolf. He wasn't there and didn't come. According to Isa, his green sports car had been seen in Kilbole the day of the accident, the day the violin case had been left upon the Shieling doorstep. Inside, wrapped up with the broken fiddle was a note. 'This will mend,' was all it said.

When Felicity knew that there was only pain and no fingers beneath the bandages she did not cry.

Myra had written a long and convoluted letter intending to be a comfort. The gist of it seemed to be that it might be a blessing to be spared the ignominy of being second rate, of being excused the anxiety of mediocrity and of learning that, despite being endowed with talent and equipment, the struggle to be top was hopeless.

Ailsa had delayed her college entrance for a year and stayed in Germany to learn the language and be near Dieter. That plan, at least, seemed to be working well.

'Mother. Why doesn't Wolf come?' Felicity asked. 'I must know. What has happened? Has he had an accident too? No one will tell me.'

'Wolf Duncan? Did you not know? Goodness me there has been such excitement while you have been ill. I am so sorry, I thought you must have heard.' Sheila had resolved to be bright. Myra's letter had goaded her into attempting a glad Pollyanna attitude; the time for mournful Cassandra was over. After all, no one had died. 'Wolf has got married. He has married some heiress with pots and pots of money. Whatever do you make of that? I think it was a shotgun affair but nevertheless it can't be bad. Fancy that wee boy as a wealthy husband and a father. Oh dear me, I must be getting old.'

The blood drained from Felicity's face as she turned from her mother and wept.

Part Three

I

SINCE THAT AUGUST night at Tulliebrae many things had
happened but little had changed in Felicity's soul. Nearly
a year had passed, her hand and her life had been patched quite
well but her spirits were still fragile and her heart in fragments
beneath the repair.

Penny Blackburn never did train to become a nurse. She took
a first-aid course and got a morning job in a private kindergarten
which was perfectly all right, according to Joan. The nicest
possible girls worked in London day schools: the hours and
holidays were good and their charges had such a decent class
of parent. Penny wiped noses and bottoms and stuck plasters
on grazes, which almost satisfied her heroic urges without
sacrificing her leisure or comfort. All she really wanted was to
get married and have loads of children, which utterly petrified
most men, who took fright when they saw the beckoning and
vacant ring finger, and took off with threatening wedding bells
tolling in their ears. Penny passed the time whilst waiting to
snare a husband by planning her wedding. Desperation meant
she might settle for anyone even though she still carried a candle
for unavailable Wolf. Rob Green came a very close second in her
hit parade but she was in London and though he would be taking
over his family farm in Oxfordshire one day, he remained for the
time being on his bachelor acres near Kilbole. Not yet twenty,
she was terrified of dying an old maid. Her willingness to be
pounced upon had yet to gratify her sexual curiosity. She became
loud and hearty, in demand as a seat filler and sober chauffeur,
a reliable sort to take on a picnic, good for a laugh but not for
bedding.

In July 1967 Rob Green invited Felicity to join his party for
the second Perth Ball. At first Felicity had refused. She had got

into the habit of refusing everything and for almost a year she had hardly left the Shieling. She was an object of pity. No one, she was convinced, would invite her anywhere except out of a sense of duty or macabre curiosity. Sheila and Magnus were in despair. They had tried everything to lift the leaden blanket of their daughter's depression, while she showed no interest in anything, lying on her bed and staring at the cracks in the ceiling till she saw them with shut eyes.

Sheila tried to coax her to take an interest in music again. There are more ways to be a musician and enjoy oneself than by playing first fiddle. Ravel wrote the Concerto for the Left Hand for his amputee friend Paul Wittgenstein, and Bernard Shore changed instruments after losing fingers – but Felicity would listen to none of it. She set her face away from all the classical repertoire and tuned in permanently to the vapid banality of pirate radio. The Muddy Buddies had erupted, burst and dispersed like so many other instant pop phenomena. 'Silent Worship' became *passé*, reverting to a pleasant parlour ballad. Felicity began to smoke and would puff thirty to forty cigarettes a day till the house stank and her bedroom was filled with ashtrays overflowing with stale stubs. Sometimes she forgot to eat and then gorged on rubbish till she was sick. Sheila tolerated everything with stoicism and watched her hair turn white as her daughter wasted her young life in unreachable grief.

Ailsa's involvement with quasi-spiritual nonsense and flower power was just a passing fad. As she and Dieter were a serious pair they were both set to continue their education the following autumn. They were thorough in all they did and had set about dropping out with alarming dedication. Now, with equal efficiency, they were preparing to drop back in. The only part of their youthful spree they were not giving up was their devotion to each other. Ailsa would continue her studies in Germany; they might even get married. Sheila and Magnus had always been certain that Ailsa's strange phase would eventually pass. Felicity might be lost for life.

Magnus had exhausted his patience as a doctor and had seen much that was terrible. He loved his eldest daughter, he was devastated by her condition but in the great scheme of human tragedy she didn't score highly. 'Get up and get washed,' he had said one May morning. 'Even if you have a headache, a bellyache or an urge to weep rivers of self-pity I won't be doing with it.'

He handed her an old picture book that he used to read to her as a child. It was Edward Lear's *Nonsense Alphabets* and contained the story of A who tumbled down and hurt his Arm and would not be comforted by any of the other letters till Z decided that they had all heard quite enough of A's sad disaster and had him nailed up in a Zinc box.

Felicity took the book and turned the pages as the memories returned of happy times when comfort came easily and love was never double-tongued. 'Look,' she said. 'There is King Xerxes!' King Xerxes had been Felicity's favourite

> 'X was King Xerxes, whom
> Papa much wished to know:
> But this he could not do, because
> Xerxes died long ago.'

'There you are,' said Magnus. 'Not being able to know King Xerxes never bothered Papa for long. Look what he does to E the little Egg upon the breakfast table, he eats it up as fast as he is able.'

Felicity laughed for the first time for ages. 'Do you remember what Papa said about U the silver Urn full of hot scalding water?'

'Of course,' Magnus replied. 'Papa said, If that Urn were mine, I'd give it to my Daughter!'

'Oh I do love you, Dad.'

'Good. Now off we go. There are some people I want you to meet.'

For the next few months Felicity went with Magnus to the Cottage Hospital and helped in the wards. She read *People's Friend* to those who could no longer see and listened for hours to tales of children long departed and happy times recalled by patients on the point of leaving life altogether. Felicity had always hated sickness and bad smells. Now she began to realise that morbidity and infirmity were not necessarily character flaws nor the result of personal stupidity. By trying to involve herself with others she almost succeeded in blotting out the memories that strangled her thoughts, taunting and haunting her with the knowledge that things might have been ordered differently and much better.

Angelica's baby would have been born in early spring of 1967. Where she and Wolf lived, whether the baby had survived, if it was healthy, even its sex were things she dared not ask.

There are two Perth Balls with a rest day in between. Penny, unlike Felicity, had been asked to both and had spent a vigorous evening bouncing through all the reels on the first night and trying to lure Rob or any other virile male into a sweaty clinch in the darkened night-club. On the second evening, when she saw Felicity she knew she was defeated. There was no contest. Felicity was still lovely, too gaunt to be pretty but exuding a magnetism no one could give or buy for Penny. The self-assurance and confidence were diminished certainly but the depths of brave sadness gave her the irresistible fascination of a tragic young widow, a heroine to wring all male hearts.

'I hate her,' said Penny to herself while smiling fit to split her face.

Felicity seemed unaware of everything. She made conversation and danced like an automaton. She wore a plain red dress with long kid gloves.

'I didn't know you smoked,' said Rob.

'It filled a gap,' she replied.

He put his arm upon her shoulder: where Penny was fleshy, Felicity had bones. 'I am sure there must be something better for gap-filling than cigarettes.'

'I expect you are right, Rob. What did you have in mind?' she asked.

'Oh, this and that.'

Penny saw and knew her luck was out, yet again. Rob was smitten and Felicity could collect him any time she felt inclined.

Later, after a particularly strenuous Reel of the Fifty-First Penny and Felicity met in the queue for vital soft drinks. Smoked salmon and rollicking dances had given everyone desert thirsts.

'Penny, you must tell me what has happened to Wolf and Angelica. Where are they and what about the baby?' Felicity had primed herself with Dutch courage before asking the questions she dreaded.

'The baby – goodness me he must be staggering about by now. He is called Henry and is utterly divine. I adore babies, don't you?'

Truthfully, Felicity said she wasn't much struck on babies. She wanted other information. Penny gulped at a glass of orange and continued. 'Henry was born in Canada, you know. Angelica's father fixed it all for them – house, job, the lot. The Von Hoffers have been very kind and of course are thrilled with their grandson. In fact I have heard that their next grandchild may be due in the spring. Oh blimey, I'm booked for the Perth Muddle with Roddy, I must dash. See you later.' All that was true, except for the bit about the second baby, which was purest speculative fiction.

Later in the loo Felicity overheard Penny talking to a friend as they repaired their faces.

'Where is Felix these days?' said a girl whose voice Felicity recognised as belonging to one of many Carolines.

'Still in Australia, still hating it I'm afraid.' (Felix had been dispatched to the property of a remote relation, with instructions to study sheep. This he did with a bad grace and was despised and scorned by all within a hundred miles of Cessnock as the 'Gentleman Jackaroo'.)

'And the Canadian contingent?' the Caroline enquired.

Felicity strained her ears to hear the real story.

'Brilliant, marvellous,' Penny replied. 'Canada is the best thing that ever happened to them. Gorgeous house, big job, lots of money, parties, holidays, staff. You wouldn't believe the difference in them both, such a wonderful break after all the trouble last year. I hope to go and visit them shortly, they have asked me to stay as long as I like.'

'And will you go?'

'Try and stop me. My job can wait. Apparently their part of the set-up is swarming with the most dreamy bachelors.'

'Oh you lucky cow, Penny.'

The attendant tapped on the cubicle door. 'Are you all right in there?'

'Fine, I shan't be a tick,' Felicity replied. When she did

emerge the others had gone. 'Sorry, I was having difficulty with my dress,' she said to the attendant as she put her gloves back on. She had seen the pitying disgust upon the older woman's face on noticing her truncated fingers.

'You should have said, hen. I would have been delighted to give you a hand.'

Felicity smiled her thanks, ignoring the tactless expression. She was inwardly miserable but outwardly she beamed. Disappointment was now the normal state of things. At least Wolf was happy, that should be a comfort. It would give joy to a saint but Felicity wasn't one of those. She was angry and hurt, incapable of rejoicing in his good luck.

January 1968

'The good fortune of the girl is quite out of all proportion to her deserts, in my opinion.' Fay Braid confided her thoughts to her husband in a shrill whisper as they sat in the front pew of St Mungo's awaiting the opening bars of the Old Hundredth.

All People That On Earth Do Dwell would do their damnedest to sing unto the Lord with cheerful voice regardless of the organ's asthma. The church was packed: Kilbole liked a wedding and happy endings.

The whole place had been scandalised and appalled by Felicity's accident and treated the loss of her future as a public disaster. For famous sons and daughters, Kilbole would have to continue to trot out Robert Burns's cousin, a smallholder of scant merit and James John, the inventor of a useful rivet. Very little had happened in Kilbole since an outbreak of cannibalism in the fifteenth century and a nearby cleric being put to the sword. A celebrated musician would have kept Kilbole on the map; a crippled one just fuelled local gossip.

'I am not in favour of marriages taking place on the rebound,' said Fay to Lionel. She had eyed the opposite front pew and hoped to goodness the groom's family knew what a risk they were taking by permitting this alliance. 'Felicity was taking drugs, you know.'

'She was,' Lionel agreed. 'But not on purpose.'

'Bah! Stuff and nonsense, Lionel. You cannot believe such

whitewash. The girl was stupefied by her own hand. Why else did she smash her way out of a greenhouse? Answer me that.'

The minister beamed from the sanctuary steps. Sheila turned to smile at the approaching procession. Magnus stout and proud with Felicity's gloved hand through his arm was having a job to keep his generous features piously solemn, but the bride's face was quite obscured by her grandmother's lace veil and Sheila knew, yet did not like to admit, that while it remained concealed, Felicity need not contrive to look happy. Behind Felicity and her father came Ailsa in fuchsia velvet with frills, a skinny stick of rhubarb in pursuit of the cream silk train.

'Well, well. I see we are wearing white. How appropriate, I don't think,' said Fay shaking her head. The aquamarine petals on her unsuitably summery hat quivered like a nettled sea urchin.

'Off-white, dear,' Lionel corrected.

'Not off enough.'

There was the matter of the ring. Where could it be put? Not on the third finger of Felicity's left hand, that was for sure. Felicity seldom let anyone see what lay beneath the glove.

Ailsa fetched her sister's bouquet and returned to her place having noticed where Dieter stood, stiff and serious, his blond hair tied back neatly, his beads, for once, discreet. Ailsa had often worn flowers in her hair but they had never before been twisted into a tidy florist's wreath to perch upon her as if she had been crowned Best Heifer or Queen of the May. Since travelling to the East with Dieter she had let her hair grow long again.

'That Ailsa must be an awful disappointment too,' said Fay. 'Fancy Sheila and Magnus letting her take up with a German hippie. No daughter of mine would have been permitted to behave that way, and no mistake.'

'Probably not, dear,' Lionel replied, glancing sideways at Felicity's slender back, down which thirty-six covered bobble buttons queued beneath the old lace.

'He is kind and he loves me,' Felicity told Myra Pennyfeather when explaining about her engagement. 'I am very lucky.'

'No my dear, you are realistic,' Myra replied. 'I'm afraid I would prefer it if you could have distanced yourself from the practicalities and continued to dream.'

'You don't dream, do you, Myra?'

'All the time, Felicity, all the time. Dreams are all I live for. Without them I would evaporate. You must not dream any more, I can see that, you have a job to do. You have a chance to be happy by making someone else happy. You have a chance to have a family, with whatever joy or sorrow that may bring you.'

'Do you wish you had a family, Myra?'

'Only when I find I have no one left to drive me mad.'

Felicity and her mother had both stayed with Myra Penny-feather for a few days of wedding shopping. It had been hateful being back in Prince of Wales Drive, the memories were agonising. As Sheila was always there neither Myra nor Felicity mentioned what had taken place in the summer of 1966. Both were waiting for the proper moment for the other to raise the subject. At the end of the visit nothing had been said but Felicity scanned the platform at Warren Street as the tube passed through for Euston, just in case, even though she knew Wolf no longer lived there.

Myra refused to come to the wedding, perhaps on principle, certainly from thrift. There was no chance of the Blackburns accepting the invitation as they were all abroad. Felix was still disrupting New South Wales and Penny, newly back from Canada, had gone skiing till the spring.

While in Montreal, Penny had visited baby Henry and become a most enthusiastic aunt. Angelica had been admitted to the art history faculty of McGill and was finding her studies in that field even more absorbing than physics, her previous passion. Meanwhile Henry, who was a most beautiful child with bubbles of brown curls like a Bronzino cherub, was cared for by a Quebecoise girl who only spoke to him in French.

Most of Penny's Canadian visit had been spent in Kingston and Ottawa with her parents. Digby had been promoted to a big job with a bigger salary and a gorgeous well-staffed house. Notwithstanding the demands of his elevated position, there was always time for plenty of parties and holidays – skiing, fishing, hunting, everything was on tap for the Brigadier and his family.

Swarms of bachelors were available. Penny had been near to heaven and Joan felt she was already there, provided she could forget about Felix.

Cedric Tullie continued in the best of health and was emphatically not asked to the wedding. The orchid he had sent following the accident was dead; one of those had been quite enough.

Hanne did not accompany her stepson though she had given Dieter many instructions to take endless photographs of everyone, even Lionel, so she could show her husband the cause of her dismissal from Kilbole and the means by which she had been available in Ulm at the right moment to become the second Frau Doktor Schmidt. Hanne had written to Isa begging her to describe everything but there was sparse hope that Isa would write any more than her usual terse message next New Year. Isa was the only one who spoke her mind about the wedding. Felicity wished ardently that Isa's mind need not be spoken. 'This wasna' meant. I always said that things wouldna' go right for you, hen.'

Isa was once more in outside catering. Her job had been to get the cake assembled upon its Pearl and Dean pillars and it was while she was doing this on the very wedding day morning that she had seen fit to suggest Felicity might be wise to think again and call it all off. However, she did concede that Felicity made a bonny bride on seeing her in her wedding dress. 'It is still a shame, though. You should have minded well what I always said.'

Felicity needed no reminding.

'I would have danced at your wedding if you had been marrying yon Wolf.'

The Gantry Close choir had been recruited to sing because Felicity had once played in their orchestra and Sheila was still part of the music staff. The school had expanded and now included girls who craned their necks from the chancel stalls to see the bride and groom greet each other. They had watched it done thrillingly in the movies; this was a decided disappointment.

The final verse drew to its sluggish close. 'From men and from the angel-host, Be praise and glory evermore.'

Felicity Campbeltown married Robert Green.

★   ★   ★

171

Isa had returned to complete the clearing up. The heated tent which had stood in the Shieling garden had been dismantled and only the stray glasses had to be counted and the wedding cake stand returned to store once all the hired linen had been listed for the laundry. It didn't take long. Isa had cleared up more weddings than most people would ever attend and was quite happy that none of them had been her own. She was passing through the hall when the bell rang, and as no one else was about, she opened the knobbled glass door.

The young man on the step looked weary and dishevelled.

'What are you doing here?' Isa asked.

'I got off the boat at Greenock this morning, I've been in Canada.'

'Aye, and doing well for yourself, by all accounts.'

'No, Isa. Doing very badly. I had to work my passage.'

'What has happened to your fine wife and wee baby?'

'Gone.'

'What do you mean?'

'She only wanted me to marry her to give the child a name. Once that was done I was told to go. The marriage, such as it was, is being dissolved.'

'And the money?'

'What money?'

'The money they gave you. The job, the house – all of that?'

'I didn't take any of that for myself, only while Angelica was with me, up till the time the baby was born. After that I've been on my own. I have got nothing. Nothing at all.'

'Oh man, man, what a de'il of a fix we are in,' said Isa. 'Oh my poor wee man. I don't know what to say.'

'I've come to see Felicity, Isa.'

'You are too late, Wolf. She is away off on her honeymoon.'

Dieter and Ailsa were eager to leave Kilbole but Dieter felt he ought to finish one more film before they caught a train south (Magnus and Sheila had forbidden hitch-hiking and it was not worth arguing). He had taken five films and was now reduced to snapping Magnus's chickens and Sheila's latest Scottie, Vat 69.

'This is where Hanne used to work,' said Ailsa. 'You had

better take a photograph of that, though Glamis Towers used to be much bleaker before they gave it all that gloss paint.' Two lions flanked the front steps and had been alarmingly spruced up by having the insides of their mouths painted red. Their teeth gleamed Pepsodent white.

'This *Schloss* is where my stepmother was servant?'

'She was a nannie, and it's not a real *Schloss*.'

'Architecturally it is curiously made but I am thinking that is not practical.'

'Flicky and I thought the Wicked Queen lived in a turret and could cast spells on us if we didn't curtsy every time we passed the gate.'

'But this is most fanciful.'

'We were children, Dieter. Wolf didn't seem to mind, but then it was his home.'

'Ah yes, this Wolf of whom I am hearing so much when I am being reprimanded by my stepmother. Wolf is perfect, no? Wolf who does not make a mess, Wolf who makes no noise, who does his homework, who is polite, who goes to bed and says his prayers. I am being most blacked off by this Wolf.'

'Browned off,' Ailsa corrected. 'Actually he was very nice, I liked him, much more than Rob. I wish Flicky had married him.'

'But such things are no longer possible. Anyway would not your sister have become browned off with one so quiet, so tidy and so frequently at prayer? My film is now finished, let us go.'

Ailsa did not make a curtsy at the gate which was guarded by reconstituted stone griffins. A young man in jeans carrying a rucksack stood in the entrance gazing in at Glamis Towers.

'Ailsa?'

'Yes. I'm sorry.' She looked at the youth who was as unkempt and tattered as any other impoverished tourist. Suddenly she saw the small boy with crooked teeth and protruding ears beneath the man's stubbled face and shoulder-length hair. 'Oh my God, you must be Wolf!'

She kissed him. Ailsa kissed everybody in the interest of universal peace and cosmic harmony. This kiss, at least, meant something. It gave Wolf hope. It would be wrong to give up now.

'Dieter, look! This is Wolf.'

The men shook hands. 'I am most pleased to meet you at last,' said Dieter.

Ailsa put her arm through Wolf's. 'What Dieter means is he is so glad to see that you are dirty and untidy and normal. Look at his knees, Dieter! Those jeans haven't been worn through by too much praying, not unless Wolf prays on his bottom. That is a whopper of a hole on the backside. Oh Wolf, you need a nanny. Where are you living now, where are you going? I thought you were married and richly prospering not alone and palely loitering.'

'I'm living nowhere and going nowhere. But at least I am being nothing on my own.'

'Nonsense, you can come with us. Can't he, Dieter?'

Later that day all three left together.

Sheila asked Wolf to take the violin with him. It was mended now and Felicity would never play it again. It could return to Hanne.

'No,' said Wolf. 'I want to think of it here. Felicity can give it to her children.'

2

In years to come Felicity asked for an explanation.

'What else could we do but keep quiet?' Ailsa replied. 'You were in Madeira doing your best to be happy, searching for rapture in the bridal suite. What do you honestly suggest we should have done? Left a note maybe through your new front door saying "Welcome home, and by the way your true love came a-wooing while you were on your honeymoon?" Don't be ridiculous. Keeping quiet about Wolf was the kindest thing we could all do. Even Isa agreed and she doesn't hold with fancy footwork, as well you know.'

'Kindness can kill,' Felicity replied. 'Wringing necks of wounded birds is kind. Kind shepherds shoot old sheepdogs when they are no longer useful. Isn't kindness just another form of cruelty when it is the easy way out?'

'All right then, put it this way. What if you had known about Wolf turning up, what would you have done? Parted in noble agony while the credits rolled or gone all operatic and killed yourselves? Left poor Rob back-pedalling to bachelorhood? It would have taken years to unravel your marriage. You might have been pregnant, for God's sake.'

'I wasn't.'

'You might have been, and then what would have happened?'

'Things might have been different.'

'Of course. Sometimes, Flicky you are a real tit. Now admit it, we were right to keep the secret, weren't we?'

'I don't know, Ailsa, really I don't.'

Ever since the wedding Felicity had been serene and resigned like a nun relieved to have shut herself away in the sanctity of her final vows. Her life's path was henceforth to be fixed and circumscribed. It had been her choice to marry Rob. Anything better was finished, behind her, packed up and stowed away as memories. Rob loved Felicity to the best of his ability. He was honest and straight, he deserved steadiness in his wife.

Magnus told Sheila not to worry, Rob Green was a fine fellow and their little girl would soon forget all silly fancies, especially once she had a demanding family to keep her busy and turn her hair white.

'Oh not yet, Magnus, she is just a wee thing still.'

'And one day, when her hair does turn she will be almost as beautiful as her mother.'

Sheila threw one of Fay Braid's bead-work cushions at Magnus and felt better.

The Blackburn relatives in remote New South Wales sent Felix home in the summer of 1968. They had endured enough. They reported in a sharp letter that he was reckless, stupid and utterly irresponsible, thus severing all future family conviviality. Felix, they added, was thoroughly un-Australian and no longer welcome.

'What a world we live in!' Joan had exclaimed on reading of her son's banishment while basking on the shores of a Great Lake. 'How can a nation of convicts possibly be in a position to judge others? Un-Australian! Well, I should hope so too.'

Digby had been slightly less forthright. 'It appears that Felix has been doing a lot of drinking.'

'Of course he has,' Joan replied. 'Most of the place is desert.'

'Drinking, amongst other things,' Digby replied.

'Get him into the army, Dingo, and all will be well,' said Joan. 'He is hot-blooded and youthful. Wonderful young men have always been like that only normally they have got the aggression out of their system by war-mongering and subduing horrid pagans.'

'The army may not want him, Joan.'

'Not want your son, Dingo! Of course they will want him. You give the orders, you are as near as dammit to being a general. I always thought that was what generals were for – ordering things. If you don't, I will.'

When Felix got home it was obvious that no fighting force

would accept him. He was sallow and emaciated, alternately manic and lethargic, hopelessly stoned and utterly broke. He went to live in Penny's flat for a while so she could keep a sisterly eye on him but he stole from her and sold her stuff to feed his habit. Penny had the horrible task of telling her parents that their only son was a junkie.

He was admitted to the cream of detoxification establishments where skilled and expensive therapists tried every method to wean the wealthy of their dependencies. Field House had its successes. Felix could have been one of their star graduates but within a week of being discharged from there the police brought him back to Penny, weeping, sweating and shaking in the grip of narcotic-induced horrors. Field House did not cater for those without the will to help themselves to cleanliness and refused to readmit him until he demonstrated a desire to change.

Angelica had come home to London with her little Henry. She was to continue her studies at the Courtauld. The Von Hoffers loved their grandson for his glorious looks and enchanting temperament, but not for his surname. Their only likely grandchild was a pleb. Angelica's marriage could be annulled as Wolf had been no more than a supportive companion to her for as long as she needed him. He had gone when asked, taking nothing and demanding no support of any kind.

Despairingly, Digby cut off all funds from Felix, who was then driven to desperate lengths in order to provide himself with a steady drip-feed of cash to finance his addictions. Angelica wanted to be a solitary celibate, free to study and have her baby brought up with every assistance, except that of a father.

Little Henry's maternal grandmother wished ardently for a patrician grandchild and his grandfather could pay.

Penny saw a way round all these problems. It seemed so easy and simple, provided the plan was carried out in the spirit in which it had been plotted – unadulterated cynicism. She also kept a hopeful candle lit for Wolf. He would come for her. She knew he would. A Gypsy Rose Lee with a crystal ball told her that she would eventually get her dearest wish, if she was patient, which was quite satisfactory and only cost one pound ten and sixpence.

October 1970

'You must have a bath.'

'I had one an hour ago at home,' Felicity replied. The nurse made her jumpy, recalling boarding-school matrons and hassles about hairbands and bowel habits.

'You must have a bath in this,' the nurse insisted, handing over a sachet of livid gelatinous liquid.

The bathwater turned saffron as if the Hare Krishna cult had used an unsatisfactory batch of dye. Felicity looked down at the landscape of her body. Two outer hills topped by brownish cairns and sloping away from a central valley blocked by an enormous pallid mound, a child's picture lacking only a spiky sun and flying birds of Ms and Ws. She couldn't see the area the nurse had threatened to shave and wondered when she would ever look down again and be able to greet the tops of her thighs.

Beneath Felicity's distended belly-button, the baby lurked contentedly secure, most reluctant to be born because the way out was draughty and tight and uninviting; better by far to slumber on in happy darkness amongst the familiar warm pulsations.

'It is castor oil for you, Mrs Green,' said Sister with relish.

'Oh no, I'd be sick.'

'We'll see what Doctor says about that. You will be having an enema anyway.'

The longer she stayed in the bath the better. However, the windows were ill fitting and early autumn was whistling through every crack in the building. Magnus had insisted that Felicity be a patient of Scotland's best gynaecologist, with whom he had played rugger in his student days. The great man would arrive at Greybank Maternity Hospital once things were happening; other lesser mechanics would deal with the banalities.

A young man, newly qualified, induced labour by breaking the waters. Felicity wondered if he could possibly feel like sex ever after spending his days focused upon a rich assortment of vaginas.

Calving cows and lambing ewes didn't seem to deter Rob, who

was a three times a night man. Felicity did a lot of thinking on her back. Rob didn't demand enthusiasm from her any more than he expected rapture and imagination from his cattle, not even when the bull rather than the AI man planted next year's calf.

Mother Cow and Mother Person share the same gestation period. Rob had calculated his baby's Expected Date of Delivery from the tables in the *Farmer and Stockbreeder Yearbook*. The baby didn't seem to know about this. Felicity was three weeks overdue and her blood pressure soared. Only Magnus was aware of other complications: his friend the prop forward had most unethically confided that his old team-mate, the shortest scrum half in Scotland, had a daughter with the very devil of a dodgy cervix. Felicity was looking forward to being a mother and getting rid of the bump. Sheila was ecstatic, she longed to be a granny. Her white hair suited her well for the part.

Rob sat beside the high, hard bed and worried about his thirty acres of wheat still standing. Next year it would be different. The move to Oxfordshire would be a wrench but at least the rainfall might be slightly less and he might be able to make hay without having to leave it soaking and rotting while summertime storms wept torrents and wrecked the winter fodder. He was also looking forward to prising Felicity from the close vigilance of her protective parents. He wanted to have his own family to himself.

Magnus and Sheila could visit frequently, he said, there was plenty of room at Church Farm, Steeple Pastern which he had inherited on his father's death. The farmhouse near Kilbole was only suitable for a childless bachelor and the land had been good for the cutting of his agricultural teeth. Now he could take things more seriously in the countryside of his own childhood. The Scottish farm had once been part of his maternal grandfather's property and would now be managed by a factor until such time as his own son could do battle there for science versus the elements. Rob's mother had moved south on her marriage in 1928 and had no intention of returning to her native land now she was widowed.

Lady Jean Green, a leathery she-spider with beady eyes, bred show ponies. She also hunted, shot, chased and fished, a real country lover and only happy when outwitting nature. She and her daughter Pricilla, Rob's senior by seven years, were moving from Church Farm to a nearby stable block where they planned to start a riding school. Lady Jean was an undaunted sixty-five and Pricilla was forty, dominated and defeated.

Rob felt awkward in the hospital, out of place amongst people who knew what was up. He was used to being in charge

'How long do you think you will be?' he asked Felicity, squeezing her good hand.

'I don't know. The pains are still very slight.'

'Perhaps that is because you are being brave.'

'I'm not brave, Rob. You should know that. We will just have to let things happen, you can't put on the ropes here, Sister wouldn't like it.'

Rob still didn't know Felicity, couldn't tell when she joked or when she was in earnest. She never complained about her hand and only mentioned it to reassure him that it didn't bother her. He had never told her that it turned him off. That would not be kind but the sight of the three stumps on her left hand corresponding to the three strong straight fingers on her right hand revolted him. It wouldn't have mattered if she had been born like that, it was just the nightmare thought of them having been severed on broken glass and chewed up by lapdogs that made him heave. He was happy to have her as a placid lover, and preferred her to keep her hands to herself. He bought her many pairs of gloves and had placed the wedding ring on her third finger, right hand.

As further incentive to move south he promised her lots of musical outings in Oxford but she didn't enthuse. Felicity had the perfection of a fractured statue: she was patient and smiled a lot at grief.

'Gracious me! Have you seen this in the paper, Flicky?'

'No, Rob, what?' The pains were getting much stronger, she would have liked to have had her back rubbed firmly. She wished that Rob would not call her Flicky: that name belonged to others, not her husband who was as remote from her inner heart as a nice cup of tea was from her immortal soul.

Rob was reading *The Times*. '"The marriage has taken place quietly of Mr F.D.C. Blackburn and Mrs A. Duncan." Why are you breathing like that, Flicky?'

Felicity had learnt breathing from a book. It wasn't doing much good, but the news distracted her from the immediate pain. She had a long way to go.

'Do you think that could possibly be Felix?' asked Rob. 'He must be better, then. Good for him. I wonder where he met his woman? At the clinic, maybe. These upper-crust junkie places are crawling with people on the lookout for new mates. I imagine she is a cradle-snatcher or a nurse on the make. If it is him I expect there will be more about it in the other papers. Well-connected drug addicts are a bit squalid for *The Times*.' He picked up the *Daily Express*, which he bought most days for the Giles cartoon, and turned to the gossip column.

'What was the name of the woman? I didn't hear. Oh!' Felicity puffed as she had been instructed and waited for the contraction to reach its peak and subside, which took ages.

'Mrs A. Duncan is all it says. Duncan . . . that name rings a bell. Wasn't that the surname of that Siegfried fellow? Oh wait, here is something more. Christ, Flicky you do look odd, shall I fetch a nurse?'

'No, no. Go on. You mean Wolfgang.' Even saying his name flustered her. 'He was a Duncan but then it is quite a common name, not that Wolf's Aunt Joan would agree.' A gripping muscular surge began to grow like a wave mustering itself before breaking. 'Anyway, he and Angelica have emigrated to Canada and live in loving luxury with their baby, according to Penny Blackburn.' The contraction gathered strength. 'Please, Rob, read the rest of it. Pay no attention to me. OH! OH!'

'Well, it is Felix all right. William Hickey has dug out quite a decent photograph of him . . . Look! Oh Christ, Flicky, what's up now?'

'What about her, his bride, Mrs Duncan? Oh my God!'

'Are you sure you don't want a nurse or some gas or something?'

'No, not yet. Tell me about her.'

'OK. Here goes. "Attractive" – why the hell do they always call everybody who isn't Quasimodo attractive?'

'Go on, Rob, you are driving me mad. Oh Christ Almighty!'

'Easy does it, Mrs Green,' said the nurse. 'I'll just get you a wee jag of pethidine to make you drowsy.'

'No, no! I want to hear what my husband is saying. Go on Rob, quickly. Holy God this is hell!'

'Steady now, dear, just a tiny prick,' said the nurse as if an injection was going to hurt compared to the rest of the torment going on, like throwing a cinder on a volcano.

'"Attractive ex-deb Angie, whose first marriage to songwriter Wolf Duncan has been dissolved, is making sure that her three-year-old son gets a fair share of silver spoonfuls by marrying his father, the hard-living son of General 'Dingo' Blackburn. Angie is the only child of financier –". Flicky, what's up? Help, Nurse, quick! There's something wrong with my wife!'

'There, there calm yourself. She is having a baby, things are bound to get a bit tense. Just take yourself off for a walk, she'll be fine in a bit, though the baby won't be by for an hour or more yet.'

Felicity could remember very little of what happened after that, which was just as well. All through the indignity of peering and probing, of exhortations to push, to stop pushing, to bear up or down, she could think only of Wolf. Wolf divorced, Wolf the only man in the world. Where was he? Why hadn't she been told? What had gone wrong?

She dreamt that Wolf walked beside the trolley as they wheeled her to theatre; all through the blank blackness he was there. As she came round she was calling Wolf's name. Rob was too distracted and ecstatic to notice but, despite the excitement, Sheila knew and understood.

Anna was a tidy palindromic name for a first and last child.

Felicity's depression returned. Rob was told that the 'baby blues' were normal but after six weeks of apathy, it was apparent that nothing at all was normal and Felicity was very sick indeed.

Anna throve on bottles and blossomed from a shrivelled squealer into a jolly pink chuckler in the care of her doting grandmother.

Myra Pennyfeather only used the telephone in the direst crisis. Normally she wrote rather cryptic letters using economy labels to re-use old envelopes. Sheila knew a lot must be wrong before she noticed that Myra's voice was choked.

She had read of the tragedy in the *Evening Standard* and wanted to relay the news quickly before Felicity saw it in the following morning's paper or got to hear it on the news.

'Sheila, I have just learnt of the saddest disaster. Young Wolfgang Duncan, I am sure it is him, is missing in Nepal, presumed dead. An accident of some sort, it seems, while he was suffering from a local fever. The reports are very vague, there is nothing certain yet, except a young English man with a German name has gone missing and in view of the terrible weather, his ill health and a cataclysmic series of avalanches it is assumed that he has perished.'

The report stated that the twenty-five-year-old man had trekked to a remote and mountainous area and had been employed as a voluntary teacher in an extremely isolated community.

'Thank you for telling me, Myra. That is terrible news. Such a young life, and a good one too. What a wicked, wicked waste. I will have to think about who should tell Flicky.'

'Poor lamb,' said Myra. 'Give her my love, I will pray for her.'

Rob didn't seem to understand the significance of the news. It was sad, of course it was, he remembered Wolf and had found him pleasant enough, if a little quiet, but why his death should be more shattering than any other of someone so young, was beyond him.

'I loved him, Mum,' said Felicity after she had heard the news from Sheila.

'I know, my sweet. Remember him with love.'

'I do. I will every day until I die.'

Magnus kissed her forehead. 'Does it help to know that the Lord loveth whom he chasteneth?'

Felicity said she wasn't sure and Magnus replied that it would be one in the eye for the Almighty if she rose above the chastisements. 'You must get better my wee girl, get on with your fine husband and your new family. That is where you belong now, not here. Remember that another day; you make your own life, we require no sacrifice from you. I've seen more than enough of pathetic daughters who have had to curtail their own lives to mind their aged parents. Give your best efforts to your good man and my beautiful granddaughter. Rob loves you both as much as he can. Don't let him down.'

Secretly Sheila thanked God for removing the obstacle that had blighted her daughter's happiness. Things might become more sanguine now that Felicity could mourn a dead lover and not long for a live one.

In London Penny cried till her eyes ached. She would have to rethink her dearest wish or else the gypsy had been a fraud. She grieved for the loss of Wolf but not for Wolf himself. She put his photograph on her dressing table inside a sombre frame for all to see and mark, though few people ever did because hardly anyone visited her bedroom.

Ailsa and Dieter continued their life of endless study which made them happy but puzzled Magnus, who wondered when his assumed future son-in-law would consider his brain sufficiently stuffed to permit him to use its contents to earn a wage. Ailsa wrote home rarely from Heidelberg but when she did, her letters contained facts and not much chat. However, she and Dieter were terribly distressed by Wolf's death. It was well over a year since they had last seen him; they didn't know the part of Nepal in which he had been lost. Hanne, writing to Isa in her usual flourish of green ink at Christmas, said she and Lotte were shedding many tears.

Rob and Felicity took Anna to her new home in the south in the spring of 1971 and Sheila spent the next seven years in her empty nest, alone with the husband she loved.

Magnus died of a heart attack in 1978. He had been curling at Ayr ice rink and should have known better, according to his infuriated cousin.

'A doctor owes it to his family and his patients to keep out of trouble. Not like some who serve no purpose, Lionel,' Fay Braid told her husband rather pointedly.

Magnus had been sixty, a year older than Sheila who still talked to him when VAT 69's successor, the terrier John Begg, was taciturn. Grief may have accelerated the onset of Sheila's decline. Very often she forgot what day it was and once she put the kettle in the fridge.

'Had my cousin been less inconsiderate he would never have left us all to cope with his demented wife,' said Fay on spotting Sheila at church in bedroom slippers.

3

October 1987

'I USED TO work here once, in the haberdashery department,'
said Felicity.

'Yes, you said,' Anna replied with exaggerated patience. 'You
were waiting to go to the Royal Academy. I know, I know.'

'Just like you, darling.'

'No, Mother. Not like me. I haven't been accepted yet. Don't
count chickens.'

It was Anna Green's seventeenth birthday. Both she and her
mother had taken the day off to go shopping in London. Anna
was at a tutorial college in Oxford. She hadn't wanted a party at
Church Farm and had asked if both her parents could take her
to the theatre instead. They would all meet later at the Farmers
Club before *Les Misérables*.

'Just the three of us, please,' Anna had insisted.

'That could be tricky,' said Felicity, 'what with Daddy renting
a room in Aunt Penny's house and her offering to cook us all
supper.'

'Aunt Penny isn't my proper aunt like deadly Pricilla who
I have to hack because we are glued together by blood. How
come you and Dad are such friends with her?'

'We sort of grew up together and then we all got together
again about ten years ago. Penny was very sweet to you when
you were little, you must remember that.'

'When I was little yes, but not now. I can't stand her and she
certainly dislikes me a lot and I don't know why.'

'She is jealous, Anna. Penny sees you as representing yet
another generation of rivals.'

'Rivals for what?'

'Men, husbands, fathers for children.'

'Mum, you are so blind and silly, I'm not the one in her way. So-called Aunt Penny is gross, she is pushy and interfering, almost as bossy as Grandma Green. I wish we lived near your mother instead, at least she is just dotty.'

'Poor Granny,' said Felicity. 'She would have to come and live with us if Isa couldn't carry on looking after her.'

'I'm sorry, Mum. Granny would hate to move away from Kilbole. She told me once that all she wanted was to be allowed to stay in the Shieling till she died and she couldn't care less if the place fell down around her. I wasn't meaning to be nasty.'

'You aren't, Anna. You are my light and joy, my hope.'

'And another thing, Mum. I want to go to that interview at the Royal Academy on my own. Do you mind very much? I am quite old enough, you know and it is my life.'

'No, I don't mind,' Felicity replied.

She did, though. Felicity needed Anna to succeed where she had been forced into failure and sometimes the ardour of her yearning shocked her. Felicity would have crawled to a shrine, worn a hair shirt, slit open a goat if she had been sure it would help in getting Anna nearer to the concert platform. Dousing her maternal ambition was difficult but essential, as was avoiding the pitfall of excessive parental protectiveness. Anna's success would make sense of Felicity's failure and would restore her faith in the fairness of God. However if Anna needed to go to the interview alone, so be it; she must not be thwarted. Perhaps it would be better not to dwell further upon what might have been.

Felicity had told herself repeatedly that teaching the mentally handicapped to relate to music was an honourable calling, even if it wasn't stardom. She was deceiving herself. Bashing away at tambourines had nothing on playing the Albert Hall: conducting the Sunbeam Percussionists was a sod of a job. Beethoven had said that he left his music to cure the world; Felicity kept her charges from fighting by getting them to vent their frustrations on cymbals and castanets.

'What are you staring at, Mum?'

'That woman: she looks a lot like an older version of the awful girl I used to work with here. She was called Bernice and could be smelly. Maybe if I had a sniff . . .'

'Christ alive! Will you stop embarrassing me, please. Every-where we go you seem to dig up your past.'

Since becoming prominent in the National Farmers' Union and knowing about Green Pounds and the Common Agricultural Policy, Rob had needed to spend several nights a week in London attending meetings, grappling with Brussels and such like. Renting a room off Penny Blackburn had been most convenient. Penny ran a nursery school called Henny Penny's in the ground floor of her house off Sloane Avenue. Prospective pupils had to be put on its waiting list at conception.

'Please can we not stay with Aunt Penny on my birthday either,' said Anna. 'I hate the smell of Play-Doh and all those dinky hooks for tots' tweed coats and the tiny loos for them to pee in.'

'You and I can cadge a bed off my godmother Myra Pennyfeather then,' Felicity replied. 'Her place smells of rotten vegetables.'

Myra had redecorated nothing in thirty years. Her curtains hung in tatters even before she took to sheltering stray cats once the last of the stray dogs had died. Cats didn't need to be walked and the stairs were a great burden to her now. Apart from criminal bunions and vicious varicose veins Myra was fine, though her circle of friends was dwindling daily and the materialistic Thatcherite eighties disgusted her. 'Thank God for that,' she said on hearing that Anna was destined to be a musician. 'I am delighted. I cannot be doing with these right-wing money-mad young things with their skirts round their ears, their brains full of banknotes working at broking commodities.'

Anna had wanted to see Matisse's *Snail*. A boy she admired had raved about it, so naturally, she did too.

'I can't see much in it myself,' said Felicity. She and Anna had wandered through the Tate for about an hour and Felicity had been struck once more with the fact that she was grow-ing old. At her age, when faced with Carl André or even seasoned Jackson Pollock she did just wonder whether she was being conned. She enjoyed visiting art galleries to look at the people as much as the pictures. A large woman in a turban and bottle glasses interested her far more than Craig Martin.

'What pictures do you like then, Mum?'

'That is what I like,' said Felicity pointing at Sargent's *Carnation Lily, Lily Rose.*

'Oh dear,' Anna replied sorrowfully. 'Mum! What is wrong?'

'That man, there! Look, I know him.'

'It's Henry!' Anna exclaimed. 'You might have seen him in Oxford. He is terribly clever. Pushy Penny is his real aunt, which proves genes count for zilch. Hi Henry, what are you doing here?'

'Hello, Anna. Have you been unchained from the desk or what? I've been summonsed to lunch with Mummy. She's giving a lecture on minimalism and needs more than a conceptual audience, so I have been roped in to represent the masses.'

'You are a good boy. Henry, this is my mum, only she seems a bit fazed. Mum, say how do you do nicely.'

'I knew your father.'

'Dear me, how unfortunate,' Henry replied. 'I'm afraid Dad is a bit of a disaster these days. He is living in Barbados, doing this and that, the oldest drifter since Noah.'

Henry was just like Wolf, unbearably so.

'Mother! Your chat-up lines are dire.' Anna took her mother's arm. 'Come on, Mum, pull yourself together.'

Henry smiled kindly, Wolf's smile but with symmetrical teeth. 'My parents married far too young, that is why they are separated.'

'Oh, I see. Sorry. It is just that you look so like someone else: your father's cousin, in fact. He was called Wolfgang Duncan.'

'Really?' Henry answered with bored courtesy. 'I don't think I know him.'

'He is dead,' Felicity said.

'Mum, don't cry. It must be her age,' said Anna. Henry's straightened teeth were dazzling. 'It is my birthday, Henry,' she said to distract him from her mother, who was dabbing at her eyes and sniffing. 'I'm being taken to the theatre by the rentals, we are going to *The Glums.*'

'Lucky you. I'm by way of being a bit of an amateur thespian myself,' he said. 'Only not a musical one. I'm Polonius. The producer insists on setting *Hamlet* in a laboratory monkey house, it is really bizarre. Happy birthday anyway, Anna. I hope you have a lovely evening. You too, Mrs Green.' As Henry kissed Anna, Felicity remembered Wolf's kisses and felt the tears return. She did not notice Anna shrink.

'Henry is very charming,' Felicity remarked later.

'He is a widow pleaser.'

'What is that meant to mean?'

'Oh never mind. He gets on better with older people.'

'Does everyone know you are only just seventeen, Anna?'

'Don't worry, Mother, only children are always old for their age, I pass myself off as twenty.'

Felicity smiled and thought of the beautiful Henry. 'I wish I could,' she answered.

Later, over herb tea and cannonball buns, Felicity told Myra what she had seen. 'But he was the image of Wolf, I couldn't believe it.'

'How very upsetting, my dear. You never did get over him, did you?'

'Oh I did, Myra, I have. I couldn't go into a decline for ever, it wouldn't be fair. I live in the real world, I'm not some love–lorn maiden in a book, I have real things to do and can't afford to moon and mourn for what I cannot have.'

'Some of us mourn for ever — it doesn't end, just gets more distant.'

'Sshh Myra, Anna is coming back.'

'Never mind, have another bun. Talking of books, which I realise we weren't, have you read this?'

Felicity refused the bun and took the book, a paperback by a Tom Otterburn, called *Beginning and Ending*. 'Can I borrow it, Myra?'

'No, buy one for yourself. I can't bear to part with it, it is brilliant, most satisfying. Now come on, Anna have a bit more to eat. You are exactly like your mother was at your age, all tall and thin and straight. Never change, my dear.'

Penny brought Rob to the Farmers' Club. 'Don't let me disturb you, I'm not staying,' she said, accepting a drink.

'Well at least join us for a bite before we go off to the theatre,' said Rob.

'I might do that. Thank you. It is a bit early to visit Dad yet.'

Anna's face fell. She had already heard how Penny had very kindly offered to come and pick them up after the show. At this rate she would only have both her parents to herself in the interval. There was something she wanted to say, to ask them both together, alone without strangers, and especially without Penny.

'Oh, what a treat!' said Penny swooping on a smoked eel. She was hearty and keen about everything, the sort of person who gets really worked up about gold stars for tidiness and pushing the crescent moon through the proper slot.

Digby, now General Sir Digby Blackburn, was in King Edward VII's Hospital for Officers. He was dying.

Felicity looked at Penny who chattered and gobbled simultaneously without pausing and thought how strange it was never to know for certain whether a parting was final. Penny and her little sister had been inseparable as children and yet their paths had not crossed once since Penny's parents had been posted away from Kilbole in 1958.

Ailsa had said then that nothing would ever be the same again. She had been right about that although, for her, life had turned out thoroughly satisfactorily. Unemotional and practical, zealous and conscientious, she and Dieter Schmidt had married when they considered the time ripe. As a couple they had emigrated to the States where both had good jobs and had, after careful planning, produced two children, a pigeon pair of blond Bostonians destined for the Ivy League and high office. Meanwhile all the other characters that had met to watch the Coronation on the Campbeltown television had led lives disordered by reversals and upheaval, except possibly Lionel and Fay Braid whose unfriendly co-existence remained a constant hell.

In Germany, Hanne's husband (Ailsa's father-in-law) had taken to local government and civic pomp, achieving much status as Burgermeister, the biggest cheese in the Rathaus. Joan Blackburn had lived long enough to see her husband knighted but not for him to succeed to his cousin's title. Joan had died in 1980.

At Tulliebrae Cedric Tullie continued in the best of rotund pink health looked after by Mrs Bolsover, while Bolsover himself did little and drank lots. Nanny Fount had also died in 1980 but she, unlike Joan Blackburn, had been extremely full of years.

For the last sixteen years the Greens had lived quite equably at Church Farm, Steeple Pastern. Having done nothing to topple her mother-in-law from her tip-top perch in the hierarchy of local doings, Felicity had made neither positive nor negative impact on rural Oxfordshire. She had done some training and got enough qualifications to instil musicality in the chronic sick and mentally handicapped, which she did most days at a residential home and day centre near Cowley.

Lady Jean Green had never warmed to Felicity. 'My daughter-in-law is not really one of us,' she would bellow across horse-strewn scenes. 'She is a cripple and pretty useless. She can't ride and is no good in the garden or anywhere else.' Anna had even heard her grandmother say that it wasn't fair to have had just one child and that she and her daughter, Anna's Aunt Pricilla, had vacated Church Farm on the express condition that it was to be filled with grandchildren. Felicity's mother-in-law had shown no sympathy for her when she had endured two early miscarriages, and regarded mechanical inability to breed as a character flaw. 'Poor Rob,' Lady Jean had sighed raucously at the church fête. 'The dear lamb, how he longs to be a proper father, how he needs a decent wife, not some disabled fiddler who spends her time making music with lunatics.'

Pricilla agreed with her mother. 'I wouldn't have been like Felicity,' she said, tightening her headscarf over her netted hair, adding wistfully, 'If someone had married me, that is.'

Anna had hoped that by getting her parents alone, away from home, she could air her worries. If only they could reassure her that the rumours she had overheard were lies. She could not bear the tension and anxiety of listening to dropped hints and surreptitious implications.

However, it was not possible to talk during the interval and when they left the theatre, jostling through the daz-zled crowd, Anna saw with sinking heart that Penny was waving and twinkling maddeningly from the other side of

191

Cambridge Circus all agog to be a godsend and get them safe home.

'Where to, my Lord?' she enquired facetiously.

'Home James! And don't spare the horses!' Rob replied, too pat to be spontaneous.

Felicity sat in the back with Anna. They had both enjoyed *Les Misérables* but not enough to blot up their troubles. It was a vile night and it was kind of Penny to go to so much trouble and spare them an irksome or extravagant journey.

'How is your father, Penny?' Felicity asked.

'Not long now, I'm afraid. I'll be an orphan before Christmas,' she replied Dunkirkishly. 'It comes to us all in the end.'

'Death and taxation, how true,' Rob said.

'And being an orphan,' said Penny. 'Except, of course if you die young.'

Some people do both, thought Felicity. She had not been able to get Wolf out of her head ever since she had seen young Henry Blackburn who reminded her so poignantly of Wolf the last time she had seen him at Tulliebrae, the night things went off course. Henry was the same age now that Wolf had been then.

'Can I go and see your father, Penny?'

'Why?'

'Just to be friendly,' said Felicity almost truthfully.

'Well, don't tire him,' said Penny. 'You will find he likes talking about his past if you can bear to go along with it. Whatever you do, don't contradict him. Agree with everything he says even if he wants black to be white. He is a horror to the nurses unless he is humoured. Ten minutes is more than enough, any longer and he fades.'

'Shall I take him anything? Whisky perhaps?'

'Drinking isn't good for him.'

'I wasn't suggesting an orgy, just a bottle of Scotch if he enjoys that.'

'Enjoyment and health are two different things,' Penny replied. She drove a slow relentless pace, a dead certainty: hare beating tortoise. 'Still, he won't last much longer,' said Penny, talking of her father as if he were a putrefying pot plant.

'I'll visit him tomorrow morning,' said Felicity. 'Can you wait to drive us home, Rob? Anna needs to be dropped in Oxford.'

'Sorry, darling. No can do. Cubbing tomorrow. I've got to be round at Mother's by six sharp to collect me 'oss. Take a train, there's good girls.'

Since lodging with Penny, Rob's language had become irritatingly brisk.

Even without considering Rob's early start, Felicity didn't feel she could invite him and Penny up to Myra's flat for a nightcap. They needed whisky. Herbal tea or lukewarm Liebfraumilch would not do. For once Felicity longed to have Rob in her bed. She hated sleeping in Myra's spare bedroom on the rickety divan covered with grubby candlewick, but Anna had been adamant about not staying with Penny and it was her birthday, she should be allowed to choose. Tomorrow would be better: she and Rob would be back in their home at Church Farm, alone. As the wind mounted Felicity felt comforted by that thought.

Meanwhile Penny had driven Rob back to her house, to his rented single room in her basement, a most convenient arrangement for a most obliging tenant.

Felicity manned the barricades alone, battering the howling aggressors with missiles that bounced like beach balls, bruising nothing. She lifted beams which dissolved into matchsticks, her fists wouldn't work at fighting, though both her hands were whole. No weapons exploded yet the battle thundered on. Penny Blackburn was shouting something inaudible amongst the uproar, her face distorted in unknown rage. A little voice, a grown child calling, woke Felicity. 'Mum, Mum, wake up. You are having a nightmare.'

'Oh my darling, I'm sorry. It must have been that cheese. God in Heaven, what is that noise?'

'A storm. A dreadful gale. I've never heard anything like it before. Look at Battersea Park – the street lighting is bright enough to show up the poor trees, the wind is murdering them. I was on my way to you anyway, even before I heard you crying out. Myra's pesky cat has decided to be super-terrified down my bed.'

Felicity and Anna looked out at the turmoil. Ariels, chimneypots and slates snapped and tumbled, smashing into the street. Frantic branches, still in leaf, waved in desperation before merciless execution in a hail of the hurricane's cackling gunshots. Great trees cracked apart, roots wrenched their earth with them as they heaved and fell sprawling, slain in battle, on the ground that had grown them.

'Is this the end of the world?'

'Watch out for horsemen, darling.'

'Do you take nothing seriously, Mum? Look at those trees falling, it is terrible.'

'They will grow again. Some things are better pruned.'

'Not everything, though.'

'No, not everything.'

'Mum, supposing you could get your fingers to grow again, would you be happy?'

'I'm happy now.'

'That is not an answer. The common lizard can regrow its tail.'

'Common lizards can't manage without. They can't take alternative employment, they don't read or sing or go to the cinema, they don't play Happy Families.'

'Is that what you and Dad do? Is it just a game?'

'What is worrying you, Anna, tell me.'

'Do you love Dad?'

'Yes and he loves me, why?'

'Do you love him best of all?'

'What is all this about?'

'Would you leave him for someone else?'

'No, I'm sure I wouldn't.'

'Would you ever have left him?'

'Darling, I can't answer that. It is too late or too early. Whichever way you look it is the middle of the night. Shall we raid Myra's kitchen?'

'Supposing . . . oh, well never mind. Let's hunt for biscuits, I'm famished.'

In Chelsea the windows rattled too as the gale raged about the sedate squares and terraces. Penny's basement was snug and safe.

In the morning, London awoke to find the scenery had been changed. Fallen branches littered the ground between the upended trees, parks and squares were quite transformed, suddenly appearing to be thickly planted with bushy shrubs.

The clinging leaves had formed wind-catching sails, doubling the effect of the blow's force.

Their taxi driver was full of it. Power lines down, railways and roads torn apart, great swaths of the country crippled. Tales had proliferated of cars squashed and casualty departments filled by the wounded who had been cut to shreds and stunned by debris and falling masonry. Whole parks were wrecked and woodlands decimated. Seventeen were dead.

Anna refused to come up to the wards. 'I can't be doing with sick people,' she said. Felicity wondered whether that was another gene she had passed on to her daughter. For herself, the disgust she had felt for hospitals and their contents had quite evaporated with age. Her own accident, coupled with her job, had seen to that. Nowadays Felicity was quite immune to infirmity and all the nasty smells and sights that were associated with sickness.

Digby Blackburn was in a single room. He had shrunk and withered. His stick legs scarcely rumpled the flat plain of cellular blankets but the skull beneath the thin skin still produced a most patrician profile. He greeted Felicity effusively, forever urbane and immaculately mannered. He wore wholesome striped pyjamas. Not being bold enough to kiss him and reticent about shaking so frail a hand, Felicity thrust a bottle of whisky towards Digby and wished him a chirpy good morning.

'Of course I remember you!' he said. Felicity was fairly certain this was an act, a very good one, but then he added, 'By George, you are the same stunning looker you were when you were twenty. I'd have known you anywhere,' and she was grateful for his gallantry.

Felicity, though aged, was certainly still fine looking: slender and unwrinkled and not a bit diminished by the salting of grey hairs amongst the dark.

Digby's smile was already turning into the death-head's grin with unsteady teeth of ageing ivory prominent between retreated parchment lips. Felicity recognised the smile and the sweetish smell of morbid breath. She was right to have come at once. Digby's once florid complexion was yellow – a familiar sign of an approaching end.

'I mustn't tire you, General,' she said.

'Whyever not? I won't need to be fit for anything once I've said all my goodbyes. Do you believe in the afterlife?'

'I'm not sure.'

'Neither am I,' said Digby briskly. 'Well now, tell me about yourself.'

Felicity smiled at the old man. He was talking rather like her mother since the onset of dementia, with a rational voice relaying the rubbish of a brain running down, occasionally voicing with clarity the inner workings of an instrument whose batteries were close to dud, facts held together with thinning bits of string. Staff Nurse had already warned Felicity that the General's memory was inclined to be unreliable. 'Speak to him about the old days, he remembers those better than the present.'

'But I didn't know him in his old days,' Felicity protested. 'I was only a child, and he must be at least thirty years older than me.'

'You were grown up in the sixties, weren't you?' was the curt reply.

Felicity considered for a moment and then admitted that the nurse was right. The older people get, the more recent the past becomes. Compared to the Egyptians, the Normans are madly modern. Staff Nurse was probably no more than twenty-four.

Digby eyed the whisky longingly. 'It is a little early for that,' he said, 'but it seems a shame to waste what time is left to enjoy myself.'

'Penny told me not to let you drink too much. She said it wasn't good for you.'

'No point in adjusting the mirror as the car goes over the cliff,' he replied. 'This old horse is going to the knackers and it might as well get bottled.'

Ten minutes was not long. Felicity had business to finish.

'General, I have come to ask you about Wolf. You remember Wolfgang Duncan, don't you?'

'Of course, I'm not gaga. Fine chap, one to be proud of. He went out East, you know.'

'Can you remember twenty years ago when you tried to discredit Wolf in Penny's eyes by making out he had stolen some jewellery – emeralds, I think. Can you remember why you did that?'

'Yes, I remember. Why do you ask, Felicity?'

'I was fond of Wolf, General. Very fond of him. I never believed he had stolen anything but you did say you would explain your reasons to me one day. I would like to know.'

Silence fell as Felicity waited and Digby appeared to drift off into reverie. Eventually she asked if there was anything she could do to help.

'No, not really,' he replied. 'I might as well tell you. With poor Joan dead the secret isn't so important. One thing Felicity, for my sake, please don't tell Penny. Felix knows of course, let him be the one to tell her if he wants to have a laugh at my expense once I'm gone.'

'I promise, General. I am good at secrets and I wouldn't tell Penny anything I didn't want printed in the papers. Sorry, it isn't kind to speak like that about your daughter. I do apologise.'

'Don't. You are right, Penny is very indiscreet, but you are wrong about the rest.'

'What do you mean, General?'

Digby attempted a wink and then looked askance as if he was no longer sure where or what he was. 'Dammit I've lost the thread.'

'You were telling me about why you wanted Penny to think badly of Wolf.'

'Ah yes well . . . Penny never married, you know. Never seemed able to catch men's eyes, unlike her mother.' Felicity remembered how Joan would affect a childish voice and look up at men coyly through downcast lashes. Stout Penny employing the same ensnaring ruses would be even more nauseating. 'Still, I expect it is too late to worry about Penny now.'

'Penny is'nt old yet, General, years younger than me, I'm in my forties.'

'Penny is thirty-nine and desperate,' Digby replied. 'She'll have a job to get off the shelf now. Felix is the only one of my children to get married and that fell apart. I suppose you know why Wolf married Angelica von Hoffer?'

'To save her child?'

'Exactly. Well after all that had been annulled Felix married Angelica.'

'I know,' said Felicity. 'I thought that was to legitimise their child. Henry, I mean.'

'Yes, but there was more to it than just getting the line straightened. Felix needed money, much more than I was ever going to give him. The Von Hoffers made his marriage to their daughter well worth his while, once they were certain that Cousin Cedric wasn't going to start breeding and deny their grandson his title. They liked the idea of handles and all that balderdash. You, Felicity, certainly gave them cause for thought.'

'Me, General? Why?'

'Everyone thought Cedric was going to ask you to marry him.'

'But that is preposterous. What an absurd idea. Why on earth would Lord Tullie and I want to marry each other?'

'Security, status maybe greed . . . all the usual reasons.'

'But that is just plain idiotic.'

'No it isn't!' said Digby, a flush spreading through the yellow skin of his sunk cheeks. Felicity remembered Penny's instructions: her father was not to be crossed. She changed the subject. 'You have a fine-looking grandson, General. I met Henry yesterday. He told me he had never heard of Wolf, even though he looks just like him. I thought it was him. I couldn't believe it.'

Saying Wolf's name might keep the old man on track. The minutes were ticking by but neither she nor Anna had a bus or fox to catch. Digby, however, could lose the plot at any time.

'That's the point, Felicity.'

'What is, General?'

'Young Henry looks like Wolf because they are related.'

'Yes, I know. Felix and Wolf were cousins.'

'No, Felicity. They are half-brothers.'

'Do you mean that you are . . . are you saying that you were . . . ?'

Digby shrugged his coat-hanger shoulders and spread his withered palms in a gesture of submission. 'Yes,' he answered. 'I am his father. Are you surprised?'

'I'm astonished,' she replied. 'Amazed.'

Felicity poured Digby another slug of Scotch despite his tongue already being well loosed.

'You see, I wanted to prevent Penny from throwing herself at Wolf, I wanted to put her off. I had to if I was to save them from er . . . what's the damn word?'

'Sin?' Felicity suggested helpfully.

'That too. What is the thing called? You know, you are a bright girl, been to church and all that.'

'Fornication? Lust? Carnality?'

'No no!' Digby was becoming dangerously agitated. 'What the Egyptians did, turned them all mad. You know, what they sang about in that show, *Salad Days*, you remember, the bit about Cleopatra and that chap beginning with a P. I didn't want any of that sort of hanky-panky. Bloody hell, why can't I remember the right damn word.'

'Do you mean incest?'

'Sshh! Not so loud,' said Digby. 'The whole hospital will hear, it's full of chaps from the regiment.'

'You and Miss Duncan were lovers, General?' Felicity mouthed, whispering incredulously.

Digby indicated that Felicity should come nearer as he struggled to raise himself to a more upright position.

'Yes, just once,' he confided softly. 'Odd, don't you think? But that's war for you, though in our case it was the outbreak of peace that got us together. VE Day, lots of babies must have been conceived then, people got carried away, all those flags and jumping about kissing strangers. Poor Clarice was no stranger, though, in fact at one point I had come damn near to marrying her, until I met Joanie of course. Take my advice, Felicity, never get carried away, never drink champagne on an empty stomach and never ever do anything for old times' sake or out of curiosity. Die guessing every time.'

'I see,' Felicity replied.

'I was fond of Clarice, I admired her. Everyone did, she was a splendid woman and would have been just the ticket as an army wife – but something was missing. Anyway, as I said, I married her sister and Clarice said she couldn't give a damn, that she had far more important things to do than marry a major and that there were plenty more fish and all that, only there weren't. Then on May the 8th 1945 Joan and I were staying with old Mrs Duncan and Clarice at Glamis Towers. Joan was off games, pregnant and sick; Felix was always a nuisance even in the womb. Clarice and I got quite tiddly on champagne and went out to join in the celebrations while Joan went to bed alone with a hot-water bottle. Well torchlit hokey-cokey in Duncan Park wasn't exactly our idea of fun so we got into the back of Mrs Duncan's Rolls which had been laid up on bricks for the duration and drank a whole bottle of her hoarded champagne, while we discussed how life would be now peace had broken out. Well, one thing led to another and little Wolfgang got conceived out of curiosity beneath a camel-hair motoring rug full of moth holes and smelling of camphor. I remember Clarice thanking me: she told me the experience had been most interesting, which finally convinced me I had married the right sister – but it didn't stop there. Just once is quite enough, even in a hurry in the back of a car, remember that too.'

'Miss Duncan must have been about the same age that Penny is now,' said Felicity.

'Oh no, Clarice wasn't as old as that, she just seemed old. Anyway everything was ticking over just fine inside and nine months later, there was Wolfgang.'

'Did no one else know?'

'No. I'm sure of that. By the end even Clarice had begun to believe that fairy tale of finding a little orphan boy in Germany. Poor Clarice, she would have made an excellent spy – she was first class at secrets. Unfortunately the secret she kept wasn't of international importance. She posed as a pregnant widow and had her baby amongst strangers beside the happy mothers of the first post-war children. The only time she ever mentioned the experience was when she said how unkind some people could be to mothers who gave birth to bastards. She was on the council of the Glendrane Home for Unmarried Mothers you know, a most valued member too, I was told.'

'Who knows all this apart from you, and now me?' Felicity asked.

'Bastion, my lawyer, of course, Felix and Wolf. That is all.'

'So Wolf knew this when he died.'

'Wolf isn't dead, Felicity.'

She looked at Digby, skinny and wasted, resting his head on his hospital pillow, the veins at his temple horribly protuberant blue worms. She realised reluctantly that, like her mother, he had lost touch with reality. Sheila often spoke of Magnus as having talked to her that morning, she expected him home each night, and often she believed that he had come. Black must be allowed to be white; Digby was not to be crossed.

'I would have liked to see both my sons again before I die, Felicity.'

The sick man had yellowing eyes. He twitched the covers with his bony fingers now too thin to keep his signet ring outward facing. His one-time barking voice was just a gentle growl.

'Do you know where Felix lives? Can Mr Bastion write to him and ask him to come and see you?'

'He could, but he won't. Felix wouldn't come anyway.'

'And where is he?'

'In Barbados, somewhere called Freya's Well, I think. I'm not sure, near St Lucy.'

'Have you asked Felix to come, General?'

'Penny won't let me,' he replied. 'And I don't want to rock the boat.'

Staff Nurse came in. Time for a pill or a bath or a bedpan. Whatever it was, the interview and visit were at an end.

'Goodbye, General. It was good to see you again and thank you for telling me what happened.'

'Goodbye, my dear. Thank you for listening. Remember what I said. I may be ill but my brain isn't so bad, even though I never was a clever chap.'

4

OXFORDSHIRE HAD BEEN savaged less extensively than further south, where the devastation had altered the landscape and established woodlands had been severed as if the hurricane had been a sacking army of giants. Even so, despite the lesser havoc, Rob had quite a task clearing the damage and submitting extensive insurance claims.

Their weekend alone, which Felicity had planned, never happened.

Rob's mother was in a heap about her fodder shed, which was in a heap too. Furthermore, cub hunting had been cancelled – another catastrophe for which, rather strangely, Pricilla, held Felicity responsible.

'That girl Penny Blackburn is a treasure, one of the old school,' said Lady Jean Green to the vet. 'She gave up her weekend to rush down here to lend a hand and give dear Rob's spirits a boost. She has the same instinct for doing what is right as royalty during the Blitz. Yes, she is a really good and useful egg, unlike some.'

Penny's contribution to post-tempest morale was to wring her hands with a hearty cheerfulness and eat large meals prepared by Felicity, who was quietly mourning the fallen pear tree from which Anna's outgrown swing had hung, just another childish thing no longer wanted.

On Monday morning the stock market tumbled.

'To Who? To Who?' became the owlish cry of those with shares to sell.

'We are ruined!' announced Lady Jean.

Pricilla said Felicity should sell her car, which is what she would have done, had she too been married to a man who owned a cattle truck.

While the markets continued dropping Felicity had received a call from Mr Bastion of Fry, Pride and Harping.

'Me! An executrix? There must be some mistake. The General can't ask me to do that. I have nothing to do with his family or his will. I don't know how to be an executor. I can't execute.'

'It is the General's wish, Mrs Green. He has asked me to draw up a new will to that effect. He said he was greatly taken with your integrity and good sense and felt that you alone might be able to grasp the situation in an unbiased fashion. Personally I feel the General should be indulged and have his wishes respected on this matter.'

'Wait a second, Mr Bastion. Even I know wills have to be made by people sound in mind. The General was obviously soft in his when I saw him.'

'I have no confirmation as to that, Mrs Green. He is old, certainly, and sick. He can be forgetful occasionally. Aren't we all?'

'Mr Bastion, he told me that Wolfgang Duncan was still alive.'

'There is no proof to the contrary, Mrs Green.'

'No proof to the contrary! What do you mean? Wolfgang Duncan died in the spring of 1971 just after my daughter was born. I remember it distinctly, he was in Nepal.'

'Yes well, Mrs Green. Let us say he disappeared in Nepal.'

'Seventeen years ago, Mr Bastion. How long does the legal profession require to assume someone dead?'

'Mr Duncan is almost certainly living somewhere, Mrs Green. His demise was a matter of convenience, a diplomatic death if you like. He has assumed a new identity and a new name.'

'What do you mean? Where? How?'

'Some things are quite beyond my scope or sphere, Mrs Green, and not available for my investigation. There is a bank account in Switzerland that is still in use from time to time. I have no other information. Neither I, nor my firm, have had contact with the gentleman for many years. The only thing we have done is to ask the bank to inform their client of his father's grave illness.'

'But you don't think Wolfgang Duncan is dead.'

'No, I do not. There has been no evidence to suggest that he is no longer with us somewhere, in some guise or other, probably engaged in work of a sensitive and secretive nature. Good day to you, Mrs Green. Let us hope it is a long time before our services as General Blackburn's co-executors are called upon.'

'Wait, Mr Bastion. What about the General's other children? Why can't they be his executors?'

'All attempts have been made to contact Mr Felix Blackburn but it seems he is neither able nor willing even to visit his father. There have been no transactions between father and son for many years now, not since before the death of Lady Blackburn, I believe.'

Felicity asked about Penny and was told, quite bluntly, that Miss Penelope Blackburn was not suitable as an executrix; likewise the General's grandson, who was still at his studies and somewhat under age.

Following this conversation Felicity couldn't sleep. She wandered the house at night, reading without absorbing, boiling kettles for brews left undrunk and exhausting herself with speculation. During the day she dropped off at awkward moments, even sleeping through some of the worst excesses of the Sunbeam Percussionists.

'Please Grania, I need to take some time off.'

Grania was Felicity's superior in qualifications but her junior by about twelve years and Felicity was never sure whether she found her intimidating or just irritating. Today Grania was being both as she arranged herself into an appropriate listening pose, head slightly inclined, chin supported, both hands visible and brows quizzical to denote concern. Grania was lean beneath the ethnic layers of coarse weaves and cheesecloth, seeming always to be on the grubby side with her dark comb-tethered hair greasy and lank.

'Do you, Felicity? Why?'

'It is personal,' Felicity replied.

'Would you like to share it?' Grania asked.

'No. It is private.'

'A marital problem, maybe, or is it your health?' Grania was not slow in detecting women's troubles, especially in those of Felicity's age. 'Without intruding upon your space I feel you might find it therapeutic to be more giving. Together we could address the problem.'

'All I want is a couple of weeks off. Without pay, of course.'

'What about your commitment to your clients?'

'The Sunbeam Percussionists will bang on quite happily without me, Grania. A dog with delirium tremens could conduct them just as well.'

'Do I detect a lack of self-worth, Felicity?'

'Quite possibly. But I know what my sanity is worth.'

'That comment is inappropriate. Unbend, Felicity. A proud tree cracks, a flexible one sways with the wind. There is an interesting piece on that very subject in *Therapy Month*. Have you read it?'

'No, but I've seen enough fallen trees to last me, thanks. I've also played enough xylophones and handbells and sung enough songs with the tone deaf to know that I have had a bucketful of all that too.'

Felicity's request for leave was refused. She resigned.

'What will Rob say when you tell him you have become unwaged?'

Felicity had made certain that Grania never met Rob. Rather than admit he was a land-owning Tory with rambler phobia, Felicity had implied she was married to a smallholder in poor health who grew organic vegetables.

'Better to be unwaged than unhinged,' said Felicity.

'Well in that case, you may leave now. Your attitude is not helpful and anyway, with the cuts in funding, I might have been forced to abolish your post next session. In a way you might be doing us a service, provided the underspend is not ringfenced. Your leaving party will be next Thursday week,' said Grania. She wrote a list of festive fare in her desk diary: Hula Hoops, Twiglets, Bombay Mix and Aqua Libra.

The lunchtime concert was just about to start when Felicity took her seat in Magdalen College Chapel. The chiaroscuro stained-glass figures in the lofty windows gazed down upon the small group of musicians assembled to give an hour's recital of Handel's most popular works. Felicity felt free to think. The familiar Water Music twinkled and resounded in the subdued light of autumnal sun slanting upon old stone.

Dove Sei, the unbearable agony of longing pierced her and for the first time in years she wished she could pray, wished she could really believe in a wiper of tears who could make all things new and serve out second chances.

The afternoon was warm for October and she was droppingly weary. As she nodded she heard the tenor sing 'Where'er You Walk'. Cool gales fanning glades seemed a bit of an understatement. So long as she didn't fall off her chair or snore, sleeping through a performance was not a crime.

The interview with Grania had been the confirmation of her obsolescence. She was without job, without purpose. No longer needed as a mother and helpless as a daughter, ineffective as a lover and wrecked for what she had been intended. She watched the deft fiddlers, she knew the notes and fingering. There was nothing she could do except imagine the pressure of the string against the violin's neck in her missing fingertips.

She awoke to find tears coursing down her cheeks. The tenor was singing 'Silent Worship'.

Outside the afternoon was autumnally soft. There was plenty of time, all the time she could wish, no one expected or wanted her home for ages. The serene deer had eyes of liquid light: she spoke to them because they understood nothing. In the spring, the meadow would be filled with fritillaries, which would grow again regardless of the giant trees lying with their roots exposed, toppled monarchs, their private parts now open to the public gaze, ridicule and pity. Once, according to the guidebook, these trees had been accustomed to shading the greatest men and finest minds – Wolsey, Addison, Gibbon and Wilde – as they took a turn about the grounds. Felicity did not know Oxford well, despite living so close.

She would walk. That way she might get her thoughts straight. The young man in front of her had his uncle's back view; she recognised Henry Blackburn at once. All he lacked were Wolf's protruding ears. Maybe, like his teeth, Henry's jug handles had been corrected to conform so sunshine could not glow through them as it does a whippet's hocks. Felicity had no wish for Henry to find her tearful yet again and was pleased to see that he turned to the right beyond the little bridge. She would go left.

The walk was open but still bestrewn with ripped branches as she picked her way along the shady path. She didn't know where it led but kept going and sniffed the scent of bitter smoke and heaped leaves.

If Wolf were alive, what was it to her? He could be married, a family man with a loving wife, doting children and a stable life that needed no interference and agitation. It was not for her to poke about; just because she had kept his memory sacred didn't qualify her to disrupt or distress him further. But she had to know. Every day she had thought of him, his memory was central to all she did. She loved him always. The music had opened a wound that wouldn't heal ever. 'I will love her till I die.' The tears began smarting again.

A figure approached through bonfire smoke. Felicity stepped off the path and feigned great interest in the roots of a banal laurel. Crying women are tiresome. The stranger might feel it essential to help or, in the words of Grania, reach out and share Felicity's grief. The walker passed. He was evidently trying to commit something to memory, glancing occasionally at the book he carried and mouthing the words he needed to learn. It was Wolf! It must be. It couldn't be Henry this time as he had turned the other way, gone off down the river in the opposite direction. Felicity knew then she must be going mad. Being rational, she did not believe in ghosts and yet she shook with fear. Twenty years had passed: she knew full well that Wolf would have changed, he could not possibly look like the young man who had passed, he must be aged, greying, balding.

She resolved to continue her walk. It was silly to retrace her steps. The path would finish soon, it would be interesting to find out where it ended. She had been walking for about three-quarters of a mile and reckoned she must be nearing somewhere in the region of Marston Road. Young voices laughing and shouting reassured her, there was real life to be had at the end. On her left she saw several punts bobbing on the waiting water as a happy party got itself arranged for a river jaunt. She hadn't realised that the Isis flowed so far. A bridge led to a vast grassed court and a range of sedate classic yellow stone buildings that she had never noticed before. Now she knew she was lost and was wondering what to do when she saw a man coming towards her down the dark path beyond the bridge. This time he smiled. Wolf again.

'Hello, Mrs Green.'

'Henry Blackburn! . . . but you turned the other way. How can you be here?'

'Addison's Walk is circular. We arrive where we started.'

'And know the place for the first time? So this is Magdalen again, the New Buildings. It all looks so unfamiliar. I thought I was walking in a straight line and all the time I was going round. I would have started to track myself, like Pooh and the Woozles.'

He smiled at her, Wolf's smile. 'Are you feeling better? I thought you looked distressed.'

'I'm fine, thank you. So it was you back there in the bonfire smoke.'

'I'm afraid so. You looked as if you had seen a ghost.'

'I had.'

Henry was trying to memorise Polonius. With luck, the production would go to next year's Edinburgh Fringe. Meanwhile it wasn't easy to get the rich not gaudy, the borrowers and lenders and the apparel proclaiming the man in proper shape.

'You are too young for Polonius.'

'Only children are always old for their age.'

'So Anna tells me,' Felicity answered.

'Yes, but I only pretend to be older than I am when I am acting.'

'You know her age?'

'Well, yes. Mummy told me she couldn't possibly be the same age as me. Incidentally, my mother says you haven't changed.'

'She has seen me?'

'Yes, at the Tate. She knew you immediately. She was wearing her habitual woebegone disguise. She is quite large.'

Felicity recalled the vast woman in voluminous draperies with circular horn-rimmed glasses.

'Angelica wasn't the woman with her head in a turban, surely?'

'That is the one.'

'Oh, how rude of me. I never even acknowledged her.'

'Not to worry. I don't know why, but she wasn't eager to meet you again.'

Felicity did know why. 'In that case I will respect her wishes. Oh dear, that sounds pompous, like my ex-boss who was always aerated about personal space and room for growth.'

Felicity looked at Henry and forgave Angelica for using unfair and foul methods to ensure she could keep her child from abortionists or adopters, but it was quite pleasing to experience the gratification of knowing she had also retained some guilt. Poor Angelica, she was a physical disaster: that too was quite nice to know.

'Where are you going now, Henry?'

'I am going back to Jesus.'

'Oh,' Felicity replied, floored.

'Jesus is my college, Mrs Green.'

'Aha. I understand. I thought you meant you had seen the light.'

'No, not yet.'

'Henry, let me give you tea. I am sure that is the right sort of auntish thing to do and I don't imagine it will upset your mother.'

'That would be lovely. Let me carry your parcel.'

Henry really was most awfully sweet, thought Felicity. It was sad that Anna found him creepy. She gave him her Blackwells bag to carry. It was heavy with a new copy of *Who's Who* which her mother-in-law had demanded for her birthday.

They ate fruit scones looking out of St Mary's Church crypt across the cobbled square towards the Bodleian and the Radcliffe Camera.

'You are lucky, Henry, being here. Oxford is stunning.'

'Isn't it blissful? Sometimes I just want to wallow in it for ever, become an aesthete and die.' Henry certainly wasn't a typical young man. Felicity longed to ask whether he had many friends.

'I saw your grandfather last week. He is not well.'

'Poor Grandpapa. Mummy says he is dying.'

'You ought to go and see him. He would like that. I got the

impression he is very lonely and feels he is leaving life all adrift. He wants to tie knots and cast off.'

'Oh dear. Yes I will try. It is just a bit awkward at the moment. Maybe Auntie Penny would take me with her, I am so queasy about death. One just is not used to it these days, not like in the last century when most people would have assisted at at least ten deathbeds by the time they attained their majority.'

Felicity was fairly certain that Henry would be too busy till it was too late.

'Henry, your grandfather also wants to see your father.'

'Tricky one, that.'

'Why? The West Indies aren't far, eight hours at the most.'

'The distance isn't the problem, it is my father himself. He never comes to England now, he has sort of gone native. He isn't welcome here at all. Auntie Penny hasn't spoken to him since Grandmama Blackburn died. Grandmama pretended Dad was a chronic invalid and lived abroad for his health.'

'How did your grandmother die, Henry? She wasn't old.'

'She died at Thermes-Les-Bains, she was taking a cure.'

'A cure for what?'

'Old age, I think. Anyway she had a heart attack. Grandpapa blamed the volcanic mud, but the spa said she had been playing too strenuously with her tennis coach.'

'Gracious me, I never thought she was a tennis player.'

'She wasn't. Auntie Penny said her mother's heart packed up because she got so distressed by Dad's evil ways while visiting him a month before.'

'Couldn't you persuade your father to come and see your grandfather, Henry?'

'Christ no! Darling Daddy hates me. He can't even bear to look at me.'

'Maybe you remind him too much of someone.'

'Could be.'

'Have you never met Wolfgang Duncan, Henry?'

'No. Before you mentioned him in London I had never heard of him. Mother had, though. He must have featured in her past somehow – she got quite flustered, which is not her way. Who exactly is he?'

'An uncle.'

210

'Well I never. Can I get you a flapjack? I dote on them, especially the ones with nuts in.'

He walked her to the Park and Ride bus stop. 'This is very considerate of you, Henry,' she said. 'No one has felt I needed protecting for years.'

'Wait there,' he said. 'I shan't be a tick.'

Felicity stared at the spot on which Cranmer, Ridley and Latimer had been martyred, till Henry returned. 'You look pensive,' he said. 'What is it? The questionable virtue of martyrdom?'

'No, I've forgotten to book the sweep.'

'Ah yes, well . . . I've got you a present, Mrs Green.'

'Oh Henry, how kind. You must call me Felicity. Really I don't deserve a present, not for just one scone. Can I look?'

He had been to the paperback bookshop and bought her *Beginning and Ending* by Tom Otterburn.

'A scone and a flapjack and a nasty fright in Addison's Walk. Have you read it?'

'No, I haven't. Though you are the second person to tell me how wonderful it is. Thank you very much. I will read it on the plane.'

'Are you going on holiday?'

'Sort of. Yes, I am going to Barbados.'

Now that she had said it, her idea became a concrete plan, given substance by her statement of intent.

'Well watch out for Dad. Apparently he looks like the Old Man of the Sea.'

'A friend from work. Her husband died, she needs a break and a companion. I promised her I would go with her, Rob. She is very depressed. She needs to go to Barbados.'

'Why not bring her out here for a breath of country air? That will do her good. No one actually *needs* to go to Barbados, Flicky,' said Rob.

'They do if they are Barbadian.'

'Ah, I see.'

The lie came horribly easily. Rob appeared to accept it, glad to have avoided an unwelcome house guest.

'I will only be gone for a week. Not long. I am sure you can manage.'

'I think you are mad,' said Rob. 'Places like that get hurricanes at this time of year.'

'Then I too will feel perfectly at home.'

'I suppose it is cheaper now.'

It wasn't quite as expensive as the spring but it cost enough, and that was the problem. Felicity had no money of her own beyond her meagre salary which she had always frittered quickly. After Black Monday Rob was not a good touch. Pawnbrokers wouldn't give enough for her engagement ring and nothing of substantial worth at Church Farm was hers to sell.

If only her mother were still on the spot. There were lots of things at the Shieling that could raise the required cash but there wasn't a way of getting hold of them. Isa, quite rightly, would never collaborate in that way. Felicity was in despair until she hit on ringing Ailsa in the States.

'Hi, Auntie Flicky!' Iona Schmidt, the younger of Ailsa and Dieter's two children, answered the phone. She was mighty sophisticated for one of six; her brother Campbell was eight. 'Auntie Flicky, it is nearly Hallowe'en. Me and Campbell are going to have a party with real pumpkin lanterns and scary faces and witches and frogs and spiders. Grossmutti Hanne is staying too, she is really smart with tacky paper.'

'That is great, Iona. Give Grossmutti lots of love from me. Can I speak to Mummy, please.'

'Mom, it's for you . . . as usual.'

It didn't take long for Ailsa to grasp the problem and still less time for her to produce a solution. She was a systems analyst: she got things straight. 'Dieter will lend you the money. He flies back from Prague tomorrow via Heathrow. He will post it direct to your bank. How much do you want?'

'Thank you very, very much. I really appreciate it. I will pay him back just as soon as I can, maybe if I get another job or sell something. He won't need to wait.'

'Take your time, Flicky. No worries. I don't expect he will charge you more than two and a half over base.'

No wonder the Schmidts were so orderly: they never gave way to impulsive gestures. Sometimes Felicity wondered how she and Ailsa could have sprung from the same combination of loins and womb.

'Why don't you meet me in Barbados, Ailsa. It is cleverly placed between us. You could help me look for Felix.'

Ailsa was bound to refuse, but it was worth a try. Felicity's feet were getting colder by the hour. 'Ailsa, can I have a word with Hanne, please?'

'Of course, I'll get her for you. She is being very hazardous with her home-made candles.'

Felicity asked Hanne whether she had ever heard that Wolf might still be alive.

'But Felicity, he is falling down some ravine or dying of a fever, is he not? I am remembering the incident so vividly, and am being reminded of Molly Malone.'

'That is what we all believed. I think now that maybe it was just a story to keep me happy.'

'Fevers are not happy events but many stories are told for many reasons. Ailsa is forbidding me from telling the tale of *Struwwelpeter* because it may frighten the children, though it is relating many good reasons for not being rude to black-a-moors or hounds, and Campbell and Iona are always watching programmes upon the television in which heads are exploding and other most unpleasant things occur. How is your daughter?'

'Anna is fine, thank you. She is trying to get to the Royal Academy of Music. She is playing your father's violin at the audition. Have you not heard anything at all about Wolf?'

'No, Felicity, I am hearing nothing. Oh but this news of little Anna is making me have much joy. Wish her *viel Glück* from me!'

Felicity was using the telephone in Rob's study when he walked in. 'How much longer are you going to be?' he asked abruptly.

'Just a second,' Felicity mouthed back. Campbell was in the middle of reciting all his excellent grades. 'Campbell that is wonderful, clever you. Listen, lovie I must go, your Uncle Rob needs the phone. Lots of love to all of you. Have a really terrifying Hallowe'en, won't you. Byee!'

Felicity hung up.

'Don't tell me you were gassing to America.'

'Yes, darling. I was ringing Ailsa.'

'Well don't do it again without asking me. I'm not made of money, you know. You must not waste what little I have left.'

'Don't be ridiculous, Rob.'

'I am not being ridiculous. I cannot tolerate passengers on the wagon. Pay for your own flaming calls in future. I didn't marry you to have you pissing my money up against the wall.'

'Rob, what is wrong? Have you been drinking?'

'What isn't wrong is more to the point. Of course I have been drinking, it is the only thing to do when your money is going down the drain. I'm going out to see if at least the cows are still there.'

'Wait Rob, please. Do you want me to cancel this Barbados trip, because I can, really I can.'

'No, don't let your friend down. Go and enjoy yourself. Don't worry about me. Don't worry about shooting at Undergreen, don't worry about the Opening Meet.'

'But shooting and hunting are nothing to do with me. The Millbrooks won't mind if I don't go to Undergreen with you. Anyway, you always say I am a rotten loader.'

'Stop bringing out your sodding crippled hand as an excuse for everything.'

'I don't. I never have, Rob. You know that.'

'OK I'm sorry. Just remember who pays your bills.'

'Grania was right. She said you wouldn't like it if I became unwaged.'

'Who the hell is Grania? Another of your do-gooding little friends, is she? Well she can sod off too. I'm going to have a drink with Mother.'

Rob's mother had a word with Felicity. Normally she barked at her about the weather and the price of oats but this time she decided to dish out cryptic advice. 'Never forget, Felicity, that nature abhors a vacuum.'

'I would never desert my husband at this time of year,' said Pricilla. Sadly for her such fidelity was never to be tested.

She watched the reservoir slant and disappear below as the plane banked over Staines, before following the coastline from

Southampton to Chesil Bank towards the Atlantic and the Caribbean.

Felicity settled back in her seat and tried not to think about crashing. Since Clarice Duncan's death she had never really been at ease flying. If only one could get out, pull a communication cord, ask to get off or board a lifeboat, taking to the air might not seem so final. Still, here she was, Barbados bound, her Rubicon crossed.

5

R OB COULD HAVE coped with customs, and taken charge of tipping. Felicity missed him horribly, she felt shaky with apprehension and fatigue and longed for home, Rob's dogs, the smell of toast and English chill. No amount of bubbly steel band could cheer her, a lonely Persephone on a jaunt from Hades released into sunlight with a prisoners' chorus of passengers blinking and stretching, letting the heat ease their cramped joints, stiff and travel-stale after the flight. Hibiscus and bougainvillaea clambered about the trellises leading to the terminal where Barbados welcomed visitors with long queues. Grim faces, quite different to those beaming from the posters scrutinised incomers' papers and Felicity felt she was being processed for something sinister and not at all holiday-making. The adenoidal clatter of the pounded oil drums throbbed through the airport and she was so homesick that she hoped her papers would displease Immigration sufficiently to merit her instant repatriation.

By the time she got to the taxi she had convinced herself that this whole venture was absurd and the least sane of hunts. How could she begin to find a man she hadn't seen for twenty years amongst this rich assortment of mixed races? Besides, everyone belonged to someone here; no one else was alone. She felt silly and pallid and dizzy.

Leroy's taxi was a cavern of dangling charms and scented plastic posies. As he drove to the hotel the radio announced sensational hardware bargains obtainable at Winston's Emporium and raved about some miraculous skin whitener between flashes of ecstatic gospel music. Joyful noise did not cheer Felicity even if it did please the Lord.

While Leroy screeched by a traffic roundabout Felicity looked through the navy tinted window and saw a large, irate bride standing amongst the formal planting dressed in frothing white waiting to be snapped in her whipped-cream splendour. Several small attendants, the girls in stiffest net and the boys in bow-ties, were taunting her and dodging the flailing bouquet. Poor soul, thought Felicity as the rain began to pour. Marry on Friday, marry for losses.

'Welcome to Barbados, lady! This your first visit?' Leroy shouted above the hallelujahs and the drumming downfall.

Felicity said it was.

'You on vacation?'

'I've come to look for someone.'

'You looking for a man?'

'Well yes, I am.'

'Got anyone in mind, lady?'

'Oh yes. Someone called Felix Blackburn.'

'Felix, that sure is a cool name. This man a ba'jun?'

'A what?'

'Does he live here?'

'Yes.'

'You his woman?'

'No.'

'You the mother of his children? Him done a runner?'

'No, I want to find him because his father is dying.'

'That is really bad. Ah'll get my auntie to pray for you. She's an Adventist. Them Adventists get a great heap of prayers answered every time. Every time!'

'Thank you.' A depressed lassitude was sweeping over her. She needed a bed, a drink and someone to love who would offer more hope than an aunt with a heap of answered prayers.

Tonight she would sleep. Tomorrow she would look for Felix.

The bus to Bridgetown was filled to more than double capacity, the heat generated by the packed bodies outstripping anything firing from above. Saturday was a great day out, the ideal moment for sharp dressing and hitting the capital but not a good time for a visitor to get orientated. A stout woman in a bursting blouse and Eliza Dolittle hat squashed her grandchildren against her shiny bosom to allow Felicity a sliver of space on the seat.

217

No stop was ignored: more and more passengers packed aboard the bus until it reached the terminus where its payload exploded and dispersed.

As Felicity walked towards the harbour, a flush of heat surged through her as sweat dribbled out. Her heart thumped and her legs turned feeble. She sat on the kerb and waited to recover. A flea-bitten mongrel sniffed her with disdain before turning its curly tail to saunter down the waterside. Even her mother-in-law would be surprised at the depth of her depravity now that curs also despised her. She steadied her head in her hands, hoping the nausea would pass.

'Are you OK?'

'Yes, thank you. It's the heat, I'm not used to it.'

'You had better not sit there. I thought you were a beggar.'

'Sorry.' She instinctively hid her left hand in her skirt pocket and looked up at a tanned man with straggled artificially blond hair and an earring. It was hard to age someone so lean yet wrinkled like a raisin and with such a tobacco-husky voice. 'Perhaps if you could tell me where to get a cup of coffee I might feel stronger.'

'Come with me. My friends have a café over there on Fisherman's Wharf.'

For a second Felicity thought that she might have found Felix but her rescuer's name was Adrian and he made it his business to be blatantly, openly effeminate. He lived by befriending tourists and doing a little light guiding and possibly some pimping. His health was bad, he said; the Barbadian climate was kinder, more tolerant in every way than his family in Dorking.

Felicity told him her errand and bought him a rum.

'Felix, or whatever his name is, may not want to see you.'

'You know him?' Felicity asked.

'I know most people,' Adrian replied.

'But do you know Felix?'

'Depends.'

'On what?'

'Another drink, for a start. One word of advice, my dear: don't go to the High Commission or the police, will you?'

'Why not? I was going to try both.'

218

'Just don't, OK? You mustn't stir things best left dormant. Do you understand?'

'I think so. But how else can I find him?'

'I will ask about for you. Just don't meddle. I promise I will do my best.'

'I was wondering whether he might be in the phone book,' said Felicity.

'You are very sweet, my dear. Why not search for him in Yellow Pages under U for Undesirable.'

'Why, what does he do?'

'This and that. I won't tell you, then you won't know. Give me a day and a bit of encouragement and I will find out whether you can see the man I think you are looking for. All right?'

'Yes, fine. What do you want?'

'You must be kosher. Unless you are so clever that you reckon to win through on naivety. Give me my expenses, your name and some proof of identity and I will get back to you.'

Adrian's expenses were quite hefty

'I haven't got much money, I'm afraid, I had to borrow the fare off my brother-in-law. Will this be enough?'

'I can't bear it. You are going to get yourself fleeced here, my little lamb. I'll take half of that now, give me the rest later. Don't go spending it meanwhile. I'll call at your hotel as soon as I've got some news. Relax. Enjoy yourself. That is what paradise is for.'

'I can't face the bus again.'

'You need greater stamina for bus riding. The cashier will call a taxi for you. Internal calls are free.'

A few hours of sun and sea were enough. Felicity was not designed to enjoy much basking: the sight and smell of oil-slicked bodies sickened her and she wasn't certain about what lurked in the ocean, especially after seeing barracuda on the menu. She had heard enough of Moray eels to dread a slithery nudge and the snap of trapping jaws locking on to protruding toes or, worse still, tits. Thank God, she thought, I am not a man, and shuddered. She would die of fright on encountering a stingray prowling its silent territory amongst armed urchins and would be badly rattled by colliding with shoals of flying fish. Sea bathing had never been her thing since icy childhood dips near

Kilbole where every wave threw up a jellyfish. The warm West Indian waves were breaking high and strong and as she was alone, no one would miss her if she got sucked into the undertow. By sunset she had almost finished her book. Tom Otterburn was a bewitching writer, she had been transported by him from the first sentence, carried along by a need to devour but dreading the end when there would be no more to delight her.

'Did you see the green flash?'

Adrian had appeared from nowhere and was standing beside her in the pink afterglow watching the slate-blue clouds gather into night. A liner glittering with party lights glided towards port.

'You gave me a fright, Adrian. I didn't expect to see you. What green flash?'

'Tourists are always told that there is a green flash just as the sun sinks below the water. I've never seen it myself, at least not when I'm sober.'

Adrian had news. Felicity was lucky. 'I've located your man.'

'He is not my man.'

'Your man, my man, I'm speaking in the broadest sense, like an Irishman, to be sure. Sometimes I say I'm from County Galway myself, the tourists love it. Anyway I've done my best for you. Take a cab to the fish market in St Lucy tomorrow and someone will meet you there, Jacob or Esau is the fellow's name. Get the cab to wait for an hour or so.'

All had been arranged with considerable personal difficulty, inconvenience and outlay by Adrian, who deserved a pretty serious rum.

Later on, when she was once more alone, she rang Leroy. He had given her his card when he had driven her to the hotel. LEROY'S LIMOUSINE. DISTANCE NO OBJECT. ANY TIME ANY WHERE, LEROY FOR LUXURY. She booked him for the whole of the next day.

'No problem, Lady. Sunday is a cool day for a trip. My aunt, she been praying all day. All day but the Lord not tell her nothing. Maybe he tell us we just got to go and look for ourselves. My wife is Episcopalian, she goes to church on Sunday, so she'll have another go at the Good Lord tomorrow.

That way we give him two chances and I get saved on both Saturday and Sunday.'

All along the coastline churches and tabernacles had been crammed with singing congregations of women dressed in their very smartest, topped with Sunday-best hats. Men loafed in the shade with cans of beer.

Felicity had enjoyed the journey, driving by the pretty pastel chattel houses interspersed with their gimcrack modern concrete counterparts embellished with bulbous pedimented balustrades. Some of the columns were set on a slope instead of placed to rise vertically with the steps. Children and dogs meandered about the roads. The further from Bridgetown, the more Barbados seemed well suited to everlasting lotus eaters.

Leroy had relatives in St Lucy. He was happy to wait there at the bar; to pass would have been damn rude, he told Felicity. He parked beside the concrete fish market, a weekday gossip shop but now deserted and Sunday silent. Leroy's cousin worked at the cement works just visible at the coastline's tip, and his cousin's pay needed sharing. Felicity sat on the step by the empty sea. Several young boys stared sulkily at the water willing it to whip itself into a surfable frenzy but the royal blue waves were placid and only flashed feeble foamy smiles.

'Felicity Green?'

'Yes.'

Henry had warned her that his father had surrounded himself with uncouth minders. Jacob was shorn bald with a mouth more golden than a bag of chocolate coins. Further gold bits glinted from fingers and earlobes and a hefty medallion hung upon his muscular shirtless chest. His shorts were slashed to be ragged, his feet and hands were huge and intimidating and out of kilter with his rather high-pitched soft voice.

'You have to come with me.'

Leroy waved cheerfully from the bar over the road where he was meeting more cousins by the minute.

'I'll be back in an hour, maybe two,' Felicity shouted.

'You take just as long as it takes, Lady. We got all day. All day!' was the slurred reply.

Felicity got into Jacob's Mini-Moke which was not much

more than an engine with seats attached to the chassis and they drove off, away from the gentler sea, climbing upwards and over towards the east coast.

'He's got hisself a rum shop all among the sugar cane,' said Jacob.

'Who has? Mr Blackburn?'

Conversation was pretty impossible as they careered over the bumps, raising dust well dried by the sun after the recent rains.

'Nah. Mr Duncan, not Mr Blackburn.'

Felicity started at what she thought she had heard.

'Mr Duncan?' She thought she must be dreaming. 'Did you say Mr Duncan?'

They were now descending a sharp incline strewn with loose stones. Jacob was concentrating on negotiating his vehicle and no longer chatty. Felicity decided she must have been mistaken and tried to rid her mind of the silly notion that she might be about to meet Wolf. She no longer noticed the view or the precipitous road, the potholes or the spectacular sea along that savage coastline. All she could think of was Wolf. What could she say? How should she behave? Lead us not into temptation. How much simpler it would have been had she stayed at home.

Felicity had imagined the rum shop to be like an off-licence, stacked with crates of liquor on special offer and shelves of labelled bottles. She did not expect a patched-up shack perched on heaps of stones – nor had she anticipated its proprietor to be old. He was sitting on the shady side of the porch, smoking. No customers and no visible stock were there to indicate that this was, as a hand-painted sign proclaimed, The Right-On Rum Shop. An old woman driving a couple of desultory goats had been the only other human for the last half-mile. The engine stopped. Just rival soloist birds accompanied by an orchestra of insects amongst the dancing, dusted grasses and parched, rustling sugar cane, imposed upon the baking silence.

The man got up and walked slowly towards Felicity. He was stooped and frail with over-living. Wisps of whitened hair hung from beneath the brim of a battered panama, the eyes were blacked out by sunglasses but the bags under them extended to cheeks crazed with broken veins framed by deep-gulched stubbled jowls; his thick lips were sun-dried and his fingers nicotined. His ripped shirt had, like him, enjoyed a privileged youth but his batik shorts were tourist tat. He seemed shorter than the Felix of Felicity's memory. In fact there was nothing of the self-confident spoilt youth left in this wreck. He was forty-two, twice the age he had been at their last meeting.

'Flicky!'

'Felix?'

'Don't you know me?' He took off his glasses and she saw his sad eyes beneath hooded lids with the bloodshot whites of a habitual drunk. Blue eyes, very blue, reflecting the faded collar of the Jermyn Street shirt, the same as those Felicity had seen last week pleading to see his children. Digby's eyes.

He held her arms and bent to kiss her. She turned her head away, gagging on the rank fumes.

'You used to like me kissing you, Flicky.'

'I'm sorry.'

'Why have you come, Flicky?'

She didn't know, she couldn't tell, there was nothing left but utter revulsion. In the back of her mind she knew that this journey was not just an attempt to please a dying man. She had come across the ocean for news of Wolf. Perhaps she had found much more than that. She felt a panic of confusion rising, like searching for a familiar face in a crowd of preoccupied strangers.

'Your father is dying.'

'I know.'

'He wants to see all his children.'

'Both his children, Flicky.'

'I know that Wolf is his son.'

'You see, I am a wise child who knows his father.'

'He wants to see all three of you.'

'There were only two, Flicky. Two sons. No daughters. The gallant General was not the only one to play away matches. Absence makes the heart grow fonder . . . of other people. You should remember that, Flicky.'

'For God's sake. Who are you?'

'Who do you want me to be?'

'Not Wolf. No, not Wolf. Tell me you aren't Wolf. Your teeth are wrong, your ears, all of you.'

'The teeth are new. I've had some knocks, it took more than vinegar and brown paper to mend my head . . . shall I show you the scars? No? Well fair enough, you've had a bellyful of mutilations. Here is Jacob. He knows me better than anyone now. Who am I, Jacob?'

'The boss,' Jacob replied.

'Yes, but what is my name?'

'It is writ there over the door,' he said pointing to a minute sign that proclaimed Mr Wolfgang Duncan to be the proprietor of the Right-On Rum Shop. 'That is you.'

'Good man, Jacob. Now get lost. Mrs Green and I are going to take a look at the view. I'll call when I need you. Come on, Flicky, let us stagger a few steps so you can see the sea. Don't worry, I won't push you over, I never do my own dirty work, do I, Jacob?'

Jacob flashed a golden grin.

'Jacob is awfully stupid, but all I've got. I have to lie low, people find it hard to understand me.'

Felicity shook her arm free. 'How do you live?'

'You might as well ask why I live. I suppose I live to spend money — Three cheers for the Swiss, I say and their bloody discreet banks. That is how I live now, anonymously. Time was when I could get money out of both Blackburns to keep my knowledge of their indiscretions secret. Those days are over. How did you find out about it all?'

'You told me just now.'

'About Penny, yes, but what about the other? Who told you that?'

'Your father.'

The east coast stretched straight out below them, miles of savage and treacherous sea too dangerous for swimmers, the white shore quite free of crowds.

'Isn't this the point in our conversation when you tell me I've got a lovely place?'

'I think it is hateful,' said Felicity. 'You have made it vile.'

'You are very harsh, Flicky, considering that everything has been your fault.'

'My fault?'

'Yes, yours. You had everything and your stupid pride meant you lost it. Christ, your hand is gross.'

'You gave me the drugs.'

'Me? No Flicky, the bad trip was your doing like all the rest of those disasters. Have you met Angelica's son? The result of your stupid challenge?'

'Yes, he is charming.'

'Oh is he? What a nauseating piece of precocious smugness. He makes me want to vomit.'

'He is your son.'

'I've heard he looks just like me.'

'He looks like Wolf.'

'There you go, Flicky. Disappointing, isn't it?'

'I want to leave. Now.'

'OK. You can. Go home and forget about all this. Let the old boy die in peace. I'm not coming back like that biblical prig, the prodigal son. The fatted calf lives! Why should I let Penny smother me, or renew the acquaintance of my ex-wife or receive the bloody gratitude of her self-satisfied son? Let Penny take centre stage and organise the obsequies all her own way, it will be compensation for never getting a wedding. Instead of my daddy giving her away she can give away my daddy.'

Jacob was already revving the Moke when they got back to the shop.

'What do you do all day?' she had to ask; the inertia of the place was stultifying.

'I drink, I get stoned, sometimes I read. Porn mostly. Jacob knows a good supplier, don't you my brave fellow?'

'You ought to read this,' Felicity said reaching into her bag and fishing out *Beginning and Ending*. 'Your er ... boy, Henry Blackburn, gave it to me. It is good, better than porn, I imagine.'

'I've read it. It is trash.' He snatched the book and threw it hard and high into the midst of the standing cane.

'Now I know you are Felix,' said Felicity.

'God you are stupid, Flicky. Stupid but lovely. I will always love you, you know that.'

Looking back she saw him, his arm raised and his wrecked body enveloped in a dusty cloud, like smoke.

★   ★   ★

When Adrian came looking for Felicity the following afternoon she had already decided to fly home. She had seen enough of tropical Heaven and found it hard to distinguish between it and earthly Hell.

'Mission accomplished?' he asked.

'I don't know,' Felicity replied. 'I don't know who I saw.'

'Neither do I,' Adrian replied. 'I wasn't there.'

'Tell me, Adrian. Do people talk about Felix?'

'No. Not now. There was a great to-do when his mother visited, just a month or so before she died. That must have been about six years ago at least.'

'Surely she didn't stay with him then?'

'Lord, no. She went to Sandy Lane.'

'On her own?'

'No, my dear, not in the slightest. Anyway, she went to visit her naughty little boy and the next day she flew home.'

'Why did she leave so quickly?'

'There was nothing she could do. Her son was in gaol, on remand for pushing, but thanks to some relative and colossal expenditure on a brilliant advocate there was no case to answer. After that furore subsided Felix seemed to disappear; several people assumed he had died. Healthwise he was in shocking shape.'

'Is that man I saw yesterday him?'

'As I told you, sweetie, I do not know. His affairs don't affect me, never have done,' Adrian snapped, picking at a hangnail.

'Well that is all right then.' Felicity felt that while she may have given the apple cart a lurching shove she hadn't actually upset it. 'Thank you for your help, Adrian. Can I take a message to England for you?'

'No my dear. I don't think you would deliver it. Goodbye, safe journey. Next time consider the Med for a weekend break.'

She was keen to go home to where she was needed.

Rob's voice spoke on the answering machine: he must have wanted to have a lie-in and not be bothered by early morning farm business. The long beep sounded and Felicity spoke.

'Rob, darling. It is me. I have decided to come home early.

I'll explain later. I'll be back in time to cook your breakfast. Byee!'

She was exhausted. The flight home had been short thanks to a tail wind, and she hadn't slept. The long-term car park was impossibly bleak at that early hour but once she was on the road with *Today* on the radio and the heating at full strength she knew she had done the right thing. She would give Rob a big kiss, a big breakfast and listen to his tedious hunter's tales with enthralled delight. She would shut out all other thoughts and learn to enjoy what she had got.

She rang Rob again while filling the car at a petrol station. More pips sounded before the long tone: he must be sleeping late, too tired to take his messages. She remembered that Anna had gone to stay with a friend for her college's half-term holiday.

Rob's labradors covered her with kisses and wagged their whole rumps with delight. It was wonderful to be home.

Bacon smell wafted from the kitchen. Rob couldn't have got her message, he was cooking for himself, bless his heart.

The kitchen door opened. 'Come and get it, Robbie darling!'

Penny Blackburn was holding a fish slice, ridiculous in a hideous négligée, frothing all over in whipped-cream lace, white and bridal.

6

Penny Blackburn had gone north to scatter Digby's ashes at Tulliebrae. The General died the day after Penny told him she had caught a man at last. She said he had died happy, at peace with the world. Digby had died of cancer unvisited by any son or grandson. 'You'll love Rob, I know you will,' were Penny's last words to the man she would always believe to be her father.

Penny hoped, just in case, that the will included a clause referring to grandchildren in *ventre sa mère*. Mr Bastion was being rather cagey and had appointed a younger member of his firm to assist him in his application for probate. Proving the will was going to take time and consume much of what was there to be inherited. Regrettably the late General's affairs were far from straightforward, he informed Penny gleefully after she had instructed his firm to look sharp and get a move on.

Henry Blackburn, as the only known grandchild, had gone north too but without his mother. Angelica's diary was far too full to include the disposal of a father-in-law's remains. No other family members witnessed Digby's ashes wafting over his unfulfilled expectations, nor had any been present at the cremation.

Penny was planning a gala of a memorial service, with choirs and buglers, bishops and top brass to tea at the Cavalry Club after St James's, Piccadilly. She would wear navy. Next year, for her wedding she planned a silk suit in peach.

Rob told Felicity he was committed to Penny and had been so for over a year, speaking of his adultery as if it were an ill-conceived corn contract. He apologised sincerely and Felicity realised that he was pleading for her to fight for him to stay. She didn't, possibly because she knew that she would win. No side of the triangle made mention of love but Rob looked pitifully doleful.

Felicity's feelings had been hurt. She could not believe what had happened but after the first incredulity and the subsequent furious distress she became resigned and indifferent to his infidelity and set about starting a life alone.

Rob moved out of Church Farm and went to stay in London while arrangements were made for Felicity to move into Oxford. It was all quite convenient really, considering the winter drilling was all up to date and he could easily use London as a base from which to hunt and shoot. In other words, Rob's life was not much disrupted by the new turn in his domestic arrangements. Though his conscience and his heart bothered him considerably, he reassured his mother and sister that everything was fine.

Lady Jean said she had seen the collapse of his marriage coming and, given the circumstances, what else should they have expected? They must all buck up and make the best of it; after all, it wasn't as if Rob and Felicity had children, as such. In her grandmother's eyes Anna, at seventeen, was no longer a child. Pricilla said that at last Rob had got someone to partner him at bridge, adding that had she been a non-player like Felicity and married to an enthusiast like Rob she would have made it her business to learn. Such fun they would all have in the future at Church Farm with her mother and herself making up a four with Rob and his Penny.

Anna had arrived at the Royal Academy unprofessionally late. She had got confused on her way out of the underground at Baker Street and taken several wrong turns. The queue at Madame Tussaud's was hopeless, all foreigners with blank faces and as helpful as characters in a bad dream. A busker interrupted 'Yesterday' to put her right. She put twenty pence in his guitar case and hoped his impoverished condition was not an evil omen.

'I knew your mother. We were at Fairweathers together.' The woman was kindly looking and neat, a precise and dedicated musician who had devoted her life to nurturing the talented and helping the gifted to achieve distinction. This was meant to be an informal interview but nevertheless Anna felt sick. Nerves bothered her and being constantly reminded about where her talent came from made her want to smash the violin and scream

'Listen you lot! Look here! I am me, not just a bit of Mum's knitting.'

'Your mother was such a gifted musician. She would have been a great professional.' That stung too.

'Yes,' Anna replied. 'My mother can't play any more but she is still a musician.' Inside she seethed. Did they need to imply that her mother had died with her career hopes? Her mother was gifted, her grandmother was gifted and now she, the latest recipient of this extra-special present, was lumbered with the gift too. Thanks were due for everything: she had been brought up to write ecstatic letters even when she was given the wrong kind of bicycle basket instead of the Barbie doll she had craved. Thanks to being gifted, she must make use of her talents. Then the sacrifices would be justified and Felicity would be comforted. Loss would be annihilated by the daughter starting a musical career where the mother had been forced to stop. The star is dead! Long live the star!

Anna wished for courage to rebel and give the pricks some telling kicks. She was both angry and sad. She knew what had happened between her parents. She had seen it coming, only no one had listened. She hated her father for his deceit, she hated her mother for being deceived and she hated Penny Blackburn for everything. Today, in this audition, she hated the panel, the accompanist and herself. London pigeons flapped past the Academy windows, free to fly, crap and coo wherever they fancied. They were hateful too.

Despite her mood, Anna played well. She could sense that her performance was impressive and when it was over, she was convinced of success.

However much she loved music she felt that the mantle she had inherited was a strait-jacket. It wasn't fair. Other candidates who were desperate for a place would fall short.

During the interview her violin attracted considerable interest. 'It belongs to my mother.'

'And what a joy it must be for her to hear you play. Do you know its history?'

'No, only that it had to be mended twenty years ago. It got smashed at a party.' Anna began to giggle. Said like that, it sounded as if the fiddle had an uproarious life of its own.

'That is better. Smile, Anna. You will be fine one day if you practise and work hard. However . . .' her mother's schoolfriend leant towards Anna confidentially, intending friendship and encouragement. 'We do not feel that you are quite ready to come here. You lack polish and also you seem a little bit short of dedication. Think about it and after you have thought, next year maybe, give it another go. Our standards are very high: this place only accepts the outstanding. You possibly have the makings of a competent musician. Your family must be proud of you.'

Anna could hardly believe what had happened. She had done her best, there was nothing better to come. She had failed. This could deal her mother the *coup de grâce*.

'Cheer up! It may never happen,' the porter said as she walked out into Euston Road.

'I think it already has,' Anna replied.

She could not go home, not yet. She couldn't face her fractured family with the news. The Greens would be indifferent to her failure, they never did think much to music, but her mother would be pulverised. At least Penny wasn't likely to turn up to be helpful in this crisis now that her previous staunch support had transpired to be a bulldozer poised to demolish Anna's family.

Walking back towards Baker Street, Anna decided she had better delay going home yet a bit. I am not a child any more, she thought as she bought herself ten Benson and Hedges and a book of matches. I am grown up enough to drive, to marry and to be in charge of myself. She entered the Globe and spent most of the remains of her pocket money on a double whisky. She didn't like the taste but loved the warmth and comfort. She was new to cigarettes but could just manage without spluttering. The pub was a refuge for those with bleak homes and flats without souls, lonely bedsitter dwellers homeward bound from deadly jobs gathered there for a bit of fuggy humanity. Anna tried not to let defeat strangle her hopes. Dismissing depressing thoughts with the help of a second drink she watched the television until, feeling stronger, she started for home as yet uncertain as to how she should break the news of her failure to her mother.

It was two stops to Paddington.

The whisky had taken effect and given her confidence a fillip.

The man beside her was perfectly polite. He looked at the label on her fiddle case.

'Excuse me. Please don't mind me asking, but is your mother called Felicity?'

'Yes,' Anna replied. She hoped her voice didn't sound slurred. 'Felicity Green. She used to be called Campbeltown, before she married you know.'

'You are the image of her. Are you a violinist too?'

'No,' Anna replied. 'I'm not any more. I have just failed for music college. I'm going home to tell my parents now.' She hiccuped. 'Sorry, I needed Dutch courage. Oh Christ, this isn't Paddington it is Euston Square!' Suddenly she felt no longer in control, unable to cope. Another hiccup; it sounded like a sob.

'Don't worry, you have got on the eastbound line by mistake. Change at King's Cross, I'll show you where to go.'

19 November 1987

Felicity and Rob sat in the hospital waiting room with other stunned relatives. Thirty-one people were dead, burnt to death at King's Cross. The Greens were lucky: Anna was one of the few survivors. Smoke had damaged her lungs but her injuries were slight; she could be discharged shortly though the shock would continue and the sights she had seen would haunt her for the rest of her life.

Rob tried to be a comfort by patting Felicity's hand, which she withdrew. There were worse troubles at sea, he suggested with a quiver to his voice, things could have been worse, much worse he whispered. The couple opposite were clinging to each other convulsed with grief. Felicity didn't dare speak: she hated Rob then more than she had ever thought possible. Soon he would urge her to count blessings. Muzak moaned reassuringly about rocks and islands.

Somehow Anna had been guided through the smoky maze of tunnels up into the air while others were carried down the escalator into the inferno to join those poor souls who had got off the train to a death as certain as if they had arrived at Auschwitz. Anna had seen a man on fire stumbling towards

232

her, his scalp seared and flames leaping from his mouth. She had smelled the stench of the incinerators and heard the screams of the damned.

Anna was in a high white bed, swathed in a white gown, staring straight ahead like a corpse propped up by pillows. Despite the overstretched staff's best efforts, greasy grime was still embedded in her skin, her nails were filthy black and Felicity almost choked as she kissed her, the stench of her reeky hair was so strong.

'Anna, darling, thank God you are safe.'

'Don't cry, Mum. I'm just fine. Where is Dad?'

'Over there, talking to the doctor.'

'Mum, I am sorry.'

'What about? Darling, there is nothing to be sorry for. You are all that matters. You are alive – what possible reason could you have to be sorry? You mean everything to me. To us.'

'Mum, I've lost your violin.'

'But not your life. Darling Anna, did you think I would worry about an old fiddle? We will get you another one, a better one, the very best to celebrate your survival.'

'I want to tell you before Dad gets here. I want to tell you how it happened.'

'All right my love, I am listening. Don't distress yourself. What did happen?'

'A man went back for it. I left it behind, and he went back and now he is dead.' Anna shook with sobs, Felicity held her tight.

'My darling, was he a special man?'

'No, just a man. An old man. He had been talking to me on the train.'

'Was he trying to pick you up?'

'No. Not at all. Anyway, he was old. He had known you when you were young. He said he recognised me as being your daughter: that, and the violin, he read the label. Oh God, he went back. He went back just to fetch the violin. He died rescuing a lump of wood and bits of string.'

Felicity put her arms round Anna. 'Don't you cry, darling. You don't know that he died. He is probably as alive and well as you are. Have you any idea of his name? Apart from being old, what did he look like?'

'I can't remember.'

'Was he tall or fat, did he have a beard? Surely you can remember that much.'

'No. I don't think he was any of that. I know his hands looked tanned. I remember that. Oh yes, he didn't wear a wedding ring. I always notice wedding rings on men. I hate them.'

Felicity saw that Anna was at cracking point. It wasn't fair to question her, everything would come to light in time. The list of casualties would be published soon. Then, if the poor man had been killed, they would know who it had been and would try to cope with Anna's anguish. Felicity was certain that he would have survived: no one would really go back into the flames just to fetch a violin. Anna was in shock, she mustn't blame herself for something that probably didn't happen. An old man? The only old man she could think of was Cedric Tullie and he was in Dumfriesshire scattering Digby to the four winds. Anyway, Felicity told herself, Cedric wouldn't be seen dead on the tube. She wished she hadn't thought of such a tasteless image. Uncle Lionel was another old man who had known her when she was young but Aunt Fay never let him out on the loose from Kilbole. Perhaps it had been a doctor friend of her father or one of Myra's old Fabians. There were lots of possibilities.

Rob had finished talking to the doctor. He looked at his little girl and felt himself about to cry. He took a spotty handkerchief out of his pocket and gave his nose a hearty blow. Felicity had given him the hankie in last year's Christmas stocking. She was overwhelmed with misery on realising she wouldn't be giving Rob silly presents ever again. Her anchor and stability, her passport to a secure old age, her man, her husband, all of that was gone. She was alone. She also knew now how fond she had been of Rob. Nineteen years of marriage do not end sweetly, and maybe need not have ended had she not let her silly fantasies trap her into foolish adventures.

'Come on, Anniepop. Cheer up, chicken!' Rob smiled at his

234

daughter with such tenderness and she smiled back, happy to be comforted like a child. Felicity looked away remembering her own father and how he had always been able to put things straight better than her mother who would do anything to take her children's hurts upon herself but got too involved to be an unbiased support.

'Anna has lost the violin, Rob. I told her not to worry and promised her you would buy her another one, a better one.'

'Of course. The best available, the best my money can buy my chicken, if that is what you want.'

'Thanks, Dad, but no thanks. I don't want another violin.'

Felicity gasped. 'But darling you can't be without your own instrument. You must have another one to play. Anyway I am sure the insurance will pay something towards a replacement.'

'No, I don't want one.'

'But how will you manage? What will you do when you go to college?'

'I am not going to college.' Anna looked down at her stumpy nails with their narrow rim of black mourning. 'I want to grow my nails long and paint them puce. I want to travel round the world. I don't want to be a musician. I am not some poor bloody royal, forced by birth to inherit a job they don't want to do.'

Felicity did understand: her goal was not Anna's any more. Withstanding disappointment was tough, accepting failure and the death of hope was a hard knock for a parent. She had known, but had failed to acknowledge, that only her own ambition had been the impetus behind her child. Now she understood how her own mother had felt when the accident had ended all her musical prospects. If Anna had children they must be allowed to grow up free to choose, not trapped by parental aspirations.

'I expect you will feel differently about it once we get you home,' said Rob.

'No I won't. I don't want to come home either, not now it has been wrecked.'

'Supposing Mum and I stayed together, would that make

235

you happy?' Rob put his arm round Felicity and kissed her cheek, the couple play-acting their devotion for the pleasure of their public.

A nurse smiled as she went past pushing another survivor in a wheelchair, unrecognisable behind a coating of dressings.

'No. It is too late. That is ridiculous. Why should you do something just to please me any more than I should go to some boring music college just to please you? I couldn't stand another year of watching you pretend. Anyway, Penny has got her claws into you, she won't let you go. Not now.'

'I am sure you shouldn't be upsetting yourself, darling,' said Felicity. 'I do understand, really I do. Let's get you organised. Come home for a bit anyway, I promise you Dad and I won't fight. Will we, Rob?'

Rob wasn't listening. He was pretending to study an incomprehensible graph on the bed end; he didn't seem like a man much in love. Anna was right. Penny was not going to give him up.

'Mum and I are very proud of you, Anna,' he said. 'I am sorry, I didn't realise quite how grown up you had become.'

'That is because you only had one child.'

Penny took her father's death upon her chins. She was triumphant in love and had little emotion left for being bereaved. His death had been expected, unlike her mother's fatal attack. Penny and Joan had never been close, due, quite possibly, to their vast physical differences. Joan had been a blue-eyed blonde fairy, Penny was a muddy troll. They had very little in common and Joan had always bullied Penny to take a grip, get pretty and grab a man before it was too late. Joan couldn't understand the problem and had never forgiven her daughter for lacking allure, as if sex appeal were something one could acquire along with uplifting underwear and a good manicure. Any man would do, within reason. Any man except one, and he was dead. Joan, like Sheila Campbeltown, had gone along with the popular belief that Wolf had died in Nepal. Penny had never been given any reason to disbelieve this and Digby had been delighted with the tidiness of it all. Mother and daughter did share a healthy sexual appetite but Penny's, unlike Joan's, suffered from bad packaging.

Rob didn't mind Penny being large, and enjoyed her lumbering enthusiasm. All Penny's parts were sturdy, complete and in good working order, though lovemaking was like cavorting with an ecstatic hippo whereas Felicity had been a placid gazelle.

Cedric Tullie had taken to young Henry Blackburn enormously and couldn't imagine how a philistine like Felix could have fathered such a cultivated son. Henry, to his mind, was the heir of his dreams. Not only did Henry appreciate the fine architecture of Tulliebrae but he also appeared captivated by the few remaining orchids and not at all hostile towards the last dachshund. Cedric's heir was a sensitive epicurean, capable of appreciating great art and the marquess grieved about having sold some of his best Sèvres to spare them from Mrs Bolsover's savaging duster. Being elderly in a huge house cost a fortune; the insurance alone was crippling and something had to give if Cedric was to stay at Tulliebrae till he died. Judging by his chipper condition he would last till long after the rest was dust. Some of the proceeds had been spent constructing a lift, which made all the difference now that Mrs Bolsover was no longer man enough to support him up and down stairs. Bolsover had been expelled to the gardens, where he studied seed catalogues over the vestiges of Cedric's cellar and littered the borders with loud petunias and jolly nasturtiums.

Anna had her damaged hair cut, grew her nails and decided to go to Boston to work as au pair to her Aunt Ailsa until she had earned enough to move on, or had run out of patience with the precocious junior Schmidts. It was mid-December when Felicity drove her to the airport in a blizzard.

'Mum?'

'Yes darling?'

'You know Auntie Penny.'

'Too well, Anna. What a ridiculous thing to ask.'

'Don't, Mum. Don't be flip, I'm serious.'

'So am I. Come on, spit it out. God this weather is appalling, your flight will probably be delayed for hours.'

'Penny told me that Dad was her first love and that you stole him from her. Is that true?'

'No, not exactly. Actually, not at all. Penny had a crush on someone else, long before she met your father.'

'Who, Mum?'

'His name was Wolfgang Duncan.'

'And did this Wolfgang man love her?'

'No, darling. He loved me.'

The wipers raced against the driving sleet piling at the windscreen's edge. Anna lit a cigarette and Felicity hadn't the heart to stop her. 'Did you love him back, Mum?'

'Yes, darling I did. Why do you ask?'

'I want to know. Penny keeps telling me horrible things about you. I hate it. She says you chased her old cousin and you did drugs.'

'I think you might find that Penny is trying to justify herself by distorting the truth,' said Felicity with admirable restraint. 'Bloody cow,' she added, under her breath.

'That's better, Mum. I'm sick of you all being so adult.'

'We are adults.'

'Oh yes? Did you know that the bloody cow calls Dad her Knobby Robbie?'

'Yuck!' said Felicity and felt cross and injured as if someone had criticised her child or reprimanded a family dog.

'Are you still in love with Wolf, Mum?'

'Only with his memory.'

'Is he dead?'

'I honestly don't know. Maybe he is; maybe he has changed. Twenty-one years is more than a lifetime.'

'Have you seen him since you were all young?'

'I don't know. I may have. I hope I haven't. Sorry, darling. I don't want to talk about it any more. Anyway, here we are. Grab a trolley and we'll get you checked in.'

The check-in queue was long and slow. The Christmas rush to fly away was already building and canned carols, tinsel and flame-proofed plastic greenery pervaded the shops and concourses of the terminal. Anna suddenly gasped and grabbed Felicity's arm. 'Look, Mum. Look, I know him!'

'Who, darling?' said Felicity looking round expecting to see some pop star who was probably quite unknown to her.

'Here in the paper. Look!'

GENERAL'S SON SOUGHT.

The estranged son of the late General Sir Digby (Dingo) Blackburn who died last month has disappeared. Last heard of in the West Indies in 1981 Felix Blackburn has not made himself known to his grieving sister. A double blow has struck nursery school owner, Penelope Blackburn, whose forty-two-year-old brother is now the heir to his bachelor cousin, the Marquess of Tullie. Their mother, popular hostess, Lady 'Joanie' Blackburn, died abroad six years ago.

A picture of Felix taken at the time of his arrest was printed beside the text. 'I am sure I know him, Mum.'

'Who?' Felicity studied the picture. It could have been a younger and healthier version of the man in Barbados.

'Where have you seen him, darling?'

'I can't remember. Oh yes! He looks like the man I spoke to on the train. Yes that is him, I am sure it is.'

Fry, Pride and Harping had moved their offices from Gray's Inn on merging with Kiplin and Cripplegate and were now housed in a glass and steel edifice with an art-filled atrium. Mr Bastion lamented this turn of events more acutely than most because he suffered from vertigo and could only make the journey from the lift to his office by hugging the wall and refusing to think about the deep central well that existed dizzyingly beyond the toughened glass that ran round each gallery level. His slatted blinds were kept shut to conceal the Thames panorama which was obscured by murky weather anyway on the day that Felicity called. Christmas parties seemed to be on all floors and the giggling receptionist who had directed her to the correct lift and level wore a Santa Claus red bobble hat.

'Who advised you to refuse the General's wish for you to be one of his executors, Mrs Green?'

'My husband. You may not have heard, Mr Bastion, but he and Penny Blackburn are now living together, as man and wife.'

'Good gracious!' said Mr Bastion. 'I had no idea that Miss Blackburn's cohabitee was your husband, Mrs Green. Have you instructed solicitors to act in your divorce? This firm has many excellent members.'

'I'm sure, Mr Bastion, but we haven't got as far as that yet and anyway I couldn't afford your fees. I'm here on another matter altogether.'

Mr Bastion already knew of Felicity's Barbados visit and had employed an investigator to look for the Right-On Rum Shop and its proprietor. He brightened with every complicated twist in Felicity's story of recent events. Digby Blackburn's will was to be Mr Bastion's final turn: at over seventy he should have been retired but he had no home life or hobby to make idleness attractive and the more convoluted the winding up of his schoolfellow's affairs, the more his inertia was postponed.

'And do you feel your daughter is correct in her assumption that the man who returned for her instrument was indeed Mr Blackburn?'

'I don't know. She is truthful; she wouldn't lie, if that is what you mean.'

'No no! I am not questioning her veracity, just her reliability in such traumatic circumstances. After all, you say you do not know which of the General's sons you met in Barbados.'

'Quite, Mr Bastion. Is there no further news from there?'

'None, alas. The licensed premises you visited have evidently been demolished and our investigator has failed to locate anyone called Felix Blackburn or Wolfgang Duncan or a native gentleman of your description answering the name of Jacob.'

'What about the Englishman called Adrian?'

'Not at all helpful, I fear.'

As they parted Mr Bastion and Felicity wished each other a most unlikely Merry Christmas.

*   *   *

240

Rob had an uncomfortable Christmas with his mother and sister, missing Felicity and not pining for Penny.

Henry Blackburn, his mother and aunt went with his grandparents to the Ritz where they ate lavishly and pulled crackers without conviction. Angelica looked grim in her party hat, like Marie Antoinette wearing the cap of liberty. Penny promised them a real family Christmas next year at Church Farm, with all the trimmings, she said. After all, Christmas is a time for children. Henry winced as he saw his plump aunt simper.

Mr von Hoffer paid the bill.

Henry disliked taking his grandmother on her annual Boxing Day visit to her mother's grave in Golders Green: not that he wanted to go hunting or shooting like his contemporaries, but it would have been nice to have had an invitation to refuse.

The Irvine bus ran over John Begg in 1985 but Sheila Campbeltown still talked to him and thought they went for walks, whereas in reality she spent most of her time looking out of the Shieling's windows expectantly, quite at a loss to know what or who she was awaiting. Isa could cope with the repeated questions and anxiety; to her it was a job. Felicity was too close. She felt hemmed in and frantic. Her mother was driving her up the wall.

'Well this is a nice surprise. Are you staying long?' Sheila asked for the twentieth time, her face lit with a gentle joy of delight on discovering her daughter in her house even though Felicity had arrived the previous afternoon.

'Just the week, Mother,' Felicity answered yet again and as she would at least once an hour throughout her visit.

'Shall I make you some porridge, Ailsa?'

'I'm Felicity, Mother, and I don't like porridge.'

'Your father does,' Sheila replied defensively. 'He never goes without. I made porridge for the other man too.'

'What other man, Mother?'

'The man that isn't here.'

Felicity laughed and tried to reassure her mother. 'Are you saying "he wasn't here again today, and you wish that man would go away"?'

'Don't talk nonsense, Flicky, please. The wee lad brought the fiddle.'

'What wee lad, Mother? You said it was a man . . . and I have no fiddle any more.'

'Don't muddle me, darling. The wee lad was Wolf, that was his name, he brought the fiddle for you. He stays on Arran.'

'No, Mother, Wolf used to spend his holidays there with some people called Otway. He did come by once and gave me his fiddle after the fireworks when mine got burnt on the bonfire. That was a long, long time ago.'

'Was it, Flicky? Well you know best but I am sure you are wrong. His name isn't Otway, you know, not that, just something a bit like it.'

'Duncan is nothing like Otway,' said Felicity. 'You are getting me muddled too.'

'Oh Flicky, I wish I could remember what I wanted to tell you.' Sheila's lost look passed and she began to get agitated again. 'Do you not think you should be going? You won't want to be late, you know. It is not a nice day for a boat trip.'

'I am not going anywhere on a boat, Mother, wherever did you get that idea?'

'I don't know, somewhere inside. Flicky, wouldn't it be grand if we had a good turnout?'

'What do you want to turn out, Mum?'

'My head, for a start, Flicky.'

It was not that Felicity hadn't tried, it was just that she couldn't succeed. The real Christmas tree she bought leant at a dangerous angle and shed its needles the moment the crushed fairy had been impaled on its crooked leader. The lights, which she had discovered still stored in their original ballerina box, were crotchety old-fashioned trade unionists. 'One out, All out' was their motto.

Lionel and Fay Braid came for Christmas Day and brought along their own miniature frosted plastic tree, an evil device that revolved while tinkling a parody of 'Silent Night'. 'Personal misfortunes are no excuse for not celebrating Our Lord's birth,' said Fay as she wound the mechanism.

Felicity steered her mother to the piano stool and sat beside her at the treble end. At first Sheila was too flustered, she couldn't remember anything, she looked at the notes with disbelief as if meeting them for the first time. After Felicity had picked out several simple carols with her good hand and vamped the bass as best she could, her mother began to relax. Felicity gave her an encouraging hug. 'Go on, Mum.'

Sheila's hands were stiff but after the first few notes she just managed to produce a recognisable tune: it was 'The Merry Peasant', the scourge of her professional life, played by every one of her pupils, promising and useless alike.

Fay looked up from close inspection of the monkey band in the glass-fronted cabinet. 'You should live here, Felicity, it is your duty.'

'Mum and I would fight.'

'What was that?' Sheila asked.

'I said you and I would fight if I stayed too long.'

Sheila smiled to herself, a secret shared with someone somewhere else. 'When are you going, Felicity? You should be away back to your man directly.'

'I'll be off the minute Isa gets home, Mother. I promise.'

'Where is that woman anyway?' Fay asked.

'Germany, Aunt Fay.'

'She has never gone abroad! Whatever next?'

'She is staying with Hanne. She used to work for Miss Duncan at Glamis Towers. They have remained friends. It was Hanne's stepson that married Ailsa.'

Suddenly Sheila's face lit up. 'I remember. Hanne was the girl that Lionel got fresh with in the shed on Coronation Day. What a to-do! Magnus was quite amazed. We all were. Fancy Lionel and that buxom German lass. How we laughed!'

Fay was white with indignation. 'Your mother is mad, Felicity, quite mad. She should be locked up. Come along, Lionel we are leaving.'

Felicity watched the old couple as they crossed the unraked gravel towards the gate where some joker had, yet again, changed the name from 'The Shieling' to 'The Smelling'. Lionel was carrying the presents; the tip of their tinsel Christmas tree poked out of his holdall as Fay clutched at his arm to steady herself. After nearly fifty years of animosity they were still together. Felicity almost envied them.

7

BY LEAVING KILBOLE early, before Isa returned, Felicity was sure to get to Oxford before it was dark. She did not relish arriving at an empty strange house after nightfall and groping about for switches and stopcocks. The little rented house in Hayfield Road was not yet used to her any more than she was to it. The plumbing had its whims and the locks their caprices.

The Sunbeam Percussionists were longing to welcome their conductor back. It had been humiliating asking to withdraw her resignation but Grania had been thoroughly compassionate and madly understanding and re-employed Felicity on a part-time basis, albeit at a lower rate, for which it was compulsory to be most grateful. Grania had said that major life events, grief and loss and change, must be addressed head on and shared. She was quite right of course but immensely grating.

Leaving her mother had been difficult. Sheila had become very anxious for Felicity to come and see something in her cupboard just as the car was loaded and ready to go.

'I remember now,' said Sheila. 'I want you to look at something.'

'What is it, Mum?'

'I can't remember.'

'Well I am sure it can wait. I will be up again soon and Isa will be in shortly.'

'Don't go, Flicky. I want to tell you something.'

'Yes Mum, what?'

Sheila looked about as if she had mislaid her thought like a pair of glasses. 'It's gone,' she sighed.

'Well then, so am I. I will ring you very, very soon. Be good, Mum, I do love you.'

'How kind,' said Sheila absently. 'Just put it on my bill.'

Sometimes Sheila failed to recognise her home and imagined herself in a hotel.

Felicity went south via the quickest, central route, deliberately avoiding Tulliebrae. On her way north she had been delayed by the hunt and had joined the stream of cars going up to the house. An old man wrapped up in a rug had been watching the end of the chase from the first-floor entrance at the top of the double steps. She had recognised Cedric Tullie and was suddenly terrified of being caught snooping. Mindless of etiquette, she had turned her car and driven off at speed, ignoring the rage of the hunt followers whose sport she was disrupting.

Amongst the heap of circulars on the mat when she pushed the door open in Oxford that evening were two letters, both heartily addressed by Penny. One was from Hanne and had been redirected (after being steamed open) and the other was from Penny herself demanding a meeting with Felicity. They had things to talk over, she said, things to be sorted out in an adult fashion.

'Bitch!' shrieked Felicity and flung the letter in the bin with great force. She couldn't face reading Hanne's six pages of green writing on onion paper till later. She needed to get settled into her new loneliness and used to being able to please herself, no longer concerned with keeping others well contented. She turned on the fire and sat on the floor with an apple and a lump of Cheddar wearing wool tights and an Aran sweater and puffing on a cigarette between bites. The solo life was not that bad, really it wasn't.

Two nights later just as novelty was being elbowed by melancholy the doorbell rang.

'How did you know where to find me? Come in, Henry, please.'

Henry Blackburn was standing on the pavement, getting drenched. He was neatly dressed in a good tweed jacket and cords, holding an azalea.

'You are soaked, Henry. Give me your jacket before you get pneumonia, I'll lend you a sweater.'

'You are behaving like a mother.'

'I am older than your mother, Henry. Look at your shoes,

they are sodden. You need to be nagged about the perils of damp feet.'

'This is for you,' he said handing her the pot plant. 'I wanted to give you an orchid but the shop was shut.'

'Thank goodness for that. I detest orchids. This is lovely, thank you very much. You mustn't get cross if it dies. I am not good at making plants happy. Have a drink. Whisky?'

'I'd rather have champagne.'

'I've got a bottle of white Château Tesco, would that do?'

'Housewarmings merit something better.' He produced a bottle from a carrier bag. 'Where are the glasses?'

'Henry, you are sweet. That champagne looks very special.'

'It is. My father's cousin has sent me a crate for my twenty-first.'

'For a party surely?'

'I don't do parties.'

They sat either side of the black iron grate where pretend gas logs glowed and billowed obligingly, unlike the damp misshapen branches that spluttered and smoked at Church Farm. None of the furniture in the Hayfield Road house was hers, the curtains were truly nasty and the walls were painted in natural sludge but she had wired up her music and had been enjoying *Scheherazade* when Henry had arrived.

'I love this,' he said.

'It is the sexiest music I know,' Felicity replied. 'Apart from . . . Oh God, Henry what am I saying? Champagne always goes straight to my head these days. How did you know my address?'

'My aunt has it pinned up on the kitchen noticeboard.'

'Her kitchen noticeboard?'

'No, yours.'

'Is Penny installed at Church Farm?'

'She had to sell the nursery school lock, stock and Lego. Her pupils' parents didn't like irregular morals in their headmistress despite most of them leading most exotic and disorderly lives. She has taken on the lease of Grandpapa's basement in Down Street where he lived after Grandmama died.'

'Where is Down Street?'

'Mayfair, the polite bit between Piccadilly and Shepherd

Market. It was handy for Grandpapa because it was within strolling distance of all his clubs. He belonged to six. On Sundays he ate sandwiches in Green Park. Anyway, now Penny spends most of her time in the country.'

'Has she taken over everything, including my husband?'

'No, not yet, especially not him. He looks miserable.'

'You are just saying that to be tactful.'

'No, it's true. He looks dreadfully cowed.'

'Poor Rob.'

They sat in silence while Felicity thought about what she had just said. She was sorry for Rob, she always had been. She had married him to be her lifebelt, not her life's love to sail away with in a beautiful pea-green boat and now Penny was using him as a ferry to carry her to the comfort of family life. She smiled at Felix's son. 'I am sorry, Henry. I forgot to say how sad I was about your grandfather.'

'I never did visit him before he died.'

'I rather thought you wouldn't.'

Henry looked a bit downcast and then came to what Felicity assumed to be the real purpose of his visit. 'Aunt Penny wants to know who you saw in Barbados.'

'Oh yes? Is she getting you to be her messenger?'

'No she is not. I want to know too.'

'Henry I know it sounds ridiculous but I don't know whether it was your father I saw or, just possibly, someone who used to be like him, but greatly, horribly altered. Let me get us some blotting paper. Would an egg sandwich do? I've no flapjacks, I'm afraid.'

'You remembered my weakness?'

'Yes. And I must thank you for giving me *Beginning and Ending*. I've lost it, I'm afraid. It had an accident in Barbados, but after I'd finished it. You were right, it was wonderful. Has Thomas Whatsisname written anything else?'

'Tom Otterburn . . . no, not yet, at least not under that name. He is in his forties and travels a lot, according to the blurb.'

'I don't remember reading anything other than the text. Well, he's young enough to write much more.'

'Forty isn't young.'

'It isn't old, for God's sake.'

'Your Anna thinks anyone over thirty is geriatric. How is she? To have experienced that fire must have been terrifying for her, for all of you. She was very lucky to have escaped. There were so few survivors.'

Felicity told him about Anna's job in the States and about how she was suffering from recurring nightmares.

'Like flashbacks after a bad trip?'

'I suppose so. You don't take drugs, do you, Henry?'

'Of course not. Mummy said you were a bit of a swinger once, though.'

'Once and once only, Henry. Your father laced my drink with LSD. It was appalling. That was how the accident happened, when I lost my fingers. I don't like talking about it. I stick to this now,' she said raising her glass. 'Is there any more left in the bottle?'

'Masses,' Henry replied as he poured them both another glass. 'Does Anna talk about what happened to her?'

'A bit. Henry, tell me is there any news of your father?'

'Nothing at all. He seems to have vanished like Mephistopheles in a puff of smoke.'

Felicity cringed at the thought. Since Anna's departure she had scanned the lists of casualties and survivors but nothing in the aftermath of the King's Cross fire seemed to indicate that Felix or any other person known to her had been a victim. Anna must have been mistaken about the photograph, over-emotional and understandably harrowed with a fanciful imagination. Felicity didn't want to discuss her daughter's anguish with Felix's son.

Henry handed Felicity an ashtray. He didn't smoke. 'There is one man who no one has claimed. They are trying to reconstruct his face from the evidence of his remains in case it triggers someone's memory.'

'But this man wasn't what you'd call old, was he?'

'Everything is relative.'

A clammy grip squeezed her heart as she quickly changed the subject to music. Before Henry left he had arranged to go with Felicity to an organ recital at Exeter College the following week.

Hanne's writing was hell to decipher. Lotte Schmidt who (in

Hanne's words) was still being singular but living as a man and a wife with a lover who Hanne's husband, the Bürgermeister, was not much liking, was visiting London and would be wishing to renew her acquaintance with Felicity. No date or address was included amongst the flimsy pages so it was lucky that Lotte managed to make contact at all.

Lotte was prominent in corporate logistics and had been invited to deliver a paper at a conference on trans-European heritage management. 'Your housekeeper told me your Oxford number,' said Lotte in near-perfect English.

Felicity liked the idea of Penny being mistaken for her housekeeper. Husband keeper, home taker, marriage breaker, more likely. Poor Lotte would be disappointed to find that not only did Felicity have no housekeeper but she scarcely had a house to keep. They met on a thoroughly objectionable evening, damp and chilly with a sharp wind skirmishing round Oxford station.

'Felicity, hello. I have no difficulty in recognising you. You are not changed at all.' Lotte was the epitome of woman making good. Perfectly and sensibly groomed, beautifully and appropriately dressed and abounding in what women's magazines call poise. Felicity, by contrast, was an attractive mess, an artless wild flower, beside a well ordered house plant. She would not have recognised Lotte ever, the change in her was so great.

'I see you are surprised. I think your were expecting me to have two plaits and a dirndl skirt,' said Lotte kissing Felicity on both cheeks with confident politeness.

'Yes Lotte, I'm sorry, I was.'

'Maybe if I sing one of my mother's songs concerning Banbury Cross or Pussy Cats going to London you will be at ease.'

'No no, not that! It is wonderful to see you, I just had no idea you would be so grown up. Silly of me when you consider there is only about eight years between us. How is your mother? I haven't actually seen her since Ailsa and Dieter got married.'

'My mother is still the same, only she is very cross that I have given her no grandchildren yet.'

'She has Campbell and Iona to keep her happy.'

'America is far away and the children are so sophisticated,

they are not biddable like *Kinderlein* who dance in rings and play clapping games.'

'Are there children like that anywhere, Lotte? Actually I believe even my daughter Anna finds her niece and nephew a bit bumptious.'

'Bumptious! I love that word, straight out of a school story where wrongs get righted and the sneaks receive their come-uppance.'

'Your English is phenomenal, Lotte.'

'I had a good teacher, I want to tell you about him, that is one of the reasons I have come to see you.'

Lotte declared herself thrilled to be staying in the one spare bed in Hayfield Road. 'I am not at home in the country, Felicity. This is delightful,' she said tactfully as she saw the full extent of Felicity's new home. 'I do not think my mother knows all your troubles beyond the fact that you are parting from your husband. Maybe I did not listen well. I try to become deaf whenever she talks about marriage. My spinsterhood is a very delicate issue with her.'

'I have given up trying to explain that my marriage is over to my mother.'

Felicity suggested half-heartedly that Lotte might enjoy a harpsichord recital in the Holywell Music Room.

Lotte said she would prefer to stay in: she was tired and had seen enough heritage and discussed enough of its management to deserve a night off. She gave Felicity a squashed box of home-made biscuits that her mother had insisted she bring: the spicy crumbs smelled of ages ago, happy days of nursery teas and doorstep sandwiches.

'Help yourself to a drink, Lotte. There is a corkscrew here if you want to open the wine now.' Felicity had put her hand over the receiver while she talked to Lotte before resuming her conversation. 'Sorry, Henry, what were you saying? . . . Yes, I have got a friend to supper . . . Yes, Henry a girl friend, why? . . . Yes I promise you, she is called Lotte, come and see if you like . . . What is this interrogation, are you a spy for your Auntie Penny hoping to find me *in flagrante*? . . . Oh Henry, for goodness' sake. Yes I would love to go to that with you.

Merton on Thursday at seven-thirty? Perfect, I will see you there. Bye.'

'Have you got a lover, Felicity? Or am I being blunt?'

'No, Lotte. To be blunt, I haven't. Anyway, even if I had the chance, I don't want one.'

'Are you in love with anyone?'

'That is a very blunt question.'

'I ask you this because I used to hate you, Felicity.'

'Me, Lotte? Why? What had I ever done to make you do that? We haven't met since you were twelve. I hope you don't hate me now.'

'I could not now, I have no right. I should not have ever done so either. But I couldn't help it.'

'Like falling in love? How most odd. You must explain. I'm not being rude but to be honest, I don't believe I have thought of you much more than once in twenty years. You didn't even get to Ailsa's wedding as far as I can remember.'

'I was travelling. Australia was too far away to justify such a journey.'

'Quite. Have you travelled a lot?'

'A bit. Now I am based in West Berlin but I studied in the States and for eight years, up until two years ago, I worked in Holland. That is where it happened.'

'What happened, Lotte?'

'I met Wolf.'

Felicity clutched the edge of the table to steady herself. 'Oh, Lotte!'

'See. Now I think you understand why I hated you. Look at you, you and he are both the same – you are obsessed with each other. No one can get between you.'

'But Lotte, at that time I thought Wolf was dead.'

'So did most people. He was living a new life, with a new name. He has taken several new names and identities but he can never rid himself of his infatuation with you.'

'Oh Lotte, I can't bear it. But don't stop, tell me more. I must know. Is he greatly changed?'

'He is older, but I think his personality hasn't altered except with experience.'

'He hasn't become a drug addict, an alcoholic, a bitter, vile villain?'

Lotte laughed. 'No, none of these things as far as I know unless he has deteriorated rapidly during the last couple of years.'

'He hasn't gone to live in Barbados?'

'No. He would never go there except to make sure that his brother is provided for.'

'Wolf maintains Felix?'

'Yes. I'm telling you he is a very good man. I loved him. Why are you crying, Felicity? He loves you, you must find each other now, you belong together.'

'Where is he?'

'I do not know. Wait, he will come. Be patient.'

'Why hasn't he tried to find me before, Lotte?'

'He knew where you were, Felicity, and he knew you were married. He assumed you were happy and had no intention of disrupting your life or that of your family. His feelings went too deep for friendship.'

'Did your mother know about this, Lotte?'

'There are many things that my mother must not know. She is indiscreet, enthusiastic. Imagine her reaction if I told her I was living with her favourite charge. She would be ordering up hats, baking wedding cakes and knitting small garments, singing cradle songs and frightening the poor man as he had never been frightened before, and with the life he has led, believe me there have been many incidents to terrify him. Wolf, or Will as I knew him, has led a hazardous existence but even he is not equal to my mother's plans for my wedding. The nature of our work was not public property. My mother would compose a part-song for counter-agents and stitch E for Espionage on to vests.'

'Is that what you both were? Spies?'

'No.'

Felicity laughed. 'Sorry, that was an idiotic question.'

Lotte continued: 'Anyway, I decided I could not conduct a love affair while my mother was on alert to ring bells and throw rice. Besides, I knew our relationship would not last. Wolf, my dear Felicity, was always loyal to you. He smiled at you over my shoulder, he made love to you, not me, in our bed. I was just a stand-in, like an actor who fills spaces when the real star is absent. I relayed news of you to him from my mother, who always displayed your Christmas cards most prominently. He knew only good of your family life with Anna and Rob. Your smiling faces on the photographs of my half-brother's wedding to your sister betrayed no unhappiness.'

'Wolf saw that?'

'Yes. Our relationship was already fragile but it ended when I discovered he had cut out your face and kept it by him always. In the end I left. He was not sorry. He had been called away to do some work and when he returned, I was gone. He never looked for me, though I left many clues. All that is over. I have Georg now and he is not haunted by ghosts.'

'Lotte. Supposing he has met someone else. Maybe he is married with children by now.'

'It is possible. He is almost certain to have changed his name. While we were together he called himself William Schwartz most of the time. He used other names for some of his work but now . . . he could be anyone, anywhere.'

'If only he had known,' said Felicity. All those years of getting on with life, of putting up with substitutes, of pretending, flashed before her. She had deceived Rob all along the way; she had deceived herself. At least she had been spared the anguish of thinking the man she loved was alive during those moderately pleasant sessions of lovemaking, no more gratifying than a decent meal when slightly hungry. She remembered the nights when she had gone to bed early to avoid Rob and the times she had faked delight when he made love to her. She had faked everything: she didn't want to hurt his feelings. She had cared so little about her lack of enjoyment that she never sought help from anyone or any book. Sex could inflame her like great music, great art or a gulp of alcohol but it had lacked the essential ingredient that could raise it above mechanical gratification and transfigure it into love. After Rob had finished she felt satisfied, happy to have been entertained and to have had her immediate needs met. She had never got to Heaven.

'Lotte, I am sorry. I did not know. Had I known Wolf was alive and where he was I just can't imagine what I would have done. I might have been tempted to leave my husband long ago, or stayed on and been a good hypocrite.

You see, I cannot blame Penny or Rob for enjoying themselves.'

'I remember Penny was quite unattractive when she was
young. Is she still afflicted by a bad complexion and excessive fat?'

Felicity said that she was.

'But you are still a beautiful woman. Your husband must
be mad.'

'No, Lotte, not mad, just not prepared to be second best. You
know the feeling.'

Lotte left the next morning; she would be back in Berlin for
her afternoon round of meetings. She said she was pleased to
be returning to Georg, the architect with whom she shared
her bed. Georg and Lotte had an excellently convenient and
sensibly satisfactory relationship with the option of converting it
into something really lasting. For the moment, the negotiations
were at the preliminary stage.

Wolf might come, he might not. It might be too late. Quite
possibly the magic would evaporate in the light of reality. What
is known of courtly lovers after the quest is done and the lady
won? Living happily ever after is a giant order. Felicity told
herself all these things and was not comforted.

Every morning she awoke hoping. She jumped to answer the
telephone and never let the post lie long. The world revolved
and even the disappointed nights eventually developed into fresh
days. Hope was her fuel: without it she would have subsided into
the torpor of depression.

Penny was marking out her new territory. 'You are all I have
got now, Robbie darling and I mean to have you to myself.'
She occupied her time with bundling all Felicity's things – her
clothes, her books, her photographs – into empty Coarse Calf
Nut and Surelay Pellet bags before wheeling them off to the
vacant bull pen to incubate moulds. 'The piano takes up so much
room,' she sighed as she showed Rob the wonderfully chintzy
festoons she had installed in the drawing room. 'Don't you think
it could be sold?' Only empty photograph frames stood upon it
now awaiting new occupants.

'No, Penny, I'm sorry. That piano is for Anna.'

254

'Of course, my love. How silly of me. I am longing to be a really nice stepmother, as well as the other sort.' Penny smirked and looked down at her round but fruitless belly.

Rob pretended not to hear and went off to see whether the slugs were as bad as he feared. They were, which may have been why he was unreasonably cross about finding hanging loops inserted in his wellingtons and the cloakroom hooks labelled Rob, Penny, Dogs, Anna and Visitors. Rob hankered after Felicity. Penny knew this and was narked.

The Percussionists ran riot, clattering their castanets and bashing their cymbals at random. When the whole class refused to sing 'Lord of the Dance' Felicity took them out for a game of Grandmother's Footsteps which deteriorated into a roughhouse. 'You are not with us, Felicity,' said Grania. 'Have you something you wish to share?'

Felicity had a secret hope and it was not for sharing with anyone.

I must be mad, Felicity thought, on realising the full stupidity of what she had done. Why, for God's sake, had she let herself be trapped into inviting Penny for lunch? She could kick herself for having issued the invitation when Penny had rung requesting a meeting. 'Your place or mine?' Penny had asked breezily.

Instead of replying that she had rather thought both places were hers Felicity had lost her head and suggested Penny should come to Oxford. 'I am so glad you are prepared to be grown-up about all this,' said Penny.

On the appointed day Felicity looked out on to Hayfield Road and tried to derive inspiration from the terrace of brick cottages opposite. She waved at pregnant Thelma pushing Damon in his buggy on her way to Mirabelle's play group; she watched the bin men collect the black bags; she made another cup of coffee.

The telephone rang. It was Henry asking Felicity if she would come to his first night as Polonius.

'Of course, if I can.'

'Good. You can come to the party afterwards too.'

'But I am far too old for that. The party will be for your friends.'

'You are my best friend, Felicity.'

Sometimes Henry worried her. Oh well, back to the kitchen, she didn't want Penny to think she existed entirely on egg sandwiches and apples, which was in fact the case.

Henry rang again. Could Felicity hear his lines? 'Not until I have got rid of your aunt. Then I will see what I can do.'

'How about supper? I could take you somewhere really special to make up for having that harpie breathing your air.'

'We'll see. Call in later. Now I must get on. I am making a fish pie.'

'Are the fish off?'

'Utterly putrid and festering, laced with arsenic. See you later. Bye.'

Penny pursed her lips as if to kiss Felicity but was left poised to pounce upon air and a turned back.

'Come in,' Felicity commanded and Penny followed her into the sitting room which served as hall and dining room also. She sat beside the unlit fire and scrutinised the mantelpiece for invitations. There were none; only a flyer for a jumble sale and a postcard from Boston.

'I was wondering when you were coming to fetch your things,' said Penny.

'Why?' Felicity replied. 'I don't need them at the moment.'

After her final miscarriage Rob had given Felicity a Persian cat. Mr Mogford had been her personal property, but typical of his race, he had been most disloyal and independent and continued to live as and with whom he pleased. 'I really do not think Mr Mogford would like moving in here, he is very old and set in his ways,' said Felicity.

'I am afraid that cat is dead,' said Penny. 'He ate slug pellets.'

'You might have told me.'

'You didn't tell me about visiting Felix in Barbados,' Penny countered. 'Nor did you tell me why you visited my father when he was dying.'

'That was private. Your father promised to tell me something.'

256

'And did he?'

'Yes.'

'Is that why you went to Barbados?'

'Yes. Your father wanted to see both of his . . . er . . . children before he died. I tried to persuade Felix to come home.'

'So you did see Felix?'

'I did.' Felicity was now convinced this was true.

'How was he?'

'A wreck.'

'You are talking about my brother, remember.'

'I am only telling you the truth, Penny. It would be stupid to say he was well and prosperous and sent lots of love because he wasn't and he didn't. Anyway my absence in Barbados seemed to suit your plans very well. Such a lavish nightie – you looked like a prima donna cooking Rob's breakfast.'

'There is another thing,' said Penny, ignoring Felicity's last observation and getting up disapprovingly to tip a full ashtray on to the artificial logs. 'What have you got to say about my father's will?'

'Why? Nothing! Your father's will is nothing to do with me.'

'I understand Daddy wanted you to be an executor.'

'Yes but Rob told me not to, so I refused.'

'My Rob?'

'If you like, Penny. But I had been under the impression Rob was mine then.'

'Did you ask Daddy to leave you Mummy's sapphire brooch?'

'Of course not.'

'Well he has. Explain that!'

'I can't.'

'It is Blackburn property, it should come to me. I am his daughter, after all.'

So the will told no secrets. That at least was good news. Felicity was relieved: with luck, Digby had taken the truth of Wolf's birth to the grave too.

'I don't want sapphires, Penny. You keep it.'

Penny was a bit winded by that. She had expected Felicity to put up better defences. 'No, it was Daddy's wish but you must leave it to Anna. She will be my stepdaughter, after all.'

'Here, have some fish pie. You used to hate it when you were a child.'

Penny prodded the mess and pushed it aside. She crumbled her second bread roll, while Felicity lit a cigarette. 'Oh dammit, that is the telephone. Excuse me.'

Ailsa was ringing from Boston where it was early morning. Instead of diminishing, Anna's nightmares were much worse and more frequent. She needed help. Ailsa was coming over anyway and would bring her niece home.

'What about the children?' Felicity asked.

Campbell and Iona were being taken skiing by Dieter. It would be a good chance for them to bond with their father, Ailsa said. Felicity felt Grania might find much to share with her little sister. 'Poor Anna,' said Felicity. 'Can I speak to her?'

The doctor had been called and had sedated her. She was sleeping dreamlessly and deeply. Penny had been listening to Felicity's side of the conversation. When she heard Anna's name she left the room and went upstairs, presumably to find a loo. Christian Aid rang the bell and while Felicity answered the door, Penny quickly lifted the receiver beside Felicity's midget double bed.

'Sorry about that, Ailsa. My neighbour wants me to bring water to Africa. Please go on. Are the nightmares still only about the fire?'

'Yes, but her major problem is with the man she spoke with on the subway.'

'She thinks he was Felix, doesn't she?'

'That is right. She is sure she is responsible for his death,' Ailsa replied.

'Tell her there is no evidence at all to support her theory. No one even faintly like Felix has been found.'

'She has heard that there is one man unaccounted for.'

'Oh no. Poor Anna. If only I could help.'

'We can't do anything more for her here. She must come home.'

'Of course.' A passing delivery van did not muffle the sound of the upstairs receiver being put back on its cradle but Felicity was too agitated to notice. When the sisters had finalised the plans for Anna's homecoming Penny was back downstairs preparing to leave. The fish pie was untouched.

'I would have asked you to take the leftovers to Mr Mogford,' said Felicity sorrowfully but Penny didn't hear, she was in a hurry to go. Felicity did nothing to stop her.

Henry had a theory about Polonius and the arras, which he illustrated with Felicity's curtains. It was still quite light when Thelma passed pushing Damon home from shopping. A man's bicycle was obstructing her path leaning against the front of Felicity's house. Thelma was going to drop in and ask for cast-offs for the Oxfam jumble but, seeing the curtains closed, she decided to be tactful and call another time.

8

'LET HER GO, she needs space. Do not intrude.'
    'But Ailsa, you have brought Anna all the way home so
she can be looked after, cured of her night horrors or whatever,
and here you are, newly through Immigration, when she gives
me a kiss and two hundred fags and dashes off to London.'

'Don't say fags, Flicky, you could be misinterpreted, and you
must give Anna freedom to grow. She has her own needs and
identity now and a boyfriend called Pip.'

Ailsa was cool in practical navy, a frequent traveller and utterly
used to airports. Felicity had met her sister and her daughter with
lots of excited waving and a bunch of foolish flowers. Ailsa and
Anna had been quite pleased to see her, she supposed, even
though she had parked the car miles away on a level normally
only visited by criminals and lunatics.

Ailsa linked arms with her sister. 'Don't hassle her, Flicky.
Pip is a nice guy, they met in Boston, he is a well educated
jazz musician and really mature.'

George Melly hove unbidden into Felicity's mind. 'How
mature, Ailsa?'

'Oh, late twenty-something, going on thirty. He's gotten
himself a good job in London and he is great on sax.'

'What?'

'He is a saxophonist. They did a show for charity at New Year,
Sexophanie and the Sax Offenders and made lots of bucks for
our local Arts Festival.'

'Who is Sexophanie? Ailsa?'

'Oh come on, Flicky. Don't act the heavy parent. Anna was
good, real good. Didn't she tell you about it?'

'No, Ailsa. I thought she was being your au pair, not a
chanteuse in a dive. I also thought she was sick.'

'Not exactly sick, Flicky, but she could use some therapy.'

Ailsa was to spend two days in Oxford with Felicity then go north to visit her mother before flying back to the States from Glasgow.

Ailsa had a Filofax which enabled her to get personally organised. In it she kept her whole life in order and saw her existence mapped and regulated within specified boxes. Ailsa talked about windows of opportunity and allotted set periods to be a mother to her children. Quality time was an entirely new expression to Felicity, whose life trundled onwards within the pages of a diary bought at a charity bazaar.

Ailsa was quite right to be bossy. Felicity was drifting into a lackadaisical mess. She hadn't even got a solicitor to act for her in the divorce.

'You are impossible, Flicky. What have you done? Nothing! You have the rest of your life to think about. You must fight for every cent. Are you quite incapable?'

'That is not kind,' Felicity replied.

'Nor is the world, nor are ex-husbands with new families to support.'

'I don't like to think about that possibility,' said Felicity.

'You must, though. Also you must think of your car licence, your TV licence, your poll tax, your insurance.'

'Stop it, Ailsa.'

'And what about your pension?'

'Have a heart, I'm only three years older than you.'

'Yes and behaving like someone going on twenty-one. It is obvious, Flicky,' she said. 'You must get Rob to buy you a prime piece of real estate in the best location and then you can let it out and go back to Kilbole to care for Mother. It makes sound sense.'

'But what about Isa? I can't sack her. What about my career?'

'Isa is over seventy, Flicky, she should be retired. Working part time shaking handbells at the disadvantaged is not a career, it is an occupation.'

'I hate Kilbole, Ailsa, especially with Mum as she is. I haven't the patience.'

'Well then she must be put in a home and the Shieling turned

261

into a boarding-house to pay the fees. I wouldn't sell it now, the market is falling. You must be realistic.'

'Ailsa, what do you and Dieter do for fun?'

'Fun is very important. We prioritise times for it. Why do you ask?' Ailsa appraised Felicity from top to toe. 'How come you keep your figure, Flicky when you eat junk and never work out?'

'I worry,' Felicity replied.

'About what? Not your divorce, presumably. I've never met anyone so unconcerned.'

'For one thing, I worry about Anna.'

After her initial seduction had turned sour, Angelica Blackburn had always loathed Felix and hated marriage. It was fairly certain that neither of hers, the annulled one to Wolf or the failed one to Felix, had ever been consummated and she certainly had no intention of going in for that sort of thing again. Her life was spent amongst artistic intellectuals; her grasp of conceptualism and minimalism was well respected. Her views were sound and her criticism considered most important.

She worried about her son and then worried even more about her bourgeois concern for his sexual preferences. Her world was filled with homosexuality, about which she was entirely at ease except when she began to suspect that her own child was gay. Her joy was genuine when Henry made mention of a female friend. Angelica imagined her son discovering sex in the arms of a serious young woman, a historian maybe, at Somerville. Having been unable to find time to watch Henry as Polonius, she had not discovered the real identity of his girlfriend.

One day, as a sniff of spring wafted about London and bulbs were starting to brighten the parks, Angelica had bumped into Penny Blackburn in Harley Street looking mighty coy. Penny had insisted that they went to tea at Sagnes in Marylebone High Street to satisfy her sudden craving for marzipan.

'How are you getting on with your stepdaughter?' Angelica asked. She ate cream horns and watched Penny bite off the head of an extremely yellow early Easter chick.

'She isn't my stepdaughter yet, Angelica, and I haven't seen her since she returned from America. Rob says she is being distant, but I have a way with children.'

'Isn't she grown up? I thought Henry said she was at Oxford with him.'

'She is at a crammer, not being clever, Angelica. Felicity pushed her into trying to become a musician but failed. Such a mistake to overstretch the young. The child needs lots of fresh air and decent people to mix with. I will do my best by her, when I can spare the time.' Penny glanced downwards but Angelica made no reference to either Harley Street, marzipan or Penny's busy schedule.

Penny decided that she must indulge in a stridently green Kermit the Frog. 'Anna was utterly dominated all her childhood by Felicity, who hoped her little girl would be a replacement for herself. I've told Rob that any child of ours will be brought up normally and go to Pony Club, not concerts. Too much culture at an early age can make people odd, you know.'

'I was taken to lots of concerts,' said Angelica. 'In the Albert Hall on Saturdays.'

'That is because your grandmother was foreign,' said Penny kindly. 'Anyway I did hear something very interesting concerning Anna Green and the fire at King's Cross. In fact I should have rung you about it but it quite slipped my mind what with one thing and another.'

Penny related what Rob had told her about the man on the train and how Anna had asked him to go back for her violin. 'And the most amazing bit of the whole event,' she said to Angelica, 'is that Anna is convinced the man was Felix.'

'Why on earth didn't I know about this?' asked Angelica. 'Does a wife mean nothing?'

'Well my dear, you aren't a very keen wife.'

'Nevertheless I have more than a passing interest in knowing whether or not I am a widow.'

'Felix wasn't amongst the casualties, there is no need to get agitated.' Kermit had been devoured but green lingered on Penny's teeth. 'Felicity is the one to blame. If she hadn't been so obsessed with her own thwarted ambitions the child would never have asked anyone to risk their life that way. I expect Anna was more frightened of her mother than the fire. I suppose you know that Felicity said my father asked her to get Felix to come and see him.'

'Is that the reason she went to Barbados?' Angelica asked.

'Looks like it. Though to my mind she was reckoning on stealing your husband. After all, she knew that Rob was hopelessly in love with me and she would do anything to get a title. She's like that,' Penny replied. 'Also Felicity is a terrible spendthrift. She might have thought Felix was in for a fortune. Anyway, she managed to wheedle dearest Daddy into bequeathing her one of the best bits of Blackburn jewellery. Mummy would turn in her grave. Poor Rob is having a dreadful time sorting out Felicity's settlement, she is such a greedy grabber. He may even have to sell some land.'

'Surely not, how terrible. Still, you have got plenty of money. That should be a comfort to him.'

Sometimes, even now, Penny could see why her mother had always considered the Von Hoffers to be incurably vulgar.

Once in Scotland Ailsa assessed the situation and got her mother on to the waiting list for admission to Glamis Towers Eventide Home. Meanwhile she could attend as a day patient. She instructed Isa to start packing up the Shieling with a view to disposal and visited Sheila's doctor demanding a prognosis. Mrs Campbeltown was deteriorating rapidly, she was told.

Ailsa told Felicity these plans but said she would send a fax confirming everything once she was back at her Boston office.

'I don't have a fax machine,' said Felicity, who was quite overwhelmed by the speed with which Ailsa could get the world up and about.

'Wake up, sister. Get real! My secretary will mail you.'

Ailsa's secretary was a dope and used the Church Farm address, which meant the letter arrived two weeks later at Hayfield Road, redirected and tatty. The paper inside the envelope was sticky with un-American Marmite.

Anna reappeared once Ailsa had gone. Felicity did not ask where or with whom she had been as she was fairly certain that she would neither get the truth nor like the answer.

'Welcome to furnished lodgings! Anna, this is your place to

use as and when and how you like. You belong here. Come and go as you wish, treat it like a hotel.'

'Mother, most of my friends get a hard time from their parents for doing just that.'

'I'm sorry Anna, I just wanted you to know that this is home.'

'No it isn't,' Anna replied. 'My home is at Church Farm.'

'I understand,' said Felicity.

'Well if you understand why can't you be there?'

'Because, my darling, I do not belong there any more.'

'Why didn't you fight, Mother? Why don't you try to win?'

Felicity thought for a while and then answered quietly, 'I no longer want to win.'

'It is a game to you,' said Anna. 'A silly game that can be forgotten.'

'I won't forget, Anna, believe me,' Felicity replied. 'But I must forgive. There are two sides to every marriage.'

'Don't give me that crap.'

Felicity hadn't expected Anna to return so full of indignation. She had dreaded misery, horror, guilt, neurosis even, but not anger. Anna had come back to look for her home and found it gone.

At Church Farm Rob's words were almost identical to Felicity's in Oxford. 'Of course you belong here. This is your home.' He had missed his daughter so much that it ached. He hadn't wanted to destroy her happiness. Penny was prepared to be understanding, to be kind and helpful, welcoming and loving but Penny was always going to be an impostor. Anna hated her. She didn't even like to think of Penny touching the mugs hanging in the kitchen or taking a bath in the Church Farm baths, using the lavatories or polluting the air of home with her mouthwashed breath.

Anna loved her father most fervently but he had betrayed her trust and spoiled everything for ever and always. She didn't hate the baby that might be expected around Christmas but she loathed and detested all those who had caused it. With those she included her mother.

Felicity did her best with Hayfield Road. She had made Anna a room and given her the means of independence. She did not intimidate her daughter with catechisms and took pains to let her be an adult, which only resulted in Anna wanting to be a child again. Anna realised she had been bucketed out into the world before she had outgrown her prematurely demolished nest. There was something repulsive in finding that her parents had got on with life without her. As an only child she had been the focus of their existence; now she was peripheral.

'Make yourself at home,' they said, trying to be hospitable to the stranger.

She detested Henry Blackburn's solicitous devotion to her mother almost more than her father's absurd lust for Penny. Rob was a man, they can get odd fancies. Henry was just a boy, a wimp, a craven, fawning sycophant, a joke amongst her friends and Felicity was an old woman in her forties. The concept was repugnant and thoroughly nasty or utterly hilarious, Anna was not sure which.

The newspapers published a picture of the reconstructed, unclaimed fire victim. The unknown dead man had a benign, even anodyne, face, well shaped with good bone formation, almost aristocratic and unanimatedly noble in appearance. He observed the world with sightless oval-lidded eyes, a slight smile on his lips that appeared wise and to know more than spectators could gather from his burnt corpse.

Felicity looked at the page and gasped.

'Mum, what's wrong? What have you seen?' Anna asked.

'Nothing, darling. I've just remembered something I'd forgotten.' She picked up the paper and hurriedly left the room. Upstairs, locked in the bathroom Felicity looked again at the man. She told herself the picture could be of anyone. He had the face of a statue, an example of *Homo sapiens* found in biology textbooks and first-aid manuals, not a real person. Everyman could look like that: a mask without personality, it could have belonged to a hero or a criminal, loved, loathed or merely tolerated, missed greatly or completely unmourned except perhaps by his mother, if he had one.

The face haunted her. The man's calmly detached smile had seen another world from which there was no possible chance of return.

266

The forensic artists had done a brilliant job from no more than a charred skull stripped of skin, without ears or eyes or hair, none of the bits that distinguish one average man from the next.

Anna hammered on the locked door. 'I want to go and see Dad. Now.'

'I'll drive you over later.'

'I said now. I need a car.'

'You need to pass your test first, then we'll see. I dread you driving round on your own.'

Anna cried like the tired frustrated child she still was. The fragility beneath the armour plating was frightening. Her infancy was knitted with her maturity and neither faction could dominate the childish soul still resident in the prematurely experienced adult body. Felicity remembered being homesick for her teddy even when she had known what it was like to share her bed with a man. Parties had never really seemed to come up to the mark without jellies in waxed cases no matter how sophisticated the spread.

Felicity dropped Anna at the front door and noticed that Penny had planted the pair of tubs that flanked it with a horrible bright selection of flowers that would make mellow Church Farm look like a pub. Given the chance a late frost would do for the mixed petunias even quicker than the farm cats.

'Where are the dogs?' asked Anna.

Penny had found her sitting in the Church Farm kitchen, the contents of the fridge and the larder ranged about. She had scratched up a meal from cereal, chocolate biscuits, Ribena and burnt toast. Charred crumbs clung to the butter and a trailing sticky string had dribbled over the current *Farmers' Weekly* from the golden syrup tin, out of which stuck a yoghurt-smeared spoon.

'Hello, Anna. I wasn't expecting you,' said Penny. 'How lovely to see you.'

Anna ignored the pleasantries. 'I said, where are the dogs?'

'In their run, Anna. They make the house so grubby with their muddy feet and moulting coats.'

Anna got up and, leaving her meal half eaten, stumped straight to the yard and released the dogs. They were really pleased to see her, there was no side to them. Gratifyingly filthy and shedding hairs by the handful, they were directed into the house to help Anna wreck it.

'I haven't come to see you, Penny, so you needn't hang about. I'd rather be left alone in my own home. Where is my father?'

'He's gone to a meeting in London, Anna.'

Anna loosed a volley of obscenities at Penny blaming her for Rob's absence and her wasted journey.

'Actually I want to talk to you,' said Penny. Her round face was dangerously florid. 'There are one or two things I feel we should get straight. Ground rules and all that.'

'This is not your ground,' Anna replied, lighting a cigarette.

'I wish you wouldn't bring your mother's filthy habits here,' said Penny ostentatiously producing an ashtray. 'It is a lethal habit. Even passive smoking can do harm.'

'Good,' Anna replied. 'Mum says you smoked like a furnace when you were young.'

'I dare say your mother is to blame for your manners too. Furthermore I would have thought that you, of all people, would be aware of the fire risk.'

Anna stayed silent and flicked ash into her Ribena.

Penny sat down opposite Anna and reached across the table for her hand. Anna's nails were long and painted black; Penny had fingers like sausages and had crammed her mother's ring on to her engagement finger. 'I want you to know that I realise how guilty you must be feeling, Anna but please believe me I do not think you were as much to blame as your mother.'

Anna withdrew her hand the moment it was touched and exhaled smoke into Penny's face. 'Very well, if you are not going to co-operate, I will have to come straight to the point. Do you know who this is?' Penny produced an enlarged photograph of the unknown fire victim.

Anna looked away.

'Look at it. You know that man, don't you?'

'No.'

'You may not know his name but you have met him, haven't you? Haven't you?' Penny put her face so close that Anna saw it as one mass of coarse pores like wet Aertex.

'You met him on the train the night of the fire. Didn't you?'

268

'Did my mother tell you that?' Anna asked. She was shaking with anger and fear.

'No, I found out from a far more reliable source. You admit it, don't you? This is the man you sent back to die.'

Anna was crying. She couldn't answer: all her fight and nerve had gone.

'I will tell you now who that poor man was. He was Felix, my brother, my only brother. My poor dead mother and father's only son. Angelica's husband, Henry's father. Your mother chased after him to Barbados and lured him to come to England and then you got him killed. Burnt to death. Have you any idea of what that must be like? Do you realise what you have done? I hope you never ever have anyone to love as much as I loved my darling brother.'

'It isn't true, I didn't know,' Anna screamed. 'I didn't kill him, I knew nothing!'

'You do now. Look, here is another picture of him when he was alive. See – the two are identical. Where are you going?'

'Away from here, back to my mother, anywhere.' Anna got up from the table and ran out of the house, the dogs chasing after her longing for a walk. 'Go back!' Anna commanded them. 'Go back. You can't come where I'm going.'

She ran down the short drive to the lane and there she found Felicity waiting in the car.

'Mummy! Why are you here?'

'I thought I would stick around in case you needed me.'

'Thank God you did. Oh Mum, what can I do? Penny thinks I killed her brother.'

'I thought she might. I presume she told you the man in the newspaper was Felix?'

'How did you know?'

'Instinct, my love.'

'Was he Felix, Mum?'

'I don't know.'

Felicity saw a tractor approaching down the road and she had no wish to meet any of Rob's men just then. Over the years they had all become her friends so greetings would have been awkward for everyone. She started the car and drove away waving cheerfully to Bert as if all were extremely well. Once on the main road she continued. 'I promise you, even if the man you met was Felix, it was not your fault. Blame me if you must but don't please blame yourself and poison your youth with needless guilt. What happened was terrible but the man had free will, he chose to go back. Nothing you could have done would have prevented him. It wasn't your fault, my darling.'

'How do you know? You weren't there,' Anna replied.

'I wish to God I had been with you.'

'If you hadn't made me try for the Royal Academy none of this would have happened,' said Anna. 'You knew I was never going to be as good as you.'

'I'm sorry, but that isn't true. You could be very good if you wanted. I only wished you to have the chance.'

'You pushed me.'

'I'm sorry you see it like that.'

Resentment and anger melted as Anna clasped her mother and sobbed as if the world had ended and it was all her fault.

'Please Mum, don't leave me. Please don't go away, I'm sorry for being so bolshie, really I am.'

'I think I understand, I hope I do. I will stay in Oxford for as long as you need me, I promise. You can come and see me, stay with me, live with me or just ring me any time of the day or night.'

'Thank you. I've got to tell you something more.' Anna twisted round in the front seat till she was facing Felicity. The black rings round her eyes were only make-up, the face beneath was fresh and very young. 'Did I tell you what the man's last words to me were?'

'No, Anna, tell me now.'

'I must rescue that violin, for your mother's sake.'

9

C EDRIC TULLIE'S CRATE of champagne was a mere precursor to Henry Blackburn's twenty-first birthday which loomed over the spring of 1988 threatening the young man's composure, ruining his concentration. The elderly Von Hoffers felt something seriously festive should be done to mark their only grandchild's coming of age, something expensive and shiny, preferably involving top-notch friends who would, quite naturally, be the lifelong companions of a future marquess. Henry told his grandparents he would prefer a family affair, which hurt their fragile feelings. The Von Hoffers assumed quite wrongly that Henry deemed his many friends too grand for his grandparents, whereas the truth was that Henry's friends were sparse.

Angelica, who for all her protestations of indifference to ephemera had, without official justification, added 'The Hon' to her cards and chequebook with startling speed, sided with her parents as usual. Though she had never enjoyed a single party in all her forty years, she looked on them as essentials like regular dentistry and clean underwear.

'You must have a party, Henry,' she told her son. 'Your great-grandmother had a birthday party every year and she lived till she was ninety-six.'

Henry absorbed this non-sequitur and groaned.

At Hayfield Road Henry confided his anxieties to Felicity while she was having a rare spate of cookery.

'Cheer up, for goodness' sake,' said Felicity, who found Henry's precious self-absorption quite enervating at times. 'At least you have only got to eat a delicious dinner, drink too much and thank everyone for having you. Consider those tribal fellows who have to endure macabre mutilations and kill lions or paddle about in hot cinders.'

'Will you come, Felicity?'

'To your birthday dinner? No, Henry, thank you. You know your mother doesn't want to see me, I brought nothing but grief to your grandparents. My daughter is accused of causing your father's death, your aunt has stolen my husband and the whole boiling were once of the opinion that I was out to trap your distant aged cousin and scupper your chances of ennoblement even though you were embryonic at the time. No Henry, I would sooner have supper in a snake pit.'

'You will have to meet them one day, Felicity.'

'Come Judgment Day, maybe. Now look here, I've made you some really sticky flapjacks, these will stiffen your sinews.'

'Oh Felicity, you are divine. You and I will celebrate properly when this atrocious party is over.'

'Think of England, Henry!'

'No Felicity, I'll think of you.'

Ailsa had told Anna that she mustn't mind her mother having a walker. 'They are great for the lone female, Anna. Utterly inoffensive and non-threatening. Look on Henry as your mother's pet dog or a smart accessory that pulls her outfit together and makes an entity of a concept.'

'Henry makes me sick,' Anna had replied.

As it was, Henry's twenty-first had to be cancelled. His father's body was found in Barbados unearthed by scavenging dogs not far from the Andromeda Gardens. Angelica, as non-prostrated widow, identified Felix's body and rather enjoyed the experience, which she later used for a series of lectures on the morbid art of decomposition in collaboration with a rising artistic star concerned in putrefaction.

Nobody could accuse Anna of being a murderer any more. That role had been played by someone with a grudge far, far away over the Atlantic. Felix's end had been as squalid as his life. He had been shot and dumped in a makeshift grave, the victim of some disaffected narcotics merchants whose deals had gone awry.

Anna was so happy that she sang for joy and hammered Myra's

piano till *Gaudeamus Igitur* shook the park pigeons in the treetops. She was exuberant with relief. The blame that had been laid on her for causing Felix's death was lifted. She knew of no other person claiming to know the identity of the burnt man: he was a stranger, no one special and nothing to do with her.

Anna liked living with Myra despite the stench of crumbling cat. She even warmed to being temporarily vegetarian. Fear of death and dying bothered her; she had never been at ease chewing on parts that had walked about when whole. In Prince of Wales Drive she could make loud music to distraction and disturb no one as the mansion flats were substantial, built of staunch material and the neighbours weren't put out by noise. Myra was now well recovered from having her second hip replacement the previous November and was quite fit enough to exercise her splendid new joint in Battersea Park. It made a lively change for her to have young in her flat again. Few callers visited her now. In fact one person, who had climbed the stone stairs and knocked on her door while she was in hospital, assumed from the desolate air of the place that it was permanently abandoned and deserted, its owner dead or gone away.

Myra made no demands and never asked questions when Anna wished to be left alone, nor did she pry. If Anna wanted answers, she gave them to her honestly and without embellishment, volunteering nothing unless asked. Anna didn't ask much; she needed encouragement and reassurance, both of which Myra gave her liberally.

On the rare occasion that Anna became pensive Myra helped her to expunge the memory of the stranger at King's Cross by suggesting all sorts of people who could have spoken to her in the train and saying that the death mask was inconclusive and looked nothing like anyone she had ever known in all her seventy years. This was Myra's only lie. She did know who the face resembled: it was her secret and she would stay quiet unless or until Felicity felt strong enough to talk to her about it.

Felicity rejoiced in Anna's exoneration. Behind her happy smile of relief there was a black dark empty chasm. Just one flicker of hope was left but that guttered and died when a letter came from

Lotte saying that yes, the unknown man, the gentle lifeless mask, could easily be and probably was an accurate reconstruction of what had been the living love of Felicity's life. So many factors fitted. The scar on the skull which had been the result of a climbing accident, the replacement teeth and traces of nicotine were all accurate. Wolf had been just within the possible age range and only a little taller than the victim's suggested height.

Wolf is dead, really dead, Felicity told herself over and over again and yet, like doubting Thomas, she wanted tangible proof.

Childhood prayers promised Heaven, a better place where loved ones reunite in bliss. She found herself praying that there was a home for little children beyond the bright blue sky, a happy land far far away, but no one seemed to be listening or hear her prayer.

'The most important thing, when getting divorced, is for the parties to talk to each other,' said Grania when Felicity asked for a morning off to meet Rob. Grania was right as usual, she knew what should be done despite her lack of personal experience of divorce. Grania's relationships were either fruitful or meaningful; never both.

Since the mean misery of spring had drifted into an aimless summer Felicity had taught herself to accept that Wolf would never reappear now.

Within a year or two, sooner maybe, she would be free of all ties and at liberty to start living again. She would travel and see the places where Wolf had been, there would be no need to be careful or cautious. She could risk whatever she liked. Having missed youth the first time she would wring her middle years for adventure and new experience so that in the end, if she survived, she would have more to remember as she faded, than memories of having settled for second best.

Rob came to Hayfield Road. He rang the bell and dithered on the narrow doorstep. It was May and falsely summery.

Felicity opened the door tentatively fearing a researcher of markets or vendor of daft brushes. She was wearing a cotton dress that had become a great favourite over the years because it only came out when the weather turned warm.

'Roses, how lovely. Rob, thank you. You never brought me flowers before.'

Rob kissed her: she smelled poignantly familiar. He had always liked the dress, it made her look young but not ridiculous. She was lovelier than he remembered; even her hand didn't distress him when she took the flowers and buried her nose in them.

'They are the Schoolgirl roses off the south wall, the ones you planted when Anna was five. They always come out weeks ahead of the rest.'

'I remember. Maybe it is something to do with Emma Hamilton being buried there.'

'Anna's hamster, of course! Perhaps I should diversify into dead rats as the vital purchase for the modern gardener. God knows I will have to find something profitable to sell soon.'

'Oh Rob, is farming that bad? Come in. Look, it is an awful mess, living alone has done nothing for my tidiness. Penny would give me a rocket and a black mark.'

Rob wrongly assumed the clutter belonged to his daughter. 'Is Anna here?'

'No. She is living more or less permanently with Myra Pennyfeather in London. She says she likes it there and Myra adores her company. They have a great empathy, like the ideal grandmother and granddaughter.'

'Her boyfriend is still in Oxford, though.'

'Which one?'

'Henry Blackburn of course.'

'Oh no, Rob. You have got the wrong end of that stick. Anna can't abide Henry.'

'I see, I must have misheard. Lots of people are called Green, after all.'

'Did you think Henry and Anna were an item? How funny. Well well.'

'An item?' said Rob. 'What is an item?'

'You and Penny. That is an item.'

Felicity gave Rob a mug of instant coffee. After so many years she didn't need to ask about milk and sugar. Two dozen florist's roses stuck stiffly out of a goldfish bowl on the windowsill; Rob's garden flowers she put in an earthenware jug on the centre of the

275

table. What Rob had to say was going to be tough. He coughed and spluttered while he tried to get started.

'Flicky, I'm sorry.'

'What about in particular, Rob?'

She had not expected him to cry. 'There, there,' she said putting her arms round his paunchy trunk and laying her head against his chest. She did love his checked country shirts, his spade-shaped fingernails and his lingering aroma of happy herbivores.

'Oh Flicky, I do love you.'

'I am very fond of you, Rob.'

'But not love?'

'No, not all of you. Anyway you have got a new love now, and a baby on the way, I hear. What would Penny say if she saw you like this?'

Penny's pregnancy was finally confirmed though conception must have happened at least three months after she had first displayed symptoms of her condition. Willpower and wishful thinking had anticipated fact, ingenious science and dedicated effort had finally come up with a positive reading, at which point Penny's attentions had switched abruptly from her mate to her brood. Rob was banished to the spare room for the duration and Penny took to busy nesting.

Rob took Felicity's good hand in his. 'Oh God. Oh Christ. What a bloody fool I've been.'

'Poor Rob. It is a wee bit late for second thoughts,' Felicity replied, withdrawing her hand and offering him a cigarette.

'I know. Damn the baby.'

'Don't, Rob. Don't say that. Another child is what you have always wanted. You know that. Your mother should be pleased. I bet Penny is ecstatic.'

'You could say that,' Rob replied. 'And you are right. I did, I do want a family but now that it has happened I feel just like a bull put out to grass after his semen has been teased from him. I might as well be a mail-order sperm producer.'

'All this was your choice, Rob, not mine.'

'Flicky, I'm broke.'

'Really, Rob? Properly broke, begging by the wayside type broke or down to your last two hunters type broke?'

'It is bloody serious. I might have to sell up here as well as in Scotland, or at the very least split the land, sell Church Farm and move in with Mother and Pricilla.'

'But Penny will rescue you, Rob. You get the full family package when you take her on, including spending money.'

'I don't want to marry her for that, or any other reason. I want you back.'

'It is much too late for that.'

'Is it? Please, Flicky. It would make life so much easier. I would only have to pay token maintenance for the child, I wouldn't have to dispose of the farm.'

'I am not a hedge against bankruptcy, Rob.'

'I didn't exactly mean that.'

'Rob are you honestly telling me you can't afford to divorce me? Is that serpent of a solicitor Ailsa found for me that wily?'

'It isn't funny, Flicky. Not at all, you mustn't be so heartless. Yes I can't afford anything like as much as the serpent is asking but it isn't just that. I don't want to divorce you, not any more.'

'I am not a clever deal, a sound bargain, a tax dodge or a bit of rollover relief. Nor do I wish to be on your herd basis or any of those other devices you farmers use to keep yourselves in your smug country houses.'

'Flicky please, remember why I married you.'

'Why? You can't have done it for money.'

'I loved you.'

'Oh Rob, think again. You pitied me.'

'Flicky, please. If that is what you think please take pity on me now.'

'I will not stay married to you for any reason, Rob, least of all pity.'

'Supposing I promised never to be unfaithful again, never to let Mother or Pricilla over the doorstep.'

'No, Rob. Not even if Anna pleaded with us to stay together, which she will not.'

'She won't? Are you sure?'

'Yes. Quite sure. Isn't that a bit of a relief? You can't dither any more, I have made your mind up for you. I don't want to hurt your feelings but I am really rather happy living in this little

277

heap. I never belonged in the country, not all the time. I miss it now, when summer is coming and the birds are tweeting, but I can always go and look at other people's flowers, and smell the blossom in the Botanical Gardens and coo about ducklings in Worcester if I get nostalgic and have none of the agony fretting about foxes, magpies, greenflies and all those blights. Anna tells me Penny has put her stamp on Church Farm: nothing of me belongs there any longer.'

'Flicky it's true, I can't bloody afford to divorce you. I can't even pay the rent on this place. You have got to move somewhere smaller. Come home please.'

'No, Rob. I want to stay here in Oxford somehow even if I have to apply for a better job.'

'But what can you do?'

'Lots of things, Rob. Missing a few fingers doesn't mean I am useless at everything, except of course as a violinist. By the way, I believe, but I am not sure, that Anna is thinking of trying for the Academy again.'

'You'd like that, wouldn't you, Flicky?'

'Yes, of course. But only if that is what Anna wants for herself. I am afraid most people seem to think I pushed her too hard when she was little.'

'I know you didn't, Flicky.'

'Well then Rob, why don't you say so instead of letting me be pulverised by hurled brickbats and endure all the criticism and take the blame for being a ruthless and ambitious parent.'

'I want you back, Flicky.'

'No, Rob. I am going to respect my own integrity.'

'What the hell does that mean?'

'It is Graniaspeak for no thanks, I'm happier on my own.'

'Grania?'

'My boss, Rob. You remember, I've told you about her before.'

'Oh, I see. I thought perhaps you had . . . No, never mind, forget it.'

'Oh Rob. You are so silly sometimes. Just because I wasn't perhaps as hungry for sex as Penny apparently is, doesn't mean I am alternatively inclined.'

'Penny has lost her appetite. You are right, I am silly.'

'Poor old Rob. Never mind. The shooting season starts again in a few months; that always puts a spring in your step.'

'Flicky, you are the only woman who understands me. Please think again.'

'No, Rob. You don't understand me at all.'

Oxford was ending for Henry but not with a bang. He didn't celebrate with riotous balls and nude jumping off bridges clutching bottles of champagne. He became morose. The milk train of talent spotters had been down to scout around for brilliant recruits and had offered him a splendid job in merchant banking, which he had turned down. He wanted to spend his life in Oxford being clever and had no wish to serve his donnish apprenticeship anywhere else, certainly not in recently planted groves of academe, no matter how prestigious their faculties.

'Everybody bombarded him with advice and implored him to find a job. '"Find Yourself Something to Do Dear, Find Yourself Something To Do!" Christ Almighty my family are driving me nuts.'

'Well I suppose you can't sit in the sun for ever, Henry.'

'Not you too, Felicity. People never had this sort of trouble before. Aesthetes and intellectuals didn't have to do squalid jobs. Did they?'

'They did, Henry, unless they had patrons, were well endowed or went to war for a cause. Only the absurdly rich just drifted about thinking, though even they generally got involved in some sort of set and formed movements or, at the very least, dining clubs. If it is solitude and contemplation you want you had better become a monk.'

'Only if you become a nun and I can be Abélard to your Héloïse.'

'Nuns are not my thing.'

'And monks aren't mine. I will just have to become a writer. I will start my great novel tomorrow. Will that suffice, do you think? I will buy myself a beautiful new fountain pen and several notebooks with hard covers this very day to show I mean business. When great-cousin Cedric dies I can retreat to Tulliebrae and become vastly celebrated as well as noble. Can you really see me teaching the Tudors in the Midlands or selling debts to Eurobankers in Dock-lands?'

'What will you write about, Henry?'

'You, Felicity. You you you. Is there anything else?'

'Henry, you are in great danger of becoming a silly ass.'

Every night Felicity rang her mother. There was little point in running up such a monstrous bill because no matter what, Sheila always said the same thing.

'Well this is a surprise! I haven't heard from you for ages. I am getting on like a train.'

One day the train stopped.

Sheila was found lying on the floor, half-dressed and in a coma, by Isa who immediately summoned help and got her ambulanced into hospital. Ailsa had been told that her mother was deteriorating but no one had imagined it would be so rapid.

Felicity drove north faster than she had ever driven before but when she rang the hospital from Carlisle she was told her mother had died. Peacefully, curled up like a baby in a high cot with a waterproof sheet, amongst kind strangers.

There was no point in hurrying now.

Felicity turned the car towards the west and drove to Kilbole via the coastal route. The midsummer sun was setting late beyond the islands, silhouetted grey, hard-edged against the fading flame. The same lumps, the same rocks, buoys and the white lighthouse solitary amongst squealing, wheeling gannets: none of that had changed since Felicity's childhood when she and Ailsa explored the shore with Felix, Penny and Wolf. They had played there in chilling caves and frightened themselves witless with stories of cannibal troglodytes. They had teased sea anemones with pebbles and gazed in disgust at the stranded jellyfish evaporating on the sand in mottled blobs.

Felicity stopped the car as the sun disappeared and cried all alone for her mother. She could have done more; she should have been there. If only she had stayed longer, gone the extra mile, given back more than she had taken. It was too late for so much and too late for her to do anything for so many – her father, Digby, Joan, Felix and now her mother and Wolf. All dead and alone in the end.

Felicity was on her own to live as well as die.

The church was gratifyingly full for Sheila's funeral. She had taught music to most of Kilbole for many years and was remembered with affection by her pupils, none of whom had gone far as musicians as very few had possessed a vestige of talent. Only two real stars had shone and both of them had fizzled out. Sheila always remembered the joy of teaching both Felicity and Wolf. Often she forgot what had happened to them, which was, in a way, another joy. From time to time her dementia had catered for happy endings. 'It is a good turnout, I'll grant you that,' Fay Braid shouted down Lionel's ear. 'More than one would have expected, given the circumstances.' She directed her remarks at the front pew where both Sheila's daughters stood like two slender black columns beside their tubbier husbands.

Felicity had been surprised that Rob had come. Initially she was disturbed by his presence but he was such a comforting support that she found herself being really pleased to have him there. It couldn't have been easy for him to get away during haymaking and the Royal Show. Rob had become very fond of his mother-in-law. Sheila had never intruded and never imposed and had managed to ignore his own mother's snideness and disparaging references to the Campbeltown inferiority, treating the insulting snobbishness with apparent indifference.

Only once, when Joan Blackburn had ceased all friendliness with the Campbeltowns the minute she and Digby had been posted to more elevated parts, did Sheila ever let her feelings be hurt, though only her husband had seen she was deeply injured. Magnus had understood and made her laugh at such fickleness.

Sheila possessed simple faith and believed absolutely in an afterlife which she would share with Magnus who, for several years now, had been living with her in her muddled mind. Felicity prayed that her mother would not be disappointed.

This was Dieter Schmidt's third visit to St Mungo's and the third time he had sung the Old Hundredth in it to the accompaniment of the cranky organ. The first time had been for Felicity's wedding, the second for his own. He had not been able to get to his father-in-law's funeral so this was his first experience of the organ at its most lugubrious, which was entirely fitting for a funeral. In 1968 he had worn beads and his hair in a ponytail, six years later he had been dressed in hired morning suit with hair cut short, in 1988 he was wearing sombre black and had no hair left to speak of but much much more money.

Rob wore his father's black coat and bowler hat, both of which had done many rainy graveside stints and inclement Remembrance parades, acquiring a greenish tinge in the process.

Anna sat in the pew behind with the Braids, but Isa, who had devoted these last few years to caring for Sheila, refused Felicity's invitation to sit at the front and put herself at the very back of the church. Isa didn't hold with 'greeting' at funerals which was why she shrank into the darkest corner nursing a sudden attack of hay fever. The man beside her offered her his handkerchief which she accepted, promising to wash and return it to him but, as she knew neither his name or address, this seemed quite unlikely. He appeared to be lame and had a beard. Isa couldn't do with beards ever since she had been billeted on a particularly nasty foster father who resembled the Player's Navy Cut sailor.

Sheila's two daughters were the only women at the graveside. As Felicity saw her mother put to rest beside her father she was overwhelmed with sorrow for all those who lay alone. For herself, she would choose cremation: she did not want to be boxed up to rot in isolation.

Rob, Dieter and Lionel assisted the undertaker's men by holding cords. After they had lowered the coffin Rob came to Felicity and held her steady. She hadn't expected to be so very much in need of his support and was most grateful. He kept his arm round her till they left the graveyard, shielding and protecting her from the sympathetic stares of curious onlookers.

'A pity her dear mother did not live to see this day,' said Fay Braid to the remaining congregation waiting at a respectful distance. 'Felicity's marriage problems hastened poor Sheila's death without a doubt. The young have much to answer for. Still, all is well now. I doubt my niece will not appreciate her luck in having her man standing by to take her back.'

'Sheila is with us yet, in spirit,' mused Miss Pease, a one-time matron at Gantry Close.

'Really Mildred,' replied Fay in shocked tones. 'You let Billy Graham go to your head.'

'That was thirty years ago, Fay.'

'Mud sticks, Mildred. Now where is Lionel? I fancy it is time we went for the tea.'

Later, over a scone of stone in the Glamis Room of the Duncan Arms, Fay took Felicity aside and told her that she must not reproach herself.

Ailsa spoke to the catering manager in the strongest terms about the scones and obtained a discount.

'I believe, sir, that you knew my stepmother,' Dieter bellowed at Lionel. 'You shared an interest in horticulture.'

'Whatever are you doing with a man's hankie, Isa? Have you got a sweetheart at last?' asked MacBrayne's widow.

'Never, Aggie. You'll never find me entertaining yon caper.'

Penny and Rob had not parted happily. She could not see why he should race north to bury his (almost) ex-mother-in law at such a time when he was needed at home to run errands and bring comforts to the mother of his second family. Rob was needed on the farm too but nothing would persuade him to stay in Oxfordshire. His workforce were reliable and responsible, capable of acting on their initiative, and Penny must be too. She turned her cheek from him as he bent to kiss her goodbye. He would be away for a week.

After a day, the electrics fused in the kitchen end of Church Farm. Somehow not one man on the place could help. Hay needed making there and then; life or death it meant and no time over for larking about with fuse wire. Nobody knew of a friendly electrician for miles, which was odd considering the sophistication of both grain drier and milking parlour. Mrs Green always renewed the fuses herself with no difficulty and without all her fingers. Mrs Green was a remarkable woman, they said; then, to a man, they got on their tractors, turned on their radios and sped off to ted and bale and listen to Wimbledon. Even Diana, chief of the local questing divorcees, couldn't help. 'Too sad,' she said. 'My little red car is in dock, I am utterly grounded. Sorry!'

Penny had to resort to her nephew. 'Henry, sweetie, it is Auntie Penny.'

'What is wrong? What do you want?' he replied tersely, not at all keen on having his afternoon's viewing interrupted.

Penny explained her crisis.

'It is too silly, Henry, but I am absolutely terrified and simply can't bring myself to tinker with switches and wires. I can put up shelves and paint but electricity leaves me cold.'

Tennis was the only sport to interest Henry even slightly, but relatives, however appalling, had to be humoured.

All Henry's calamities got dealt with by his old college scout who was delighted to have a trip into the countryside in the Von Hoffers' wondrous twenty-first birthday present, a car, split new, low, fast and dark green.

Mr Beer coped with the fuse in a trice.

'That is quite some car, Henry. Your father once had one very like it,' said Penny without adding that Henry had probably been conceived on its leather seats.

'I've got something else to show you, Aunt Penny.'

'Oh Henry, who gave you that? What a beautiful watch, is that another present?'

'Look! Is it familiar? There is an inscription on the back.'

Penny's eyes were sharp, she was still too young for glasses. She took the watch in her hands and read.

'How did you get that, Henry? Was it sent?'

'No not sent, Aunt Penny. It was delivered. I don't wear it all the time, it is too special.'

'You were given it in person?'

'Yes,' Henry replied. 'It was brought down from Scotland. We met in London.'

Mr Beer was anxious to leave. During that afternoon Penny discovered enough to remap her life and Henry decided it would be wiser to put the watch in the bank.

Rob did not stay on in Kilbole after the funeral but raced south to Stoneleigh where he had a lofty role to play as steward. The Royal Show had featured large in his summer calendar for many years and he was well in line to becoming Honorary Director one day. He would need a wife for that, and Penny was tailor made for the part.

Felicity had found the gregarious enthusiasm for agricultural

284

feats, rural competition and jostling for social supremacy irksome. She had also shown her distaste for pomposity so it came as a shock when Rob found she had been popular and was missed. A surprising amount of people asked after her with affection and told Rob to give Felicity their love. Nobody mentioned Penny. Those who knew kept Rob's affair quiet, putting it down to middle age along with fast cars, thicker waists and forgetfulness.

Amongst the heaps of accumulated post that greeted Rob on his hungover return to Church Farm the morning after the exuberant finale of the show was a letter from Penny. She had gone. Their affair was over There was to be no child. She was sorry.

Rob thought for a while and wondered whether he too was sorry. His head thumped a bit but through the fog he discerned that he was relieved. Then he realised he was delighted and utterly thrilled to be unhooked. He pounded his desk, scattering junk mail, cheques and bills alike and, having alarmed his dogs with a great shout of joy, set off with them to vanquish his hangover and celebrate his freedom in the Royal Oak.

Felicity knew at once that something had changed. Not only was her post no longer redirected to her in Penny's hand but it was uncreased, well sealed and bore no telltale traces of blotted steam.

Grania insisted that Felicity take some more time off work, saying that she must give herself permission to mourn. 'Grieve!' Grania commanded. Felicity did not find that grief obeyed orders; it crept up on her at bad moments. Binge's Elizabethan Serenade demolished her, as did the smell of burnt jam and little yapping dogs. Remorse racked her as countless incidents of her neglectfulness emerged from the back of her conscience. There was nothing to be done except to grieve.

Felicity did not only grieve for her mother.

The envelope had been posted in London and bore the previous day's postmark. Penny's actual letter had been written the day after Sheila's funeral.

Penny used short words. Years of infant teaching showed: one expected anything of length to be broken down by syllables.

'Don't look for me' (it started) 'I have gone away. It is for the best. I know that you and Rob must belong together, you need each other. I must not let my own feelings stand in your way. I have lost the baby. The strain of it all has been too much for me. I give up, you can have your husband back. You need him more than I do. I do not matter. Try to forget me, that is all I ask.'

Felicity read and reread the letter. It was as clear as a public notice. Penny's magnanimous condescension was no private matter.

Henry saw the letter on Felicity's kitchen table as he was putting some lilies in the sink for a drink. He always brought flowers, and lilies were just the thing for a new orphan. He had stayed on in Oxford intending to research his great novel which was going to involve Medusa's snakes, Circe's swine, Socrates and the distillation of hemlock in twenty-second-century Tokyo, the whole work pivoting upon Henry's private hypothesis that the poet Keats would have been a resurrectionist, had he lived.

He read the letter, he couldn't help it, and turned pale with rage. 'My bloody aunt! The scheming, patronising bitch. First she pretends she is in love, then she pretends she is pregnant and then, when she gets bored, she plays the sainted martyr.'

'I think she may have meant it. Really meant it, Henry,' said Felicity. 'Poor Penny, how dreadful to have miscarried.'

Henry replaced the letter in the toast rack. 'Mother is absolutely certain there never was a baby. Penny pretended the whole thing – cravings, big belly, the lot. Besides, don't miscarriages take up time and space? People notice them going on; women don't just lose babies like biros.'

'But that is even worse. She has given up everything and got nothing in compensation. I feel awful.'

'Why?'

'Well I feel sort of obliged.'

'Obliged to do what? Not return to Rob, I hope.'

'Well yes, I do rather.'

'Live with me. Be my love. Please, Felicity. You are the only woman I have ever loved and ever will love, apart from Mummy sometimes.'

Felicity laughed. 'My, what a caution you are to be sure.'

286

'I'm serious.'

'Sorry, Henry,' said Felicity more warily. 'You can't mean it.'

'I do. Look, I am kneeling, I am imploring you.'

'Come on, Henry, you will have to do better than that! Enough of this nonsense.'

He clutched her knees and bowed his head as if in prayer. 'Please, Felicity, this is not a joke. I really mean it.'

'Now you are being ridiculous. Get up, Henry. This isn't funny any more.'

'It never was. I am in deadly earnest. I worship you.'

'Don't. Don't ever say that!'

'Why not? It is true. I worship you. There, I've said it again. I will always worship you till I die.'

'Henry, I am the one being serious now. Listen to me. Only one person has ever said that to me and that man is the only one I will ever love, have ever loved. Do you understand? Nobody else has meant as much to me and never will.'

'Are you talking about my uncle?'

'Yes. How did you know? I thought you had never heard of him.'

'I asked, I was told.'

'You owe your life to him, Henry. He married your mother to prevent her having you aborted.'

'Interfering bastard. I hate him. If I had never been born I would never have had to suffer.'

'You'll get over it.'

'You haven't, Felicity.'

'All through my marriage I thought he was dead and he thought I was happy. Now that everyone knows I am unhappy he really is dead, at least I am almost one hundred per cent certain he is dead. I suppose I can tell you now, Henry. The man that spoke to Anna on the night of the fire at King's Cross wasn't your father but his brother. He is, or rather was, the only man I loved. I knew I was right at once when I saw the reconstruction of the unknown man's face. His ex-girlfriend bears me out. The family resemblance between you, your father and your uncle is very strong, but I think you look most like Wolf.'

287

'No I don't,' Henry shouted. 'I don't look in the least bit like him. I am much taller and I don't have —'

'Don't have what, Henry?'

'Nothing. It doesn't matter. Anyway, I know I don't look like him.'

'But you have never seen him, Henry, have you?'

'Of course not.'

Part Four

I

M YRA PRAYED FOR her dear friend's soul at mass and lit candles to St Cecilia knowing full well that what she was doing was better than going to Sheila's funeral or sending exorbitant flowers to rot upon a Presbyterian grave.

Apart from the haunting reconstructed face, Anna could no longer visualise the man who had guided her from the fire. Only his voice stayed with her: it was deep and without accent, sounding similar to but more self-assured than that of Henry Blackburn. Nine months had passed since that awful night. When she was at her lowest, just before the birds awoke she would imagine she was hearing him telling her that he would go back for the fiddle, for her mother's sake.

Felicity had told Anna that her first and truest love had died long ago and he had been the one who had given her the violin. Perhaps the man had been a ghost, a guardian angel she had encountered unawares. Would a ghost have aged? Did angels smell of French cigarettes? That was it, she had just remembered – the man had carried with him the delicious and exotic scent of Gauloises. She wondered whether that sudden memory was worth passing on but then the sun came up and her life went brightly about its business. Every day did dawn brighter, whatever the weather.

Anna became reconciled to her parents living apart, finding comfort in knowing the rift was over and not a hideous threat any more. The worst had happened and it wasn't, on the whole, too bad, especially now that Penny had walked out. Anna found she didn't really mind if her parents patched up their marriage or not. They were civilised and polite while apart; together they might be awkward after such a long separation. Only statutory events like Christmas seemed to present awkward problems.

She was delighted that there was no baby. Having Penny as a stepmother in her home would have been sufficiently dire without a teeny half-brother or sister puking all over it. She too was pretty sure that there never had been anything other than greed swelling Penny's belly.

The subdued sorrow of her grandmother's funeral had cast a brief, insubstantial shadow of depression over her but now she had heard that Henry Blackburn was off on a protracted tour of great art with his own mother she felt happier than ever. Henry and Angelica would make a somewhat Forsterish pair as they trailed through the corridors of culture. Anna could forgive Felicity anything except her tolerance of Henry. An attractive mother is an asset but one with an adoring youth in tow is an embarrassing liability, especially when the young man is a wimp.

When Anna rang with thrilling news Felicity was not at home to hear it. Myra did her best to celebrate Anna's great moment but a secret surprise needs to be imparted with fanfares, not left dangling upon an answering machine.

'I hate Henry. God but I loathe that creep!' Anna shouted, replacing the receiver.

Felicity had not been able to talk to Anna because she was indeed with Henry. 'One last evening, that is all I ask before I go away.'

'Henry you are going on an arty tour with your mother, not to your death.'

Henry had become increasingly tiresome since his studies ended. Out of work and inspiration he loafed about writing frightful drivel overflowing with adverbs. Even Felicity, who wanted to be kind, could think of nothing encouraging about his dialogue in blank verse between a gorgon's snake and one of Hydra's heads. He spent too much time being languid waiting for brilliance and fluency to chance along.

The evening was overcast and close as they drove through narrow lanes tunnelled between dense, overhanging trees. The Thames valley looked like toy countryside, pretty and preserved but lacking the muckiness of real rural life. All the houses had names and those that were not really old conspired to look that way. Henry's car was quite at home amongst such affluence but Felicity felt awkward and disturbed by the memory of another time when Henry's father had tried to entice her with dinner by the river.

At Henley the tents were dismantled. She remembered what Felix had said about young men rowing backwards to the cheers of old ones in pink socks and tarts in hats. She had still never been to Henley Regatta but Anna had gone with friends this year and hadn't bothered to tell her mother till it was all over, compounding Felicity's redundancy as parent.

They sat outside beneath an awning as the evening began to darken and thunder sounded very distantly. The garden flowers became more vivid in the close grey of sunless dusk; blown roses and peonies disintegrated in the strengthening breeze on to newly mown striped lawn. A swan, on its own, glided downstream haughtily ignoring a busy, fussing duck family out for a dabble here and there. Henry ordered champagne and Felicity wished he hadn't.

Henry worried about his book which was not getting written. He thought a bit and scribbled, but nothing jelled. The plot limped and the characters meandered to no purpose. However, it wasn't literature Henry wished to discuss.

'Felicity, I want to tell you something.'

'You are warned, Henry, I'm not here to listen to anything embarrassing. Tell me, how is your mother?'

'I want to tell you some bad news, Felicity. You must brace yourself,' said Henry ignoring Felicity's civil question. 'Listen, you must be brave. I have had it confirmed, officially confirmed, that the body of the unclaimed man is really that of Wolfgang Duncan. His life and work were so secret that no one can shout about his death or indeed who he was when he died. It is him, Felicity. You have my word. I haven't just been drooping about these last few weeks, like nephew like uncle, if you like. Just remember that I will be in deep trouble if what I have just told you is ever discovered so don't ask me how I found out. At least you now know for certain that the man is dead.'

The first large raindrops fell upon the table, spotting it with dark dots and they, or sad tears, splashed into the champagne making rings among the bubbles.

Felicity smiled at Henry and blew her nose. It wasn't fair to make him spend his money on another's gloom. 'Thank you, Henry. That was kind. I needed to be certain and now I am. Anna must never know. Will you promise me that?'

'Only if you promise not to go back to your husband.'

'I don't want to discuss that either.'

'But I do. This is my party. I can choose.'

'Very well. I am not sure. Will that do?'

'No. Listen. Any man who has behaved like Rob did with my awful aunt is bound to do it again. It is the same thing as first blood to a hound or heroin to a lost soul like my father. You can't stop the rot.'

'Maybe not, but then again maybe I wouldn't mind.'

'If you don't mind it is even more important that you don't do it.'

'Rob and I are used to each other, Henry. I'm fond of him and I think he loves me, in his way.'

'That isn't good enough. Why don't you wear that brooch my grandfather left you?'

'I don't like to, Henry. It isn't right for me, it makes me feel like a scheming adventuress who muscled in on a dying man and stole his descendants' loot.'

'Balls. I'm his descendant and I would love to see you wearing it.'

The rain was pattering steadily now, changing the brown river water to steamy pearl. As Henry took Felicity into the conservatory dining room the floodlights came on beneath the weeping willows, illuminating their thick leafy trailing tails that danced in the growing wind.

They ordered and Felicity was horrified at the extravagance, knowing full well that she had not got enough money even to offer to go Dutch.

The thunder sounded closer. Night changed to brief day as lightning shot through the sky.

'Felicity, I've got a present for you here, to go with the brooch. Will you wear it for me?'

'No, Henry. No. Put it away. I will not take anything from you.'

'You are taking nothing. Just giving yourself. Please let me give you this ring in exchange. Will you marry me Felicity?'

'Christ no, Henry!'

'Why not?'

'Because I am twice your age.'

'By the time I am forty-two you will only be sixty-four, and that is that problem halved.'

'Because I don't love you.'

'But I love you and you love someone who is dead, no one else.'

'Because everyone would be disgusted and horrified.'

'So what? When have any of them thought anything about your feelings?'

'Because there is more to marriage than playing house.'

'I have taken a vow of celibacy.'

'Henry you are ridiculous. I haven't.'

'But you are old.'

'Not too old for sex. Oh God, this is a silly conversation. Let's change the subject yet again. How is your mother?'

'No. Felicity you haven't given a good reason for not marrying me. We could live together happily, travelling, writing, reading, going to concerts, being rich and beautiful and somewhat intriguing and no one would goad me into going with ghastly girls or speculate about my sexuality because I would have you to be my love and my life, my real only ever wife.'

'You are a ridiculous child and I've been a thorough fool to let you get infatuated. Stop being an idiot, please,' she said rather too loudly to be discreet and looked at Henry as she tried to suppress her hilarity. 'I shouldn't laugh. It isn't kind.'

Behind him a potted orchid stuck out its tongue. The storm had started properly now. Wild branches waved in a frantic ecstasy scattering small willow leaves like sparkling confetti flashing golden in the floodlights. Henry looked more like young Wolf than ever as he gazed back across the table enduring Felicity's mockery while the flower jeered over his shoulder.

'I can't wear your ring, I haven't got a finger for it. Look!'

But she had. Her left hand was there upon the damask cloth complete with all five fingers, young and smooth with no ageing signs of forty-two years' wear. The fireworks exploded outside in the screaming night and the plant reached down and bit Henry on his protruding ear, he seemed to gasp and Felicity saw that he had crooked front teeth. 'God, Oh Christ Almighty! Help me! Wolf!'

She ran out through the glass doors just as the power was cut. She stumbled and lay face down upon the soaked grass shaking with terror till the storm abated and a doctor, who had been dining too, tended her and got her put to bed so she could recover overnight.

In the morning, she awoke to find her bill had been paid but Henry was gone. She took the bus home from Reading and felt conspicuous wearing her smart black dress in Gloucester Green during the morning. She was too old for that sort of thing in summertime Oxford.

The answering machine was full of blank calls, all from Anna. 'Where were you, Mum? I rang and rang and you weren't there all night.'

'I'm sorry, Anna. Really sorry. Please tell me your news.'

'It is old news now. Dad knows but I wanted to tell you first. Now it is spoiled.'

'No, darling please. Let's meet tonight, I'll catch the train.'

'I'm busy. Pip is taking me out to celebrate.'

'Celebrate what?'

'I have been accepted by the Royal Academy.'

'Oh my love . . . you are wonderful . . . What can I say?'

'Don't bother to say anything. Bye!'

Henry wrote once saying he never wanted to see Felicity again ever. She thought of writing back and then decided it was best to leave things be. Besides, the letter had come from Paris and heaven knew where next Angelica had planned to visit on her grand tour. Also Felicity knew that Henry would feel better if he gave himself the credit for having ended their non-existent affair. It would do him good to be in charge of his past.

The summer went by without making itself much felt and seemed nearly over before it got started. The best-run charities, the promptest herald angels, had circulated their catalogues of Christmas necessities while the plums were still unripe.

Kilbole's sharpest estate agent got on with selling the Shieling before the autumn. Rob, frustrated by temperamental weather and the vagaries of the market, was absorbed in snatching at his harvest. He had missed getting his barley away on the early shipments, unlike his alert neighbour who was happily equipped with sunny wife, brawny sons and the latest mighty combine harvester. Rob's family were no help, any of them. Every time it rained his mother and Pricilla thanked heaven for softening the going for their horses.

Felicity was lonely in Oxford on her own.

The flashback faded till it was just a half-remembered nightmare but she was guilty of leaving Henry feeling stupid and insulted. She understood the despair of youth and pitied him. She missed his companionship sometimes, but not his cloying adoration. There were no more flowers. The azalea sickened, shed its brittle leaves and died: she put the skeleton plant in the bin but kept the pot for Christmas hyacinths out of habit.

Felicity's sanity was maintained by her job and a growing affection for the frightful Percussionists and their desperate band. Her wanderlust had evaporated with the loss of hope. She had no Grail left to seek, no quest and no dim star.

As she was leaving for work one wet morning she found Rob approaching down Hayfield Road.

'I've come to talk to you. Can I come in?'

'Of course, but just for a second.'

'Bloody rain. It is ruining everything. I thought I might as well come and have a chat now. We won't be able to cut till at least the afternoon.'

'I'm sorry, Rob, I have to go to work, I'm late as it is.'

'But this is important.'

'So is my job. I've got pupils expecting me.'

'Pupils? Surely you can't teach people music? I mean you can't demonstrate much, can you?'

'Five fingers on two hands aren't necessary for percussion bands and singing.'

'That doesn't sound important to me. Can't you wait a bit while I have got time to talk.'

'No Rob. Grania will kill me.'

'Oh the wretched Grania, you seem more in awe of her than anyone else.'

'She thinks farmers rape the countryside. Now I must go. How about lunch? I could manage that.'

Rob looked up at the sky where a blue patch was poking through the grey. 'No chance, I haven't the time to waste. Tell me, when are you moving back?'

'Back?'

'Yes, back home. After all, there is nothing to stop you now. The place is in an awful mess and I need you. I can't afford to pay your rent any more, you know that.'

Felicity looked at her husband and wondered if this was how he had seduced Penny, with a barrage of practicalities.

'I can pay my own rent, Rob. I wish you wouldn't treat me like a spare part to be fitted when your machinery conks out.'

Rob spoke to Grania. He did remember hearing about her: she wasn't his sort but she might know what was wrong, especially as she supervised Felicity most days. He simply couldn't understand why Felicity wasn't packing up and moving back. It made such good sense as well as being a sound economic strategy.

'You must woo her, Rob,' said Grania. 'You must give her space and self-respect, make her feel valued.'

Rob disliked Grania instinctively; the woman was patronisingly professional and unreasonably familiar. Still, maybe her advice was worth a bash. 'One bunch of roses is not enough,' Grania opined when Rob told her of his earlier efforts.

The next time it rained he brought Felicity a soggy bouquet of mournful Michaelmas daisies, four beetroot and a marrow.

Still she refused to come home.

Michaelmas daisies proliferated all over the house in Hayfield Road. They weren't up to the standard of Henry's flowers but their sheer volume began to wear her down.

Rob brought eggs and a pre-season pheasant that had collided with his car. He even took her to Elizabeth's without groaning about the price provided they drank the house wine. Penny kept her word and remained gone. Rob had heard nothing of her and done nothing about finding her.

'Don't you think she might need you, Rob? Losing a baby is

a real tragedy even when people are happily married. It must be terrible for her, all her dreams are destroyed.'

'It wasn't a real baby. It was wishful thinking or a false alarm.'

'Poor Penny,' said Felicity.

'Rubbish, poor me for being tricked. She left me, I didn't kick her out.'

'Rob, that is heartless and horrible of you.'

He apologised to keep the peace. A cheated wife pitying a scheming mistress was a complex concept but Rob was prepared to be compliant for the good of his cause. 'Please, Flicky, please darling. Let's start again. I promise I will make you happy this time.'

'You didn't make me unhappy last time,' Felicity answered truthfully. When she had been with him, nothing had plummeted or soared. Her life had trundled steadily forwards only taking little lurches over minor bumps along the road.

'Are you saying that there will be a next time?'

'Yes Rob, perhaps, if that is what you really want.'

Felicity was over forty after all; there was nothing to prevent her return to Rob. Being single for the next forty years could be bleak: traipsing about the globe searching for Wolf's relics was a touch stupid. Rob's mother and sister were only little pitfalls and furthermore, being reunited would be domestically convenient and tidier for Anna. Rob was right, it made sense. She would think about it.

Felicity pawned the Blackburn brooch to pay her solicitor's thumping fees. The divorce was shelved, which soundly irked the serpent whose fangs had been nicely sharpened for profitable battle.

Cedric Tullie died. Suddenly Henry Blackburn was the country's most coveted catch, a prime piece of eligible bachelorhood. Young, strong, clever and solvent with the healthy good looks of a man devised by an advertising agent to promote the trustworthy universal acceptability of a credit card, Henry had everything needful like good manners and clean fingernails.

Henry lacked carnal magnetism and friends. He also had trouble with women. Anna's friends were older and more knowing but she had the confidence to bluff her way and the personality to make her age irrelevant. She got on well with a crowd and was attractive without being a threat and was equally at ease with both sexes. Anna's new friends introduced her to far more exciting and sophisticated places than Felicity had ever frequented.

One of the Sax Offenders had said that her legs were perfection, which meant megatonnes more than any reassurance dished out by her parents. She liked noisy parties now and loved being admired. It was especially heavenly to make people laugh.

The staff at Raffles recognised her, which gave her a buzz.

'Fancy Henry Blackburn being Catch of the Month,' said Fred Beaminster who had known him at school. 'We all had him as a confirmed bachelor, if you know what I mean.'

'You all had him?' asked a slender commodity broker called Phyllida who lived off nicotine and champagne.

'Christ no. What a thought! We weren't into that sort of thing, Phylly.'

'Just testing! He certainly looks dishy.'

'Looks, perhaps . . . but what of the performance?'

'Well there's a thing. What indeed?'

'Henry was never bad at Oxford either,' said a girl of astounding brain called Daisy.

'But was he good?'

'Oh very, very well behaved.'

'I didn't mean that,' replied Rupert, an emergent merchant banker.

'He was my mother's toy boy,' said Anna.

'What? Really? Tell us more,' said James. 'One is intrigued.'

It made a very good story, everyone laughed a lot. Anna might not have given such a funny performance had she known that James was in journalism.

Instead of cheerful banter in the newsagent's the shop went quiet when Felicity walked in to buy her *Daily Telegraph*. She had to get the first two clues of the easy crossword each morning or else she felt the day couldn't start. Yesterday they had been 'Heifer' and 'Vest'; today the first word was 'Altar' but Mrs Smithers, who worked the till and loved to help, was not prepared to provide the necessary 'Native'. She sniffed and took Felicity's money without a word. She and her friend resumed their excited chatter once Felicity had left but stopped abruptly when she re-entered having forgotten to get some pencils as prizes for her best pupils who had almost perfected 'Oranges and Lemons' on maddening handbells.

'Your name is Mrs Green, isn't it?'

'Yes, Mrs Smithers, Felicity Green. I've been living round the corner in Hayfield Road since last Christmas. I'm leaving soon, going back to the country. Sorry, I must rush. I'm late for work.'

Mrs Smithers was making an awful meal of putting six pencils in a paper bag. 'Are you a social worker?'

'Yes, sort of. I teach music mostly.'

'Fancy,' said Mrs Smithers, giving her friend a telling look.

The friend held the door open for Felicity. Its bell pinged righteously.

'Wait a second. Is anything wrong, Mrs Smithers?' A sudden awful thought occurred to Felicity: maybe she had inadvertently shoplifted, something she always dreaded doing in moments of distraction.

'Well if you don't know, I'm not going to be the one to tell you, I'm sure.'

Felicity didn't look at the tabloids stacked beside the counter.

Grania said that in view of the cuts (always around to be blamed for austerity) Felicity was to be made redundant, immediately.

'Are you sacking me, Grania?'

'I am telling you to go. You must understand, we have very vulnerable clients. It would be wrong to give rise to any kind of scandal.'

'What scandal? Why is it everyone seems to know something that I don't?'

'Haven't you read the papers?'

'I bought the *Telegraph*.'

'Well maybe the Torygraph protects its own. Perhaps it considers itself above gossip.'

'Grania, I demand to know what all this is about. I have been working all day with people who can't read, and some who can hardly understand but who can respond to music. I have done

301

my best and so have they, it has been rewarding for all of us and now you are telling me to abandon them for some reason that I do not know about. Has someone trumped up some charge against me? Am I being accused of abusing my pupils? If so I have a right to defend myself.'

'Look at this, Felicity.' Grania produced the evening paper from her Peruvian canvas bag. '"NEIGHBOURS TELL OF OXFORD ANTICS . . . 'The curtains were always shut,' says single mum.' "MAKING HAY IN HAYFIELD ROAD."'

Felicity looked at the headlines aghast. 'I don't understand. What the hell is all this about?'

Grania rummaged further and produced a couple of the more sensational dailies, the sort that had busty females on page three and to whose editors Grania wrote many outraged letters, deploring such abominable exploitation of her sisters.

'"TOY LORD SLAMS GAY SLUR."'
'"THE TOFF AND THE SEXY SOCIAL WORKER."'
'"ROMPS WITH LOVER OLDER THAN HIS MOTHER."'
'"We had it off in Oxford," confesses new marquess.'

Grania was quite clear about where Felicity stood on unfair dismissal. There was no point in fighting and no chance of success even with a sackful of serpents to plead her cause.

Back at Hayfield Road the neighbours were enjoying themselves. Men in anoraks with aluminium ladders had converged and flashed whole filmfuls of Felicity scurrying to her house where she let herself in, locked the door and, once again, shut the curtains.

Rob was not at Church Farm; he was away for the weekend, shooting pheasants in Norfolk.

On Sunday the papers had a gala.

A Blackburn family member revealed the obsession of the ex-junkie who posed as a social worker. A driven woman with one goal, that of being Lady Tullie. First the sixties swinger had tried trapping the late Cedric when he was fifty and she was just a groupie aged twenty with a drug habit, then, following a bizarre accident in which her fingers were severed while she was high on LSD, in her forties and newly estranged from her husband she had visited Cedric's assumed successor in hospital, taken a view, saw he was dying, persuaded him to change his will and flown to Barbados to trap his son Felix. She failed again, Felix was murdered and, nothing daunted, fixated Felicity, the music teacher from Hell, threw herself at the next generation and seduced Henry Blackburn. 'They were at it like rabbits,' a neighbour explains. 'Dustbins full of bottles tell of champagne life style.' 'Local florists denuded', 'Lost weekends', 'Love amongst the spires'. 'Social worker's orgy of sex and shopping ends with drunken collapse at top people's restaurant as young lover flees.'

Rob opened the back door of the farmhouse. 'What do you want?'

'I've come home.'

Felicity had resolved to give Rob all the time and attention she had denied him before. She would gather blackberries and make sloe gin. She would go in for better gardening and join the WI. She would learn to work the computer, put the cow records straight and keep an eye on grain futures. For Christmas she would ask for a new cat.

Rob told her to go away. He couldn't patch with defective material. It was expecting too much of him. He could not survive the jibes and sniggers. His love had died, their marriage had been sunk by a swamp of scurrilous print. His solicitor would be in contact. The door was shut.

Felicity left Church Farm for the last time, failing to notice the nippy little red Golf parked in the yard, half hidden by Rob's Range Rover.

Sold, the board proclaimed. That confirmed the deed was good and done. The Shieling, like Church Farm and Hayfield Road, was no longer home. Until she got to Boston, Felicity's home was in a suitcase.

The Shieling had been bought by a prosperous couple with plans for pool and patio. Inside, the house would be gutted of its shaky fittings, all rattles and creaks would disappear with the outbreak of Provençal kitchens, fitted bedrooms and a real bar to be built in the snooker room devised by knocking the study and the playroom into one. Felicity was glad she would not be there to see any of these coming marvels. She sang to break the silence. The condemned doors and floorboards grumbled when disturbed, crabbit and resentful of having their solitude invaded.

New taps and smarter cisterns would soon oust the resident dripping and clanging wayward plumbing which had to be humoured before consenting to flow or flush. Felicity's reputation had preceded her. Even the girl in the Minimart, the one-time sweetie shop and source of forbidden bubblegum, had looked at her oddly when she bought coffee and biscuits there.

Tomorrow she was going to drive south and the next day fly to America where Ailsa had agreed to accommodate her in exchange for housekeeping and child minding providing she quit smoking. That had been easy. Tolerating blanket bombardment by the sharp young Schmidts would be a tougher challenge but she longed to go, she wanted to get lost. Anonymity was what she craved, not an infamous celebrity for having achieved nothing but a lascivious reputation.

An agent had offered to handle Felicity's publicity and been put down sharply. 'I am not going to earn appearance money like a retired racehorse opening supermarkets.' There was more to it than that: she could set herself up on the earnings she could command while the scandal was still live. 'Let it die as soon as possible,' she had replied to the man's persisting temptations. 'None of the accusations thrown at me are true, I am utterly innocent.' She was the first persistently vertical *grande horizontale* this cashmere-suited publicity hound had encountered. He ran his excessively be-ringed hand through his blow-dried hair and suggested that in that case Felicity should sue. She had refused and he had departed sorrowfully, lamenting his lost commission. 'The only fame I wanted was as a musician. Any money I might get out of the Blackburn family would be no better than immoral earnings.'

Anna was bludgeoned by remorse for having started such an interesting hare at a time when the public was eager for frivolity to relieve autumnal gloom. Newspapers needed spice, something breezier than accidents, disasters, Olympic mediocrity and fake shrouds to keep their readers agog. Felicity's lusts and ambitions made vapid and brief but entertaining copy for the scandal-starved, whose famine had been relieved by Anna's timely handout.

It was highly likely that Penny had been generous too, a most helpful source of information, though no mention was made of her by name.

When Myra Pennyfeather's last cat died she decided to leave Prince of Wales Drive for warden-controlled ground floor living. Arthritis mutilated her hands. Her piano was sold for very little but her fiddle was Anna's for as long as it was needed. Anna didn't need Myra any more; she had a promising future and a mixed flat above some Greeks in Cleveland Street. Myra felt fulfilled and offered thanks to Mary the Mother of God for letting her be instrumental in nurturing Anna's talent. Seeing her accepted by the Academy was the greatest joy in all of Myra's life and compensation for having missed out on other things.

Anna and Felicity were reconciled but Anna found it hard to be forgiven so readily and so quickly exonerated from any blame for her mother's troubles. Anna didn't side with either parent: she had many more intriguing things to keep her humming.

★   ★   ★

Felicity waited. Fay and Lionel Braid were due to call at five and Isa was coming at six. The lease on Hayfield Road had expired and what little furniture she had retained was sold. Originally she had hoped to store stuff in some friend's garage but friends had become distant lately, their garages suddenly full.

The proceeds from the sale of the Shieling and her mother's will were slow to materialise. Meanwhile Dieter had lent her more money to tide her over. She had redeemed the Blackburn brooch and sent it to Mr Bastion with instructions for it to be given to Penny.

At five precisely Felicity leant forward dutifully to kiss Fay Braid's cheek but the old woman shrank back. Lionel took Felicity's good hand in his as if to shake it. She felt his finger tickling her palm as he lunged towards her and planted a slobber on her ear. Only swift evasive action prevented his mouth landing on hers.

'Don't worry my dear, your old uncle understands,' he said with what looked nastily like a leer. His teeth had become ill-fitting and he was forced to close his mouth with a snap.

'Lionel! That will do.' Fay was shrivelled and bent with age but still meanly lean. Her words shot from her like staples from a gun and were just as piercing. 'We are not staying long, Felicity. Personally I cannot imagine why you have come up at all. Boswell Brothers are quite capable of packing up these last bits and dispatching them to your sister.'

'Isa asked me to come . . . to say goodbye.'

'There was no need . . . Lionel! Stop that!'

Felicity saw her uncle's off-putting wink. 'I also came to collect the monkey band, but I can't seem to find it. Do you know where it is, Aunt Fay?'

'I have it safe,' Fay replied.

Felicity hadn't expected Fay to take such trouble and was flummoxed by her consideration. 'Thank you, Aunt Fay, I was worried in case it got pinched or broken.'

'No. It is out of harm's way.'

'When can I come and collect it?'

'Felicity, your mother left the band to me. It was her wish.'

'But Aunt Fay, she has it written in her will. The band was to be mine.'

'Wills indeed! How materialistic you are. Your mother was most particular that we should have it.'

'Could I possibly persuade you to leave it to me in your will, then?'

'Your mother specifically told me you were never to inherit it. It was wrong for you to dwell on deformity: her very words, as I recall. She felt you had succumbed to a morbid fixation since your accident and that an ensemble of freak musicians was not a healthy bequest.'

'Aunt Fay, that isn't true. All I wanted were those monkeys, I loved them. They were part of my ridiculously happy childhood. Please Aunt Fay, if you won't leave them to me perhaps you would let me buy them off you, at the proper value of course.'

Lionel adjusted his hearing aid which issued a shrill whistle. He had been looking at the soon-to-be-bulldozed garden at the end of which the remains of a rotting summerhouse still stood despite seventy years of battering weather. 'You should see the fine gazebo we have had put up in our garden, Felicity. It is the latest model and can switch about to follow the sun. We bought it with the money your aunt made in selling your mother's wee monkeys. We sit in it and remember her with quite some affection, you will be glad to hear.'

'You had no business doing that, Aunt Fay.'

'You, Felicity, have no business talking to decent folk at all. I feel soiled by even speaking to you. Your behaviour has damaged our standing in this town irreparably. The least you can do is disappear quietly, taking nothing with you but your shame and leaving us decent folk to enjoy what few years we have left. I am entitled to take what I like, it is the very least I can expect for the trouble you have caused and the damage you have done to the fine names of Braid and Campbeltown. Now please will you direct me to where I can uplift the violin. My niece's little daughter takes lessons next year and I understand your own daughter has given up.'

'Anna has not given up, but my violin, the one I used to play before the accident, was lost in the King's Cross fire.'

'There is a violin in this house. I saw it with my own eyes. Have you sold it or removed it?'

'No. I have seen no violin here since . . . well since I got married.'

'Lionel will look for it in the outbuildings. I will search upstairs.'

For her years, Fay was as nippy as a darting lizard.

All the outhouses had been cleared long since. A perished pile of fishing nets was all that remained in MacBrayne's old potting shed.

Lionel padded up from behind, stealthily on rubber-soled feet.

'I do understand, my dear.'

Felicity jumped with surprise then shuddered with revulsion at the sound of the insinuating voice.

'I understand perfectly, all about needing a bit of hanky-panky. It is just a pity you forgot the eleventh commandment, Felicity. Thou shalt not be found out.'

'There never was anything to find out, Uncle Lionel.'

'Come now. I know you have been a naughty girl. Perhaps I ought to smack your botty.'

'Stop that at once. You are being repulsive.' Felicity recalled the incident of Hanne and Lionel on Coronation Day and the hints that had been dropped about his affair with Joan Blackburn and felt sick. He had small pink-rimmed eyes of a peculiar unhealthy amber, like a goat but with round pupils.

'There is plenty of what you fancy left in me yet, even if it does take me all night to do what I once did all night.'

Fay appeared through the french window, plainly infuriated.

'You have behaved disgracefully, Felicity. I promised the violin to young Lynn and I never break my word.'

'Aunt Fay, believe me. There is no violin, not any more.'

'All I could find was a tea service.'

'I am giving that to Isa.'

Fay sniffed and called for Lionel as if he were a dog. Lionel liked to think of himself as a bit of an old dog in which there was yet much life, a gay dog in the old-fashioned sense, a lecherous old dog full of tricks who could switch on bitches, not a dirty old dog in need of destruction.

'Well goodbye, Felicity. We will not need to meet again I trust,' said Fay as a Parthian shot.

'Give your old uncle a kiss bye-bye.'

'I'd rather die,' Felicity replied, shutting the door in Lionel's expectant face.

Isa presented herself at the back door carrying an immense holdall. From its size Felicity deduced that poor Isa might be expecting to carry away a substantial present and hoped the tea service would come up to her anticipations. She looked exactly the same; she had never been young and had not aged. Isa was herself, unique and unassailable, capable and resigned to her often drab life observing and assisting at the dramas that entered those of her many employers like a Greek chorus of one. She had just turned seventy but her hopes for herself were no more pessimistic than they had been when she was seventeen.

Felicity was brisk and falsely jolly, half expecting Isa to be cold and disapproving like the rest of upright Kilbole.

'I wanted to thank you, Isa for all you did for Mummy. I don't know what Ailsa and I would have done without you. You were wonderful and I know Mum was very fond of you.' Sheila had not remembered Isa in her will even when she had been of soundest mind but her daughters had agreed to give Isa a 'present' of some money pretending that it was a legacy and therefore not an insult. The tea service was just a personal memento.

'Your mother was a fine woman, and your dad, he was a bonny man.'

'I know.'

'And you, you are a fine good woman too.'

'Me, Isa? Most people seem to think I am the Whore of Babylon.'

'Ach away. They don't know their right from wrong. Just a load of dirty-minded ninnies. You are never bad, just a bit silly sometimes. I've always said that, only no one would listen. Now don't go greeting now, you have been through the worst.'

'You can't imagine how pleased I am to hear you say that. I wish there was something I could do for you, Isa. Something better than giving you a tea service even if it did belong to one of my grannies and has hardly been used.'

'Och hen. That is awful kind of you but you wouldn't be

offended if I didna' take it, would you? I've been left that many tea-sets over the years that I've nae room left in my press.'

'No, of course not, Isa, but I'm afraid there isn't anything else left.'

'No I know that, but I've something for you.' She delved into her bag. 'I was here sorting the cleaning when your auntie yon Braid woman and her man came and helped thierselves, so I took the liberty of saving something for you.' She gave Felicity a small parcel. 'Take care, hen. He is very fragile.'

The monkey fiddler had been Felicity's favourite. 'Oh clever, clever you. Thank you very, very much. Oh I love him so. Thank you again. Let me give you a kiss.'

'Now, will you do something for me?'

'Of course, Isa. Anything.'

'Will you take me over to Arran? I want to see where I came from. Will you take me to see Lamlash the morn's morn?'

'I can't tomorrow, Isa. I have got a plane to catch from London early the following day.'

Isa's face seemed to freeze into a mask of disappointment. She looked betrayed and let down, her one request denied.

'I am sorry, Isa. Really I am. But you see I have my ticket bought and Ailsa is expecting me. She has even found time to meet me at the airport.'

'Well that's it then. Goodbye, Miss Felicity. I wish you well. I'll away the now.' She picked up her holdall and made for the door.

'Oh Isa please don't be like this, and for heaven's sake stop the Miss bit.'

'I'll please myself, thank you.'

'Here Isa, use the front door. Please let me see you out.'

'I wouldn't want to bother you, Miss Felicity. You with your busy life. You've got a lot to get done.'

'Isa I promise I will take you the next time I am up here.'

'Very well. I'll watch oot for you as Hell freezes.'

'Oh Isa. I can't help it, really I can't.'

'I'll just have to not fret then, I guess. I really wanted to take you over there with me. I had my reasons but then you know your own mind now. Mrs MacBrayne went with the Women's Guild without me this month past. I was away to

310

my bed with flu and couldna' travel. I was that put oot, but there it was.'

'Perhaps the Women's Guild will go again soon,' Felicity suggested.

'Och no. They were not struck on the place at all. Aggie MacBrayne said there was just lots of marmalade in fancy pots to buy and the midges ate you raw. You could see the Pavilion and the County Buildings frae over the water but that was no great affair.'

'Why do you want to go then, Isa?'

'I'm old, I'm minded to see where I began.' Then, barely audibly, she added, 'There was something else there that I wanted to get sorted, that might have been for you.'

'You've done enough for me, Isa. Supposing I paid for you and Mrs MacBrayne to go together one day. Would that do?'

'Aggie has been and she blethers too much. I've plenty money of my ane, thanks. I don't need folks giving me days oot as if I were some wean frae the Gorbals. Goodbye Miss Felicity and good luck.'

As the sky darkened after a glorious sunset the branches of the suburban trees rustled in a southerly breeze. Felicity fancied she could smell the sea as she walked past Duncan Park. Thirty-five years ago she had been allowed to stay up late for the Coronation fireworks there. The golden Queen had wept sparkles. 'Long May She Reign,' the Provost had shouted through a megaphone most loyally. Felicity remembered with awe the tearful golden rain and Queen Salote of Tonga getting drenched, for ever afterwards associating both spellings with the same meaning. Those modest fireworks had been benevolent and harmless as a summer shower.

Felicity longed for bed and oblivious sleep but knew for certain the coming night would be wakeful and uncomfortable.

At three in the morning, when the stupid blackbird, successor to many misguided generations, was singing its soul into the night turned day by the bright street lamp, Felicity could take the fitfulness of insomnia no longer and got up to make tea. She was troubled and anxious, not only by her personal unhappiness, but by Isa. The extra mile, she had not travelled the extra mile.

Poor Isa had never seen her roots: that was all she had asked for and all she had been refused.

Isa's flat was up a stone staircase above the Conservative and Unionist Party office and had a view of the War Memorial from the front and what had once been Oldman's knacker's yard at the back. Isa was reminded of mortality on all sides. She had been conceived upon the foothills of Goat Fell and her mother had been dispatched to Glendrane Home for Fallen Women where she died giving birth. Isa's father was killed on the Somme. She scanned the long list of names on the memorial and wondered if he had been one of these fallen men; she liked to think he was the model for the statue standing so straight and proud upon the plinth. She had been brought up in the Quarriers Home before going into service with old Mrs Duncan at Glamis Towers.

Felicity rang Isa's well-burnished bell at seven-thirty.

Isa answered immediately; she was up and bustling, ready for another samey day. 'Miss Felicity. What is it?'

'Isa, I'm sorry. Of course I will take you over to Lamlash. I dare say we will be back before dark. I will just have to drive through the night. It will be no bother.'

Isa's face relaxed into one of her very rare smiles. 'You'll not regret it, hen.'

'Good, Isa. I'm glad. I've never been to Arran either.'

'This will wipe the smirk aff Aggie MacBrayne's face. She has been superior and secretive ever since she came hame from the excursion. I'm telling you she is just one big gossip.'

They had a strong cup of tea in Isa's kitchenette and Felicity heard several too many examples of Aggie's inquisitive ways.

All the time Felicity was thinking how she could get everything done before tomorrow. Of course Anna would come to the airport and say goodbye if only to take over the car. Maybe she would come anyway, out of affection. Felicity wasn't certain of that.

The Atlantic is no more than a pond these days. It was not as if she were being transported or fleeing oppression; she was not setting sail across hostile waters on a boat hung about with cabbages never to return. Even so, even so it is a great leap to travel over the ocean with just a single ticket.

'There was this body at your mother's funeral,' said Isa starting her story. 'Och, you're no paying attention, Felicity.'

'I am, Isa. Please go on . . . you were saying . . .'

'There,' said Isa a few minutes later. 'That is fixed up, then. You can deliver my package, I have the address by me.'

'What package, Isa?'

'Oh my, have you no been listening?'

'I'm a bit tired, Isa. Sorry, I couldn't sleep. Explain it all again to me on the boat.'

'Right you are. Now then, I have something for your wee girl. Something I know she will like. I found this in your mother's bedroom hidden behind your father's leather suitcases before your aunt sold them to decorate a fancy restaurant in Troon. Don't ever go there, Felicity they charge you twice as much as other places for just a wee messy bit in the middle of your plate. I was that distressed to hear that your dad's things are hanging about in a place like yon.'

Isa produced a bundle wrapped in an old striped beach towel and tied up with string.

'What is it, Isa?'

'I'm no saying. It is for your Anna. We'll take it with us if you don't mind.'

'But I can collect it here when I bring you back,' Felicity said as she saw Isa stuffing it into her holdall.

'Och no, I'd be happier having it by me. You never can tell these days.'

313

3

FELICITY AND AILSA had been dreadful travellers as children, throwing up on all outings despite being dosed with Quells and having a chain dangling behind the car. The Campbeltowns had never risked taking their daughters over the water after a messy excursion to circle Ailsa's own Craig on her seventh birthday.

Arran was getting closer; Felicity wasn't sorry. The boat's frothy, ginger-beery wake was flecked with crusts as the café staff threw their rubbish to the gulls. The boat stank of salty tea, chocolate, fish and cheese. Once, when they were all little, Felix Blackburn had shocked the adults by announcing that sick was the favourite food of jellyfish, it made their tentacles grow. This thought made Felicity feel no better. Why did her mind retain that rubbish and not logarithms or the purpose of the ablative? Heaving, she remembered also that Nelson was seasick every day, which was quite discouraging.

The fan belt had worn through just outside the harbour. Not a bad place; after all she could have been headed south, in the middle of the night, stranded in remoteness, prey to all sorts of horrors. The garage was handy, the mechanics could cope and all would be repaired by the time the ferry re-docked. Despite everything, Isa was not prepared to leave her holdall with Felicity's luggage in the car. One heard such tales, she said, of thieves and felons, not to mention spontaneous combustion. It would seem that Isa was headed to become a bag lady.

Standing at the prow, Isa was a figurehead in hand-knitted hat, a secret smile upon her thin lips. She loved the sea and revelled in the wind buffeting her cheeks to a rosy healthiness.

The tower on Gantry Close was clearly visible from the ferry, its Gothic pinnacle rising above the rusting trees, instructing the wealthy to be sure and award all building contracts to God. The mainland dimmed while island features became clear. The specks she had seen across the bay turned into buildings, and traffic moved along the coastal roads beside the defined fence lines of the lower fields. Soon she would see the sheep and then she would know that it was going to rain because, according to the age-old joke, if you saw sheep on the hills rain was imminent but if you couldn't see them, it was raining already. The island of Isa's origins was becoming real, not just scenery for the staging of picture postcard sunsets.

At Brodick Felicity insisted on brandy. Isa drank more tea and they took the bus along the coast.

'Would you like to retire here, Isa?'

'No, I would not, I'm no a one for being isolated. It's bonny, I grant you but I couldna' thole waiting on the boat to get me off.'

Goat Fell was purple fringed below its stony summit, and dahlias still brightened the roadside gardens soon to blacken in the first frost.

Even after eating three courses of indifferent lunch at a seaside café on the road to Whiting Bay, time dragged and Felicity began to find her good deed increasingly irksome as Isa's enthusiasm for discovering the land of her fathers became subdued. She kept looking back trying to spot anything of Kilbole but Holy Isle sheltered Lamlash from the Firth just as the hills on the mainland denied Kilbole a sight of the sea. Isa was hankering for her home, she had seen her roots and found them wanting. She was experiencing the anticlimax of discovering the house with the twisty windows to be only magical when viewed from a distance.

Felicity had no home for which to hanker.

'Well hen you had better get on with my wee errand,' said Isa putting on her hat and picking up the pound coin Felicity had left as a tip. 'Yon service wasna' worth a bawbee,' she said in the hearing of the spike-haired waitress.

'What do you want me to do, Isa?'

'I want you to deliver this letter.' She showed Felicity a thick envelope, beautifully but illegibly addressed to someone in Isa's copybook hand.

'I'll walk with you to the road foot but no further, I'm too creaky to go up to the hoose itself. It is not far from here, we passed it in the bus.'

'How do you know? If you've never been here before?'

'Aggie told me. The Women's Guild outing came by this way and she was that annoyed when the driver refused to stop to let her have a snoop. She thinks that yon's the place I keep my boyfriend. Och, Aggie can be awful stupid at times. She reads too much.'

'Well then, Isa, let's get along. We don't want to miss the boat. If no one is there I'll just post it through the door.'

'You will do no such thing. You just chap and ring till you get an answer, do you understand? I'm not having valuable packages left in folk's letterboxes.'

'But I thought it was a hankie, Isa.'

'Maybe, but you mind what I say. It isnae a coupon frae the co-op, Felicity.'

The afternoon was warm enough to stroll and enjoy the view but Isa was too agitated to appreciate any of it. Late-hatched midges hung in clouds over the bracken loosing volleys of stings at all who passed along the road, sheep bleats and lark song backed seagull complaints. The sea was ironed flat; jellyfish might be out of luck when Felicity and Isa crossed back to Ardrossan.

An iron gate hung lopsided from loosened hinges between rough stone posts. The steep drive was overhung with runaway beeches that had once, a century ago, been intended as a hedge. Up beyond the trees, there was a house and that was where Isa told Felicity she must go. 'Yon hill is too much for me, hen. There is time enough till the boat, so don't hurry. I'll maybe take the bus when it comes along. Here, take this bag, I canna lug it any further. Good luck.'

'Why?'

'I've a kind of feeling you may be meeting an old friend of yours up there.'

'Who?'

'You'll see. Now off you go.'

'Isa, who is it? Why are you being so cagey?'

'Go on with you. I'm not telling you anything, away and find out for yourself.'

The drive was mossy where the stones had become overgrown. Isa was right: it was not an easy climb, and it was made more troublesome by the wretched holdall. Felicity hid it behind a rhododendron gone native and carried on up towards the house.

She was mildly intrigued. Who could this old friend be? It was obvious Isa had all this planned, she was engineering some kind of reunion, trying to be kind. Poor Isa. What a waste of time. No one from the old days gave a fig for Felicity now except for the titillation of knowing they had been schoolfellows with a ridiculously unsuccessful whore.

As she trudged upwards flapping her arms to deflect the bugs she suddenly thought that maybe . . . Oh my God, what a stupid idea. Henry had sought and found proof that Wolf was dead beyond question. She was tired and overwrought, silly ideas would make things worse. Of course the occupant of this house must be someone from Kilbole who had loved her mother enough to go all that way to the funeral. The congregation had signed a book on entering the church. Felicity tried to remember who they all were. Some of the names had been quite unknown to her.

From the envelope she could make out the letters T and O in capitals followed by a little t and possibly an e. The package was addressed to either a Mr or a Mrs T. Ot something. Wolf used to be sent to a holiday home on Arran run by a Captain Otway or Otterway. This could be the place. The Captain was dead, she knew that. Maybe his widow lived on. The Captain's wife had been called Little Eva, like in *Uncle Tom's Cabin*, all part of the joke. Felicity's childhood had been teeming with really old people, women mostly, widows or bereaved girlfriends from the First World War who lived on well into their eighties and nineties, the mild and uneventful south-west coastal climate being held responsible for their longevity. It was quite possible that Little Eva or her family had become friendly with Sheila after Felicity had moved south. Isa probably did not realise that the Otways were all unknown to her.

The house was stone built, its gables trimmed with rotting

crenellated barge boards reminiscent of railway stations hon-
oured by Queen Victoria. A dead flagpole stood upon the
sheep-trimmed lawn and a fuchsia grew unchecked beside the
outer porch. The blasted remains of a scraggy monkey puzzle
punctuated the view over the woods to the shore, balding spikily
like the brush on the boot scraper. Felicity pulled on a rickety
doorbell. Her heart was pounding. It had been quite a climb
from the road: that was why her hands were clammy and her
stomach full of flutterings, there was no other reason for this
agitation, she told herself, just the exertion.

She heard footsteps approach. Strong steps, not an elderly
shuffle, but she would not turn till the door opened. She stared
at the sea but saw nothing. The door opened. She turned.
A face looked round the crack enquiringly. They recognised
each other and the door slammed shut. Felicity stood upon
the step dumbfounded, her nose just inches from the blistered
paintwork. The shock had winded both caller and called upon.

'What the hell are you doing here?' Penny Blackburn eventually hissed, through the letterbox.

'I don't really know,' Felicity answered. She had seen the
hatred in Penny's light brown eyes. 'Isa from Kilbole asked me
to deliver this.'

'Why?' Penny asked tersely.

'I'm not sure about that either. Penny please, I had no idea you
were here. Please open the door. At least let me see that you are
all right.'

'What is that to you?'

'I know how awful it is to have a miscarriage. I have been
worried about you.'

'There is no need. I am fine. Now please go away.'

'Just let me see you. I can push this package through the
letterbox but it is silly talking like this.'

The door opened enough for Felicity to see Penny's round
face and to notice that, above her dirty bare feet, her ankles,
which had never been coltish, had become swollen pink bolsters.
She was holding the door steady with puffy fingers.

'What is in that packet?' Penny demanded as if expecting it to
be a bomb.

'A hankie, I think. Someone lent it to Isa at Mum's funeral.'

'Who?'

'I don't know. The name begins with "O". Could be Otway, like the couple who ran the holiday home here.'

'Yes, that's right,' Penny snapped. 'My landlord.'

'Well can you deliver it to him for me? Isa was most anxious about it.'

'Yes, yes. Now please go.'

'Penny, are you sure you are all right? You look dreadful.'

'Have you come here to crow, Felicity?'

'No of course not.'

'Where is your car?'

'On the mainland. I am going to catch the bus back into Brodick.'

'Well you had better hurry. Turn right at the road for the stop, not left, do you understand.'

'But that is the wrong way.'

'It is the only bus stop. Do what you are told. Why haven't you gone back to Rob like I said?'

'I am not going back to him,' Felicity answered.

'Why not? You should, I'm not there to stop you.'

'There was more than just you in the way, Penny.'

'No there was not. You must go back to Rob. That is what I want.'

'Yes Penny, like world peace and a cure for cancer. It isn't so simple. Rob and I are not sticking ourselves together again. I am going to America, tomorrow.'

'Good. Well stay there.' Penny wasn't looking at Felicity; her eyes were focused on the bay. 'For God's sake Felicity, hurry up and go away.'

'Goodbye, Penny. I hope you get your life sorted out soon too.'

'What is that to you?'

'I am sorry for you,' Felicity replied.

'I do not want your pity. Just leave my family alone, you have done more than enough damage.'

Felicity started back towards the leafy burrow of the avenue.

'Wait!' Penny shouted.

Felicity turned. 'Yes, Penny?'

'You do know Wolf is dead, don't you?'

319

'Yes, Penny.'

'Properly dead this time, not like before.'

'Yes, Penny.'

'And you realise that your Anna is to blame.'

'No Penny, that is not true. Anyway I thought all that was highly secret.'

'It is, but I got to know. I'm not stupid. However, Anna is not responsible, you are. If you hadn't been such a bad parent, if you had gone with Anna and helped her, if you had shown any love at all for your child Wolf would not have got off the train at King's Cross to show Anna where to go. She would not have been so frightened of you as to make him go back for your stupid violin and be burnt to death.'

There was no virtue in asking Penny where she had got her information. Absolutely nothing more could be done.

Finding Isa gone Felicity ignored Penny's instructions and turned left along the Brodick road and then realised she had forgotten to pick up the wretched holdall. Swearing loudly she turned back and fetched it from beneath the bush. Just as she had regained the road the bus sped by and no amount of waving and cursing could persuade the driver to stop for her. She was going to have to walk it right speedily.

Isa reached Brodick just as the boat was docking. It would sail again in an hour; meanwhile she would test the standard of tea at the Harbour Café. Only a few people disembarked, returning to their island homes from a day on the mainland.

Mrs Nisbet was quite overwhelmed by the volume of provisions she had bought at the supermarket where she was convinced she saved money despite having to pay the boat fare to get there.

'Och thank you very much, mind yourself with they messages dear, them tins is awful heavy.'

'I've no car with me, Mrs Nisbet, or I'd give you a hurl home,' said the man who had helped her on to the quayside.

'Nae bother, dear. I'll give Sandy a ring. He will be away for me in his van just directly.' Isa saw the red-faced woman come into the café and sit down exhausted. She counted eight bulging carrier bags in all. 'Oh my,' said Mrs Nisbet. 'I'm gasping for a cup of tea. Will you no join me in a scone, dear?' she shouted after the man.

Isa hadn't seen him, but she heard his reply. He had also left his case to be retrieved later.

'No thanks, I've a bit to walk yet before I work up an appetite.'

'You're lucky. I get hungry after walking roond ma hoose!' Mrs Nisbet gurgled as her body settled like an unmoulded jelly. She sat with her legs wide apart and addressed Isa, the only other customer.

'Oh that is a grand man, yon fellow. He came here to recuperate last year, he'd been in some awful accident, he was that sick but he's great the now. He stays down by and writes books. Do you read yourself?'

'My friend reads books, but it does nothing for her,' Isa replied. 'I only read the weeklies.'

'Me too,' said Mrs Nisbet. 'Are you here on your holidays Miss –'

'Ard. Please call me Isa. Another cup of tea, Mrs Nisbet? There is time enough before the boat goes.'

'I will that, Isa, thank you. The name is Morag and I'm minded you'll bide here quite some time yet, there is bother with the boat's guts which may take a wee while to sort. You had better take another scone, for you will be late hame the night.'

A little distance in a car becomes a trek on foot. Thumbing a lift was her only choice. A van stopped; in car years it must have been about as elderly as its driver though both were still reasonably agile.

'I don't usually thumb lifts,' Felicity explained.

'I don't usually give them, but you look safe enough to me,' the van driver answered. He was a gnome in every way, lacking only pointy hat.

'I rather thought I was the one taking the risk,' Felicity replied.

'Oh you are wrong there. You might just be a decoy, with an army of Hell's Angels waiting to pounce oot.'

'No fear of that. I need to catch the boat at Brodick.'

'I'm away there myself to uplift the wife.'

Felicity introduced herself to her driver, who was Sandy Nisbet. He knew and was known to all the long-term islanders. Never taking his hands from the wheel, he greeted everyone with a sideways nod and a loud 'Hello there!' An unlit cigarette was stuck to the bottom lip of his sunken mouth. Sandy had few teeth and less hair.

A loud tooting came from behind before a filthy green car overtook Sandy's van on a blind bend.

'Good God!' said Felicity. 'That is Penny.'

'You know yon woman that is staying up by the now?'

'Yes I do. I didn't know she was living here though, not until this afternoon that is.'

'I fancy her landlord will no be best pleased to find her still here. He was wanting her away long ago but you canna throw your relatives on the streets these days, especially not in her condition.'

'Is she not well?'

'She'd be right enough if she was a wee bit younger and not so stout and if she had a man of her ane.'

'What do you mean?'

'Did you not see?'

'See what? She only opened the door a crack.'

'Och well, it is not something you can keep secret for ever, I fancy. There will be a wean before Christmas, according to the wife.'

'Penny is pregnant? Still pregnant?'

'Aye. It's terrible. She was raped, but she'll not say who by. I reckon it must have been a right dark night at all events.'

Felicity felt a surge of indignation: poor Rob did not deserve that.

'Penny wasn't raped. That isn't fair.'

'It is not nice for the wean to think that it got itself made in that fashion,' Sandy replied.

Felicity asked, 'Did you say her landlord is a relative of hers? Is he something to do with the Otways who used to run a holiday home here on the island?'

'Och no. The Captain and his wife are both gathered. The new owner is a man called Otterburn. He writes books and I know for certain, kin or no kin, he wants yon Penny to take herself off double quick. He hoped she'd get herself sorted and away before he came back frae London. He is due home any day. Anyway, between you and me I think she has no plans of flitting at all and is minded to stay here with the bairn and drive Tom demented. That is his car she is in right now. Poor Mr Otterburn,' said Sandy. 'He has got himself lumbered.'

'Is her landlord a writer?' Felicity asked.

'Aye, he is that right enough. He gave me a book of his, but I haven't read it, I must confess. It's laying in the lobby yet.'

'Does he live alone?' Felicity asked.

'Aye, until his lodger fetched up here. He must have had a wife or the like at one time for his book is dedicated to a lady. Just that, no name just a lady. Morag, that is the wife, was quite taken with the mystery.'

'*Beginning and Ending* is a wonderful book. I loved it.'

'Well, well, I would not know about that myself. He autographed our copy ye ken, Morag was that pleased. She is a great one for having things personalised.'

They were just within sight of the harbour when Sandy braked suddenly. 'What's going on here? Och take a look at that!'

Penny was sitting pinioned behind the steering wheel of the hissing car having collided with a stone wall and crumpled the bonnet to a crushed wreck. Steam was escaping from the engine and she was screaming furiously, making altogether too much noise to be seriously injured.

'Christ Almighty, my ankle!' she shrieked as Felicity and Sandy got to the car and managed to force the driver's door open. 'Help, somebody help me!' she screamed. Then on recognising her rescuer she yelled at Felicity, 'Go away! Go away, leave me alone, get out, you bloody woman!'

Ignoring her commands, Felicity helped Sandy ease Penny out of the car and supported her bulk to a seat on the verge. She was appallingly cumbersome and heavy. The car had skidded out of control: her left foot had been hard on the brake as the car hit the wall.

'Hush, Penny. You are going to be fine. We'll get you to a hospital just as soon as we can. Try to be calm. Think of the baby. Everything is all right,' said Felicity attempting to persuade

Penny to quieten down. 'I think she is in shock, Sandy, have you a rug or anything to keep her warm? Then can you get her to a doctor.'

'Aye, right enough. I'll take her to the hospital straight away. Morag can wait. You must go on, or you will miss the boat.'

'That doesn't matter,' Felicity replied. 'Really it doesn't.'

'Yes it does!' shrieked Penny. 'I want you to go. Go away now. Quickly. I don't want you here. I hate you!' With that she sank her teeth into Felicity's left hand so hard as to draw blood.

'My God Almighty! Look what she has done!'

'She can't hurt me Sandy. Not now. Don't worry.'

'But your fingers!'

'An accident. Long ago, it doesn't matter. Only the baby matters now. Be quiet Penny please, I am going I promise. Look, the boat is already at the quay. Just take care of the baby, please, for Rob's sake and its own. Don't get upset and hurt it.'

A small collection of onlookers materialised and were quite disappointed to find that Penny was not about to give birth on the roadside. Willing helpers made her as comfortable as possible in the back of Sandy's van, laying her down upon two sacks of Arran Pilot potatoes. Even as he was driving her off to the War Memorial Hospital she could be heard shouting at Felicity to hurry up and get off the island.

The ferry was still moored down at the harbour.

A bearded man with a slight limp came up the hill and stubbed out his cigarette as he approached the wreckage. He smelled of French tobacco but his voice was English without an accent.

'What on earth has been going on here?'

'An accident,' Felicity replied.

'I can see that,' he said. 'That is my car. Who was driving it?'

'Are you Mr Otterburn?'

'I am.' He looked at Felicity standing with her back to the sea and the sinking sun shining full in her face. She couldn't see his look of recognition as she shaded her eyes against the glare and tried to explain what had happened.

'Penny Blackburn passed me on the road. She was going like a bat out of hell, I think she must have been anxious to meet you off the boat. You are her landlord, aren't you?'

'Yes, I suppose you could call me that. What has happened to her?'

'Sandy Nisbet has taken her to hospital in his van. She has hurt her foot. I hope the baby is all right.'

Tom Otterburn didn't seem much concerned about either his car or the casualty. He smiled. Teeth show up much more when fringed by beard and his were real beauties.

Felicity smiled back and said apologetically, 'I've known Penny for ever. She hates me.'

'And I know who you are,' he said.

'I'm sorry.'

'Why?'

'It is terrible to have a notorious reputation, especially one that is untrue.'

'Your hand is bleeding.'

'It is nothing. Just a scratch.' Felicity pulled her sleeve down to conceal the stump fingers and the new injury. 'Sorry, I normally wear a glove to hide my hand.'

'I'm lucky, I'm able to grow a beard to cover my wounds,' he said. 'You ought to have a dressing on the tooth marks, though.'

'You weren't meant to see those,' Felicity replied. 'I'll get cleaned up on the boat.'

'Are you going away?'

'I must.'

'Where are you going?'

'America tomorrow, and after that God knows.'

'Why?'

'There is nothing for me here. Only my daughter, and she doesn't need me now.'

'Your daughter is very like you.'

'How do you know Anna? Oh of course, you were the person who spoke to Isa Ard at my mother's funeral. Sorry, I am being so rude.'

'No you aren't. Actually, I had met your daughter before, and seen you both together with your husband. I was very fond of your mother. She adored you.'

'And I should have done much more for her.'

'I am sure you did all she wanted. Believe me.'

'Did you visit her?'

'Only once. I took her something before last Christmas.'

'That was kind.'

'She told me all about you and your wonderful family.'

'Poor Mum. She was well away with the fairies. She never really acknowledged that my father was dead. She lived in a world of her own. Most of the time I think she was happy, I hope she is now. Thank you for giving her such pleasure . . . and to me . . . I loved your book, really I did.'

'Good. I hoped you would.'

'I had no idea you were related to Penny or Felix. I saw Felix in Barbados last year. I tried to give him your book, I thought he would enjoy it.'

'What happened?'

'He threw it away, he said it was crap.'

'That sounds like Felix.'

The boat's hooter sounded. 'Excuse me, I must go at once. Isa will be frantic. Goodbye, I'm sorry about the car.'

'Don't go!' he said.

'I must,' she replied, turning away.

'Please stay!'

She ran down the hill and up on to the boat. 'Just made it! God, Isa, that was a near thing.'

Isa looked crestfallen. 'I was hoping you'd be staying on.'

'Isa. You weren't to know, but Penny is the last person on earth to want me to be her friend. I'll explain on the way home. I must get my breath back first.'

'Where is my bag?'

'Oh Christ! Isa, I'm sorry – I've left it beside the car up there. Oh God, how stupid of me. I am so sorry. We'll ring the police, we'll get it back I promise.'

'You must fetch it.'

'I can't, Isa. Look, the boat is about to go.'

Preparations were under way to cast off; the hooter gave a final blast. Morag Nisbet had come out of the café to wave when a man limped past her down the quay.

'What's up, Tom dear? Sandy will be along soon, you are awful flustered.'

'Sorry. I can't stop.'

Isa stared at the little town and saw the figure limping towards the boat. 'Wait!' she shouted as the last link with the shore was about to be severed. 'Hold on. Stop! One minute, please just one minute.'

'We canna hold the boat, Mrs.'

Isa pushed Felicity towards the gangway. The rail was just closing as the man got to the dockside.

'Your bag! You left your bag,' he shouted.

'Show her what is in it, man!' Isa shouted back.

Felicity stood bemused, amazed. Then she saw.

The man was holding up a violin.

'Go to him, Felicity. Go now,' Isa commanded.

A little figure in a knitted hat was all alone upon the deck.

A strong arm held Felicity as they stood watching the boat retreating across the widening water over the rosy evening sea.

'What is Isa doing?' Felicity asked.

'I believe she is dancing,' Wolf replied.